D0062641

C O O P E R

R I V E R

A N D

ADGER'S WHARF

Castle Pinckney

POINT

To Ft. Sumter 3³/₈ miles

Ferry to Mt. Pleasant

Ferry to Sullivan's Island

The Cigar Factory

STORY RIVER BOOKS

Pat Conroy, Editor at Large

The
CIGAR
FACTORY

A Novel of Charleston

MICHELE MOORE

Foreword by Pat Conroy

The University of South Carolina Press

© 2016 Michele Moore

Published by the University of South Carolina Press
Columbia, South Carolina 29208

www.sc.edu/uscpress

Manufactured in the United States of America

25 24 23 22 21 20 19 18
10 9 8 7 6 5 4

Library of Congress Cataloging-in-Publication Data
can be found at http://catalog.loc.gov/.

ISBN 978-1-61117-590-5 (cloth)
ISBN 978-1-61117-591-2 (ebook)
ISBN 978-1-61117-840-1 (paperback)

Text from the poem "They," by Siegfried Sassoon, is printed with permission as it appears in the manuscript located at the Fitzwilliam Museum, Cambridge.

Excerpts from Slave Songs of the United States (Song #61, "I Want to Go Home"; Song #64, "Many Thousand Go"; and Song #66, "The Sin-Sick Soul") come from *Documenting the American South* and are printed with permission from the University of North Carolina at Chapel Hill Library.

Excerpts from newspaper articles appearing in chapters 2, 25, 26, 31, and 34 appear with permission from the Charleston (S.C.) *Post & Courier.*

The map images beginning and ending this book come from the 1861 "Map of Charleston Harbor Forts" by George T. Perry, provided courtesy of Library of Congress and adapted for use here by Paul Rossman, 2014, © Michele Moore.

CONTENTS

For my grandmother Alice Cahill Moore; my parents, Jack and Anne; and my father's great-aunt, Miss Aggie Blake

Growing up in Atlanta, I would often hear people say, "Your father has an unusual accent; where is he from?"
May this story provide an answer.

"Tobacco manufacturers are exposed to a strong narcotic odor . . . men breathe an atmosphere strongly impregnated with a poisonous substance, yet become insensible to its influence."

C. Turner Thackrah, "Effects of Arts, Trades, and Professions on Health and Longevity," 1832

FOREWORD

I first visited Charleston as a fifteen-year-old boy under the tutelage of the magnificent English teacher Gene Norris, and ever since then the city has gripped my imagination with a glittering, magical fascination. When I came there in 1961, a full century after the firing on Fort Sumter, Charleston still seemed haunted by its own stunned heart, yet it was generous with its luminous beauty. It has played a large part in every novel I've written, and I've always thought that if I could explain the city to myself, then I could tell the story of the whole South as I've watched it play out during my own time on earth. But Charleston remains an insolvable mystery to me, an astonishment of what is felt but not often seen, a suffering paradise with an often greater gift for self-delusion than for self-examination.

I've long considered my fixation on Charleston as one of the most pleasurable forms that addiction can take. Since my time there as a Citadel cadet, I've collected works on the city's history, its mansions, its churches, its secret gardens, its cuisines, and its culture, and I've tried to read every book by the many novelists who have grappled with the myriad charms, complexities, and contradictions that lie beneath its spire-proud, bell-tolling landscape. By now I know the menu of the three o'clock dinners and the annual gathering of its golden debutantes and the strict customs of its aristocracy, but I knew much less about the lower classes, white and black, that form the largest part of Charleston society. Then I read *The Cigar Factory* by the gifted writer Michele Moore, who tells the story of two working-class families and brings to life a dynamic vision of Charleston from their street-level perspectives, one that breaks new ground on every page.

The Cigar Factory is a large-hearted novel with a cast of characters wholly original in the vast, tempestuous literature of Charleston. It is a courageous book that takes chances with language that I wouldn't think of taking; but I will always be grateful that Michele Moore took as her ambitious objective to tell a story in which the truth of language and the truth of lives hold equal sway. The dilemma of how best to cast southern speech onto a page has bruised the souls of a hundred novelists who have tried in earnest to set down those melodies. White writers who have attempted to imitate the voices of the black folk of their childhoods have found themselves eviscerated by critics who hear only condescension and the darker tones of ridicule in such techniques. Nor have white southerners found it amusing to see the soft, furry edges of their own speech put down with hundreds of apostrophes and clever misspellings when their native sons and daughters record their most private thoughts in dialogue that elicits laughter in the two-bedroom flats of New York. Hollywood actors have done such a number on southern accents over the years that the mere suggestion of southern speech is almost shorthand that a cretin or racist or villain or buffoon or bore—or, on rare occasions, a hero—has entered a scene.

Undeterred by this, Michele has given her readers a genuine and enrapturing attention to historical diction and speech patterns in her debut novel that is more reflective of the spirit of the place, the people, and their distinctive common past than anything I've ever encountered before in southern letters. The black characters all express themselves effortlessly in the Gullah-Geechee dialect that once dominated the everyday speech of the children and grandchildren of slaves who were first sold in the flesh-peddling market that still stands in Charleston today. This lost, poetic language has never left the landscape, and it has found itself resurrected as a field of study by linguists, sociologists, and historians in recent decades. In an author's note on the language, she explains her fearless resolve to use it with authority and authenticity, and she offers an intimate dictionary of Gullah phrases. Gullah is a melodious combination of the West African languages of captured tribes, navigating through the thickets of the King's English. That she brings it off, and does so brilliantly, is a tribute to her artistry and an articulate testament to the integrity of her historical narrative.

If this were not a noble enough strategy, Michele Moore does the same thing with her white characters. Anyone who has spent significant time in Charleston knows that the accent of the white folks in that city is singular, inimitable, original, and a trifle strange. In my freshman year at the Citadel, a local young plebe named Hoby Messervey came to my room and asked me, "Do you have a noose and Korea?" Later, I discovered that Hoby was asking if I had a copy of the Charleston paper, the *News and Courier*, but that was only after I told my mother that poor Hoby had a speech impediment. The languages of southern whites and blacks have blended into each other over the centuries, and neither group has come out speaking like the denizens of Kansas or Minnesota; this is especially true of Charleston and the lowcountry. Michele takes us into the heart of that Charleston dialect, another example of her appreciation of the intricacies of a culture sculpted by its complex biracial past.

But ultimately it is the generous narrative of *The Cigar Factory* that makes this novel transcendent. It is a novel about this bright, conflicted city that is set among the lower classes of both races, who are on the cusp of uniting around a common plight, a unity that we are still seeking to foster and sustain generations later. Michele begins her story with innocent children at play in 1893 and ends its journey with working women standing together shortly after World War II. This book also is a rarity in the rich annals of southern fiction in that it tackles the complicated subject of the labor movement as it struggled to find a beachhead among southern workers. In the past ten years, I've read Doug Marlette's *The Bridge* and John Lane's *Fate Moreland's Widow*, two marvelous studies of labor unrest that took place in the textile mills of the Carolinas. But both of these novels celebrated the struggle of poorly educated white workers before the storms of integration swept through the states of the Old Confederacy. Michele's laborers are still poor as dirt, but they are both black and white, and nearly all of them are women. She has discovered a brand new subterranean Charleston as she takes her readers into a Dickensian world of backbreaking, lung-destroying work where the constant exposure to the dust of tobacco leaves changes your skin and the smell of your body. Thanks to her descriptive power, you will never look at a cigar the same way again.

The book traces the story of two families, one white and one black. The white family is made up of poor Irish Catholics whose matriarch, Cassie McGonegal, is one of the most difficult heroines you will ever encounter in fiction. That you fall in love nonetheless with her stony, bitter, off-putting nature is a great achievement of the character and writer alike. Cassie's orphaned niece, Brigid, becomes the second generation of McGonegal women to walk through the doors as a trainee at the cigar factory, but she brings with her the sustained hope that her future, and that of her son, will be made brighter by the mystery of the byzantine sexual and social politics that suffuse the working days of all the factory women, no matter their color.

Michele also re-creates the lives of the African American workers, the daughters and granddaughters of slaves, who enter the factory by separate doors and are dressed in smocks of washed-out blue to distinguish them from the white girls decked out in green and white. As the African American parallel to white matriarch Cassie McGonegal, Meliah Amey Ravenel, who goes to work at the cigar factory as a young mother, becomes the admirable protagonist who is still holding on to her own nervy desire for a life of consequence even while faced with a pay scale that allows her to put bread and vegetables on her table, but rarely meat. There is a gallantry inherent in her struggle. Her husband, Joe, is a captain in the storied mosquito fleet, and Meliah Amey learns to barter fish and oysters as she struggles to keep her son in school. A shared sisterhood develops among the black women, who suffer constant abuse at the hands of the white foremen as the entire factory fumes and roils as the daily quota of cigars is met, no matter how much overtime it requires.

It is the secret Charleston that Meliah Amey and her family occupy, and she drifts from the body-wrecking labors of the factory to the salt air of Charleston streets where she moves from the old market of Charleston to the alleyway of St. Michael's to buy food for the evening meal, to listen to the talk and gossip that floats up and around the flower venders, the basket weavers, and the servants who work for the white families gathered at the end of the day. Together, they are able to communicate to each other in a language half-born in tribes decimated centuries ago. It is in the life and conversation of Meliah Amey and her fellow African American Charlestonians, as well as in the overtones of that same language in white speakers, that we hear the achingly poetic music of speech that is now being studied and celebrated by linguistics scholars. In Gullah a sun sets as it *lean for down*, a man going crazy is a *head tek way*, and *noko-noko* means that I'll have nothing to do with you.

Throughout the novel, there hangs the terrifying fruit of another powerful word new to the language of Charleston at this time—*union*—which strikes repulsion and fear into the hearts of the factory owners. Yet the same word contains a subversive note of deliverance and empowerment for the women who prepare the cigars from the dark green leaves for packaging in the well-made boxes that will send them on their way. In the airless universe of this factory, the working women of Charleston find one of the only outlets in the Holy City that will enable them to help feed their families. That a moving solidarity arises among these struggling women comes as no surprise, but the reader's response to their grit and spontaneity in the face of abominable conditions and maltreatment is the stuff that makes fiction so necessary and so timeless.

It is a desperate city of Charleston that Michele Moore captures, but one that is also both on the move and on the rise. It is a Charleston unmapped in fiction, now Michele's territory alone. *The Cigar Factory* held many surprises for me, from the call of the seagulls, to the building of the first Cooper River Bridge, to the destruction of the mosquito fleet, to the Ferris wheel at the Isle of Palms, to powerful glimpses into the hardscrabble lives of Irish immigrants, to a deeply felt empathy for the lives of black workers who grew up with former slaves in their families. The novel ends with a faint song of hope, but also with hard-won and lasting lessons of humanity earned by virtue of wounded hearts and callused hands. In *The Cigar Factory*, Michele Moore *speaks true-mouth* in her brave, authentic, and, I believe, controversial book that equally reveres the lives of black and white working-class Charlestonians. In that act, she has also given birth to a literary vision of Charleston that has never seen the light of day so brightly before.

Pat Conroy

A NOTE ON THE LANGUAGE

Until the great migration of the 1920s the majority of Charleston's population consisted of persons of African descent. European immigrants arriving in the lowcountry prior to this time would have acquired the English spoken by those around them, whether by their dah (nursemaid) or by their neighbors, vendors, or coworkers along the wharves. Housing in Charleston was never segregated by law.

The linguist Lorenzo Dow Turner noted that the English 'th' sound does not exist in Gullah-Geechee nor in many West African languages. Coincidentally, it does not exist in French or German, either. In pronouncing English words containing this sound, both the Gullah-Geechee speaker and the West African substitute voiced [d] and voiceless [t]. For example, "they" is pronounced *dey*, "them" as *dem*, "with" as *wit'*. Also, [v] is pronounced [b] or occasionally as [w]. *Gone* may be used for all tenses of go. *Gwi* is future tense for will. The final "r" is not pronounced. Possession is shown by proximity and not an apostrophe as in English. Auxiliary verbs are often absent; repetition and double negatives are common. Groups of words may be used to describe a characteristic of a thing or person. Tone can be used to convey tense or a special meaning, and tone does not go up at the end of a question as in English. However, tone does go up at the end of a statement.

It has been my observation that in varying levels of intensity and consistency, aspects of the West African based Gullah-Geechee language and associated communication styles can be heard in the speech patterns of many older Charlestonians regardless of race or class. Linguistic scholars, including Dr. Katherine Wyly Mille, acknowledge the significant influence of West African pronunciation, grammar, and vocabulary on overall Charleston speech. However, linguists draw a distinction between Gullah-Geechee Creole and Charleston English dialect.

The presence of West African–influenced speech is central to this story. Yet, how to portray the language on the page, given the well-known difficulties associated with dialect? Foremost among these difficulties, dialect has historically been applied unevenly and used to show condescension. Additionally, the typographical oddities and misspellings alienate many readers. The poor apostrophe is weary from the load it has too often been forced to carry. Therefore, I have chosen to rely on a different strategy, and whenever possible to give the apostrophe a rest. Dialect is portrayed in snippets—a single word, a random phrase, an occasional paragraph, particularly when a new character is introduced or during an emotional outburst: auditory navigational aids, if you will, bell buoys placed every so often as channel markers within the Gullah-Geechee/Charleston English spectrum. You are invited to listen for the sounds and rhythms of *de mores* beautiful language whenever a Charleston-born character is speaking.

GLOSSARY

Abbreviations

G: West African/Gullah
CE: Gullah-influenced Charleston English

Adu: Yoruba/G, very black
Ajani: Yoruba/G, one who wins after a struggle
Andunu: Wolof, we are not united. G, I was not with you
Bay-uh: CE, beer and bear; pronounced the same
Becuz: G/CE, because
Bin yah: G/CE, been here
Bo-it: G/CE, boat
Buckruh: Ibibio/Efik/G, white man. High buckruh: rich white man
Dah: G/CE, nursemaid/nanny or servant. Ewe, mother, elder sister
Dayclean: G, the sun has risen/broad daylight; pronounced *dey klin*
De mores: G, the most
E/e: G, pronoun for he, she, or it
Ebuh: G, ever. Evuh: CE, ever
E luke'luke bird: G, a grayish-brown marsh bird
E time fuh gone: G, it's time to go
E eye tie up on yuh: G, he/she can't keep his/her eye off of you
Enu fole: Ewe/G, to be pregnant
Faw-ibe: G, five. Faw-ive: CE, five
Fuh true: G/CE, truthfully
Fus' daa'k: G, first dark, twilight; or may say "sun lean"
Gafa: G, evil spirit. Mende, spirit soul, idol
Gho-iss: G/CE, ghost
Gwi (or gwine): G, going, or would; also, future tense for "will"; "gone" may
    be used for all tenses of "go"
Haint: G, a ghost or restless sprit that will sit on a person's chest at night,
    and take the breath away, leaving him exhausted and weak in the morning.
    Also known as a Boo Hag or a Haint Hag.
Harr-y-kin: CE, hurricane

Head tek way: G, lost his/her mind, or he/she is crazy

He'lenga: Mende/G, the period just after dark, the sitting-together time

Hol' um cheap: G, having no respect for someone

Kamba'boli bird: G, a speckled bird who sings when the tide is rising.

Kofi: Twi/Ewe/Fante/Gold Coast/G, basket name for boy born on a Friday

Ma'magole: Mende/G, elderly white woman

Marriage'um: G, to mix or blend

Mek so?: G, why?

Mek so yuh duh worry?: G, why are you so worried?

Mores: G, most. De mores: G, the most

Noko'noko: G, I'll have nothing to do with you. Gold Coast, nothing, nothing

Oonuh: G, you. Yuh: CE, your, or another form of "you"

Olowo: Yoruba/G, a person who commands respect

Pawpus: CE, porpoise

Pizen: CE, poison

Puntop: G/CE, up on top, or on top of

Sibi bean: G, lima bean. Sivy: G/CE, lima bean. Seb: Wolof, bean

Study e head: G, think hard about something

Sun-Lean: G, sun begins to decline

Sun-lean-fuh-down: G, sun is setting

Sweetmouth: G, flattery, bribery

Tana: Yoruba/G, to light a lamp. Bobangi/G, to be beautiful

Tangledy: G, tangled; confusing

Tata: Kimbundu/Kongo/G, father

Tek foot een han': G, to hurry; take his/her/your foot in his/her/your hand

T'engk: G/CE, thank

T'ink: G/CE, think

Trute: G/CE, truth

True-mouth: G, one who will not lie. Sometimes pronounced Trute-mout'

Trus-me-Gawd: G, an undependable homemade boat

Tummetuh: G/CE, tomato

Wa'yiba: Kimbundu/G, bad person

Wuk: G/CE, work

Wulula: Kongo/G, to rescue from great danger to life

Sources

Emory S. Campbell. *Gullah Cultural Legacies: A Synopsis of Gullah Traditions, Customary Beliefs, Art Forms and Speech on Hilton Head Island and Vicinal Sea*

Islands in South Carolina and Georgia Gullah Cultural Legacies. 3rd edition. Hilton Head, S.C.: Gullah Heritage Consulting Services, 2008.

Virginia Mixson Geraty. *Gulluh Fuh Oonuh (Gullah for You): A Guide to the Gullah Language.* Orangeburg, S.C.: Sandlapper Publishing, 1998.

Ambrose Elliot Gonzales. *The Black Border: Gullah Stories of the Carolina Coast.* Columbia, S.C.: State Company, 1922.

Katherine Wyly Mille. "Charleston English." In *The New Encyclopedia of Southern Culture,* vol. 5: *Language,* edited by Michael Montgomery, Ellen Johnson, and Charles Reagan Wilson. Chapel Hill: University of North Carolina Press, 2007.

Lorenzo Dow Turner. *Africanisms in the Gullah Dialect,* with an introduction by Katherine Wyly Mille and Michael B. Montgomery. Columbia: University of South Carolina Press, 2002.

Michael W. Twitty "Quotes Part Two: New Gems." Afroculinaria. 20 Oct. 2011. Web. Accessed 27 Jan. 2015. http://afroculinaria.com/2011/10/20/quotes-part -two-new-gems/.

PROLOGUE
July 1893

The sun leaned for down bringing shade to the waterfront. On the other side of the river from where Cassie McGonegal stood, light—low on the horizon—spread across the harbor entrance and surrounding Sea Islands. It was the slack of an ebb tide and there wasn't any breeze worth mentioning. Sounds of men working hard traveled easily up and down the Cooper River: the thump and thud of stevedores emptying a ship's hold, the shouts of long-shoremen moving cargo on the dock, the slap of oars as the Mosquito Fleet rowed home to Adger's Wharf. Cassie's younger brother Charlie stood upon the remains of an old bateau that once belonged to the Negro fishermen of the fleet. The weathered boards kept Charlie from sinking into the pluff mud. Reluctantly, Cassie stayed on the pier, wishing she had her own hook and her own piece of line.

"Help me, Cassie," Charlie called. She clambered down from the pier, careful to step onto the boards, never-minding her dress and how angry her mother would get when it had to be washed again so soon, never-minding her doubt that there was anything on the other end of his line besides an even bigger clump of marshgrass than the one he had caught earlier. Together they pulled, refusing to let go even as the line cut into Charlie's palms. They kept pulling until finally they brought up the nicest, biggest, and most beautiful—flounder.

Excited to show their parents what they had brought for supper, they ran through Ansonborough's narrow streets.

"She Crab! She Crab! She Crab!" the huckster cried as he pushed his cart down the dirt lane, nodding as he passed the vegetable lady with turnips and carrots sticking out from the basket on top of her head. A grown man offered Charlie seventy-five cents for the flounder, but he turned him down.

They were out of breath and walking by the time they got to Anson Street and Johnny McCready jumped out from behind a palmetto tree wearing his Buffalo Bill cowboy pants without a shirt, putting on like the tough guy he was not. Johnny would do about anything to get attention, and he was bigger than any kid his age. He and Charlie were friends, but Cassie thought of him as a braggart and a show-off. Some said he was destined for a stage. A-little-bit-lace-curtain was how Cassie's mother described the McCreadys. Johnny asked if he could buy the flounder. Charlie hesitated, then told him no and kept on walking.

"Hey, Red," Johnny hollered. All the boys called Cassie's brother Red on account of his hair. "Fish dat big feed de whole family. I'll give yuh my cowboy pants fuh dat fish," said Johnny. Charlie stopped and turned around. His dungarees were worn and faded and he'd told Cassie once if not a dozen times how much he wanted a pair of cowboy pants like Johnny McCready's.

Charlie motioned toward Saint Stephen's Church.

It was a summer evening—only a few months before she would begin working outside the house at the cigar factory. She was eleven and Charlie nine. And there in Saint Stephen's garden, Cassie watched with a clinical curiosity as Johnny McCready stepped out of his cowboy pants and stood before them in all his God-given glory. Charlie handed over the stringer, and Johnny, covered in front by a mighty fine flounder, walked off with his head held high.

Being far more modest than his friend, Charlie went behind an oleander bush and changed into his new pants.

Long shadows raced ahead of them at every turn until they arrived home. Cracks from the earthquake and pocks from the shelling during the war had left the masonry of the house the McGonegals rented much in need of repair, but no more or less so than the others on that particular block.

Laughing, Cassie and Charlie burst through the door with a story they couldn't wait to tell.

"Don't be running in here, carrying on like a bunch of wild pickaninnies," their mother scolded from her perch in front of the window where she kept an eye on the coming and goings of the street.

"You didn't ketch no fish. You couldn't ketch a cold," their father sneered from his chair in the nearly dark parlor. "Only a damn fool would trade dem fancy pants fuh a little fish."

"No little fish! A flounduh, big!" Cassie insisted, showing with her hands how big. She crossed the slanted floor to the sideboard where the lamp beckoned to be lit. She debated if it would be worth listening to him holler if she did so before it was completely dark inside. He parsed out the kerosene as if it were the last cup of fresh water and they lived in a lifeboat in the middle of the sea with only the slimmest chance for salvation.

"Well, what good does it do us?" said her mother, disappointed. "Why don't yuh go ketch anudduh one so yuh own family can have a nice fish to eat fuh suppuh?"

They were focused on the loss of the flounder and might not pay attention to her lighting the lamp early. Cassie struck the match and put it to the wick. The light revealed dust upon the crucifix. She wiped it with her finger, blessing herself afterwards for good measure.

"Did yuh steal dem pants? Shooo! Only a damn fool would believe a boy your size could ketch a decent fish wid a han' line," the father insisted, his face turning mean in the yellow glow of the lamp. Cassie motioned for Charlie to show their father his hands and how deeply the line had cut him. But Charlie was too proud and too hurt to stand up for himself.

For the first time—though hardly the last—Cassie McGonegal declared to anyone bothering to listen, "Only a damn fool would evuh want to get married."

PART I

1917

Charleston, South Carolina

Chapter 1

AUGUST 1917

Cassie McGonegal lay awake, her body as still as the night air except for her fingers moving assuredly over her rosary beads the way she moved through life, one decade passing over the other among the glorious and sorrowful mysteries.

She feared that Brigid had been born with too much Egan blood, lending her a mousy disposition and pale, almost sallow, skin. Now, at eighteen, Brigid had finally nudged past five feet in height, but she remained thin to the point of being delicate, not low and sturdy like most McGonegals.

When she completed that rosary, Cassie blessed herself and lightly kissed the crucifix. Sleep was a foreign country on the other side of the ocean, someplace on a hill high above the eternal damp. Speaking softly, she began another round, the Geechee unmistakable in the sound of her voice: "In de name of de fathuh, de son, and de holy gho-iss."

Two weeks prior, Cassie got word that a German U-boat in the North Atlantic had sunk the *Magnolia*, a schooner ship that employed her brother Charlie in the transport of sea island cotton from Charleston to Liverpool. She and Brigid had said countless rosaries and Cassie had spent a full day's pay on candles at Saint Mary's Church.

No news of miracles arrived. Only the telegram Cassie found waiting for her that evening. Charlie's body had washed ashore on Ireland's Cruit Island. Fishermen buried him in a little cemetery alongside some British sailors similarly delivered by the tide the month before.

The tears pooling about her ears had a cooling effect. She did not want to dwell upon her loss. Cassie was a practical woman. She added a late intention for the Lord to protect her sense of touch from the creeping numbness and to keep her fingers fast and sure. "Don't lemme lose my jawb," she blurted out. "She's all mine to look aftuh." She raised her head up in bed, making sure that she had not wakened her niece with her outburst. The movement stirred her phlegmy cough, and she reached for a handkerchief in which to spit.

If the Lord would help her to do a little better than the expected quota of a thousand cigars by the end of every workweek come Saturday afternoon, then maybe she could bring home $11.00 rather than $10.50. The 50¢ came about they said because of the war. Wages were going up, but so was the cost of everything else. If she saved that extra money, then maybe next year she could afford another place. A place with a proper bedroom for Brigid so she wouldn't have to sleep on a cot in the kitchen. Maybe even have a water closet of their own so they wouldn't have to go down the hall to use the toilet. But she'd have to be sure of that money. She couldn't risk getting in over her head. What if her hands failed her? That happened to Maria Poverelli. That's how come she stayed on West Street. She didn't start out that kind of girl. Without fast hands or a head for figures and words, not many body parts left for a girl to hire out. Seems Charleston men had an endless need for the services provided by Charleston girls on West Street. Holy City, my behind, thought Cassie.

If her hands failed, what sort of work could she get with no more schooling beyond the fifth grade? The coloreds got all the laundry, cooking, and cleaning jobs. If she were to ask a South of Broad lady for work, the lady would tell her flat out how it is. She'd say, "That's Negro work and we insist on hiring Negro women to do it."

Cassie reassured herself that she could feel even the slightest ridge or groove in each of the rosary beads. It had taken years for her to learn to feel how tight to press the filler leaves into a bunch when rolling a cigar. Press the leaves too tight and the smoker would have to pull rather than puff. Too loose, and the cigar burned too fast. If only it were her eyes causing trouble. Making cigars required a delicate sense of touch and nimble fingers. She could do it with her eyes closed. But she could not do it if her fingers went numb. Everything would be all right, she told herself. Her hands were sound enough and they would remain so. She would manage. Somehow she would manage. McGonegals always did.

Silvery droplets formed against the window screen. The only light challenging the darkness came from the gas lamp on the corner of Elizabeth Street. "You always said Chaa'ston won't evuh change and that it didn't matter so long as they never sold off the *Magnolia* for some steamer because you'd refuse to work below deck in a boiler room. Well, Brother, I wouldn't be surprised if you were part of the very last crew to sail across the Atlantic with a load of Sea

Island cotton to sell to England. I wouldn't be surprised one bit. Oh Charlie, may the wind be at your back," she said softly. "Who'd have thought that this would be how you'd return to the motherland."

The tide turned just before sunrise and with it came a most welcome breeze. Cassie rose at five, went down the hall to the water closet, filled her pitcher from the tap, and brought it back to the apartment for washing up. As she dressed for work, she smoothed the fabric of her uniform with her hands before pulling her smock over her head. She went to the mirror to pin her cap into place. Except for the smell, the uniforms might have been mistaken for those of nursing students. Mr. Rolands insisted that all "his girls," as he called them regardless of age, wear a clean pressed white uniform with a green smock and a green cap. But after ten-hour days six days a week, even after washing, the uniforms bore the smell of ammonia from processing tobacco. A blue blood might exit a store posthaste to avoid the acrid stench of a cigar factory girl, but the shopkeepers on King Street knew that such a girl's credit was as good as her smell was bad.

Cassie stood at the mirror pinning her cap into place when she heard the Negro street vendor sing out to announce his arrival on the block.

> *Swimp, swimp be raw raw*
> *Swimp today, swimp to-ma-ra*
> *Shaa'k stake don't need no graby*
> *Shaa'k done eat my baby*
> *Swimp, Swimp be raw raw*

Having her hands over her head caused her fingers to go numb. She put the pins down on her dresser, staring at them as if they were the problem.

> *Swimp, swimp be raw raw*
> *Swimp today, swimp to-ma-ra*

"Brigid," she called. "T'row on your housecoat. Get a dime out of my purse and run get us two plates of swimp." Cassie opened and closed her fists, bringing the feeling back into her fingers. "De flavor's in de head. Mek sho dey got de head on." She heard the rattle of plates in the cabinet. "Hurry Brigid, he's almost to de cornuh."

Cassie let her arms dangle loose, shaking her fingers until the feeling returned. When Brigid came back in the front door, Cassie was surprised to see that she was wearing her Sunday dress and shoes.

"We need ice," said Brigid, securing the lever on the icebox door after putting the plates of shrimp inside.

"The milk bottle empty; how come?" asked Cassie.

"I poured it out on the stoop. Looked like it had a piece of hay in it to me."

Cassie wanted to curse. Twenty cents gone for nothing. But she couldn't blame the girl. Typhoid fever had taken Brigid's mother a few years back. They said it came from the milk bottles being washed in contaminated water. "Any other good news dis mawnin?"

"Stove oil, we're low," the girl added reluctantly.

"Anything else?" said Cassie.

"I'm going wid yuh today," said Brigid.

"Chile, get on back to bed."

"Aunt Cassie, I've graduated high school. It's time for me to find work."

"Shoooo, chile, you the first in the family to graduate high school. Your daddy didn't want you working at the durn cigar factory. Brigid, you could be a secretary for some lawyer down Broad Street. Gawd, chile, why you wanna work at the cigar factory?"

"The war's changing everything, Aunt Cassie. I heah the shipyard may hire girls and darkies soon. Why should I do office work for faw-ive dollars a week when I can get ten mek'n cigars?"

"Shooooo! Cigar factory's hard work," Cassie scoffed. "A lot of girls can't tek de smell—mek'um sick. You gonna get a headache like you been drinking hard liquor all night. Some days so hot, you got to wear a rag on your head like a colored woman to keep de sweat out yuh eye. An dust, chile—Oh Lord—I'm telling you, dust gets everywhere. Brown tobacco dust in the air, on the floor, even in your drawers, and that's the Gawd's truth! You gonna get a phlegmy cough like I got that won't evuh go away. Tek a long time to learn to mek cigars. They don't pay you ten dollars a week to learn. No chile, they pay you four dollars a week to learn because it tek months—months—to learn to roll a wrapper leaf one direction. If you wanna mek top dollar, you got to learn to roll a left *and* a right wrap. An that tek years—I say years—to learn."

Cassie stopped. Young Brigid suddenly seemed in possession of a full tank of McGonegal blood.

"Shooo!" said Cassie, turning away. "You got to live your own life. Don't mek no difference to me, but if you coming, we got to go. Mr. Rolands don't tolerate girls being late."

They walked north several blocks before turning east on Columbus. With its current nearing peak, the tide rose quickly in the harbor and surrounding marsh. Stiff palmetto leaves scraped against one another in the steady wind. Cassie's cap came loose. Along the way, other women joined their brisk-paced walk. The women were their own incoming tide and their ranks swelled with each passing block—white women in white uniforms with green work smocks, and Negro women in blue uniforms and blue work smocks. Some of them brought their children to work with them. And there were men too, white men and colored, but their numbers were far less than the women. The men did not wear a special uniform.

The cigar factory workers came from all the neighborhoods downtown: they came from the alleys behind the homes south of Broad, they came from the Borough, they came from Harleston Village, they came from Eastside, they came from up on the Neck, they came together from the walkways of the trademark Charleston single houses, all of them walking together to the waterfront and the corner of Columbus and Bay Street.

The workers grew in numbers such that in the final block before the factory they were too many for the sidewalk and they had to take to the dirt street.

"Miss Cassie, I met a boy works on the ferryboat *Commodore*," said one of the girls. "He says this Sunday, me and him can ride the ferry for free. We gone spend the entire day at the Isle of Palms."

"Nuttin for free, chile," said Cassie with a wry smile. "Don't you forget, nuttin for free."

"Dat boy gone get fresh on de Ferris wheel," said another.

"Shooo! Boys get fresh with me on the trolley from Mount Pleasant before we even get to the Isle of Palms," chimed another who was trying to apply face powder while keeping up the pace. The young girl caught Cassie's reproachful eye and put it away.

"Fixing up for the men in this place can only bring trouble," said Cassie.

"But, Miss Cassie, my skin's turning a funny color," she insisted.

"It's from the tobacco," said Cassie, noticing that Brigid seemed shocked by the chatter. "In a few more years you gone have this same gray color I got. Save your money for powder til you really look like a gho-iss."

"Mawnin," said a Negro woman just a few years older than Brigid.

"Good mawnin," Cassie answered enthusiastically. "Tell that man of yours them blue crabs I bought from him were grand. Chile, I declare those were the best crab cakes I evuh made."

"That's cause yuh don't beat'um to death. Some folks stir and stir til it nothing but mush. Mush. Yuh got to be easy with it."

"Fuh true," said Cassie. "De less yuh handle it, de better de crab cake."

Brigid in her sailor-suit tunic and dark skirt looked on in amazement. Cassie knew that Brigid rarely saw her being lighthearted at home. After nine or ten hours of work, followed by fixing dinner, and washing and pressing her uniform, Cassie had few kind words and even fewer smiles left in her body.

As they neared the massive red brick building on Bay Street, the sound of the women's voices rose with the sun over the Cooper River.

"This way if you wanna job at de cigar factory," yelled a white man standing at the corner. "This way if you wanna job."

Brigid started in his direction and Cassie grabbed her by the arm. "No, not you."

"Man say go that way if you wanna a job." Brigid pulled away from Cassie. The girl took only a few more steps before she stopped. "What're they doing ovuh there? Do I have to line up like that?"

Cassie knew the scene was not a pleasant one to watch, but it was a fact of life. She wanted to turn young Brigid away from it, but she thought it best to let her stare. Cassie said a quick prayer that Brigid would not get foolish notions in her head. When Cassie observed a girl leaning that direction, she would admonish her as she did then with Brigid. "Heaven got to be the reward for the hell on earth. Sooner or later it mek a kind of sense and till it does, keep yuh mouth shut or yuh gonna be out of a jawb an that's the Gawd's truth." Then Cassie lowered her voice even more. "Mr. Rolands hires Negro women to work down the basement. He lines'um up that way so he can pick the ones look like they willing to work hard."

Mr. Rolands walked up and down the line of potential employees with his hand on a thin stick as if it were a riding crop, and when he touched one on the shoulder with his stick, she turned around for him to check out her backside. Sometimes he made one bend over or show him how high she could reach up over her head. If he nodded his head, that woman was hired.

"Aunt Cassie, will I have to bend over for him if he touches me with that stick?"

"Brigid, if Mr. Rolands asks you to bend over, then yes, you bend over. But I don't spect him to ask you. Now I got to get to work. Don't want that weasel Schmidt having any ground on me. And Brigid, we always enter the building using the Drake Street door, never Bay Street; you hear what I'm saying?"

Brigid nodded.

"Mr. Rolands's office on de second floor. Tell his secretary yuh my niece and that yuh wanna talk to him bout a jawb. He's nevuh been disappointed in anyone I sent, so please don't be de first."

Chapter 2

Brigid had long known life's two central lessons for becoming a valued member of the McGonegal clan: first and foremost, earn your keep. Followed by the close second, never let yourself be had. So it was with great pride the next morning when Brigid pulled the green smock over her head and walked out the door, no longer the lily-livered child she knew her aunt thought her to be, but, instead, as a cigar maker—someone people would respect, perhaps even her cranky Aunt Cassie.

When she walked onto the factory floor, Brigid had to force her eyes open against the burning sting of ammonia. Her throat tightened. A nervous feeling of suffocation rose in her chest. She wanted to run over to one of the windows, throw it open, stick her head out, maybe even jump. Anything for a breath of fresh air.

"Watch out," said the nurse, touching Brigid on the elbow to keep her from bumping into the stock boy pushing a cart stacked high with tobacco. "The doctor's ready to see yuh now."

Brigid wiped the sweat from her face before pressing her handkerchief to her nose.

"I'm used to de smell," said the nurse. "It's the dust I can't stand," she added indifferently.

Brigid had never seen a doctor in an office before. If she were sick, her aunt sent for the colored woman, Miss Huger. Miss Huger—*Hugh-Gee*—never had proper training, but she could heal, that was for true.

The nurse motioned for her to have a seat on the exam table. Brigid didn't speak, her nature being inclined toward extremely quiet. She maneuvered inside the curious metal arms protruding from either side of the table, and lifted herself up.

"Evuh had yuh blood drawn?" the nurse asked.

She shook her head. The nurse wiped the inside of Brigid's arm with iodine before piercing the skin with a large needle. Brigid willed herself not to pass out.

"Yuh married?" she asked.

"No," answered Brigid.

"Engaged?"

Brigid shook her head.

"Got a steady fellow?"

"No fellow at all," answered Brigid, feeling embarrassed by her apparent shortcomings.

"Evuh had relations?"

"Pardon me?" Brigid did not understand the question. Her arm continued to bleed and the nurse handed her a rag to staunch it.

"With men, you know—relations?" said the nurse directing her gaze toward Brigid's lap.

Speechless at such an implication, she could only shake her head no.

"Alright," said the nurse, "slip out your uniform and your drawers then lie down on the table and put your feet in them stirrups. He's got to examine you down there."

Down there?

A gray-headed man in a white coat came in the room. "Evuh had bad blood or any social disease?" the doctor asked, his breath smelling of cigar smoke.

"No, doctor," she said, her legs shaking despite the oppressive heat and foul air.

"Evuh stay on West Street?"

Brigid felt his hands touching her where no one had ever touched her before. Then it got worse and she wanted to cry out.

"Answer the doctor's question, chile," said the nurse.

"No, my aunt told me never go on West Street," she answered frantically.

"Relax yuh muscles. Tensing up that way only meks my job more difficult," said the doctor.

"Hail Mary full a grace, de Lord is wid dee," Brigid urgently prayed.

"There we go, I'm done. Good job," he announced, sounding pleased with himself. "Royal Cigar is about to invest four hundred dollars in wasted tobacco training you. That's a lot of money, isn't it?"

"Yes, sir, it is," she managed to say, her voice barely audible.

"We have over a thousand girls wuk'n fuh us. Think of that, four hundred dollars we spend training each one. That's why we gotta mek sure you're not in de family way and that you don't have a social disease. We're not like them textile mills up the country. Noooo! You can be proud to wuk here. Now listen to me, if I hear you ain keeping yuh se'f morally fit, then I'll have you report for anudduh exam. If something is missing—you understand—you come see me."

"Thank you, doctor," said Brigid, looking away, ashamed to look him in the eye. She pulled the sheet a little higher.

"Our girls are as fine as any over at Ashley Hall School. Don't let nobody tell you different."

The doctor and the nurse left the room with Brigid blowing her nose and dabbing her eyes on her all-too-worn handkerchief. She wanted to dive into a breaking wave, let the sand churning within scrub her clean. Instead, she put her uniform back on, this time noticing the insignia of Chief Papakeecha in full headdress on her smock. He faced left rather than right and she thought that odd; he appeared to be looking back over his shoulder rather than ahead.

Brigid climbed the stairs to the third floor, where she found row after row of long wooden tables as far as the eye could see. The girls sat elbow to elbow, their work areas separated by a board that allowed them to stack their cigars. Brigid's head throbbed while her eyes burned. Particles of brown tobacco dust floated in the sunlight. She felt the dust beneath her feet. Saw footprints made in it across the wooden floor. A thin film of brown dust covered everything: the worktables, the walls, even the windows, which were kept closed so the breeze would not dry out the tobacco. Aunt Cassie looked up, not in greeting, but merely to verify if Brigid were still standing.

Brigid walked toward the back of the floor where a sign read: NEW GIRLS. Dust caught in her throat and when she coughed her eyes closed and she bumped into a worktable.

"Watch it, will yuh?" the young woman barked. "I'm cut'n wrappuh leaf."

"Come close, ladies. My name is Mr. Schmidt. I talk strange; I'm from up North. I'm the foreman for the third and fourth floor. This here's Miss Sweeny and she's going to be training you ladies. Everybody smile." He was looking at Brigid as he said this, and she wished he would turn away. Something about his look made her feel as if he knew about what the doctor had done. But he would not look away, and Brigid, wanting to be good and do right, met his eye and smiled.

"That's better," he beamed, "hate to see my girls frowning. I know it smells but if you're good with your hands, it will soon smell like money.

"You've been selected to learn a job that requires a fine skill. We got niggers down in the basement to stem and cure the tobacco, and they put the boxes together up on the fifth floor, but you girls are special—you girls are the most important workers in this factory because you actually make the cigars we sell." He smiled. "Welcome to Royal Cigar, ladies." Then he locked his hands behind his back and strolled off down the aisle.

Brigid smiled. It was her nature to do as she was told.

"Listen to me now," began Miss Sweeny. "First thing yuh gonna do in de mawnin is come ovuh yah tuh de stock boy's counter tuh get yuh tobacco. The stock boy, he write down de weight of de filluh, de binduh, and de wrappuh leaf next to yuh name. Yuh got to mek at least—I say at least—one hundred cigars from every pack yuh get. That's one hundred cigars that pass inspection, yuh understand? If de cigar don't pass, we dock yuh fuh wasting tobacco."

Brigid longed for a BC Powder. She watched Mr. Schmidt walking about the floor. One girl sitting on the end of the aisle pushed her knife off the table after he walked by. He turned and smiled as the young woman made a production of standing up and bending over to pick up the knife. Mr. Schmidt continued down the aisle, his fingers waving at her from the clasped position behind his back.

"How many times she drop that knife when he walk by?" said someone toward the back.

"Bet she short an looking for a little filler to meet quota," said another.

"Oh yeah! She looking fuh sump'n," said the first. "I'd rather get docked than let Schmidt fumble my behind. Shooo!"

"Schmidt always looking to steal a pinch," said yet another.

"It's Mr. Rolands's son you got to look out for. He wants more than a pinch."

"Crab Claws, that's what we ought to call Schmidt," said the first.

The women laughed. "Oh yeah! Look out, a debble crab running cross the beach."

"Kick'um back in de watuh fore de wave runs out an we stuck wid'um."

Giggles and whispers went up and down the rows: "We going to call Schmidt Crab Claws."

Brigid watched a girl whisper into Cassie's ear. Her aunt did not laugh, nor did she pass the word any further.

"Three types of tobacco go into each cigar: Filler, binder, and wrapper leaf." Miss Sweeny raised her voice to get attention. "Start with your binder leaf. Lay it down and smooth it out so it's ready when you got your filler shaped."

Compared to binder leaf, the filler felt coarse, almost crunchy, reminding Brigid of autumn leaves in Hampton Park.

"Put the filler leaf in the palm of your left han'," said Miss Sweeny. "Close your fist to give it shape. Now add another leaf puntop the first. Close your fist to shape it, that's right. Tips face the same direction. Now add another, yeah, that's right. Shape it. Gone use six filler leafs. Six. Don't press too much. Girls, listen to me. Keep the same space between each of your filler leaves. That space is for the air to pass through when the man takes a puff. Not too tight, not too loose either."

The place did not smell like cigar smoke. To Brigid, the air she breathed in consisted of a cross between horse piss and kerosene.

"The sweetest taste comes from the tip of the filler leaf. We wanna man's first puff to be his best. That's why the tips got to be on the lighting end of the cigar." Miss Sweeny studied everyone's progress. "Don't press so hard. You choke it," she admonished Brigid. "Okay, now put them pressed filler leaves on the corner of that binder leaf you already got smoothed out. Then roll it up like this." She held hers up for them to see. "That's called a bunch. A bunch."

From the main area of the floor, Brigid heard someone say, "New girls slow you down. I don't want one next to me."

Followed by, "I hear Miss Cassie's niece is one of um."

To which the other answered, "Oh yeah. Wonder if she's a sourpuss like her aunt."

"Alright," announced Miss Sweeny. "Everyone should have a bunch. Put that bunch in your mold to shape it. Miss Cassie's niece, what's your name?"

"Brigid," she answered timidly.

"Brigid, you relying too much on your eyes. Get the feel of it."

The women on the floor let out a cheer.

"Okay, okay. I guess I can spare fifteen or twenty minutes," a girl announced before she stepped up on a crate, pulled a newspaper from her satchel and began to read aloud, spelling out words from time to time if she could not pronounce them.

"*Allies strike powerful blow in West, smashing Germans in Flanders . . .*"

"If you gonna listen, you better learn how to keep your hands moving at the same time," Miss Sweeny huffed, clearly disapproving of the girl reading aloud. "Your aunt work hard to beat quota every week. Miss Cassie's one of the fastest cigar makers we got. Luella up there, she fast but she won't go over the quota. She'd rather waste her time acting the fool."

Luella continued reading. "*'Women of South Carolina need waking up,' declared Miss Jennie White, a volunteer nurse of the American Red Cross. Miss White is in Charleston visiting her brother while she awaits to sail for service in France . . .*"

A collective "ahhhhhh" went up across the floor.

"I wish I could be a nurse," said one woman.

"Don't we all," said another.

"You got to have schooling to be a nurse."

"*'Most of the wounds are caused by—s-h-r-a-p-n-e-l . . .'*"

"If I were a nurse, I'd wanna marry a doctor so I could stop being a nurse," said another.

"*'I saw men who were in very critical condition and upon whom there was no in—indi—indication of a wound. Scores of them are stone-deaf . . .'*"

"Gonna be them shellshocked ones coming back to Chaa'ston looking for a girl."

"Don't interrupt," shouted another. "Let her read. We can talk about it when she's done."

"Wrapper leaf is more valuable than your firstborn child," said Miss Sweeny, trying to compete with the story of the Red Cross nurse.

"*Many soldiers suffer from frostbitten feet. Amputation is often necessary . . .*"

A collective gasp went up, including from Miss Sweeny.

"*We need those woolen garments that your Red Cross societies are going to knit . . .*"

"Treat wrapper leaf like it was the family Jewels," declared Miss Sweeny.

Brigid smiled politely, but she couldn't stop listening to Luella and the article about the nurse. The cigar makers kept right on working; if anything, they seemed to work faster with a good story to occupy their minds. If only her head would stop hurting and she could learn to be fast like her aunt. Working at the cigar factory was more interesting than any law office or bank. In an office, there might be one other girl and all day long they would have to keep quiet. The most they would say would be "Yes, Mr. Vanderhorst," and "Yes, Mr. Ravenel," and "Yes, Mr. Manigault."

"Wrapper leaf comes from Cuba," Miss Sweeny drudged on. "Look out the window there and you see the darkies unloading the ship. Wrapper leaf is so delicate you got to keep it under a damp cloth on your table til you ready to use it."

Miss Sweeny carried on so about wrapper leaf, Brigid thought of the white cloth as a holy veil.

"*Poor people of London can't afford to buy knitting wool; however, wool is purchased by women of more means and given to poorer women who go to sewing rooms . . .*"

"That's us," someone piped up. "I'd knit for our soldiers if some South of Broad lady would buy me the wool."

"You can't let it dry out and you can't let it get soggy. You ruin wrapper leaf," Miss Sweeny paused for emphasis, "Mr. Schmidt gone dock your pay envelope."

Brigid blessed herself before lifting the moist cloth.

"Chile, don't get smart," said Miss Sweeny.

It was sheer like a silk stocking and the color of coffee with cream. If she had touched anything more fragile before, Brigid could not recall. And the veins, how curious. Mysterious even. And then, because all the fuss over wrapper leaf seemed silly, Brigid laughed out loud. "Excuse me," she whispered, repentantly.

"'*Women of South Carolina need waking up . . .*'"

"Put the shiny side of the leaf down. Then step on the foot pedal to raise the die. That creates suction and holds the leaf down so it's easier to cut. Take the knife and run it along the edge. That's how you cut wrapper leaf. Used to be took months—I say months—to learn how to make that cut, but with these suction tables, we can train a girl in eight weeks. Next thing, look at the leaf, you got to see which way you gonna roll it. You ever look at collards? Same as tobacco. If the veins move out to the right, that's a right roll. Begin on the left and roll to the right. That's it, let the spirals overlap slightly."

Luella began another article.

"*Congress urges Southern states to conform their child labor laws to the laws of the United States . . .*"

"I don't think the colored should bring they chillun to stem tobacco."

"Why not?" another one asked a few rows back.

"You girls better be worrying about your own jobs and not anybody else's." Mr. Schmidt's voice boomed out all of a sudden. Brigid didn't know where he had come from but he was now striding up toward Luella standing on her crate.

"Luella," he said, angrily, "I told you not to read those sorts of articles."

"Mr. Schmidt, I'm proud of my reading. Lots of girls in here can't hardly read at all, but that don't mean they don't deserve to know what's happening in the world."

Brigid couldn't believe it. A girl not much older than herself was standing on a crate, eyeball to eyeball with the boss, and not apologizing for making him mad. Even more shocking was that Schmidt didn't say another word. He turned quickly and got on the freight elevator and left the floor. A cheer went up. Watching her was like seeing a movie star step out of the screen and into the audience. Luella was the most courageous—the most amazing—girl Brigid had ever met. Luella took a bow and went back to reading them the paper.

"See this tag you got hanging off here?" Miss Sweeny held up her cigar for all to observe.

"This little cup has gum paste in it. Dip your finguh in there and slide it along that tag while your turning the cigar like this—now, you don't even see it."

"Here's something everybody wanna hear," said Luella. "*Hop at the Isle of Palms. Avail yourself of the final op—op-por—opportunity—to dance at the resort this season. Four to eleven-thirty P.M. September seventh . . .*"

The rapidly moving hands of every cigar maker, except Brigid's Aunt Cassie, went momentarily still.

"Some girls lick the tip or lick they finger and run it up and down like this to fix that tag."

"Miss Sweeny," said Brigid, feeling she must compliment the teacher, "your cigar is beautiful."

"Yeah well, maybe it is, and maybe it ain, but getting that tip tucked right is hard to do."

"Music by the Metz Military Band. Program to include Bellini's Overture to Norma . . . Sump'n, sump'n I can't even begin to pronounce . . . and Wagner's Song to Evening Star. Ferry steamer leaves city one P.M., and every two hours thereafter until ten P.M. Last train leaves Isle of Palms eleven-thirty P.M., and the last ferry back to town will leave Mount Pleasant at midnight."

Hundreds of women, including Brigid, drifted into an ammonia-enriched reverie, picturing the life of a Red Cross nurse, and a soldier in uniform asking her to the last dance of the season at the pavilion on the Isle of Palms.

"Then take the ring gauge for whatever shape you're asked to make—this here a Corona, and it uses a forty-two ring gauge. See how the cigar slides easy back an forth? No wiggling round or nothing like that."

Brigid felt dizzy watching Miss Sweeny's ring-gauge demonstration.

"I'm telling you," Miss Sweeny resumed. Brigid wondered where the woman found the breath to keep talking. "You gonna sweat, curse, and cry trying to learn to tuck that tip. Now let me tell you sump'n. I'm gonna tell you what the man gonna do. That tip you struggled with to get just right? The man gone bite off that tip an spit it out befo he even lights the durn cigar! Say befo he even lights the durn cigar!"

Chapter 3

When the workweek ended Saturday afternoon, Cassie and Brigid got in line to receive their pay in cash from Mr. Rolands, who sat at a table outside near the Blake Street entrance. Despite the troubles with her hands, Cassie managed to get five over the quota to earn $10.75. She didn't approve of young Brigid working at the cigar factory, but she did appreciate that together they would have $14.75 to take with them to the market.

Blake Street was a muddy slop from an earlier rain. No one wanted to walk in the road and all vied for the small sidewalk on either side. Cassie and Brigid pulled up their white uniform dresses in a futile attempt to keep the hemline clean.

"We smell to high heaven but we got to take the trolley to the market or there won't be anything left," said Cassie. "This ain a proper job for you, Brigid. People going to look down their noses at us dressed like this—stinking like this."

"It'll be alright, Aunt Cassie," said Brigid, dodging a particularly large mud puddle. "Wind's coming out of the north. The fertilizer plant is making it smell like rotten fish all over town."

Cassie sniffed. "I can't hardly even smell anymore."

A trolley approached. Brigid and Cassie weren't the only ones going from the factory to the market. Because the Negro workers came out the Bay Street door on the south side of the building, they were naturally closer to the front door of the trolley when it stopped, and the white workers, having come out the Blake Street entrance on the north end, now found themselves closer to the rear door. The trolley waited as the white and Negro women became entwined, trying to board through the proper door.

"What a mess!" huffed Cassie, as she and Brigid worked their way to seats near the front of the car. Cassie could remember as a little girl getting on the trolley through whatever door was closest and taking the nearest seat. The Negroes did the same and no one was worse off for it. Then the countrymen politicians and Ben Tillman changed everything with the Jim Crow law. In those moments—with the sun blaring down, everyone tired from working and just trying to get to the market before the last crumbs were gone, well, in those moments, she believed that the Jim Crow was the absolute most ridiculous idea any man ever thought up.

"How's your headache?" Cassie asked Brigid as the car rocked and swayed further downtown.

"Not as bad as yesterday."

Oh Brigid, thought Cassie, always trying to put on a good face. Even if she was a bit mousy, Brigid wasn't a complainer. Cassie knew the girl didn't feel well. She hadn't had an appetite since the day she started work. Cassie decided to look right away for a bargain on some stew meat. They hadn't had meat since the week before and Brigid looked like she needed a good meal.

Buzzards lined the roof of the City Market. Signs posted on North and South Market Street warned: Five Dollar Fine for the Killing of One of These Birds!

"E ain got no mo beef. Oonuh bin yah mo sooner fuh beef. Lam' shank all e got now," said the Negro man working with the butcher.

"Well, I couldn't get here more sooner," said Cassie, irritated by the idea she chose to come to the market so late on a Saturday. "Give me fifty-cent of lam' since yuh out of beef."

"T'ree tummetuhs, tek how much?" Cassie asked at the next stall.

"Ten an faw-ibe cent," the man replied.

"Gimme the ones without them flies puntop," said Cassie.

The Negro street vendors came through the neighborhood most mornings with their cart selling fish or fresh vegetables, but Saturday at the market was the only time for buying meats. On Saturday, many farmers came in their boats from Wadmalaw, Kiawah, Yonges, and Johns Island, bringing a variety of vegetables and fruits. By that time of day, however, many had already packed up and gone, wanting to take advantage of the tide for the trip back to the islands before dark.

Amid the buzzing of flies and the relentless press of the late August sun, Brigid and Cassie made their way about the stalls, buying bananas, okra, sivy beans, corn, and five pounds of rice.

"Iceman won't come on Sunday," said Cassie. "We better stop with what we got here." Brigid found two boxes and they divided the food between them to carry home. As they were nearing the stall where Cassie had bought the lamb, they had to stop short when a large section of carcass landed on the cobblestone street a few feet in front of them.

"I'd have waited ten minutes," Cassie snapped at the butcher, "if I'd known you was gonna throw it out." The buzzards wasted no time.

They made their way to King Street.

"Miss Sweeny put me next to Luella today," said Brigid as if she had been seated next to the Queen of England. "Why didn't you tell me bout the Bank? Luella explained it to me. I wanna make my cuts good enough to have extra to deposit. Then one day, if I come up short an need a little wrapper leaf, I can make a withdrawal. I think it's grand how the girls look out for one another. Luella says if too many people go over the quota, they move it higher and everybody becomes a nervous wreck trying to keep up."

"Luella not looking out for you. That girl going to get herself fired one day. Listen to me, some girls always scheming how to beat the company. Us against them. No matter what they call it over the years—the Bank, the Breadbox, whatever—it's a bad idea. I work to take care of my own. Shooo! I worry bout my own family's suppuh table, that's right, my own family's suppuh table."

"Aunt Cassie, I appreciate everything you do for me. I mean it; I'm grateful to you for taking me in."

"Don't sweetmouth me. I'm telling you that Mr. Rolands, the daddy now, the daddy Mr. Rolands is a fine gentleman. Ever since he come down from New Jersey, he's treated me fair. I wanna treat him the same way back. Brigid, you got to learn to live your own life; I'm just telling you how I see it. To change the subject, Mr. Rouvalis is putting a new heel on my Sunday shoes and I need to get over there before he close."

Amid the clop-clop of horses hooves and the hiss and clank of a trolley, came the call of a trumpet followed by a trombone's response.

"Mother of Gawd," declared Cassie, seeing the sidewalk up ahead blocked. "We're shot at every turn."

"I love the Jenkins Orphanage Band!" Brigid shifted her box of groceries to reach into her work-smock pocket for a penny. Mr. Daniel Jenkins raised money for his Negro orphanage by teaching the boys to play music. Wearing worn-out hand-me-down Citadel uniforms taken up at every seam if necessary, the boys performed for spare change on street corners throughout downtown. Each time the band played, they were "led" by the smallest boy in the group, who stood in front "conducting" with his baton.

"Listen to it," scoffed Cassie. "They start out too low. Sounds flat. If worry made a sound, that'd be it. Shooo! Look at them proper girls imitating the pickaninny dance steps. They call that music? I swaytogawd they playing more than one song at the same time."

As the sound of the clarinets, horns, drums, and trombones rose among the shops on King Street, people came out to listen and watch the show. Cassie's feet hurt and she began to worry the meat might spoil in the sun. The other side of the street didn't look any better. The horse-drawn dray of the ice seller was stopped beside a restaurant. Then right in the middle of the road a trolley car came to a grinding metal-on-metal screeching halt. The conductor began directing all the passengers to disembark.

"I wanna get by this foolishness. Let's take Queen over to the next block," said Cassie, hefting her box of lamb-shank, bananas, and rice higher.

Brigid's eyes nearly popped out of her head.

"Did you see a ghost or did someone shoot you?" said Cassie, completely irritated with everything and everyone at that moment. "Don't be so timid all the time."

Brigid didn't say a word. She repositioned her box of groceries and followed her aunt to the infamous West Street.

Women—Negro, white, and all shades in between—appeared like hidden decorations, not always obvious to the eye at first, but on second take, Cassie would see one, or a portion of one, looking out an opened window, leaning over a railing, or just inside a doorway. Somewhere, a piano played and then stopped, played and then stopped. The yards, if not a tangle of oleander and fig vine, were littered with empty liquor bottles, chickens, and even an occasional milking cow. The chickens, cows, and trash spread out from the yard into the muddy street.

"No sense staring down," said Cassie. "Hold your head up an look around."

A white man in a nice suit and hat closed the metal gate behind him, and seeing Cassie and Brigid, awkwardly tipped his hat while keeping his head down, anxious to get beyond them on the sidewalk.

"You should be ashamed," Cassie called after him, as he passed. She watched him scurry away. "That was Mr. Shaftesbury from the bank."

The piano started again.

"Bosoms falling out all over the place," said Cassie. "And we look the fool in these durn uniforms. Bet they think we from the Temperance League or sump'n."

"Welcome to West Street, ladies," called a red-headed woman leaning out from an upstairs window, her breasts unbounded and free to the afternoon sun.

"Thank you. Good afternoon," Brigid called back. Seeing the look on her aunt's face, she added softly, "I didn't wanna be rude."

"Tell me if you see Maria Poverelli," said Cassie. "I always liked her, even if she did let herself get into trouble."

They were about to pass the back end of a cemetery. When Cassie raised her hand to bless herself, she noticed a young white girl walking toward them with something strapped to her back. A Negro man followed close behind her. As the girl and the man turned to enter the cemetery gate, Cassie saw that what she had strapped to her back was a small dirty mattress. Cassie blessed herself again, motioning for Brigid to do the same.

"Cassie McGonegal," a man's voice called out from a first-floor porch. "I'll be damn if it ain Cassie McGonegal walking on West Street. I got to say hello." He was a big red-faced Irishman and he jumped up from the swing, leaving the attention of the ladies to another gentleman, and came out to the sidewalk to greet Cassie.

He made a grand gesture of taking off his hat and bowing before Cassie and Brigid. "Good afternoon, ladies. Cassie, let me express my deep sorrow to hear of yuh brothuh Charles's passing. Young lady, we haven't spoken before. Your fathuh was aces in my book. And one of the finest sailors, too. All the captains ever worked wid'um will tell yuh de same. He was aces. May Gawd rest his soul."

"Gawd rest his soul," said Brigid and Cassie.

"Mayor Grace," said Cassie, "do you think Father O'Shaughnessy approves of you spending your Saturday on West Street?"

"Ah, Cassie, I've always loved how you struggle to find the kindest words for a man. I'm here on business true, but not the sort you're thinking. But I'm glad you brought that up, because tonight I'm launching my campaign for the next term with a speech at the Hibernian Hall. Why don't you both come?

The Bourbons stole my second term from me, but I aim to win it back. I've got the Irish vote. I'm convinced I can unite all the laboring people here in Chaa'ston: The Germans, the Italians, the Jew merchants, the stevedores and longshoremen. Hell, I wouldn't mind if we let the darkies vote in the Democratic primary again. But the Bourbons won't ever let that happen. No, they'd rather see us rot in genteel poverty and disease than clean this town up and invest in the future."

"You never lose your fight, do you, John?" Cassie and John had grown up together in Ansonborough. John Grace would never be canonized, but Cassie McGonegal and the rest of the Irish descendents would always support him because he was "our own."

A cow walked by, its udders dangling low. Behind it, soft clumps of manure fell into the muddy street.

"If you get reelected," asked Cassie, "will you clean up this street, an I ain talking bout that cow."

"Since King Charles gave the Carolinas to the Lords Proprietors, the men of Chaa'ston have sought out prostitutes to do what their wives prefer not to do, and that's the Gawd's truth."

"John, before my very eyes just now, I saw the most awful sight. Awful. A young white girl taking a colored man. Why, it's happening in the cemetery as we speak. Christ, have mercy!"

"Cassie, when we went in the surf as kids, didn't I always tell you don't ever try to swim against a riptide? You got to go sideways to a strong current or you'll drown. I'm telling you, from South of Broad to clear up on the Neck—the men of this town support integration so long as it's limited to the whorehouses of West Street."

"It's not right, John, and you know it," she persisted.

"Everybody knows the longest funeral procession in the history of South Carolina was for John C. Calhoun, but let me tell you sump'n, the second longest procession was for a Madam by the name of Grace Piexotto. She ran a house right ovuh dare on Beresford Alley. I ain gonna swim against a riptide. But I will try my best to make sure no other girl like Brigid here loses her mother to typhoid from contaminated milk bottles. And again, let me express my sympathies, Miss Brigid, for you having lost both parents so young." He was getting redder in the face and sweat rolled into his sideburns. "We're better off keeping these establishments on these two streets alone. We know where they are. We can get the girls tested for social diseases. If we broke this up, and the girls—"

"Hold your breath, John. I can't vote so it don't make no difference if I agree with you or not," snapped Cassie.

John Grace laughed. "I miss you, Cassie." He wiped his face with his handkerchief. "The women up North are pushing hard for the suffrage. Come to the Hall tonight. I think a cold bay-uh would do you good."

"I don't drink beer, so no thank you. If I don't get this meat in the icebox soon, I'm gonna die from one of them diseases you like to worry bout."

They were almost to the corner when Brigid suddenly turned and ran back down West Street, carrying her box of vegetables, calling out, "Mr. Grace, Mr. Grace," and when he stopped, Cassie was shocked to hear her niece ask him, "What time is the meeting tonight?"

Chapter 4

That evening, wearing her smartest gingham frock, Brigid rode the Meeting Street trolley by herself to Hibernian Hall. Aunt Cassie wanted no part of such a thing, preferring to spend the cherished Saturday night sitting on the front porch darning a pair of stockings, and keeping an eye on a pot of sivy beans steaming on the stove.

Stepping off the trolley in front of the imposing white-columned building sitting atop a flight of stairs, Brigid was reminded of a picture in one of her schoolbooks: Mount Olympus, where Zeus himself lived.

Brigid hesitated before the gate adorned with a small golden harp. Her insides felt nervous. Could it be the well-traveled lamb they had for supper? The feeling wasn't entirely of a bilious nature. She likened it more to the sense of fear she had when she was a child and her father insisted she swim out to him even though the water was over her head. As she made her way through the rise and fall of the waves, she heard his voice shouting encouragement, "That a girl." When she reached his outstretched arms, he shouted happily, "Now I don't have to worry when yuh go in de surf alone." She would never forget his smiling face as they floated together before swimming back to shore.

Standing on the sidewalk that evening, she missed her father. This was the sort of political meeting he would have attended. "That a girl," she heard his voice calling to her as she began to ascend the steps, passing between the scroll-topped columns, and beneath another, larger, golden harp, before entering through the wooden double doors.

"We have no more true liberty than our cousins back in Ireland," John Grace thundered from the podium. Brigid genuflected out of habit before stepping into the only aisle with an empty seat. The woman next to her handed her a program, and like everyone else, Brigid used hers to fan herself.

"I pray Gawd every day to free Ireland from the tyranny of British rule, just as I pray for us to be free from the tyranny of the Broad Street Boni. That's what I call them. The Boni, the ones born into wealth who control everything in this town: our banks, our law firms, and our elections, too!" The crowd applauded and cheered. "Both my grandfathers—both of them, you understand—both my grandfathers fought for the Confederacy in that foolish war that brought us only devastation. And for what? The boys of the South died fighting to prolong a way of life for a privileged few. Now, pestilence is Chaa'ston's comeuppance for her role in the mortal sin, yes, I say mortal sin, of fighting to prolong slavery in America."

The applause was not as robust as before.

"The average life expectancy of a white person in Chaa'ston today is thirty-six, an for a Negro, it's twenty-two. You don't even wanna know where we stand on infant mortality. We have an open watuh tank on Wentworth Street and all day long buzzards sit puntop it. The Negro alleys are nothing more than open sewers running alongside the very wells from which they drink. Let me tell yuh sump'n, typhoid and consumption are blind to skin color.

"If I'm elected mayor, I will ban livestock within the city, pave the streets, and extend sewer and waterlines into the Negro alleys. I will get rid of the foul odor that permeates our Holy City."

Brigid joined the crowd and rose to her feet, swept up in the enthusiasm for the burly, red-faced Irishman.

"I will make the College of Chaa'ston free for all white males!"

Brigid found little to clap for in that one.

"I am committed to the city purchasing the rotting waterfront wharves. We must restore our port to its former place of prominence on the East Coast. The Boni look to the past and say, how can we get it back? How can we maintain a system of cheap labor shackled to the legacy of slavery? The economy based on exportation of Sea Island cotton and rice is over. The future is in industry. The future is in rebuilding our port and improving access to it. The future is in bringing tourists to our beaches."

Everyone stood up again and cheered.

Brigid had never thought about the future. Not in the grand way that John Grace spoke of it. Ever since she had started to work at the cigar factory, she felt her life starting to turn. It was more than the wages she took home; it was something else. As if her ordinary life now held possibility, maybe even the possibility for happiness. Fearful of the disappointment sure to follow giving in to such a notion, she blessed herself and said an Act of Contrition.

"Our peninsula is too isolated. We need a bridge from downtown to Mount Pleasant. We need that bridge to provide access to other towns along the coast. If elected mayor, I will push a progressive agenda for *our* people, the working people of Chaa'ston. If elected, I promise to build a bridge across the Cooper River."

An Irish band struck up a Donegal reel. John Grace raised his fist in the air, ready to lead the charge. Men made a fast break for the bar. Ladies Brigid knew from Saint Mary's parish came up to offer their condolences on the loss of her father.

The band was quite good and Brigid smiled and clapped to the rhythm, glad to be away from the dreary little apartment. That was when she noticed a particular young man upstairs near the railing. She looked away, mortified, when he saw her looking at him. She became painfully aware of being there by herself. Loneliness overcame her joy. She went to find the ladies' room. Once there, she took her time, tipping the Negro woman the only nickel she could spare and still have trolley fare to get back home. Brigid checked her hair in the mirror, looked down to make sure her drawers weren't showing beneath her dress. The sound of the tin whistle rose above the Bodhran drum.

She felt silly for coming downtown alone. Her Aunt Cassie was right. Political meetings should be left to the men. The only way out was through the crowd. She pushed into the throng.

Halfway across the main hall she ran into the young man from the balcony, the one who had ruined her evening by looking at her after she had looked at him. He was short, barely taller than she, with skin so reddened by the sun, it was nearly purple. She tried not to meet his eye as she stepped around him.

"Excuse me," he said, stepping in front of her. "Yuh feeling alright, miss?"

This caught her off guard, and she looked up. "I'm fine," she said, wondering why in the world he would ask.

"You were in de head a long time. I figured you was feeling bilious so I got you a bay-uh to help yuh digestion," he said, extending the glass for her.

She hesitated a moment, pondering this unusual introduction. "Thank you," she said, accepting his offer of a beer.

"Manus O'Brian," he said, and nodded.

"Brigid McGonegal," she replied.

"Please to meet you," he answered.

The band started a slower song, a romantic ballad, and this increased the awkwardness between them.

"What parish you go to?" Brigid asked.

"Saint Patrick's," he answered.

"Saint Mary's," she said, before he asked.

"What'd you think of his speech?" Manus wanted to know.

"I liked it fine." Brigid answered quickly, not wanting to say more for fear of sounding foolish.

"No, really," he persisted, "I wanna know what you thought about it."

"Me? I don't know," she stammered. What difference did it make to him what she thought? She'd never met a boy who asked such things.

"You believe Gawd's punishing Chaa'ston wid all dis disease we got now on account of slavery time?"

"Shoooo! My people are working people. We never owned no slaves."

"Mine neither," he answered sharply. "But I'm asking you, do you believe what he say bout slavery being a mortal sin?"

"Tie yuh mouth," she scolded him while looking around nervously. "We're not spose to talk about such as that. It ain fitting conversation."

Anger flashed and receded across his face. He spoke with regret in his voice. "No one heals himself by wounding another says Saint Ambrose. Pardon me if I offended you." He turned to walk away. The crowd blocked his path. He touched a man lightly on the arm, trying to get by.

"I'm not that easily offended," Brigid called out. Manus turned around. "My mother died from typhoid fever. They say it come from the milk bottles being washed in dirty water. If John Grace can stop the typhoid fever, then I'm all for him. Far as that other stuff he talked about, I don't know bout any of that. But I know I'm sick of dis bay-uh—you want the rest of it?"

"Sure," he said, taking her glass and finishing the drink in one long swallow. "Ahhh," he said, suppressing a belch. "Temperance destroys de mind and kills passion." He wiped his mouth on his sleeve and smiled. "Thomas Aquinas."

Brigid added the words of Aquinas, along with the charming look on Manus's face, to the growing tangle of thoughts inside her head. One thing about being a cigar maker, she would have plenty of time for unraveling the knot.

In the lull between songs, John Grace could be heard saying to another man, "You crazy. Why send our men and our money to defend Britain an France when people here in Chaa'ston are dying from the filth of poverty. I say let Britain rot."

"And I say John Grace is full of crap," said the other man.

Grace's first punch knocked the man sideways, and his second to the nose sent blood flying.

The fracas spread and Manus put his arm around Brigid, shepherding her toward the door.

They rushed down the steps and out onto the Meeting Street sidewalk, both of them perspiring heavily in their dress clothes. Palmetto fronds scraped against one another in the steady onshore breeze. A crescent moon clung to the night sky.

"I hope nobody gets shot this time," said Manus. "Where you stay, Brigid?"

"I stay on Elizabeth Street with my Aunt Cassie," she answered.

"I'll wait with you til the trolley comes," he said. "I'd walk you home but I got to get to work. Gonna help my uncle unload a steamer that's due in from Cuba tonight."

"I work at the cigar factory," said Brigid, feeling proud as she said it.

"Maura O'Brian, my cousin, she work there. You know her?"

"No," she answered, disappointed, "but I just started."

Her trolley approached slowly from the south. Brigid wished it would break down and not come any closer. When it stopped, Manus didn't say anything. "Nice to meet you," she said, pulling herself up onboard.

"You and your aunt wanna to go to Sullivan's Island tomorrow afternoon?"

"I'll have to ask her," she said, as the driver released the break.

"I'll come to Saint Mary's in the mawnin," he said.

"We go to nine o'clock. Aunt Cassie prefers the Low Mass." The train started to roll. "Prayer ought to be short and pure." And as it picked up a little speed, she called out, "Saint Benedict—I think."

When Brigid took her seat, she saw Manus, still on the sidewalk watching the car moving away. She leaned out her window and when he saw her, he waved. She smiled, waving back, forgetting to be fearful of such happiness.

Chapter 5

Cassie had darned only one pair of stockings before her left hand went numb. For that reason, she now found herself walking into Sunday Mass wearing black stockings with brown shoes. Only her veil matched her stockings, but at least her shoes had new heels. She preferred Low Mass. No singing, no grand procession, no sermon, either. No fuss, just Father O'Shaughnessy getting down to the business of the sacrament while she herself meditated and prayed in relative peace and solitude.

Brigid and Cassie took their seats, kneeling quietly before the service began. Brigid kept fidgeting and Cassie knew it was on account of the young man she had met the night before. If the girl had any sense, she'd concentrate on learning to make a good left wrap cigar. That would be something worthwhile. Brigid didn't listen to her the way she used to. No, not anymore. Not since she'd been sitting by Miss High-and-Mighty Luella. Well, some duties were still clearly up to Cassie, and that was the only reason she had agreed to join Brigid and that no-doubt ne'er-do-well young man after Mass for an outing to Sullivan's Island. Cassie glanced at Brigid, eyes closed tight, her head bent in unusually deep prayer. What might she be praying about with such devotion?

A teapot of a young man genuflected beside the pew. Despite Cassie's look, he continued, tripping over the small board as all those unfamiliar with Saint Mary's pews were prone do to. He knelt and blessed himself.

"That's Manus," whispered Brigid to Cassie.

"Well he can't sit here," Cassie whispered back. "That's Mrs. Murphy's seat. Visitors sit in the back."

Cassie bowed her head and closed her eyes. When she heard the thump thump of the kneeler, she knew that he had gone.

Father O'Shaughnessy and an altar boy entered from the side of the sanctuary and everyone rose. As the priest knelt at the foot of the altar, Brigid gave her aunt a look, motioning her head to Mrs. Murphy's empty seat. Cassie knew full well that Mrs. Murphy was in Atlanta for a wedding and wouldn't return until Tuesday. That was not the point.

Father O'Shaughnessy finished his prayer, then reverently kissed the altar. "In nomine patris, et filii, et spiritus sancti." The congregation joined him in making the sign of the cross. The priest faced the tabernacle as he spoke—as he would throughout the Mass, offering the sacrifice to God on behalf of the faithful.

"Dominus vobiscum," recited Father O'Shaughnessy. The Lord be with you. To which Cassie, Brigid, and the rest of the congregation responded: "Et cum spiritu tuo." And also with you.

With Mass underway, Cassie began saying her rosary. The soft blanket of familiar sensations enveloped her: the solemn clank clank of the incense smoker, its regal smell filling the church, the immeasurable comfort of the Latin words falling upon her ears. Cassie cherished this time of being still within the house of her Lord.

Kyrie eleison
Kyrie eleison
Christe eleison

The call and response continued from the Kyrie through the Credo. Father O'Shaughnessy moved from left to right and back to the middle of the altar. He read the Epistle and an excerpt from the Gospel—both in Latin.

He offered the memento for the living and commemoration for the dead. He beat his chest three times, proclaiming: mea culpa mea culpa mea culpa. The altar boy poured wine and water over his hands, and at last it was time for Communion. Cassie joined the line, and waited for an opening at the altar rail. When one came available, she knelt down, blessed herself, and bowed her head, ready to receive.

Normally she kept her head down while walking back to her pew, but curiosity about this Manus O'Brian got the best of her and she decided to look up and see where he had decided to roost. He was sitting next to John Grace— who had a black eye that morning and looked rather ill. Their row was about to stand to get in line. She turned back just as she was entering her own pew and couldn't help from noticing that the young man had remained seated and the hulking John Grace was forced to climb over him. Cassie glanced one more time before kneeling and sure enough, Manus O'Brian was not going to Communion.

She knelt, unable to say her normal prayers, speculating as to why the young man might consider himself unfit to receive the sacrament. Perhaps he broke the proper fast with a late-night snack or an early bite of biscuit? Maybe even a cup of tea that morning? She thought about the venial sins that might keep a young man in his pew on a Sunday morning. What if it wasn't venial at all? Don't think such a thing, she told herself to no avail. What if he had a mortal sin on his soul?

Dominus vobiscum

She pushed up from her knees, her mind picturing the most unholy of possibilities in vivid detail. She cut her eyes to Brigid, looking for signs of complicity. Seeing only her niece's persistent innocent manner, Cassie concluded that if anything had happened last night, Brigid was not ashamed of it. At least not enough to feel she needed to go to confession before receiving Holy Communion.

Ite, Missa est
Deo gratias

Yes, the Mass is over, and thanks be to God, thought Cassie.

That afternoon, as the *Sappho* backed away from the Gaillard Street wharf, all hands sprang into action. Grunting and hollering, the men maneuvered twelve water-filled barrels about her decks in an attempt to increase stability for the side-wheel steamer prone to listing. This circus-like water barrel shuffle, unique to the *Sappho*, never ceased to fascinate Cassie.

The grand homes of High Battery came into view near Oyster Point. When the *Sappho*'s gears strained into forward, the side-wheel slowly turned and made its way along the waterfront to where the Ashley River joined the Cooper. The trash, the filthy wells, the buzzards—none of these were visible from onboard the *Sappho*.

"From this view here," said Manus, "No city is more beautiful to me. Not Havana, San Juan, not Genoa, or for the fact of the matter, not even Paris."

Cassie harrumphed. "Any port you ain made call?"

The three of them stood on deck, watching downtown recede to starboard, and the ferry turned again, this time heading east across the harbor to Sullivan's Island.

All the ferries were jam-packed on Sunday. Most people would take one to Mount Pleasant or Sullivan's and then board the Charleston & Seashore Railroad, continuing on to the Isle of Palms, a relatively new resort, proud to be "the next Coney Island." In contrast, Sullivan's was only a four-mile trip from downtown and a much quieter place to spend the day. Many of Charleston's Irish families had built small one- and two-room summer cottages there, and of course, the wealthy families had their share of larger places overlooking the water. Besides the summer cottages, the island was home to Fort Moultrie, presently a very busy place because of the war. The island had one elegant building at Station 22: The Atlantic Beach Hotel with over a hundred rooms, six turrets, and full verandas upstairs and down. The McGonegals might never be able to afford a night in the hotel, but setting up a picnic on the beach in front of it was the next best thing.

Being unfit for Communion notwithstanding, Cassie had to admit the young man had decent enough manners. He insisted on carrying all their bags, the beach umbrella, and two jugs of tea. The tide was out and so they walked a good ways across the sand before settling on a spot to spread out their blankets.

After changing into their swimming clothes at the bath house, the three of them sat in silence eating the boiled-egg sandwiches Cassie had made.

Muscles protruded from Manus like mountain ranges all over his body: Back, chest, arms, and even his thighs. Brigid could not stop staring, and Cassie found this unbecoming to a young lady. "Look, a pawpus," Cassie announced, pointing toward the water, even though she hadn't seen a thing and merely intended to distract Brigid.

Brigid, always trusting, turned, shaded her eyes with her hand, and dutifully scanned the water, waiting for the porpoise's fin to break the surface again.

"He sure is staying under a long time," said Brigid.

"Where your people stay, Manus?" Cassie asked.

"Eastside mostly. My mother, she passed some time ago, but my father and I stay on Bay Street."

"You related to Maura O'Brian that works in the cigar factory?" she asked.

"Maura's my first cousin," he answered. "She hates that place."

"Don't say nuttin bad bout de cigar factory," Brigid interrupted. "No no. Not in front of Aunt Cassie you don't."

Seagulls hovered and cawed, *Hiyak—Hiyah-Hiyak*, hoping for a scrap of food.

It seemed to Cassie that Maura O'Brian would do about anything to have a reason to show her behind to Mr. Schmidt. Always dropping this or that tool when he was around. Girls like Maura would eventually get themselves into trouble with one of the foremen and have to quit.

"They don't put up with foolishness," said Cassie, cutting her eyes to her niece. "Manus, tell us bout yuh s'ef. How you earn a living?"

"Right now I'm helping one of my uncles at the Columbus Street dock. But this is just temporary." Manus drew a circle in the sand with his big toe.

"Longshoreman?" Cassie huffed. "That's Negro work. And worse, that's union Negro work. Don't tell me you joined a darkie union?" Cassie shook her head in dismay, despite the look of outrage on young Brigid's face.

"Well, to be straight about it, I'm working as a stevedore. We handle the cargo while it's still on the ship, but soon as it's set down on the dock, that's when the longshoremen take over. I'm no scab Miss Cassie, no way. I'm a member of the National Union of Seamen and I work on the ship when it comes in, not on the dock. The longshoremen don't allow anybody that's not in their union to handle the cargo once it's on the dock."

"Oh Lord! You mean to tell me that the Negroes wouldn't let you work on the docks with them? I declare I ain never. May Gawd strike me dead before I let a darkie tell me where I can and can't work." The very thought of that upset Cassie so much she turned to face the other direction on the blanket.

"Now hol' on, Miss Cassie," said Manus. "The ILA does alright by them colored men. They earn a decent living. If you ask me, I think the cigar makers ought to join a union, and that's a fact."

"Well, nobody asked you," replied Cassie, her cheeks burning from the young man's insolence.

"Tide's coming in," said Brigid, trying to change the subject.

Hiyak—Hiyah-Hiyak

Oh, how Cassie wished these duties had not fallen to her. But since the girl didn't have a father or a mother, somebody had to ask the important questions.

"Manus, how come this job you got is temporary?" Cassie pushed on, ignoring Brigid, who looked as if a fishbone were stuck in her throat.

"I'm a member of the Irish Volunteers with the U.S. Army. We been down in Mexico chasing Poncho Villa. But you know, that didn't go so well and President Wilson called us back. We ship out next month for France."

Finally, some good news, thought Cassie. He would leave soon for the war. She could not suppress her relief. The last thing someone as impressionable as Brigid needed was a boy preaching a bunch of Bolshevik malarkey. Cassie looked to Brigid as if to say, *There now, no need to bother with this one.*

"Tide's coming in," said Brigid.

Hiyak—Hiyah-Hiyak

Manus, his face serious, his eyes on Brigid, began a recitation.

> *I must down go to the seas again, for the call of the running tide*
> *Is a wild call and a clear call that may not be denied . . .*

And when he finished, Brigid clapped, the look upon her face spoke volumes, reminding Cassie of something from another poem. A poem that Luella of all people had read to the girls, something about a heart being made too soon glad.

"I know those fellows pulling that bo-it down to the surf," said Manus. "I'm gonna give them a han'." He started to walk away, and then turned back. "Hey, Brigid, you wanna come?"

She reached beside her aunt, pulling her bonnet from the bag. "Quit cut'n yuh eye et me," said Brigid, her Geechee accent stronger than usual.

Cassie had never known her niece to take such a tone with her before. Maybe it was about time. Neither of them were getting any younger.

Brigid pulled her sun bonnet tight upon her head and ran down the beach to join Manus.

Chapter 6

It was the Feast of the Assumption, a holy day of obligation, and Brigid, her Aunt Cassie, and several of the other Catholic girls did not arrive at their work stations until after nine. Brigid took her seat next to Luella, pulled her small-handled cigar knife from her smock, and cut the string on her tobacco bundle.

"Wish'd us Lutherans had special days," said Luella, tightening the handle on her mold press. "What I can't believe is what I heard. I heard your aunt's the one got permission for all the Catholic girls to come late on the special days. Miss Cassie don't mess with no foreman. Nooo! She want sump'n, she go straight to Mr. Rolands."

"She hol's respect for Mr. Rolands," said Brigid, smoothing out a piece of binder leaf. Luella became quiet. "Luella, listen, I met a fella this weekend. He's smart about all kinds of things, even though I don't think he's had much schooling. He's got lots of poems memorized and he recites them with different voices, you know, so you stay interested. He's in the Army and I been thinking bout that article you read us. How the soldiers need wool hats and socks. I've made up my mind to knit him a pair of wool socks."

"My boyfriend's over there. He sent me a soldier's poem from de papuh. I wanna read it, but I ain so good at reading poetry." Luella nimbly rolled a wrapper leaf around a bunch. "Maybe you should read it to them, Brigid. Maybe you could read with different voices so they stay interested."

"Not me," exclaimed Brigid. "I could never stand up in front of everyone an read. I didn't mean to sound like I don't like the way you read. Luella, I'd love to hear you read a poem by a soldier." She was thinking of Manus, like she had been all morning, and something written by a soldier would let her know what being on the front might be like for him.

"No more books," Luella declared. "I'm staying with short stuff. I once read them a book, *Jane Eyre*. Took me an entire year—a year—to get through it. I was near goofy from making cigars fast enough to have extra time every day to read to the girls." Luella smiled with pride before licking the fold and securing the tip of a cigar. "This place like Lowood School if you ask me. I was happy to do it. See, I only got myself to look after. If I went over every week, shoooo, they'd just increase it for everybody else. They would. Helga over there, she got her mother to feed an tek care of. She wouldn't nevuh meet the quota—nevuh—without what some of us faster ones can put in the Bank."

They worked in silence, but Luella was born to talk.

"I think even your Aunt Cassie enjoyed *Jane Eyre*. I swaytogawd I do."

Brigid wished the girls realized how hard her Aunt Cassie worked just so Brigid could finish high school before finding work. When her mother died and her father was away at sea, it was Aunt Cassie who took her in. What would she have done without her? Her thoughts drifted back to the young girl on West Street, the one with the mattress on her back.

36

Luella took her bunches out of the mold and placed them in the bundling rack. "Sam, that's my boyfriend's name, he been down to Tampa an he told me the Cuban men who make cigars down there make enough money to pay a man to read to them every mawnin. Every mawnin! Boss can't say nothing bout what the man reads, neither. He reads newspaper articles about strikes and what have you. Then he reads from a book. Sam said he was reading them *The Three Musketeers* when he was there. That's how I got the idea to get ahead so I could read to the girls."

Brigid tightened the handle on her press and started another bunch. "How come men in Tampa make so much money?"

"Well, first off, they make what's called a clear Havana cigar. The whole thing's Cuban tobacco: filler, binder, and wrapper leaf. But the main reason they make so much money is because," Luella leaned even closer than they already were and lowered her voice, "them Cuban men belong to the union."

"Luella, why don't we join the union?"

"Because," Luella answered, looking around nervously, "the cigar maker's union won't let women join, that's why."

"Crab Claws!" announced a girl one row back.

"Don't let nobody hear you say that word," Luella whispered to Brigid.

"What word?" she whispered back.

Luella giggled before whispering into Brigid's ear, "Union."

Although there was no way Mr. Schmidt could have heard Luella, as soon as she whispered it, he turned around to look at them.

Even Luella kept quiet. Brigid let her mind roam back to Manus. He had invited her to go to the Holy Rosary picnic with him. The week couldn't go by fast enough. She hoped the Red Cross Society would be open on Saturday afternoon when she got off work so she could pick up the wool for his socks.

"This fella you met," said Luella, never silent for long, "is he handsome?"

"Yes," said Brigid. "He boxes and he's got muscles popping out all over him. You know how most boys only care bout your pieces an parts? Let me tell you, Manus ain like that. I swaytogawd Luella, he's not. He wants to know what I'm thinking."

"Keep your fingers moving," Luella cautioned. "You got to learn to work and talk at the same time. That's better. Bring him a few smokers. Every man enjoys a good cigar."

"Luella, you don't mean—" Brigid looked around—"you don't mean for me to steal a cigar, do you?"

"Course that's what she means!" said a girl sitting on Brigid's other side. "Everybody takes a smoker when she's trying to impress a man."

"That's for true," said Luella. "I'll help you pick a couple of good ones from what you got there."

Mr. Schmidt and Miss Sweeny were talking, and Brigid kept quiet, pondering the sin of stealing a ten-cent cigar, wondering how much longer she would have to spend in purgatory on account of it, and would it be less if she confessed the act to Father O'Shaughnessy? Then it occurred to her to take an extra smoker for him, too.

She had not fully decided on committing the act when Luella and the girl on Brigid's other side both announced, "Crab Claws is gone." Luella added, "Miss Sweeny is arguing with the stock boy." Then both girls sorted through Brigid's stack of cigars, selecting the four best ones.

"Not bad," said Luella. "When you get faster, you gonna be good." While the one girl watched to make sure Miss Sweeny remained distracted, Brigid lifted her uniform and slid the cigars into her underdrawers, three for Manus and one for Father O'Shaughnessy.

"Pick up some filler leaf right now," warned Luella, "don't let your han's be still or she'll notice an come over here."

"Lord, have mercy!" Brigid sighed, and smiled for having done something naughty. "My head's pounding." And when she began to cough, and cough, it was her coughing that attracted the eye of Miss Sweeny.

"Everyone gets that cough," said Luella. "It's the dust." The sound of women coughing was as constant as the clock's tick.

The girls who had come late worked through lunch. Brigid longed for a BC Powder. Later in the afternoon, when Luella was well into her second bundle of tobacco, she decided she could spare five minutes to get up and read the poem.

"My boyfriend Sam sent me this poem from a newspaper in England. It's called "They" and a soldier named Siegfried Sassoon wrote it."

"Siegfried!" shouted one woman. "He a German soldier?"

"No, he's fighting for our side," said Luella. "Hey now, watch what you say bout my Deutschland. I got a cousin fighting for America and lots of German boys from the Borough signed up so, you know, don't be talking bout my cousins, or I won't read anudduh word." She stood up on an empty crate.

The Bishop tells us: "When the boys come back
They will not be the same; for they'll have fought
In a just cause . . ."

Brigid listened close, filled with pride to think of Manus returning home wise and strong from the lessons of war. But then the poem turned.

"We're none of us the same!" the boys reply.
"For George lost both his legs; and Bill's stone blind . . .
you'll not find a chap who's served that hasn't found some change."
And the Bishop said: "The ways of God are strange!"

The dust, heat, and stench overwhelmed Brigid and she ran from her work station into the stairwell. Such a horrible poem; such a horrible, horrible vision. The war that brought the better pay might ruin the only chance she ever had for happiness. What if Manus came home blind, deaf, and legless?

Mr. Schmidt came walking up the stairs and saw her there.

"Brigid," he said, his voice concerned. "You alright? Here, take my handkerchief and wipe your face."

When she took it, he smiled, dipping his head, waiting for her to smile, too. "That's better."

He was being so kind. She felt bad for joining the others in calling him names.

"I've watched you work. You learn quick."

He wasn't even reprimanding her for being away from her work station. "Thank you, Mr. Schmidt, I want you to know how much I appreciate—"

Then he was on her, grabbing and pawing at her most private places and trying to kiss her hard on the mouth. She struggled but he pinned her against the wall.

"Eee! Eee!"

Brigid heard the banshee screech of Aunt Cassie, her cigar knife drawn and coming fast toward him.

"Let her be or I cut yuh. I swaytogawd, I cut yuh damn throat right now."

"White trash," scoffed Schmidt, pushing Brigid away and straightening his shirt collar. "You're no better than a basement nigger," he said and walked away.

Miss Sweeny opened the door to the stairwell. "What's going on here?" she demanded to know.

"Ain no problem," called Cassie. "No problem at all."

"Then get back to work," she said and turned away.

"Did you give him reason?" Cassie asked.

"No, of course not. Never!" Brigid pleaded. "I smiled when he smiled, but I was just being polite. I didn't mean anything—"

"Don't look a man in the eye and smile if you ain willing to take what comes of it. Listen to me, I know of what I speak. I was a lot younger than you when I come here to work."

Brigid started to cry.

"Hol' yuh se'f together, chile. Did he hurt yuh?"

Brigid shook her head, no. She wiped her face on her sleeve, taking big gulps of air to keep from crying.

"They pay us to mek cigars, not to listen to foolish talk and poetry. Now go on back to work and don't say nuttin bout this, yuh hear?"

Brigid started up the steps to the landing. She turned back, expecting her aunt to follow.

"I'll be along. Go on back to work," Cassie insisted. "Go on now."

Chapter 7

A few weeks later, on a warm and breezy Friday evening, Brigid waited while Manus paid the fifty cents for two round-trip tickets aboard the *Commodore* from Charleston to Mount Pleasant. They boarded the ferry and made their way to the upper deck to enjoy the tarantella being played on mandolin and guitar. Mr. Sottile employed Italian musicians to entertain his passengers. Back when Luella read to the girls about the final hop of the season at the Isle of Palms pavilion, Brigid never would have believed that she might actually be invited to go. Yet, here she was with Manus standing close enough that even the smallest wave caused their shoulders to briefly touch. The wind picked up with the approach of sunset and the thought of rough water made her smile.

The *Commodore's* engines idled at the foot of Market Street. They waited for a Navy ship to pass by, like the one that would soon take Manus and the Fifty-Fifth Field Artillery to England. And when the Navy ship passed, they waited for the *Arapaho*, one of the Clyde Line passenger steamers arriving from New York.

At last, the ferry boat swung out into the Cooper River for what should have been a fifteen-minute crossing. But at times like that, when the harbor was full of traffic, it could take much longer. And then there would be the thirty minute trolley ride from Mount Pleasant to the Isle of Palms. Brigid didn't mind the delay. She wanted to savor every moment of the night ahead.

"I got you a present," said Manus, producing an envelope from his jacket pocket.

It was a picture taken of the two them at the Holy Rosary picnic. Manus in straw hat, bow tie, and dark jacket, by the side of a large oak tree, his arms outstretched as if trying to push the oak over. And on the other side, petite Brigid, in her favorite gingham frock, appearing to be pushing back, preventing the massive tree from falling. She had thought it silly when the photographer suggested they pose that way. But now she was happy to have a picture of them together, something to look at every morning and every night of each day that he was away.

"Thank you so much," she said, looking at him in a way that she had never dared before.

"Manus," she said, not yet accustomed to hearing herself say his name aloud. "I got you sump'n, too." And she took the wool socks she had knitted for him from the deep pocket of her dress.

"Ah, Brigid," he said, "I'm gonna need these."

"I hear the winters are—" she stopped, not wanting to speak of the horrors Luella had read to them. "And these, too," she said, handing him the three cigars.

"Yuh mek dese?" He ran one under his nose. "Thank you, Brigid." He met her eyes only briefly, as if embarrassed for the show of kindness.

"You're welcome," she said, smiling. Yes, I made them, she thought to herself.

They were moving slowly. "It's beautiful, this time of evening. The old darkies, the ones still living on de islands, they call this time he'lenga. Maybe because it makes you want to linger, you know sit down and visit with somebody."

The sun went behind a streak of cloud, and the sky over downtown turned from glaring white to gunmetal gray. Manus pointed for her to look. Just off the bow, two porpoises leapt from the water. The wake of a passing Navy ship caused the ferry to list. Their shoulders pressed together. Manus's muscled arm against her delicate one, together and apart, pressing and releasing, over and over, until, regrettably, the waves subsided.

As the ferry approached Castle Pinckney, a former fort and prison for Union troops, the *Commodore* slowed again to an idle. Brigid stood up to see what sort of vessel had been given priority. To her surprise it was the Mosquito Fleet just now returning to their dock at Adger's Wharf. Late for them, she thought. She loved to see the patchwork sails of the Negro fishermen's small boats, each with a colorful and distinct eye painted upon the hull that was said to ward off evil spirits from the deep.

"Them darkies got they own way for rigging a sail. They some brave men. I mean it, brave men. They row out every mawnin to the Blackfish Banks. Blackfish Banks be faw-ive miles beyond the jetties. Say beyond the jetties. They don't have a compass or nothing for navigation. I don't know how they do it when the fog or a storm comes up. Saint Peter himself must have taught them men how to fish and how to handle them little bo-its in the open sea, an that's the Gawd's truth."

When all the boats of the Mosquito Fleet had passed, the red sun slipped out from below the clouds, hovered briefly, then dove into the Ashley River. Brigid saw the familiar buildings of downtown in silhouette against the orange sky. The steeples of Saint Michael's and Saint Phillip's presiding over the mansions of East Battery as well as the brothels of West Street.

"I've never been to any of them cities you talk about, but I can't imagine any place more beautiful than Chaa'ston come linger time."

The trolley took them over the Pitt Street Bridge to Sullivan's Island. It lumbered along, passing the grand Atlantic Beach Hotel at Station 22, and then finally crossing the bridge at Breach Inlet over to the Isle of Palms. The lights of the Ferris wheel towered above the trees.

To stretch their legs after the trolley ride, Manus and Brigid walked along the boardwalk. Brigid saw some girls she knew from the cigar factory and she liked that Manus was courteous, taking off his hat, and saying, "pleased to meet you," and so forth. Of course, Brigid couldn't forget that her Aunt Cassie had observed the same trait in Manus at the Holy Rosary picnic, and later warned Brigid to watch out, saying, "He the sort gonna be a street-angel an a house-devil."

Brigid looked at his curly hair blowing in the evening breeze, his stern furrowed brow, sizing him up, trying to figure out if Aunt Cassie was right.

The waves curled and crashed, racing up the beach.

"Tide's awfully high," said Manus. "Must be a storm coming."

He brought them each a plate of fried fish and a glass of beer. They sat at a table near the pavilion, where the band played a Sousa march.

Brigid wondered if he was scared to be going to war, but that was not something she would ask. The fact of the war was there with them, more prominent than the wind off the ocean, the crashing sound of the waves, the smell of popcorn, or the brass horns of the band. They did not speak of the war or of his leaving. They didn't speak at all, and even Manus did not break into recitation as he was so often prone to do.

They rode the Ferris wheel, something Brigid had never done before. Their car swayed in the wind. The pavilion lights shown out upon the water, the white caps extending well beyond the breakers.

"De watuh nervous," said Manus. "Currents going different directions. Only a fool would get in that watuh tonight with them rip currents."

"Is that light out there a ship?" she asked.

"Yeah," he answered, "he won't go much further with them lights on." And just as Manus spoke, the lights went out on the vessel. "What I tell you? German U-boats been seen off the coast last week. The Navy yard makes us a target."

The Ferris wheel had gone too high. Brigid hadn't wanted to see the war when they reached the top. But there it was. And tomorrow he would report to the base, and a day or so after that, Manus would board a ship and enter into that utter darkness spread out before them as far as the eye could see.

Her eyes watered. She swatted a tear away, embarrassed. "It's the wind," she said.

They went back to the dance pavilion, where the band played a variation on a theme from Bellini's *Norma*. Manus went to buy another glass of beer. Brigid had never heard such a romantic piece of music. Her parents couldn't have afforded dance lessons and if Manus did happen to ask her to dance, she could only rely on the few steps she had learned from Donna Sottile at school.

They drank their beers in silence, swaying slightly, taking small steps in place from time to time when they could not resist the rhythm.

"Our next number will be a waltz from Drigo's Serenade," the bandleader announced.

"Would you like to dance?" Manus asked her.

"I don't know them kind of dances," she said.

"We'll go slow then," he promised, taking her hand.

Each dance cost a nickel and dancers had to walk through a turnstile to pay at the start of each song.

As she put her hand on his shoulder, she asked, "Where did a boy who stays on de Eastside learn to dance Mr. Manus O'Brian?"

"New Orleans mostly, Havana some," he said, smiling, as if he were recalling a very pleasant memory.

Brigid felt the brush of wings. How many girls had danced with this street-angel before her?

For the next hour, they spent one nickel after the other until Brigid managed a passable waltz and a proper, if slow, foxtrot.

The crowd had thinned considerably by the time they stood respectfully on the dance floor while the Metz band played the finale, the national anthem. Brigid's wistful thoughts gave way to panic when she noticed that the clock said 11:30, the departure time for the last trolley back to Mount Pleasant.

As the long last note was played, she and Manus took off as fast as they could.

"My aunt will kill me if I don't come home tonight," she said.

"Kill me, more like it," said Manus, as they made their way down the boardwalk to cut over to the trolley stop.

Brigid began to cough, the phlegmy cough she got at work. She had to lean over when she couldn't stop coughing, trying to clear her lungs.

"We can't stop. We got to keep walking," Manus pleaded.

"The dancing made me short-winded." Brigid took a few more steps before stopping again. People rushed by, knowing the train would wait only a few minutes. "Manus, go! Hol' de damn car fuh me," she insisted, leaning over to cough.

No one ever ran so fast before. His straw hat fell off his head. She coughed one more time and this time she was able to spit and get a decent breath. She picked up Manus's hat as the trolley quietly began to roll. Close behind was Manus, running after it.

He didn't stop, even as the trolley moved further and further away. Even as it disappeared into the dark night altogether.

Brigid sat down on the bench under the shelter. She wondered what time they would turn off the electric light bulb there. She looked around and not a soul stirred. Her skin felt salty and sticky as if she had been in the surf. But the breeze was steady and strong and she was glad for it as it kept the mosquitoes at bay.

"What a pickle," she said aloud. She did not feel like crying. In fact, she was angry. How could he have left her there? A house-devil through and through, she thought, and if she ever saw him again, she would—well, anyone who would do something this awful, she didn't want to see again. "Oh! Mother of Gawd!" She threw his hat in the sand, took the photograph of them from her pocket, ready to rip it in two. But then she stopped.

The wind blew harder, making her hair a mess. The dance was considered the last event of the season, and there were very few people left on the island. There was one hotel but she didn't have any money. Maybe they would give her a room on credit. If she didn't show up for work she would lose her job and not be able to pay the bill. Don't think about losing your job, she told herself. Don't think about what you can't change. The only decision left to make was whether to spend the night there on that bench and take her chances with whoever might be prowling about, or to walk back to the hotel and take her chances with whoever might be there. She thought of her aunt saying, *Nothing's for free*, and she decided to stay put on the bench for the night.

"The first sorrowful mystery is the Agony in the Garden."

When she was five Hail Marys into the Crowning of Thorns decade, she heard something in the distance. When the wind would die, she heard it again and it sounded like horses' hooves. Louder and louder the sound grew closer, but she saw nothing in the darkness. The closer it came the more urgently Brigid prayed, until suddenly a Negro man driving a horse and dray came into view.

"Whoa!" called the man, pulling back on the reins and coming to a stop amid a spray of sand directly in front of her. Manus jumped down from the back and seeing his hat on the ground, stooped and picked it up. His bushy eyebrows were still furrowed as if he might yell. But he didn't.

"I chased that train all the way to Breach Inlet," he said. "I thought he'd slow down before he went over the bridge and that'd be how I'd catch him." He must have seen the look on Brigid's face. "Don't cut yuh eye et me dat way! No ma'am. I chased that train all the way to Breach Inlet. Breach Inlet!"

Brigid didn't know what to say so she didn't say anything.

"This here Comer Pinckney," said Manus.

Brigid nodded her head in greeting.

"I've employed Mr. Pinckney to take us to an old Sewee Indian he knows might be willing to row us down Hamlin Creek and over to Mount Pleasant. If we can get there, I'll find somebody to take us cross the haa'buh to town."

Brigid still didn't say anything. Manus just stared at her, as if he expected her to say something, and when he realized that she had nothing to say, he continued, "We got another hour on the ebb. We should hit it on the slack between the Cove and the village at Shem Creek. If we're lucky, we'll have the start of the flood to help us cross the harbor. Wind's crazy tonight," he said, looking around. "Keeps shifting round, but I think we got time before whatever's out there comes ashore." He stopped. Still she did not speak. "So that's my plan." And when she remained silent, he added, "Brigid, you got a better idea bout what we gonna do sides spending the night on de island?"

She stared at him for a long time, saying nothing. He stared back at her, two rather quiet people, sizing each other up on the Isle of Palms, well past midnight. They weren't on any Ferris wheel going round in a set path. No chile, they were on their own, just the two of them, and how it was gonna be was up to them, nobody else. Only Mr. Comer Pinckney and his horse to witness, and neither of them gave a damn one way or another how Brigid McGonegal and Manus O'Brian decided to spend the night together.

"No, Manus," she said at last. "It sounds like a good plan." She was going to trust him with her life. There wasn't anything else left to say. Manus lifted her into the back of Mr. Pinckney's dray, and they set off to find the old Sewee Indian.

A full moon emerged from the clouds, casting a yellow glow over the marsh grass. The Sewee had even less to say than Manus and Brigid. When they came out of the Sullivan's Island Cove into the harbor, the waves picked up and occasionally splashed over the gunnels. Brigid thought of her Aunt

Cassie and how she must be worried sick. And what if they overturned? No one would ever know.

The Sewee took them to the old village of Mount Pleasant. He and Manus jumped out to pull the boat up on the shore.

"I'll tek two dollars an a cigar," he said pointing to the cigars in Manus's shirt pocket.

"Two dollars! Man, you crazy. That's all the money I got. I won't have nothing to pay to get us cross the haa'buh."

Brigid saw the man eying the wool socks hanging out of Manus's pocket.

"Hell no!" he snapped. "I ain letting you have my socks."

The three of them were silent. Brigid didn't know what to say but she wished the others weren't as quiet as she. The flood tide was starting to come in and a wave rushed up the oyster shell–covered beach. Brigid's shoes and stockings got soaking wet.

"Okay," the man said at last. "I'll tek yuh two dollars an dem three cigars an go to West Street. But you got to row. I'm give out."

Manus heaved-to with the oars as the Sewee puffed his cigar with deep satisfaction. Brigid felt a great sense of accomplishment. A product of her skill was helping to get them back home.

When they came around Crab Bank, a spattering of lights from downtown became visible. The swells caused the boat to pitch. Manus flattened the oar to the side of the roll, bracing the boat upright again.

"Out of the rolling ocean the crowd came a drop gently to me—"

Manus recited as Brigid silently prayed the rosary.

"Watch for ships," yelled Manus over the sound of the wind. "Hold on, hold on!" Again, the boat pitched, and again, Manus braced to keep them upright.

Brigid took comfort in the look upon his face. As he worked the oars, negotiating the wind-driven waves, his expression was not much different than the one upon his face when they crossed the harbor so many hours earlier on board the *Commodore*.

Once they were past Castle Pinckney, the break in the wind allowed the incoming tide to carry them North without as much effort on Manus's part. He resumed his recitation.

"The irresistible sea is to separate us. Be not impatient—a little space—know you I salute the air, the ocean and the land, every day at sundown for your dear sake, my love."

Brigid was somewhere in the Descent of the Holy Ghost upon the Apostles decade when, upon hearing the words, "my love," she completely lost track of how many Hail Marys she had said.

"Enough Whitman," the Sewee interrupted. "You waited too late. The tide's too strong now. We won't make the Market Street dock."

"I ain late fuh nuttin!" Manus snapped. "Shooo! I'm the one getting us across wid dese swells and a storm coming on. We going go to Charlotte Street!"

"Charlotte Street," the man snapped back. "West Street near the Market. I don't wanna go that far north. I can't row against this current."

"Too damn bad," said Manus, just as the wind kicked up again. Manus rowed hard and fast to prevent a wave from hitting them broadside. "Shooo! Man, you can row or walk back downtown, don't make no difference to me, but we going go to Charlotte Street first."

Manus had a temper, Brigid could see that. She folded her arms across her chest. Her dress was more than a little damp and she was beginning to feel the chill.

As they neared the pier at the foot of Charlotte Street, the wind became even stronger. Brigid realized that getting off the boat and up the ladder wasn't going to be easy. Manus struggled to get close enough for the other man to take hold of the ladder. The old Sewee went up it fast as a jackrabbit.

"Hell's bells, you horny idiot," Manus yelled, still combating the swell. "You forgot to take the line with you. Brigid, grab this stern line—Now! Son of a bitch." Manus fought to keep the boat from getting pushed away from the pier. "Wait for this gust to die—get ready, you gone have to give it a good heave."

She had never done such a thing before, and the boat kept pitching. Already it was too far from the ladder for the old man to get back in to help. She looked him in the eye, aim for him, she told herself, aim for him, and then she threw the line.

He caught it and quickly wrapped it around a cleat. "The bow line, Brigid! T'row de bow line—Now!" When she had done this and they were secure, Manus motioned for her to go before him up the ladder. Under no other circumstance would she have risked such impropriety, but such concerns belonged to another girl, the girl she had been before crossing the harbor.

Charlotte Street was deserted. The gas lamp on the corner at Elizabeth danced and flickered in the wind. Brigid saw the light was on in the apartment. She felt sick, knowing how worried her aunt must be.

"Should I go up?" he asked.

"No," she said, "I better go alone." She started for the door, then stopped, turning back to Manus.

"You know I take the train to the base in the afternoon. You wanna get a cup of coffee or something before I go?"

"I have to work," she said.

He looked on the verge of saying something. She wanted him to say something. They were standing very close. Brigid wished they were back in the rowboat fighting the harbor swells. He'lenga came to mind. She wanted to linger until he said something, until he asked her something.

But he did not ask anything of her, nor did he take her in his arms even though she thought she might die for the want of it.

"Tek care yuh s'ef," she said, stepping back before turning to open the metal gate. Her hand was on the porch banister before she dared to look back. And when she did, he was nearly to the corner, walking fast. When he reached the lamp, he began to run.

Chapter 8

Cassie had stayed up praying past 2 A.M. At that point, with nothing else to do but wait until morning to go to the police, she poured herself the rare glass of Jameson and dwelled upon the torments of family love.

Her father was railroad man with a coal-stoked temper burning within. Men of the sea might be mean or sweet sloppy drunks. Railway men were always mean when they drank, and too often, even when they didn't. He beat the fight out of Charlie in more ways than one. How her brother grew up to be such a patient and kind man was beyond her. He was far more patient than she; of that, Cassie was certain. Brigid took after him. Cassie and Charlie were still quite young when their father finally picked a fight with the wrong man. He died an ugly stinking death in his bed three days later. For years, that smell lingered in the silence of his absence. Without her job at the cigar factory, the three of them would have been put out on the street.

When a stroke left her mother an invalid, Cassie struggled to take care of her. Miss Huger, God bless her, was a saint, but she couldn't come every day. Charlie wasn't yet married and he was away for months at a time. Cassie worried herself sick whenever she had to leave her mother alone. "At last," she remembered thinking to herself, "mother will be speaking the truth when she says I don't do right by her." But then a strange thing happened: her mother stopped complaining. After a lifetime of hems never being straight enough, coffee never being strong enough, or chicken never being done enough— suddenly, words of gratefulness came easily to her mother. And this unexpected kindness scraped off a scab years in the making. Cassie was at work when her mother passed all alone, leaving behind a raw loving place of inadequacy that would never fully heal.

And with each passing hour that she waited for Brigid's return, Cassie smelled grief coming closer and closer. And oh, the immensity of this one might just do her in. Then Brigid came through the door with an incredible story involving an old Indian and a trus-me-Gawd boat. Cassie listened, not saying a word. The girl felt plenty bad, that was plain enough to see. Cassie contemplated various immoral acts, deciding that even the worst would not have taken until after 4 A.M. to complete.

"Well, if you're not telling the trute, then it's between you and the Lord." With that, Cassie went to bed.

Cassie woke to her alarm clock and rain landing softly on her face. A ship in the harbor blasted its horn. "Oh Lord," she said, realizing that it was Saturday and even though she had been in bed for less than two hours, it was time to get up and go to work. "Christ Almighty," she said, her head aching as she sat up.

When she turned around Brigid was standing there, already in her uniform and cap, holding a cup of coffee for her.

In the distance, the ship again blew its horn.

The wind whipped through the kitchen curtains, knocking a small statue of the Infant of Prague from the windowsill into the sink. Brigid went to close the window.

"Oh no," she said, picking up the statue, "the infant's head got knocked off."

"This going to be one hell of a day," said Cassie, taking a sip of coffee.

The rain blew sideways as they walked to work. The streets were muddy and by the time they got closer to Bay Street, they were walking in water above their ankles. Cassie and Brigid went up the steps of the Drake Street entrance, their shoes, stockings, and uniforms soaking wet.

All morning, bands of wind-driven rain beat against the large waterfront-facing windows. Mr. Rolands ordered the electric lights to be turned on, something he normally didn't do until the dark of winter. Between claps of thunder came the sound of girls coughing.

Cassie's neck hurt and the index and long finger on her left hand were numb. She had fallen off pace and feared she would not be able to catch up by the end of shift. It seemed to have something to do with looking down and to the left. She stopped completely, much to the surprise of the young girls on either side of her, and even Miss Sweeny took note. Cassie began rearranging her work station, placing her mold and the press on her right, to see if that might help.

She formed twenty bunches to fill the mold, and while changing positions had helped a little bit with the numbness, it had not improved her speed because it felt so foreign to be working on the right rather than the left side. She changed everything back around.

"Miss Cassie," said Miss Sweeny from the aisle, "What's the matter with you?" Miss Sweeny had become puffed up and bossy now that Schmidt was gone. The girls were saying that Miss Sweeny was doing all she could to convince Mr. Rolands that he didn't need to hire another foreman because she herself was capable of the task.

The girls on her row turned to look. Their eyeballs took it in while their hands remained busy.

"No, Miss Sweeny, I'm fine," Cassie replied. "How bout yuh se'f? You got any problems this mawnin?"

Durn if the lady isn't going to stand there and watch, thought Cassie.

Wrapping the bunch caused her the most trouble and Cassie did not want Miss Sweeny to see her struggling to roll her bunches. Cassie decided to cut another wrapper leaf.

"Why you cutting anudduh wrappuh leaf?" Miss Sweeny lashed out. "You should be able to get all them bunches wrapped with what you already got cut. You gonna run out of wrapper leaf doing like that."

"We got sorry wrapper leaf," said Cassie. "I can't work with sorry stock," she said, pressing the peddle on the suction table to hold the wrapper leaf and raise the die for her to make another cut.

"Nobody else complaining bout the wrapper leaf being sorry," said Miss Sweeny. "You better not come up short, that's all I got to say." A gust of wind blew hard outside. Miss Sweeny turned and walked to look out the window, finally interested in something else besides Cassie.

A little before noon, Cassie's left arm ached from her neck down into her hand, making her fingers clumsy. They had two more hours to go and for the first time ever she didn't have enough wrapper leaf to finish rolling her bunches. If she went to the stock boy for more, they would dock her pay. And with Sweeny being anxious to show she could be a tough foreman, she might suspend Cassie for a few days to make a point. No one would mess with Sweeny if she showed the girls that she didn't hesitate to suspend an old-timer like Cassie.

Cassie had never borrowed tobacco from the Bank. She wondered if Luella would even give her any as Cassie always made of point of refusing to contribute. Cassie knew that the girls on either side of her were well aware of the problem, but one of them couldn't stop coughing long enough to say anything and the other one was Polish and didn't speak much English.

Cassie stood up, "I'm going to the ladies' room," she said, feeling the need to justify why she had stopped working. She saw Brigid at her table working steady. Cassie felt surprised the girl seemed to be getting the hang of it. Cassie went downstairs to one of the restrooms for whites. The toilets were bubbling and backing up, but she had to take her chances and use one anyway. The water table was rising from the storm and the toilets weren't emptying. Cassie washed her hands, staring at herself in the cloudy mirror. Oh, she hated to do it, but she had no other choice than to borrow from Luella's tobacco Bank.

When she came back onto the third floor the girls were all in a commotion. Everyone was hurrying to turn in her work, and Mr. Rolands himself was on the floor, hollering about the storm.

"I just got word that the hurricane flag has been raised in Marion Square. We're closing the factory so everybody can get home before the next tide comes in and we get more flooding downtown. I'll figure something out about the week's quota, but right now we want all of you to get home as soon as possible."

Church bells rang all over the city, warning of the coming storm. Hundreds of women poured out of the factory doorways, Negro women from the Bay Street side and white women from the Drake Street side. The rain had slacked for the moment and everyone made a dash for it down the muddy street. Since the tide was still out, the water wasn't much higher than it had been when they had gone in to work.

"Shet dem bline," a Negro woman yelled to one of the other servants at Dr. Hardon's house. The downstairs shutters had come undone and were flapping in the wind. The Hardons were one of Charleston's prominent mulatto families and they lived three doors down from Cassie in one of the nicest homes on Elizabeth Street.

"Miss McGonegal," yelled Mrs. Hardon from her porch, "Thank Gawd you two made it home before the worst hits."

"You and your family tek care, Mrs. Hardon," shouted Cassie as she and Brigid hurried by. "Lord willing this harr-y-kin won't be a bad one."

Another band of rain arrived just as Brigid and Cassie reached their gate. The wind made it difficult to open at first. Then Brigid turned to run back down the walkway.

"Brigid, where you going?" yelled Cassie over the wind and the persistent church bells.

"To get the mail," she said.

"Forget the durn mail," said Cassie, continuing on for the door as Brigid ignored her.

Once inside they got busy preparing: towels were put under the door, candles taken out and matches found, water brought back from the water closet, pots, pans, and pails, were lined up and ready to be placed beneath the inevitable roof leaks.

They settled down with their rosary beads as the sound of the wind grew steady and the ping-ping of water began hitting the pots. Slowly, the feeling returned to normal in Cassie's left hand. Brigid finished the rosary at a record clip, unable to keep from glancing at the card she had placed on the table.

After reading it, she put the note down, closed her eyes, blessed herself, and then at last, she smiled.

Cassie did not have to ask. The look on her face said it all.

"I know he's strong as an ox," said Cassie, "but I'm nearly taller than he is and McGonegals ain known for our height. Shooo, that little man not even five foot."

"He's five foot, four inches. His hair is brown and eyes are blue," she said happily. "He showed me his passport."

"Your chillun gonna be short," said Cassie as a palmetto branch hit the window.

"But strong," said Brigid. "They'll be strong."

Outside, the storm winds howled and it grew dark. The candles flickered in the wind that blew through the gaps in the boards. As hurricanes went, Cassie had been through worse, but this one wasn't over yet. They sat in silence. At last she said to her niece, "Let's say a rosary for Manus. That he comes home safe and sound."

Chapter 9

The storm lashed the old decrepit house. "Listen yah," said Ray, "dis gone mek de worry leab yuh head." He began to play softly on his clarinet, bending the notes now and then, the way Mr. Jenkins at the orphanage had taught him to do.

Meliah Amey's husband Joe paced about the room, talking about the war, while she encouraged her newborn son to nurse. "Feed up, feed up teday, mo bettuh than day befo." She whispered, her voice full of the worry that would never leave her head. Holy Mary, mother of God, she prayed, let this baby be the one to live. Just then, a big gust slapped the shutters hard against the house. "Kofi, me and Tata gone keep oonuh safe." Her son's true name was Vincent de Paul Ravenel, but his basket name, the name Meliah Amey gave to his soul was Kofi, on account of him being born on a Friday.

Meliah Amey and Joe rented the three-room house located off Tradd Street, south of Broad, on Bedon's Alley. Theirs, like others in the alley, had once been slave quarters. Mr. Shaftesbury, the high buckruh who owned it, hadn't put a dime toward repairs or upkeep since his family had it built back in the 1840s. Meliah Amey and Joe shared the little house with Ray and Binah, and Binah's cousin, whose true name was Fortune but everyone called her Pea.

Joe shouted over the rattle and slap of the hurricane shutters. "De war to end all wars gone change ebryting."

Ray paused. "Already changing," he said. "Fertilizer plant pay faw-ibe cent more an hour. Dey can't eben get de men fuh a second shift." He put the horn back in his mouth, played a little riff, and then stopped. "Who going go wuk in dat stink hole digging rock when he can be in de service? Shooo! Dis war de best thing happen to us."

Meliah Amey wasn't interested in the war on the other side of the ocean. She was more concerned with the ocean right outside their door and would have preferred that Joe sit down and join her in reciting a rosary for the intention of the roof staying attached to the house. Meliah Amey didn't own a real set of rosary beads, but Joe had made her one out of fishing line and shells like his own Tata had taught him to do. Before Joe made her the rosary bracelet, she kept count in her head, the way the Sisters of Charity at the Immaculate Conception School on Shepard Street had taught her.

"Mr. Rolands gone raise us stemmers two cent on de bundle," said Binah after shifting the crate she sat upon away from the newest drip of water. She settled back into her rhythm of tying knots and coiling the grass for the basket she was sewing. "Army buying up ebryting. Say Mr. Rolands thinking bout letting us mek cigars like de white girls. When I get paid dat good money, chile, I put a new roof puntop dis old sorry house."

"Oonuh not mek de money fuh to buy no roof. Oonuh be lucky to buy one more bucket an dat's de Gawd's truth," said Pea. She was sitting on one of the two chairs they owned. "I'm sick of watuh falling on my head. I got bad luck already," she said as she opened a parasol to hold over her head. When everyone threw a fit, she closed it.

"Put this puntop your head," said Binah, handing Pea one of her sweet-grass baskets. Binah made the baskets the way her mother taught her, and her mother before, and all the way back to Angola and the days before slavery time. Binah's people stayed east of the Cooper River in an area named

Scanlonville. Lots of women over there knew how to make the intricate baskets that had once been used for carrying everything from rice to water, the weave was that tight. A few years back, Binah and other basket makers started selling baskets to a buckruh down on Bay Street, who in turn resold them to tourists from up North.

"Me and Joe going to fight for we'own country," said Ray. "When the war obuh we gone get the rights back that Pitchfork Ben and the Jim Crow tek away."

The shutters flapped open again. A bright streak of lightening flashed in the dimly lit room. Meliah Amey saw Joe cut his eyes to her, looking for support. This was the first she had heard of him wanting to join the military. She held the baby to her chest, refusing to meet Joe's eye. The oil flame flickered. The wind picked up. Meliah Amey faltered in her rosary recitation as she watched the roof strain to resist the force.

Joe blessed himself and bowed his head. Ray kept on playing.

Joe was a captain in the Mosquito Fleet and Ray was one of many street vendors who bought fish from the boats when they returned to Adger's Wharf in the late afternoon. Ray and the other hucksters sold fish right there at the wharf to the restaurants and hotels, and some people sent their cooks to buy fish and bring it back to the kitchen while it was still flapping. The fish they didn't sell went into the icehouse for the night. Before dayclean, Ray and the others would put the fish on top of a block of ice, cover them with a croaker sack, and then set out with their cart to sell them throughout the neighborhoods downtown.

The wind shifted. Glass broke outside in the alley and rain beat against the front door. They knew it had been the bottles Pea hung in the tree outside to keep the evil spirits from coming in the house.

"Look out, Pea," said Ray. "Boo hag gone be up on de porch."

"More than one way to stop a haint," said Pea. "Mustard seed. I t'row mustard seed under my bed tonight. That'll keep'um away."

Rain seeped under the door and Meliah Amey, still holding the baby, used her foot to push a rag over to soak up the water. Joe had warned that a storm was coming. He had seen the crazy rip currents, and higher than usual tides. A different sort of wind, too. Joe swore to her that he could taste a hurricane wind on his tongue.

Suspecting that the storm was close, the fleet had moored their boats and stayed ashore that day. By the time the flag went up at Marion Square, most everyone knew what was happening and the flag served only to say, "Yes, it's a hurricane."

Normally Joe spent a stormy day repairing nets and mending tackle. Meliah Amey realized that he and Ray had spent the morning at a military recruiters' office on King Street.

The wind subsided and the shutters ceased to rattle. The storm was passing. "T'engk Gawd!" they shouted, all smiling with relief. Baby Vincent stirred. Ray played the refrain from "Happy Days Are Here Again."

"I knew this harr-y-kin weren't coming straight on," said Joe, turning to Meliah Amey. "Tana, we safe." Tana was the name Joe had given his wife. In old-time-talk it meant to light a lamp.

"Joe," said Meliah Amey firmly, "Oonuh a Mosquito Fleet captain. Don't we eat good? Ain we saving money for to send Kofi to de Avery Institute? I go Mass befo dayclean ebryday an pray Gawd keep yuh safe. He look out fuh de fleet because dey feed up Chaa'ston. Eben de buckruh hol' oonuh mens high. Mek so yuh risk all dat on a chance to be killed in de white man Army?"

"Mek so?" Joe shouted. "Because of we'own son!"

"It not gone be nuttin like you people t'ink," Pea insisted, heaving a sigh and stretching back in her chair. "De Abry Institute prefer de high yellow and de brown so yo black boy ain gone get in dat school no way. And you mens don't know how it gone be, neither. Shooo! I heah de Senator an some high buckruh talking on the piazza last night with de Gubnuh. Yes chile, I say de Gubnuh, yuh understand?"

Pea cooked for the family of a state senator who lived in a fancy house below Broad on Legare Street.

"I filet seb'n flounduh, pick a basket of crab. When they on the piazza smoking they cigars an drinking liquor, I sing low. They pay me no mind, but I hear every word they say." Pea relished being the center of attention when she had news to tell. For three or four dollars a week, she sweated over steaming rice, picked pounds of shrimp and crab—all caught by the Mosquito Fleet—and her greatest reward from the job came in those moments when she imparted the secrets of the Senator's conversation to her friends and family.

Before continuing, Pea lit up one of the small cigars Binah rolled from the tobacco scraps she swept up off the floor at the factory.

"The newspaper man, he didn't think nobody not white should be given a gun and showed how to use it. The man that owns the cotton on Kiawah got all excited, say he bout to lose he shirt if his niggers be allowed to join the Army and he have to pay higher wages to have the cotton picked this year. The cotton man begged the Governor not to let any coloreds from South Carolina join up. The lawyer say that President Wilson going to let black and white train together in the Army.

"That got them all riled up. None of them want that. Then the banker say that lots of good American men gonna be killed dead in this war and maybe it better if the poor whites and the colored did the dying. Well, they all agreed to that, sept for the lawyer cause he say the French people gone put crazy thoughts in the heads of the Negroes. He say that the Negroes that don't die would come home with them French people thoughts and won't be no good for work no more. That's when the Governor say, "Our Negroes will not be allowed to join the military.""

"But we already joined," snapped Joe. "I joined the Navy and Ray joined the Army because he don't like bo-its. We report in the mawnin."

Meliah Amey gasped.

Pea took a puff and blew a few smoke rings. "I'm not finish not yet."

"This one man stay quiet and don't eat none of the food I fix. I don't know what business he own but all of a sudden this skinny buckruh jump up and say like this, 'Gentleman, think about what you're saying.'" Pea spoke in a convincing manner. "'If you only allow white men to serve in the military, then only Negro men will be left at home with our white women.'"

Pea took another smoke. "Chile, you know that put it all to rest. But before you two get excited, Senator say the colored gone do the dirty jobs and leave the real soldiering to the white boys. So you hear it from me, you not gone do nothing in the service that you can't already do right yah in Chaa'ston."

"Hush, woman!" snapped Joe. "The man true-mouth. Say my know-how with boats and the sea will get me a good job in the Navy. Say America need men like me to win this war for our democracy."

Meliah Amey had been about to light into Joe for being such a damn fool. Now his words hung in the air, raw and painful as a jellyfish sting. Meliah Amey passed the baby to Pea. Then, taking her husband by the hand, she led him to their room to be alone together for one last night.

Chapter 10

Meliah Amey took the iron from the woodstove and put it to one of Mr. Harleston's shirts. He liked a lot of starch in the collar and if she didn't get it just right, his wife would bring it back to be redone. Besides the Harlestons, Meliah Amey took in washing and mending from the Darbys of Darby's Construction, the Millmores that owned Millmore's Drugstore, and the Mickeys that owned the other Negro funeral home besides the Harlestons', as well as the laundry from Dr. and Mrs. Harbon. These were but a few of the families known in Charleston as the Brown Elite, many of whom were descendents of slave owners who upon death willed freedom to their illegitimate sons and daughters. Back in slavery time, there came to be so many of these Free People of Color living in Charleston that the state legislature in Columbia got scared of them and passed a law making it illegal for a slave owner to leave freedom in his will.

Her regular customers kept Meliah Amey plenty busy but since Joe had been gone, she had started taking in the laundry from a few of the white families who lived around the corner from Bedon's Alley.

Doing other people's laundry, no matter who they were, didn't pay much. Joe had been gone nearly two months and still no letter, and more importantly, no money. The other men with the Mosquito Fleet were looking after her and Binah with plenty of fresh fish, but money for anything else was getting tight and twice already she had dipped into the stash they were saving for Vincent de Paul's schooling.

Binah came flying in the door, peeling off her blue uniform, all excited and hollering because she had a letter from Ray.

Meliah Amey waved her hand in front of her nose, pushing away the stench of tobacco.

"Please, Meliah Amey, read me Ray letter. Please!"

"Mek so? You can read a leetle bit."

"Because them nuns taught you good. And Mr. Jenkins taught Ray. You the only teacher to me. I wanna hear what he got to say without hab'n to study my head just to make out the words. Meliah Amey, Please?"

Meliah Amey set the iron on the woodstove to keep it hot and dried her hands before taking Binah's letter to read.

Dear Binah,

We in Spartanburg training. I never seen anything like it. The crackers up here are different from our whites. They always want to fight. The food is great. I'm playing horn with guys from the 15th from New York. A Negro unit. Lt. James Reese the band leader. He write the papers to get me in the 15th with them. I never been so happy.

Meliah Amey stopped. Binah looked as if she might cry.

Big fight in town because a New York Negro private did not get out of the way for some crackers on the sidewalk. They knocked him down. Then the white GIs from New York hit the crackers. Now the Army say we got to leave Spartanburg. Say it better if the 15th train in France. Tell Pea I'm going to France and won't be no good for work in Charleston no more. You always be my girl Binah. I love you.

Ray

"Any liquor round here?" asked Binah.

Meliah Amey went back to her ironing. "Be glad you got a letter," she said.

Binah gave up searching for a bottle. "You think we ever see them again?"

Vincent de Paul woke up and started to cry. "Tie your mouth Binah," she replied. "Don't worry, they come back yah." She picked up the baby and took a seat to let him nurse.

"Rent due next week," said Binah, glancing about the dingy room.

Meliah Amey shifted Kofi to get more comfortable, feeling relieved he was a strong eater. She had given birth to two other babies, both of them girls. The first lived three months and the second just three days. Lots of Charleston babies died, even among the buckruh. The busiest coffin makers were for the littlest ones. For the entire time she carried Vincent de Paul, she had only one prayer: Please, God, do me like you done my own mother. Take me, and let my baby live.

Seemed Mr. Death was always close at hand. She and Kofi had survived only to have Joe leave to fight a war.

"Come with me to the cigar factory," Binah said. "Pea can keep the baby most days and Miss Huger down the alley could take him the other times. We can pay her with the fish the mens bring us. I know how you feel bout the way Mr. Rolands hire, but they paying $6.25 a week now."

"I won't stand on the auction block!" she said, her jaw clinched. "I won't wear the blue dress of slavery time."

Meliah Amey's grandparents on both sides had been born into slavery. Before calling herself by Joe's last name, Ravenel, Meliah Amey used Pinckney for her true name. Her mother's parents were sold to the Comings and they stayed in town. But on her father's side, before they came to town, they worked one of the Pinckney's rice plantations on the Ashepoo River. They called the area Catholic Hill on account of the Pinckneys, the Bellingers, and the Smiths, all being Catholic and baptizing their slaves Catholic, too. When the white people left after the Civil War, a former slave by the name of Vincent de Paul Davis took it upon himself to teach the children the Latin words for the Mass. He believed in the meaning of catholic: a church everywhere, always, and by all. And it was this former slave Vincent de Paul for whom Meliah Amey had chosen her son's true name.

As a little girl, Meliah Amey and her parents attended the mostly Negro parish of Saint Peter's on Wentworth Street. Even without a proper school, the Sisters taught any child who showed up how to read and write. Meliah Amey met Joe at Saint Peter's. But Joe couldn't come as regularly as Meliah Amey because he often had to help his father, an admiral in the Mosquito Fleet. Meliah Amey was lucky; she didn't have to start working outside the home until she was ten.

Meliah Amey laid the baby in the crib Joe had made for him. She put her finger down and Vincent swatted at it, smiling. She had not spoken true-mouth to Binah. Meliah Amey's head was filled with worry that Joe and Ray might never come back.

"Kofi," she said, as he took hold of her finger, "I worry bout Tata. Guess it's up to your maum now to make the money for you to go to the Avery Institute."

All night Meliah Amey heard the birds. Thousands of them, herons and warblers mostly, flying south along the coastline in advance of cold weather. Come dayclean the live oaks would be filled with the birds taking rest on their long and difficult journey.

The morning air was crisp. Meliah Amey saw the chop in the harbor and thought of the fleet and how the seas would be rough beyond the jetties.

"Think the cool here to stay?" asked Binah.

"Seem like there's always one more hot spell," said Meliah Amey.

As they passed in front of the grand marble stairs of the Customs House, an orange and black butterfly landed on Meliah Amey's shoulder. These butterflies came every year around the Feast of All Souls Day.

"The birds and butterflies know to go south so the cold don't kill'um."

"Pea keeps saying all the smart niggers heading north" said Meliah Amey.

They walked the remaining blocks without talking, each studying her own head. When East Bay ended at the field everyone called the Mall, they crossed the damp grass until they reached Bay Street, and then the cigar factory.

"I got to say sump'n," said Binah, stopping short. "If you wanna job at the cigar factory, don't stand there looking like you think he de debble." Meliah Amey turned away. Binah continued, "If you wanna roof obuh yuh head come wintertime, you bettuh not show out."

"This way if you wanna job at de cigar factory," yelled a white man on the corner. "This way if you wanna job."

Meliah Amey stood tall with her shoulders back as Mr. Rolands walked up and down the line with his stick tucked beneath his arm. The woman next to Meliah Amey was large and Mr. Rolands passed her over and seemed about to walk beyond Meliah Amey without even considering her.

"Mawnin, sir," she said, friendly but not overly so. She deferred her gaze downward when he stopped to look back over his shoulder to see who had spoken.

He stepped back to stand in front of her. "Roll up your sleeves. Hold out your arms, I want to look at you."

He ran his stick up one side of her arm, and then down the other. "You got decent muscles. Least you been working rather than doing the happy dust."

"Yes, sir," said Meliah Amey. "I work ebry day."

"Are you clean?" he asked, touching her on the shoulder with his stick, indicating that he was ready for her to turn around. "You got the running range or the bad blood?"

"No, sir," she answered, keeping her voice upbeat.

Again, he touched her on the shoulder with the stick, ready for her to turn back around.

She kept her eyes down, letting him believe she thought herself unworthy to look such an important man in the eye. She stared at his shiny shoes, thinking to herself how much she hated him. She hated him more than any other human being she had ever met.

He tapped her on the arm with his stick. She began to raise her head, catching herself just in time and looking away. But she had seen the way he smiled, nodding his head, pleased with himself.

"I love it down here," said Mr. Rolands to his assistant, Mr. Godfrey. "Your niggers are so courteous."

As Mr. Rolands moved down the line, Mr. Godfrey instructed Meliah Amey what to do next. "Use de Bay Street door. Go down de basement and get yuh s'ef enough cloth to mek two uniforms, then go see de nurse. Yuh start come Monday mawnin."

Chapter 11

"In nomine Patris, et Filii, et Spiritus Sancti," said the young priest, Father Joubert. Meliah Amey blessed herself and bowed her head.

"Introibo ad altarem Dei," recited Father Joubert as he indeed went to the altar of God. The boy serving Mass with Father Joubert responded: "Ad deum qui laetificat juventutem meam." To God who gives joy to my youth.

The 6 A.M. Mass at the small wood-frame chapel on Shepard Street was known as the fisherman's Mass because it was the earliest Mass in all of Charleston and many of the men who attended wore waders, ready to take to their boats as soon as the service ended. Meliah Amey and Joe, along with a few of the other men from the fleet, attended daily. The chapel was primarily a Negro parish, but there were always a few white fishermen, also wearing waders, seated in the back pew where visitors sat, praying just as hard as the Negro fishermen for the Lord to keep them safe upon the sea that day and for Saint Peter to bless them with a good catch.

Kyrie eleison
Kyrie eleison

When Communion time came, Meliah Amey knelt beside Arthur Gaillard, one of the other Captains in the Mosquito Fleet. The altar boy placed the paten under her chin while Father Joubert softly intoned, "Corpus Domini nostri Jesu Christi." Meliah Amey lifted her veil, opening her mouth to receive.

Back in her pew, she quietly recited the prayer she had memorized in sixth grade. In Latin, with a slight Geechee rhythm, she prayed: "Anima Christi, Corpus Christi, salva me. Ab hoste maligno defende me." She repeated, "Ab hoste maligno defende me." From the malignant enemy, defend me.

Outside on the sidewalk, the sun pushed into the sky above Mount Pleasant. It being a workday, no one lingered to chat. Arthur Gaillard stopped long enough to say hello and to ask if she had heard from Joe.

"Gawd bless him, and Saint Michael protect him," he said. "Cool weather bout here to stay. Soon we go up de Maa'sh in de bateaux fuh oshtuhs. I bring you some."

"Thank you so much, Mr. Gaillard. Now I got to tek foot een han'," she said, letting him know that she had to hurry. She walked quickly, removing her veil and putting it in the pocket of the horrible blue smock she wore over the horrible blue dress, same in color as the one her grandmother wore when she worked the Pinckney's rice fields.

She rushed into the Bay Street stairwell, eyes burning and throat tightening, every step bringing her nearer to what looked like, in the light of the half-windows, a thick brown cloud of tobacco dust. She began to cough, unable to get a good breath the moment she entered the basement.

Negro women and their children were busy tying long dry stalks of tobacco leaves into bundles. It took several children to stack the bundles so that they wouldn't fall over while curing in the upright position.

"New people over here," shouted a young white man. "My name is Mr. Rolands. You met my father yesterday when he hired you. I'm in charge of processing. He hired you, but I can fire you. I got a hundred more just like you waiting to get the best paying job a colored woman can get in this town.

I don't tolerate laziness or causing trouble. Mr. Godfrey is the foreman down here and he's going to show you what to do."

Meliah Amey's head pounded.

"We buy three types of tobacco: filluh, binduh, and wrappuh leaf," Mr. Godfrey began. "We buy wrappuh leaf fum Cuba and de filluh and binduh fum Aruba. If yuh damage our tobacco we mek yuh pay fuh it. Damage it again, we fire yuh."

"Sort de leaves by shade and grade. Dis here Scipio. He keeps an eye on de sorting and stacking. We don't have chillun on de payroll. We pay piece work. How yuh get it done is yuh own business, understand?"

The piecework system paid so little, even little hands helped to make ends meet. Letting a child go to school, even a sorry one, was a luxury few could afford. Meliah Amey prayed softly, "Lord, have mercy, please don't ever make me have to bring my Kofi in here."

"The tobacco gets fermented twice," Mr. Godfrey explained. "It stays damp down here so we don't have to add moisture to get the bacteria growing for these piles and Scipio checks to make sure the temperature don't get ovuh ninety-five. Leaves stay in these piles thirty days."

They moved to the next section of the basement, where the air was even worse because of a misting spray being applied. "Next the leaves got to be moistened. Wrapper leaf gets sprayed with plain watuh, but the filler and the binder, they need a mixture of watuh and shredded tobacco that's got to be just right, not too much and not too little."

They continued into another area. The basement was huge. "This where ya'll gone work stemming," said Mr. Godfrey. "You have to tear the leaf pro-puh so you don't waste none."

Binah looked up to smile at Meliah Amey.

He pointed to another area. "The tobacco goes through a second fermentation ovuh there and the bundles have got to stay at 108 degrees fuh sixty days. That's right, 108 degrees fuh sixty days. Yuh understand?"

Women and children gathered leaves to rotate them in the piles so they would get equally fermented.

"After the second fermentation, the men bring the tobacco in that room there and treat it," Mr. Godfrey continued. Meliah Amey wondered if all the men knew that the sign on the wall said, "Danger Do Not Enter When Spraying."

"Over there, we got women blending the tobacco leaves to make sure each cigar come out tasting the same. We pay two-cent more per pound for blending. That area beyond the blenders, that big room we keep daa'k. These bales go in there after fermentation. They stay in the daa'k for eight months. After that, the tobacco comes out here to the blenders. Sam Maybank gonna get you started stemming. The toilets for colored and the room for yuh to eat gone be up them steps on the other side of that dark area. If I evuh ketch yuh using de white girls bathroom, I'll send yuh to jail aftuh I fire yuh."

By late morning, the chill had given way to the close warmth of a swamp.

The oil from the tobacco stained Meliah Amey's fingers. She got the hang of tearing the leaves close to the stem, but she saw another woman who kept leaving too much leaf behind. The woman had three small children with her, and they stood beside her now, watching their mother.

"Like this," Meliah Amey said, demonstrating her method.

Another woman did the same. "Dis way yah. Oonuh do dis way."

The old-time talk was as thick as the dust. And all of them, including Meliah Amey were adu: very black. As much as she hated being there, Meliah Amey realized that working in the house, taking in laundry, had kept her from this beautiful sound, the sound of women working together.

Looking around, Meliah Amey was reminded of the stories her grandmother told about what it was like back in slavery time. How they were stolen from Africa and brought to South Carolina, sometimes by way of Barbados, or like Joe's family, Haiti, how back then, they spoke the different languages of their people. Some, like her own family, were from Angola, some Senegal, or the Gold Coast. But they had to learn to communicate with one another and with the white people, too. So they mixed their different ways of speaking, along with some of the buckruh's way of speaking, until all of them could understand one another in order to grow an abundant crop of rice or build a mansion downtown.

The Sisters had tried to change Meliah Amey's way of speaking, and maybe they had while she was in school with them. And when she spoke with Father Joubert or Mrs. Hardon about the doctor's shirts, Meliah Amey tried to sound more like them, but most times, she didn't think about her words, she just talked. Now, listening to the women in the basement, she was reminded of the sound of her beloved Gkumma's voice and the way they used to talk to one another. And it was only this memory that brought any comfort to her aching head and sick stomach.

"You goddamn idiot," Mr. Godfrey shouted at the woman, who continued to have trouble stemming the tobacco. "Never seen such a thickheaded woman. Come over here. See if you can do any better tying the leaves into bundles. Hell, maybe your chillun can do that much. I swear your brains must be in your feet."

Everyone stopped, their hands stilled by indignation. Meliah Amey believed there was a special place in purgatory for men like Mr. Godfrey.

"She can't bend," said an older woman. "She come yah to work because she can't bend no more to clean the floors at the hospital."

Meliah Amey stopped like everyone else.

"What's going on?" said the young Mr. Rolands walking over from the other side of the building.

They all watched as the woman, in obvious pain, tried to bend to pick up the tobacco leaves.

"My father missed one when he hired her," said the young man, laughing.

The other workers remained still as the woman struggled to pick up the tobacco from the floor to tie it into bundles.

"That's enough," said Mr. Rolands. "Go on. Take your children and get out of here." He pointed toward the stairs.

The woman did the best she could to hold her head up. With a child holding each hand, she made her way up the stairs, the hem of her drab blue dress dragging through the tobacco scraps.

"Don't forget to bring back our uniform," hollered Mr. Godfrey.

In the room where they were allowed to eat their lunch, the talk was all about the firing of the woman.

Binah and Meliah Amey sat together eating the biscuit and sibi beans they had brought from home.

"Will my headache ebuh go away?" Meliah Amey asked Binah.

"Some say they never get the headache, and some say the headache never stop."

Meliah Amey looked up to see Binah smiling at Sam Maybank on the other side of the room.

"What you doing, girl?" asked Meliah Amey with surprise.

"What it look like?" answered Binah. "Ray gone off to France, having a good time. Shooo! I wanna have a good time me s'ef." And with that, Binah went over to talk to Sam. They left the break room together.

Meliah Amey decided to go outside and get some air, as well. Before she got to the door, an older woman everyone knew as Maum Hannah—a term of respect—came over to talk to Meliah Amey.

"That man show out, do Francine bad. Hol'um cheap," said Maum Hannah. "Francine got seb'n chillun to feed up. Man done run off, and she maum cross obuh in July. She got no help. Me an them been talking. We want Mr. Godfrey to give Francine anudduh chance. It not right, what he done. We

64

gone stop work till he say he hire Francine back. We must speak like one. Ebrybody got to say yes. Wuh oonuh say, chile?"

Meliah Amey looked for Binah, wishing she was there to help. This was not a choice she wanted to make on her first day. If she said yes, she had to go through with it and risk getting fired. If she said no, she would lose the support of the other women. She closed her eyes, praying for guidance, but none came. Then she thought of the children working down in the basement, the horrible sight of Francine's children watching their mother being disgraced. She thought of Vincent de Paul having to work in the cigar factory, and that helped her make up her mind.

"Maum Hannah, I got to think of my own son. I can't say yes. I can't."

Back in the stemming room after lunch, Meliah Amey looked for Binah, anxious to find out if she was going to stop work with the others. She did not see her or Sam Maybank, either. Meliah Amey couldn't meet anyone's eye as she took a seat on a box and began ripping the leaf away from the stem. When she dared to look up again, she saw all the women and men that worked in the stemming department standing still, their hands idle by their sides.

"What's going on here?" Mr. Godfrey demanded to know. "Get to work, all of you."

Meliah Amey kept her head down, and her hands working.

"Get to work!" Mr. Godfrey shouted.

"Not till you give that woman anudduh chance," said Maum Hannah, stepping forward.

"What's going on here?" the young Mr. Rolands asked.

"They say they not going go back to work till you give that useless woman you fired this morning another chance," said Mr. Godfrey.

Meliah Amey saw Binah stealing to the back of the room and getting started stemming. Sam came in carrying tobacco as if he had been working all along.

"You're late," snapped Mr. Godfrey.

When Meliah Amey dared look again, she saw that the young Mr. Rolands didn't seem to know what he should do, and Mr. Godfrey was waiting for him to decide. She prayed: Oh most gracious advocate, turn thine eyes of mercy toward us.

"Everyone in the stemming department is fired," Mr. Rolands yelled, clearly finding his confidence. "Everyone except them three still working. The rest of you, get out. You're trespassing."

Meliah Amey didn't dare look, not even to Binah. She kept her head down, pulling leaves from the stems for all she was worth.

It was the toes of his shoes she saw first. The shoes of a white man, a buck-ruh, the young Mr. Rolands.

"You're not ignorant like the rest of them," he said, his voice different than the way he had spoken earlier. "We need smart ones like you. You look out for me, and I'll look out for you." Then she felt his hand on her shoulder, and he gave it a gentle squeeze. "Do we have a deal?"

She said nothing, not letting her hands slow or break stride. He put his other hand on top of hers to still them. She did not look up. "What's your name?" he asked.

"Meliah Amey Rabenel," she answered, her voice shaking with fear. "My husband Joe Rabenel. He a captain in the Mosquito Fleet," she said with conviction.

"Is that so?" he said. "Amy, here's a dollar for you to keep. You did the right thing and kept working. If you need something, I can help. I have needs, too. Go on, take the dollar. Do we have a deal?"

She accepted the dollar. "Yes, sir." She kept her eyes down, hating herself even more than she hated the daddy Mr. Rolands or his son.

Chapter 12

"Mek so yuh tek dat man's money?" Pea wanted to know. The three women sat together eating supper in the light of the kerosene lamp in the little house on Bedon's Alley. The dollar bill from Mr. Rolands's son lay in the middle of the table. Meliah Amey nursed Vincent de Paul.

"She didn't have no choice," insisted Binah, pushing her plate aside. "I swaytogawd, I do a favor myself for the young Mr. Rolands just to buy us sump'n sides swimp an grits fuh suppuh."

"Binah!" Meliah Amey scolded, wiping the baby's mouth with a rag.

"You should have told him to stick that dollar bill up e skinny buckruh ass," said Pea.

"Shooo! That not for true Pea, and you know it," said Meliah Amey.

"Pea, you wanna be digging rock at de phosphate mine?" asked Binah. "Now stop acting high and mighty like we live someplace we don't."

"I wanna go to New York with all the smart nigger," said Pea. "Senator say on account of the war they not letting foreigners come this country no more. Say in New York, they paying seventy-five dollars a week—a week—to Chaa'ston's finest black bricklayers. The Senator is beside he self because all the best carpenters and the masons and what have you, they all going to work up North." Pea pulled a cigar from a pocket in her waistcoat and lit up.

66

"Where you get that Panatela?" asked Binah.

"Not telling," said Pea, smiling. "But I didn't do no favor for no mens, that's for damn sure. Anyhow, that's all the high buckruh be talking bout these days. Talking bout how their smart niggers keep leaving for the North. Then a letter comes to the door from Teddy Harleston and that group of his with the name a mile long, the National Association for the Advancement of the Colored People. Now, Solomon, he can read. He come back to tell me that the letter was asking Mayor Hyde and the Senator to force the Navy Ship-yard clothing factory to hire Negro women to make the sailor uniforms. The letter say if the Negro women don't get them sewing jobs, that soon, all the Negroes going go North for the better jobs." Pea tapped a few ashes into her plate. "Didn't need Solomon to tell me what the Senator say bout that because I heard him way back in the kitchen. *I'll be damned before I do anything Teddy Harleston and the goddamn NAACP tell me to do.*"

"You keep saying the smart niggers going North?" said Binah. "If that's true, then you're stupid as we are for staying here in Chaa'ston."

"Who you talking bout being stupid?" said Meliah Amey. "Binah, mek so you messing round with Sam Maybank?"

"He and I walked to the drugstore for a BC powder. What you think we did?"

Meliah Amey didn't say another word. "Binah, would you hold Vincent de Paul so I can go get us some water?"

"Smells like he need cleaning or sump'n," said Binah, holding him away from her. "Let me go get the bucket of water and you take care of this baby."

Binah stayed gone far longer than was necessary to walk down the alley to the cistern. Just when Meliah Amey was about to go look for her, she came back in the door, a camellia blossom in her hair and smiling from head to toe.

Meliah Amey and Pea cut their eyes to one another and shook their heads.

"You never guess who I ran into down by the cistern, Sam Maybank. We going go for a walk down to Oshtuh Point and hab us a look at the ships in the haa'buh tonight."

"I don't want no trouble from the po-leeze," said Meliah Amey. "You stay away from Oyster Point."

"Well, I didn't ax you, but thank you very much," said Binah.

"Binah, this come in the mail for you today," said Pea, pulling a letter out of her pocket.

Meliah Amey added a stick of wood to the stove to heat some water for the baby's bath. Binah took the letter from Pea.

"Look at all them fancy stamps," she said, opening the letter. Meliah Amey watched her mouth moving, trying to make out the words. Binah looked up to Meliah Amey, and Meliah Amey took the letter and began to read aloud.

Dear Binah,

We now a part of the 369th Regiment. People call us the Harlem Hellfighters. If I live through this war I want to go to Harlem to play in the clubs they got. We with a French unit and been issued French rifles and rations. We even wear French helmets. Kind of like we don't belong to the U.S. Army at all. We played for the officers and their wives. They love our music. Said they never heard this razzmatazz rag we play. They call it razzmatazz jazz. But we come to fight. Not play music. We leave soon with the French Army for Champagne. They tell us write our family cause it may be the last. Binah, you the only family I got. God help me to see you again. Don't give up on me. I want us to go to Harlem when I come home.

Ray

There was a soft knock on the door. Pea puffed on her cigar. The water began to steam in the pot on the stove. Again, the knock came at the door. Vincent de Paul let out a squeal.

Meliah Amey looked to Binah, wondering what she was going to do.

"Just because a girl goes for a walk with one man, don't mean she don't still love another." And with that, she opened the door and went outside.

"Mores times, Binah be a good woman," said Pea. "But that leetle bit of sump'n else she be, that leetle sump'n else be trouble."

After Meliah Amey got Vincent de Paul cleaned up, she wrapped him in her nicest blanket. Then she put on the fancy hat and shawl that Pea's white people gave her. There was no way the sweater could fit Pea, but it seemed to make the senator's wife feel better about herself to give her poor cook her old clothes rather than throwing them directly in the trash.

"Binah's right, it's a nice night for a walk," said Meliah Amey.

"Whenever you wear that hat and that fancy covering over your dress, I know you going go walk on High Battery. Meliah Amey and Binah, your head take way tonight."

"Don't worry, Pea," said Meliah Amey, smiling a little just to make sure she still could. "I may not be smart enough to go to New York or Chicago, but I'm smart enough not to get in trouble on a pretty night." Then she picked up the dollar bill from the table and slipped it inside her pocket.

She wanted to take Vincent de Paul down to Adger's Wharf.

When she got to the Battery, there was a large party going on at the Carolina Yacht Club. The building glowed in a soft warm yellow light. An orchestra played. Now and then peals of laughter came from the open windows upstairs.

The palmetto fronds along East Bay scraped against one another in the occasional breeze. She could hear the gentle slapping rhythm of small waves against the sand below the sea wall.

"Good ebenin, Miss," said the carriage driver, removing his top hat, and taking a deep bow in his coat and tails. "Best time of year in Chaa'ston be right now. Not too hot. Not yet cold," he smiled. His name was Henry Elliott but he liked to be called Mr. Mayor. Mr. Elliott was the carriage driver for Charleston's U.S. congressman. Mr. Elliot always wore the top hat and tuxedo. Meliah Amey didn't care for him because she felt that he was a greedy Negro who took advantage of the rest of them because he had a little influence with the congressman. If a Negro wanted help for a family member in trouble, he or she could pay Mr. Mayor and he would try and get a favor from the congressman. Everyone knew that in exchange for that favor, Mr. Mayor would give information back to the buckruh about other Negroes.

"Ebenin, Mr. Mayor," said Meliah Amey, returning his courtesy.

"Fine night for a walk on High Battery," he said. "Bet that's where you going in de white lady's hand-me-downs. An with your baby, too. All you need is a hand-me-down baby carriage an you be set."

Meliah Amey kept on walking, holding Vincent de Paul to her chest.

"Two dollar, I get you a pretty one," he said. She kept walking, wanting to walk right past him and up to the railing overlooking the harbor.

"Fuh ten cent, I mek sho nobody bothers you walking on High Battery," he called to her.

"No thank you, Mr. Mayor, saving my money for my son to attend the Avery Institute one day. Maybe he gonna be a doctor when he grow up." Meliah Amey wasn't sure why she chose to tell this to the likes of Mr. Mayor, but she didn't like him putting on airs because he wore a tuxedo to work and she wore an ugly blue dress. She felt trapped and alone and wanted to lash out at someone. She wanted to say to him, to Mr. Godfrey, and to Mr. Rolands Jr., "The likes of oonuh will not beat me down."

The music turned to a waltz.

"Well," said the mayor, "you got big plans for that black baby. Mighty big plans. Listen here, they got another round of dancing yet to go. You can take a short walk on High Battery."

As if it were up to him to tell her where she could and could not go. Just the same, she went up the steps. The salty mist touched her face as soon as she reached the top.

Saint Michael's bells chimed. A steamer quietly eased into port while a Navy ship headed out. She turned Vincent de Paul so he could look out. "Your Tata left on a ship like that," she said. "He joined the U.S. Navy to fight for America. He out there somewhere. I know he thinking bout you Kofi, and I hope he thinking bout me too. We got to believe he coming back to us. Chile, nobody know the watuh like yuh Tata. He goes out there beyond all the lights you can see, out beyond the jetties that mark the channel for the big ships. He go way out but he always come back to me befo sun-lean. Always."

Vincent de Paul started to cry, and Meliah Amey comforted him. "Your Tata a strong man. He got big muscles from rowing the boat, but skinny little legs because he row more than he walk. Kofi, do you remember your Tata's arms? Do you now? I do. The Lord knows I do."

The music stopped and she heard clapping and knew she better go. Then it occurred to her. Something she would ask the mayor to do for her.

"Mr. Mayor," she said, and he was getting anxious because he knew the white folks would be coming out soon. The other carriages were pulling up and trying to get into position behind the congressman's. "I need to know if my husband Joe Ravenel, if he alright. He left out of here with the second battleship group. I haven't heard a word in over two months. Here's a dollar for you to find out for me if he okay."

He took the dollar in his white gloved hand, slipped it in his pocket and tipped the top hat. "I find out where your husband at. The mayor can get anything he wants from the buckruh."

Meliah Amey walked back to Bedon's Alley. Binah still wasn't home. She put the baby down on the bed. He reached up, giggling, and she took Joe's hat that he wore when he was out in the boat and held it just out of reach. The baby was fascinated by the shiny Miraculous Medal she had sewn to Joe's hat. The Sisters of Charity gave each child who made his or her first Communion a gift of a Miraculous Medal. Meliah Amey had one, too. She wore her medal on a chain around her neck and never took it off. She regretted that Joe was out there somewhere without his.

Then Meliah Amey got down on her knees, blessed herself, and prayed like hell for Joe to come home safe and whole.

Chapter 13

The days passed, each a little shorter than the one before. First light didn't come until after Mass when Meliah Amey turned onto Columbus Street, joining hundreds of women walking to the cigar factory. The Negroes in their dingy blue and the white girls in their white and green. Why was it, thought Meliah Amey, that some of the white girls could be friendly and pleasant but when you got them all together like that, they took on airs like each one thought she was the most special thing in the world? They were the cigar makers. Rolling the cigar had to be easy compared to all the nasty work getting the tobacco ready. And their foreman would never dare try to feel them up.

Look at them, laughing and showing out. None of them seemed particularly smart based on how they talked. If they were smart white girls they would have a job in an office on Broad Street. Yes, they were worst kind of white girls, the ones working one level above Negro work. They were the ones never to trust.

"Luella, guess what?" a white girl shrieked when she saw a friend. "A Citadel cadet says he's gonna come walk me home this evening. I swaytogawd, I can't hardly stand it."

You a fool, thought Meliah Amey. The kind of fool that believes any white man that tells her she's special. That tells her no other woman on earth could be so sweet and fine. Meliah Amey wanted to turn and tell the girl, "marriage be the last thing on that cadet's mind when he come to walk with a cigar maker."

Meliah Amey saw Binah up ahead in the crowd and caught up with her.

"Yuh head tek way to go to church before dayclean," said Binah. "I want every bit of sleep I can get."

"Vincent de Paul still sleeping when you left?"

"Oh yeah! Pea's up stirring round. Say she got lots to do this mawnin."

Mr. Godfrey made some of the Negro women making cigar boxes on the fifth floor come down to the basement to help with stemming, and none of them were at all happy about that. By ten o'clock in the morning, he had twenty brand-new women learning to stem the tobacco, and by three o'clock that afternoon, Meliah Amey couldn't tell that anything was different since the day before. She had not seen the junior Rolands, and for that, at least, she was grateful.

Mr. Godfrey weighed the tobacco each of them stemmed and recorded it in his logbook. Since they were all paid piecework, no one wanted to stop to take a break to use the bathroom. Meliah Amey had been fighting the urge for over an hour, hoping she could hold out until the end of the day. Then she decided that even if she lost five cents by taking the time to run upstairs to the toilet, it was worth it.

The bathroom for Negro women looked like it never got cleaned. Everything was nasty, and that was coming from someone who stayed on Bedon's Alley, where the only toilet they had to use was an outdoor privy. She did her business and hurried out.

Back down in the basement, she walked as fast she could to get back across to the other side of the building. The large dark area where the tobacco aged seemed like the kind of place a haint would live. The nuns tried to teach her not to believe in haints, to believe only in the devil.

He grabbed her from behind, pulling her into the pitch dark behind the tobacco bales. "I won't hurt you," he kept repeating.

Meliah Amey struggled against him, but the young Mr. Rolands took hold of her arms, pinning them above her head.

"Come on now, don't be this way."

She got an arm free and pushed his head away.

"I'm clean. You'll be alright." He managed to grab her free arm. "We're going to help each other out, remember? Now stop carrying on."

"Noko'noko!" Meliah Amey fought to free herself, pleading that she wanted nothing to do with him. "Noko'noko."

He managed to pin both her arms over her head.

"That's it," he said, "settle down. I got fifty-cent in my pocket that's yours if you be good to me right now."

His words gave her the strength to keep fighting.

He started to get rough with her. "You took my money. You aren't nothing but a West Street whore and you know it."

Her arms were numb and it was hard to catch her breath. She closed her eyes and prayed, "In nomine Patris, et Filii, et Spiritus Sancti—"

"Shut up," he demanded.

"Anima Christi, sanctifica me. Corpus Christi, salva me. Ab hoste maligno defende me."

"Are you praying?"

"Ab hoste maligno defende me."

"I never heard a nigger pray that way before," he said

"Ab hoste maligno defende me."

"Stop it!" he demanded, releasing her arms, letting them drop by her side. "I said stop it right now."

She dropped to the floor, sobbing, her arms limp and useless to defend herself. She tried to get up but slipped on the oily brown tobacco dust, landing hard on the concrete floor.

"You and me made a deal," he said. Then he walked away, leaving her on the floor in the dark room.

"He'lenga time," said Binah as she and Meliah Amey began their walk across the Mall, heading home. A silver tint descended upon Charleston, touching everything equally: crepe myrtle and camellia, magnolia and maiden hair, the bricks of Bennett's Rice Mill and the wrought-iron gate of the old planter's mansion turned tenement.

"You ain crack your teeth for seb'n blocks, said Binah on the walk home after work.

A few blocks further south, Meliah Amey spoke. "He say we made a deal."

"Your eye been leaking," said Binah, "You alright? You hurt? Should Miss Huger take a look to make sure you not hurt?"

"No," Meliah Amey answered. "Gawd answered my prayers. He let me be."

"What yuh gone do?" Binah wanted to know.

"I not know, Binah," answered Meliah Amey. "But that buckruh, e duh debble."

"Maybe I can help to get you out of this mess," Binah insisted.

"Stay out of it, Binah," said Meliah Amey. "Can't have you losing oonuh job, too. We gone need every cent me, you, and Pea can bring home to get through the cold weather."

"Listen, I got a dime in my pocket. Let's walk to the market, see if anybody selling sump'n for us to eat tonight sides swimp and grits."

"No buzzards in the market," said Meliah Amey when they arrived. "No food, neither."

They walked through the empty stalls of the market building. Some pigeons flew out from the rafters, but there were no vendors at that hour during the week.

"I bet we find the wegitubble lady that stay on Saint Michael's Alley," said Binah.

As they got closer to the corner of Meeting Street and Broad, Meliah Amey and Binah were swept up in the swell of bankers, lawyers, and the white girls who worked in their offices, a riptide in wool suits and gabardine dresses, every one of them as anxious to get home as Meliah Amey and Binah in their blue cotton uniforms smelling of ammonia from the tobacco. They stood at the Four Corners of Law, as the whites called it, waiting to cross. The intersection was so named because of the buildings represented there: Saint Michael's Church, city hall, the federal courthouse, and state courthouse. The street was no less jammed than the sidewalks. The yellow flame of the gas lamps took shape as the sun leaned further down. Every trolley car was full, and still men grabbed hold to pull themselves aboard. On the widest street in all of Charleston, carriages and horse-drawn drays, trolleys, and even a few automobiles came to a standstill.

At last they were able to cross.

Along the high brick wall of Saint Michael's Gate, the Negro women sold vegetables, kindling, and flowers. The vegetable lady sang a song to let people know what she had that evening:

> *Green Pease*
> *Sugar pea*
> *Red rose tum-metuhs*

Some carried the baskets upon their heads; some held one basket in their arms and carried another upon their head. Some walked about and some sat on boxes leaning against the brick wall. While Binah looked over the vegetables, Meliah Amey moved down the sidewalk to get out of the crowd. At the end of the row of vendors was a woman seated on a box selling flowers while making a sweetgrass basket. Her seven children surrounded her. It was Francine with the bad knees.

Meliah Amey did not know what to say. Had someone told Francine that the workers protested against the way Mr. Godfrey had treated her? Had someone told her that all the stemmers supported Francine? All of them, that is, except Meliah Amey?

Then Maum Hannah came up with another basket full of flowers. She recognized Meliah Amey.

"I don't speak with she," said Maum Hannah, turning her back to Meliah Amey.

Then a fancy horse-drawn carriage pulled up. "Whoaa," called the driver to the horse. It was the congressman's carriage and Mr. Mayor. The mayor came up to Francine. "Congressman wants me to pick out flowers for e wife. Give me the best you got and I'll make sure he buy from you ebry time."

As Francine put together a bouquet, Meliah Amey knew the rules and she did not make eye contact or try to speak to the mayor while the congressman was nearby.

"T'engk yuh berry much," said the mayor, handing the money and bowing to Francine. He cut his eyes to Meliah Amey to make sure she was listening. "Congressman going home now to take the pretty flowers to he wife."

"Two yams, and a tummetuh, take how much?" asked Binah.

"Ten cent," Francine answered.

"What Mr. Godfrey and Mr. Rolands did to you weren't right," said Binah. "When them men cross over, the Lord gonna throw them back. And when he do, the shaa'ks gone feed up on them."

Francine handed Binah a flower. And as she and Meliah Amey started to walk away, Francine called them back.

"You gots chillun?" Francine asked Meliah Amey.

"Yes," answered Meliah Amey, feeling ashamed that Francine would speak so kindly to her. "A boy."

"You got a man at home to help you? Francine asked.

Meliah Amey shook her head no, turning away, not wanting to look Maum Hannah in the eye.

"Come back yah," Francine called again.

Meliah Amey turned around. Francine handed a flower to one of her girls to give to Meliah Amey.

Men from the fleet had left some oysters and a porgy fish along with some shrimp in the icebox on Bedon's alley. "I take the fish and the oshtuhs to Miss Huger," said Meliah Amey.

"I know, I know," said Binah. "Least tonight it will be shrimp and yams." And as she set the food on the table, she looked around the dark room. "Sump'n wrong," said Binah. "Light that lamp."

Meliah Amey lit the kerosene lamp, and it became clear to them both: Pea was gone.

They ran down the alley and up the steps to Miss Huger's house. She stood by her stove, holding Vincent de Paul in one arm and stirring a pot of sibi beans with the other.

"Pea don't write good enough to leave you a note. She felt bad bout that, very bad," said Miss Huger.

"Where she gone stay?" Binah wanted to know. "She bettuh not be going back to that man that stay on Line Street."

"No, nothing like that," answered Miss Huger. "Chile, Pea done left for Detroit. She gonna work in the place making the automobiles. Say the foreigners that used to get them good jobs can't come obuh yah no more because of the war. She hear the Senator say they wanna hire colored now since colored can't join the unions."

75

Miss Huger stirred her beans another turn. Meliah Amey and Binah were speechless.

"Pea felt bad leaving you two with the rent coming due and no one to take care ah the baby. I tell she, you got to do what's best for Pea. Meliah Amey's smart. She'll figure it out. I help you when I can, but I can't keep de baby in de mawnin. Tomorrow's my day for doctoring."

"I don't know if building cars gone be steady work," said Binah as they walked back down the alley. "Very few of the high buckruh own an automobile. Seems to me they won't need many of them things to be made. It's not like a cigar that's gone after a man smokes it. When a high buckruh man buys one automobile, he won't have to buy another before he cross over."

"Listen Binah," said Meliah Amey, remembering the look the mayor had given her. "I swaytogawd I won't be long, but I need you to watch Kofi for me, okay? I won't be long."

Meliah Amey kissed Vincent de Paul on the head before handing him to Binah. "I won't be long," she called, nearly running down the alley.

The congressman stayed on Lambol Street when he wasn't in Washington. Meliah Amey ran through the narrow dark streets, anxious to see the mayor and to learn what news he had for her. She went down the alley behind the house where the carriages were kept.

Up ahead, in the half-light of the alley, she saw a man talking to the mayor, handing him money. The mayor tipped his top hat, and the man took off fast into the night.

"Mr. Mayor," she said, trying to be nice because everyone knew that he would ask for more money if he didn't like the way someone talked to him. "Ain it a nice ebenin an you looking mighty fine in your top hat." The mayor smiled. "If you don't have any news for me, that's alright. I come back anudduh ebenin." If he sensed how desperate she was for the news he possessed, if he smelled the fear running up her backbone, if he got wind of that, he would ask for more money. She saw him sizing her up.

"Well, I'll come back another time," she said. "I come back next week." She took a few steps down the alley.

"Joseph Rabenel onboard the U.S.S. *South Carolina* that left out of yah two months back. They been up an down the East Coast on patrol and training, but they fixing to start keeping longside the ships going cross the ocean."

"He alive an safe!" she said, "Thank Gawd."

"I don't know nothing bout how safe he is," said the mayor. "But when that ship left out a Chaa'ston, he was on it, and that ship ain been shot at by nobody yet."

76

"Thank you, Mr. Mayor," she beamed. She ran back to Bedon's Alley. But with each passing live oak and palmetto, she became more and more confused. Why hadn't Joe sent her a letter?

Meliah Amey could barely stand up by the time she went to her knees in prayer before crawling into bed that night. She prayed to Saint Michael the archangel for a miracle. Without one, she would have no choice but to bring Vincent de Paul to work with her.

Chapter 14

In the darkness before dayclean, Meliah Amey coughed and spat the phlegmy brown substance that had taken up in her lungs since she started working at the cigar factory. She wrapped Vincent de Paul to her body with a large piece of cloth, picked up his blanket, and headed out the door. The wind was up, bringing a cold damp mist in from the harbor. She turned away from the waterfront, hurrying toward Church Street and into Saint Michael's Place, trying to avoid the wind as much as possible.

The flower ladies had a small fire burning in a barrel to keep them warm as they prepared their baskets for a busy day in the market. Davis Gaillard stopped with his cart of fish. His brother Arthur was a member of the Mosquito Fleet.

"Mawnin Mrs. Rabenel. You going go to the Fisherman's Mass?" he beamed.

"Every mawnin long as I'm able," she answered. "One day Joe gonna come home an when he do, I don't want no break in the chain keeping him safe."

"That's right, that's right." said Mr. Gaillard. "Any word?"

"He on board the U.S.S. *South Carolina*."

"Nobody know the watuh better than Captain Joe, and that's the Gawd's truth. How'd you like them oshtuhs?"

"They were grand," she said, even though she had bartered them away.

"I bring you some more then," he said. "Got porgy today but come tomorrow we stay inside the jetties and won't go back to the Blackfish Banks till spring comes round again. But don't you worry, Captain Joe's family won't go hungry while he fighting for he country."

Mr. Gaillard continued on his way, pushing his cart, singing:

> *Porgy Walk*
> *Porgy talk*
> *Porgy eat with knife an faw'k:*
> *Porgie-e-e-e*

"Mek so yuh tek duh baby dis mawnin?" Francine wanted to know when Meliah Amey passed where she and her children were setting up to sell flowers.

"Got no choice."

"The air in that basement not fit for a baby," Francine replied.

An urge to cough came over Meliah Amey, and she had to lean over to get her lungs to clear.

"I keep the baby for you today," said Francine. "This wall block the wind and the trash fire in the barrel heat the bricks. It not bad right yah. Me nursing me youngest, so you ain got to worry bout that neither."

Meliah Amey studied her head. Leaving her baby with someone she hardly knew out on the sidewalk? Then again, she couldn't bear the thought of either Mr. Rolands or Mr. Godfrey even looking at her son, as if just their eye on the boy would risk an evil spirit getting inside his soul.

"Take how much?"

"Thirty cent," Francine answered.

"Can't pay but twenty-cent, but I get you some fish, maybe some crab, some oshtuhs, too."

"That be alright, twenty cent an some good-eating fish, that be alright." Francine pushed a sweetgrass basket toward Meliah Amey. "Wrap him up good and put him in yah. He be alright. Me and Maum Hannah watch him. I stay here. The others walk but Maum Hannah tell me to sit here with the baskets and flowers. I be here, don't you worry."

"His name is Vincent de Paul," Meliah Amey said, still holding him close.

"Vincent de who?" said Francine.

"De Paul," said Meliah Amey.

"I call him Paul," said Francine.

Meliah Amey removed her Miraculous Medal from around her neck. She blessed herself with it, and then tucked it in the basket.

Meliah Amey kissed her son on the forehead, the blood of every mother in her line pumping hard through her body. They had survived the passage, the pest houses of Sullivan's Island, and the brutality of clearing the swamps and growing the rice. Summoning the strength of all her mothers, Meliah Amey left her baby with Francine at the place the white people called the Four Corners of Law.

Meliah Amey pulled at the tobacco, trying to work even faster to make extra money now that Pea was gone. She kept thinking about Vincent de Paul, wondering if he was warm, and dry. She had thought the heat was bad, but now that it was cold and damp, that seemed worse. Every now and then a child would cry and Meliah Amey would startle, thinking it was Vincent de Paul. Throughout the morning came the sound of people coughing and spitting.

"You hear bout the change coming to the cigar makers?" asked a woman stemming, sitting on another box.

Meliah Amey shook her head.

"Won't be too much longer before they let them all go."

"We gonna start making cigars?" Meliah Amey asked.

"Ain hear nothing bout that, now."

It was hard to feel sorry for the girls working upstairs and not down there in the damp basement with the water spraying from the pipes overhead to keep the tobacco moist.

"What else you hear?" asked Meliah Amey.

"I hear two women in blending done left for the North so they short today over in blending. It pay more but you got the mens standing over you all day long because blending got to be just right. I stay down here."

Later in the morning, Mr. Godfrey came walking through the stemming room. "Need two of you to come ovuh tuh blending," he said. "Pays better if you can learn the work."

Meliah Amey had no interest in anything new and different in a week that had been one new and different bad thing every time she turned around. She looked up to see Binah and another woman all smiles and walking behind Mr. Godfrey. Binah put her hands beside her ears, making funny faces because Mr. Godfrey couldn't see her. Meliah Amey laughed and the two of them squeezed hands as Binah passed by. "Bring it home, sistuh, bring that good money back to Bedon's Alley by first dark."

Meliah Amey ate her sack lunch outside against the brick wall, trying to stay out of the wind. It was a gray day, the kind with a sneaky cold feeling. She prayed for Mother Mary to keep Vincent de Paul warm.

"Seen Binah?" asked Sam Maybank.

"No, Sam," Meliah Amey answered. "She over in blending now. I don't know when she eat."

He walked away looking sad. Sam wasn't a bad man but he wasn't Ray, either. Sam was quiet, like he was studying his head, or maybe he was a little slow, Meliah Amey couldn't decide. One thing no one would ever wonder about Ray, or Joe, for that matter, was that either of them might be slow.

When Mr. Godfrey called quitting time at the end of the day, Meliah Amey took off up the basement stairs as fast as she could. Outside, she started running across the wide-open field of the Mall but had to stop and lean over to cough and spit. That helped her get a better breath and she was off again, feeling the first rain drops landing on her face.

She turned on Calhoun going past the Harlestons' funeral home. She had heard that the Harlestons had a ballroom, where the Brown Elite had real nice parties and such for their own kind. Then the wind picked up, bringing a full-blown rainstorm over downtown. She went into the alley, hoping to make better time without the crowds on the sidewalk that time of day.

But when she reached Saint Michael's Place, no one was there, and hardly anyone was about in the storm. Meliah Amey spun around, trying to decide where to look first for Francine and her baby. Her mind jammed, trying to remember where Maum Hannah stayed, was it in the Borough or was it Tradd Street? She couldn't remember. Of course, Francine wouldn't be sitting there in the rain with her little children and the baby, but where would they be, and how was she going to find them?

Meliah Amey ran a block over to Washington Park and pushed open the wrought-iron gate and went inside. Sometimes people set up tents in there to sell tools and such when it rained, but there were no tents beneath the dense canopy of live oaks and Spanish moss.

Saint Michael's bells chimed softly eight times. Could they be hiding in one of the two highest of high buckruh churches? Meliah Amey ran back across Broad Street to search.

She went inside and began searching the pews.

"You can't be in here, now get out before I call the law," the Negro caretaker hollered.

"Where the flower lady with all the chillun go?" Meliah Amey pleaded with him.

"She smart enough to get out the rain, now go on with your stinky se'f befo you get me in trouble."

Outside in the rain, Meliah Amey leaned over to cough. She couldn't run anymore. She didn't know where to go. She walked aimlessly, trying doors to basements to see if they were open, looking up and down trying to figure out where they might have gone.

She walked so long it got dark, and the rain kept coming down. Then she thought of the covered Market. There were people, Negro and white, taking shelter from the storm in the buildings, but none of them were Francine and her children.

She had never asked the police for help, preferring to avoid them altogether.

Soaking wet in her blue uniform, she crossed Meeting Street making her way to the police station.

"Maum, Maum" she heard faintly over the sound of pouring rain. She turned to see a small boy, one of Francine's boys. "Obuh yah," he called out to her, leading her back to the front entrance of the Market with its stone portico. Tucked to one side Francine had the entire brood, a little cold but very dry.

"When it rain sideways I come here to stay dry."

Meliah Amey picked up Vincent de Paul to her chest, burying her head against his cheek, thanking God he was safe.

"I keep that baby dry all day and then you come along and get him soaking wet," said Francine, shaking her head.

Meliah Amey sat with the other children, letting Vincent de Paul nurse, until the storm passed. She paid Francine a quarter and told her she would have Mr. Gaillard bring her some fish the next morning.

She had never been so relieved to see the yellow glow of the lamp in the window of the house on Bedon's Alley. She went inside to find the house warm and smelling good, real good, like chicken cooking in a pot.

"Binah," she hollered, suddenly more happy than she'd been in months. "Come here. How much extra money you make?" Meliah Amey walked over to the table and right when she saw the letter there from Joe, Binah came out of her bedroom with a bottle of liquor in one hand and a Petite Royale cigarillo in the other.

"Binah," she said, surprised by the sight.

"We not eating shrimp an grits tonight," she said. "We gonna eat a gawd-damn chicken. That's right, chile, a gawd-damn chicken."

"Where you get that bottle and this bird? Blending don't pay that much. Binah, say?"

Binah took another sip. She wasn't drunk but would be soon.

Meliah Amey went about her business, keeping an eye on Binah, trying to figure out if whatever had happened was good or bad. Binah had brought in water earlier and warmed it on the stove so Meliah Amey didn't have to go outside to fetch it. That was nice of her. Meliah Amey bathed Vincent de Paul and got him ready for bed. She took the Miraculous Medal from his blanket, blessed herself, kissed it, and put it back around her neck.

"I love Ray," Binah said when Meliah Amey sat down after getting the baby settled. She poured herself a drink, looking at Binah but allowing her fingers to touch Joe's writing on the envelope: Joseph Ravenel, U.S. Navy. "But he over in France playing music like he always wanted. I know he got a girl."

Meliah Amey nodded, taking a sip, enjoying the burn of it hitting her empty stomach. And that chicken sure smelled good. The baby safe and in bed. A letter from Joe waiting for her. For a few hours, maybe everything was going to be nice. Maybe she and Binah would laugh like they used to do with Ray and Joe.

"I made a deal with the buckruh debble," said Binah.

"No!" Meliah Amey yelled, nearly turning over the table. "Binah, No! Don't start down that road."

"Shut your mouth, Meliah Amey. If anybody starts talking and trying to stir up trouble in the basement, I go tell him they name." Binah took a long draw from the bottle. "He not the meanest man I ever been with, that's for true. Besides, in a few weeks, he eye gone tie up on somebody else." She took a puff from the cigarillo and then stubbed it out. "Let's eat this gawd-damn chicken before I get too drunk to taste it." Binah got up from the table and went to the stove to fix their plates.

Meliah Amey couldn't wait any longer before opening Joe's letter. Twenty-five dollars in cash fell to the table. "Binah, look, he sent money to help pay the rent and buy us a load of coal! Let me read Joe's letter. Then me an you gone eat this bird an drink a toast for the war to be over soon."

Dear Tana,

Sorry I take so long to send this letter and the money. I think of you and Vincent de Paul always. The Navy not like the man said. I study my head long before I write this to you. But soon we go to the North Atlantic and maybe get hit. The Navy say colored can't be on deck. Can't be learned to shoot the guns or be on the bridge. Say Negro work down below. Some shovel coal. Some clean bathrooms. I work in the kitchen. I wash the dishes and clean the tables after the white sailors eat. I am very much shamed to tell you this. Please do not tell my men in the fleet.

Joe

PART II

1923–1924

Chapter 15

DECEMBER 1923

The coal-burning stoves did little to warm the cavernous waterfront building. Brigid wore two sweaters and a scarf around her head, but it was her hands that bothered her the most.

"Come on, Brigid," Luella snapped. "Pay attention."

"Yeah," followed Gretta. "We got to get thirty-five by eight o'clock, now put your mind to it."

When the cigar factory went to the team system, they laid off all the cigar makers—all except for Brigid's Aunt Cassie. Mr. Rolands Sr. transferred her to the packing department, where a keen eye mattered more than fast hands. Aunt Cassie never missed an opportunity to praise Mr. Rolands Sr., either. Gawd rest his soul.

"I'm sorry," said Brigid, picking up some filler leaf and pressing it into her left hand. "Manus hasn't made it home yet and I wanted him to spend Christmas with me and Patrick this year."

"Don't worry bout him," said Luella as she rolled a wrapper leaf around one of Brigid's bunches. "We in here freezing an he in Aruba or someplace."

"He left out of there last month to take a load of nutmeg and tobacco back to Amsterdam." Brigid wiped her dripping nose on her sleeve. "He sent a wire two weeks ago from Antwerp saying he'd be home by the twentieth."

After the war, Manus had a good job at the shipyard and they were living with his father in the old house on Bay Street. Then Manus's father died from the same terrible 1918 flu that took Mr. Rolands Sr. and thousands of others, too. Not long after that, the shipyard had a big lay-off. If Cassie hadn't moved in to help out, they would have lost the house to the taxes. Eventually, Manus got on with a Dutch shipping company aboard the S.S. *Arabella Anke*.

Manus was in Trinidad when Patrick was born in 1921. The following year, the cigar factory advertised: *Five Hundred White Girls of the Highest Moral Character Needed Right Away*. Not only was she tired of always having to add more rice to the soup, or worse, doing without from time to time, Brigid realized she simply didn't feel easy inside without her own bit of money coming in. She asked Manus's cousin Maura to watch the baby and went back to work making cigars.

The team system required two women for wrapping and one for forming the cigar bunches. They were expected to roll between seven and eight hundred cigars per day, except during the Christmas rush when the day stretched out to fourteen hours and the quota became one thousand. The team system put an end to Luella having any extra time to read to the girls. But the worst part of it was the pay. Because it didn't take as much skill to learn how to make only one part of the cigar, the pay dropped nearly three dollars a week.

"He only a few days late," said Gretta. "That ocean big he got to cross."

"What you trying to do talking that way, mek her feel worse or bettuh?" asked Luella. Brigid said a prayer to Saint Anthony.

"I hear the men that go down to them islands come back wanting they wives to do things in a way that ain't natural," said Gretta. "You know, in ways that God didn't intend."

Brigid kept her head down.

"Oh now, look out," Luella teased, finishing one cigar and quickly wrapping another. "You gonna embarrass Miss Muffet here. She'd have to go tell the pope if she thought she'd done something God didn't intend. Ain that right, Brigid?"

"Shooo," countered Gretta. "With that mean old aunt of hers living under the same roof, I don't know how she got in the family way even once."

"Shut your mouth," said Brigid, staying focused on forming and shaping her bunches. "The Bay Street house may be falling down, but we each got our own room with a good solid door. I say a good solid door."

Why everyone would always think of her as some sort of precious lamb, she would never know. Unless, it was her eyes, she knew she had her mother's big innocent blue eyes. Just as well if they allowed her to hide her occasional less-than-pure thoughts. Despite the cold damp, the warmth of a blush spread over her. The acts of husband and wife were unspeakable, yes, but she did not dread those nights the way some women did, as if it were just another chore, same as cleaning grease from behind the stove. No, the doing to and the having done of it all made her feel grown up and worldly.

"Hey, watch it, you're getting behind," Luella nudged Brigid. "That's why they prefer to hire single girls like me. We don't worry bout our husbands and babies."

"Anudduh thing I heard," Gretta continued, never the one to let a lewd subject drop. "Something happens to men in the British Navy when they get too far from land without any women on board. See, when they get too far from land, they start—"

Gretta hushed the moment Mr. Godfrey and Mr. Rolands Jr. stepped onto the floor.

"Never seen so many dumb homely-looking girls," said Mr. Godfrey.

"Dumb and docile," said Mr. Rolands Jr., "that's how I want them." The two men walked down the aisle between the long worktables, talking that way the entire time. Mr. Rolands Jr. was over the entire factory now.

"I wanna work someplace different," said Luella. "I can't stand how they talk about us."

"Who pay more than here?" asked Gretta, her voice muffled as she licked the tip to close the flap of a cigar.

"No place," answered Luella and Brigid in unison.

When the men were gone, the women were free to talk as they pleased.

"That fellow I know went down to Tampa again and he brought me back a paper," said Luella. "They say Royal Cigar supports the Prohibition because the taverns won't sell any cigar if it's not union-made. When the taverns closed, they got rid of the competition. I wish John Grace had won another term, I swaytogawd, I do. He for the working people like us."

"My mother say she don't care nothing bout the vote. She say politics should be left to the men," said Gretta, running her knife along the die to cut another wrapper leaf.

"Manus and I had the most ridiculous—I say ridiculous—argument over me voting for the first time. He made me so durn mad."

"You vote for Stoney?" Luella demanded to know.

"Shooo! No, I most certainly did not and I never intended to," Brigid countered. "That was what was so ridiculous." Brigid secured the latch on her mold press and started on another set of bunches. "The Temperance Ladies left a pamphlet at the door and Manus went to put it in the trash. I said, 'Hol' on, let me read it before you throw it out.' My Gawd, you'd have thought I committed a mortal sin the way he carried on. Talking bout, 'If John Grace loses, it's gonna be on account of letting you women vote.' Then he said he wasn't going to pay the buck-fifty poll tax for me to vote because I was gonna vote for Stoney. And oh, that got my Irish up, let me tell you. I said, 'Listen here Manus O'Brian, I'll pay my own damn poll tax and vote for who I want to.' Shooo!"

"You vote for Stoney?" Luella asked again.

"Thought she said she didn't vote for Stoney," said Gretta, uncertainly.

"You two bad as my husband. All I said was I thought the Temperance Ladies made a good point to say that Mayor Grace should put forth as much effort shutting down houses of ill-repute on West Street as he does toward paving roads and bringing sewer lines into the Negro alleys."

"John Grace don't want to waste his time trying to clean up West Street, that's the trute, and he sure don't care much for the Prohibition," said Luella.

"I might support the Prohibition myself if Manus spends any more of our money buying de bay-uh."

"Brigid, you talking like them Temperance Ladies. Lots of them stay below Broad," said Luella. "Paying the poll tax don't mean nothing to them, nothing. But John Grace—John Grace appealed to the working people and times are tough. Who you think gonna spend money to vote ovuh sump'n tuh eat fuh suppuh?"

Their mouths rested while their minds went to their own thoughts. No matter what, however, their hands were never still.

One of the things Brigid liked about Manus was how he asked her opinion about this or that, sometimes crazy stuff she'd never considered before: Why do you think they don't hire men to make cigars? Do you think the darkies ought to be allowed to vote in the Democratic primaries again? Do you really believe people get moved out of purgatory early if someone prays for their soul? If he was going to keep on asking her questions, well then, he needed to accept that sometimes he might not like what she had to say. She said another prayer for his safe return. The day after the crushing blow of Grace's loss to Stoney, Manus went back to sea without even kissing her good-bye.

And now his ship was late and no word on why or when it would arrive.

That night after work, Brigid decided to spend the dime and take the warm trolley down to Maura's house in Ansonborough to pick up young Patrick. Brigid rested her head against the trolley window. The shops were open late this close to Christmas. King Street itself was decorated with gaslights overhead. The soft glow of yellow lights formed a beautiful arching canopy all the way to Broad Street.

Brigid saw John Grace coming out of Condon's department store carrying an armload of presents. His second term was drawing to a close. She wondered what he would do with himself in a few weeks when he was no longer the mayor of Charleston.

The trolley stopped at Marion Square and several people got on. Brigid made room for another woman to sit down.

"Gracious, what's that smell?" exclaimed the woman as she took her seat beside Brigid. When Brigid turned to face her, the woman put her delicate handkerchief to her nose, and stood up indignantly.

"They ought to make those cigar factory girls sit in the back with de coloreds." She took another seat. "My eyes burn from the smell of her."

A Stoney, thought Brigid. The woman harrumphed one more time about the odor and the trolley lumbered on.

Brigid pulled the cord to get off at Hassell Street. She walked down the aisle, fluffing her scarf as she passed the woman who had insulted her, sending more of her stink in the good lady's direction.

"Oh Lord! Thought they'd never let you out of that place tonight," said Maura O'Brian Santolini, when she opened her front door. "Chile, come on in here an get out the cold air." There was no doubt that Maura and Manus were cousins based on their build. "I hate to wake the boy, but I know you want to take him home. I swaytogawd, I don't miss the cigar factory one bit. Not one bit."

Little Patrick rubbed his eyes, pouting and looking miserable for having been awakened. Brigid hoped after the Christmas rush she wouldn't have to work late every night. He put his arms around her neck when she bent down to put on his coat. She kissed him on the cheek. When Brigid stood up she became dizzy and took a step to catch herself.

"Eee! Eee! Brigid," Maura squealed.

"I'm alright," she answered. "Just a little dizzy all of a sudden."

"Gawd, chile," said Maura, "stay an rest."

"Thank you, Maura, but I'll rest when I get home." Brigid turned to leave. "Has David heard any news bout Manus's ship?"

Cousin Maura had married David Santolini, one of the harbor pilots who took the helm on ships coming into or out of Charleston harbor.

"Not a word," said Maura, with concern, "not a word. I pray Gawd keep him safe. I do, every day, I pray Gawd keep him safe."

Brigid went to pick up Patrick but he fidgeted and pushed away. "Suit yuh se'f," she said to him, knowing full well he would ask to be carried before they reached the corner.

It was after nine before Brigid came downstairs to eat a bowl of the fish perlo that Cassie fixed for her. Brigid could barely stay awake to swallow. Her aunt was in the living room having her tea and looking at the evening paper by the new electric light.

"Well, well," said Cassie, "here's sump'n you might wanna hear." Cassie coughed a few times, adjusted her glasses, a thing she did when she was studying her words, wanting to be sure she got them right. She spat into her handkerchief. "Excuse me," she said.

"What is it, Aunt Cassie?" Brigid asked anxiously.

"Don't rush me. Let me see here now, okay . . ." and her lips moved, and she read it a second time, "Vessels due to arrive Charleston December 24th or 25th. Let's see, here's one, yes chile, the S.S. *Arabella Anke*." Cassie smiled, happy to be the messenger.

"Thank Gawd, thank Gawd," said Brigid.

Chapter 16

Cassie woke up thinking about oyster pie for Christmas supper. She pictured herself by the warm oil stove in the kitchen downstairs. She'd be standing over the hot skillet crumbling the saltine crackers into the melted butter. In the living room, a lump of coal would have the trash burner glowing red. She'd mix the liquid from the oysters with a little Lea & Perrins, some pepper, a dash of mungwa salt, touch of sherry, splash of cream.

The kitchen in her mind got warmer and warmer while Cassie stayed in bed under her heaviest quilt with a cap upon her head. Even in darkness, she saw the curtains move as the wind off the Cooper River passed freely through the old house on Bay Street. Some days she put the entire evening paper into the various gaps and holes where she could feel the wind coming through. She only hoped that Manus took better care of the ship than he did of his own home.

Cassie needed to get up and she wanted Brigid to have a warm place to dress and feed the urchin. She prayed aloud for courage, saying the Hail Mary in her Geechee way:

> *Hail Mary full a-Grace*
> *De Lawd is wid dee*
> *Bless-it art dow 'mong women*
> *An bless-it is de fruit ah die wound Jesus*
> *Holy Mary Muthuh a-Gawd*
> *Pray fuh us sinners now an at*
> *De hour ah our death. Amen.*

Then she threw the covers aside and made a dash for the kitchen.

"I hear they may let us go by five today," said Brigid, helping Patrick to feed himself some grits.

Cassie turned to warm her front side. The problem with the trash burner was that one side of you got too hot while the other side got cold. "Shooo, if they let us go early, I'm gonna get some oshtuhs an mek us an oshtuh pie fuh suppuh."

"I love an oshtuh pie," said Brigid. "I been saving to buy some ham. If they let us go early, I'm going go to Tomboli's an buy us some ham."

"Oh Lord, I hope they let us go by faw-ive," said Cassie. "If they do, you go to Tomboli's and I'll go to the market and then Maura's to pick up Patrick." Cassie smiled, thinking of the pie she wanted to bake.

Double Claro, Natural, Claro, Maduro, Colorado, Colorado Maduro

Cigars came in one of eight different shade groupings based on the wrapper leaf and Cassie's job in the packing department was to sort them out. A Claro was light tan to yellow, a Double Claro light green, a Natural was tan to brown, a Colorado meant a medium dark reddish brown, a Colorado Maduro was a dark brown with a reddish hue, a Maduro was dark to very dark brown, a Colorado Claro was a natural with reddish hints, and Oscuro was the darkest of dark wrapper leaf.

It took a trained eye to detect the subtle but distinct differences in shades. And every cigar in the top row of each box had to match identically, and the bottom row had to be in the same sub-grouping but slight variations were acceptable.

One thing she noticed after training her eye to pick up the difference between a Colorado Maduro and a regular Maduro was that she had begun to notice the tiniest differences in all sorts of things that otherwise looked the same. When she sat on the beach, she studied the gray kamba'boli birds with the white breast, and she did the same with blue crabs before tossing them in the pot, too. One day when the weather was still warm, she even found herself staring at the marsh behind Saint Lawrence cemetery, trying to see if the grass along the edge of the marsh might be a different shade from the areas that got full sun all day long.

Double Claro, Natural, Claro, Maduro, Colorado, Colorado Maduro.

Cassie was forty-one years old, older than most any other woman she knew in the factory. She was thankful to have a job. There wasn't a day went by she didn't thank Mr. Rolands Sr., God rest his soul.

They had made a deal years ago, and he had kept his word. He was aces in her book. Aces. She wasn't but fourteen or fifteen when he called her into his office.

"Cassie McGonegal," he said, offering her a chair. "I've been watching you, and I think you're the kind of gal I'm looking for to help me out around here. See this paper I got here in the mail from New York," he handed her the paper.

Cassie sensed that he was testing her to see if she knew how to read. She could read fairly well, better than a lot of them girls back then, but all the same, she felt scared to death as she took the paper from him, wondering if she would be able to make out the words.

The top of the paper said, "Royal Cigar Factories Closed in Past Year." Below that was a list of cities and states, and beside each one a date. She smiled, nodding with a sigh of relief because she could read all those words just fine.

"All of them closed down on account of one thing and one thing only. Union agitators got in there and made demands on the company that we couldn't afford to meet. See there, at the bottom, the factory in Milwaukee? We closed it down last month."

Cassie wondered why he was telling her all this. "Would you like a chocolate?" he asked nicely, offering her a pick from the finest assortment she had ever seen.

She thanked him and helped herself, wishing she had had time to wash the tobacco dust from her hands.

"These unions are more or less like a branch of the Yankee federal government, and I know how the good people of South Carolina feel about Yankees, and I'm from the North. Right now—yes, have another chocolate—right now I can raise you girls' pay when demand is up and when it's down, I can lower it. When demand for cigars goes up, I can pay you girls more money. It's a formula we call supply and demand and it's the only way to run a successful business. You seem like a bright girl to me. I bet you understand what I'm trying to explain, don't you?"

Cassie understood just fine.

"But these unions would have the federal government telling me I got to pay you girls the same no matter how many cigars we're selling. If that were to happen, well, I couldn't afford to buy the higher-quality tobacco. Without good tobacco, people won't buy our cigars and we go out of business. Would you like a glass of ice tea?"

He was very cordial.

"No, thank you," she answered, daring to meet his eye. And when she did, he smiled. Such an important, well-tailored man had never smiled at her that way before.

He took a cigar out of his pocket, held it up to the light. Cassie studied it as well; it was a Panatela shape but it didn't look like one of hers. "Clear

Havana Panatela," he said, "Only the highest-grade Cuban tobacco in the filler *and* the binder, not just the wrapper." He bit off the tip, and struck a match, enjoying a few puffs as he got comfortable in his chair.

"I know your family depends on the money we pay you. You're not the only girl here keeping food on the table by making cigars for us. My people had to work for a living, that's right. We didn't own a plantation where we could sit on the veranda all day sipping bourbon. Can you imagine what would happen, not just to your own family but the families of all the girls working here if we had to shut down? Wouldn't you like a glass of ice tea or something?"

"No thank you, sir," she repeated.

"There's something else I need to tell you, and it's not a subject we like to discuss, but I need to be honest with you," he said, taking the cigar out of his mouth and leaning forward. "If one of them unions were to get in this factory, they would demand by law—by law, I say—that you white girls go down in the basement and stem tobacco like a nigger." He sat back hard against his chair. "There, I told you the worst of it. Can you imagine?"

"No, sir," she answered with alarm, "I—I can't imagine."

"I've been watching you. You're not like the others. You're very smart, I can see that. You keep to yourself but you work hard. I need your help, Cassie. Will you promise to come and tell me the name of any girl you hear talking about stopping work or walking out? If you tell me what's wrong, and why girls are upset, I bet I can fix it. And if you ever—ever—hear talk of anyone meeting with a union man, will you promise to come straight to me?"

Knowing so many families depended on her, Cassie agreed without hesitation.

"You're going to be a very important person to me. I'll look out for you, too, I promise. Any time you give me the name of someone wanting to cause trouble by talking to a union man or trying to get the girls stirred up, I'll have a little extra put in your pay envelope come Saturday. I'm going to look out for you, and let me guess, you never had anybody say that to you, have you?"

Cassie shook her head, never had anyone promised such a thing in her entire life.

That was way back in 1897, and he never let her down and he always kept his word. He fired Schmidt the moment she told him how Schmidt had taken advantage of Brigid. Cassie could talk to Mr. Rolands Sr. and he would listen.

Lot of times his hands were tied, he used to say, but he listened and made her feel that he was trying to look out for the girls.

Double Claro, Natural, Claro, Maduro, Colorado, Colorado Maduro.

But Mr. Rolands Jr. was a different sort. He knew about the agreement Cassie made with his daddy, because not long after his father passed, he called Cassie into his office.

"My father had only praise for you, Cassie McGonegal," was how he started off. But he didn't offer her any tea or a cool glass of water or anything like his father would have done.

"You know," he said to her, "we don't have this kind of trouble in our cigarette factories. But seems like every other month the cigar makers are upset about something and threatening to talk with agitators. What is it with cigar makers?" he wanted to know.

Cassie said nothing. It didn't seem like he really wanted her to answer anyway.

"You know the difference between a cigarette maker and a cigar maker, don't you?"

He paused like now he was ready for her to say something, so she smiled, even though she didn't like the young man's lack of manners one bit, and answered, "No, sir, I don't know the difference."

"One is made by a machine and the other is about to be. I'll let you in on a secret," he said, leaning in close, "won't be long before we have a machine to make cigars, too."

"Shooo! Oh Lord!" she hadn't been able to stop herself from reacting so. Since she came to work at the cigar factory, the company had been talking about how it wouldn't be long before they got a machine to make cigars. Mr. Rolands Sr. had told her once that they could make a machine to cut up the filler into bits rather than leaving the leaves intact and pressing them together like they did by hand, but so far, every machine they tried had chewed up the wrapper leaf, the most expensive part of the cigar.

To Cassie, a well-made cigar was a thing of beauty. She doubted a machine could ever make a cigar that a man would want to smoke. And besides, she knew that tobacco was made by God, and the leaves would always be different shades, depending on how much sun and water the plant got in the field. That was all there was to it and nothing could change that. Oscuro didn't taste mild like a Claro, but some men preferred a milder smoke than others. And then when you figured in the difference of the binder and the filler leaves and how they, too, affected the taste, well, then a person understood that the combination of tobaccos was endless, and one wasn't better than another, it merely depended on what a man liked in a smoker. When Cassie opened a box of cigars, she felt as if she were looking upon a work of art. Men expected to open a box of cigars and to find them all the same shade. If they opened a box and found a mixture of Claro, Maduro, Natural, and what have you, well, a man wouldn't pay decent money for such as that. No, a machine would never be able to sort the cigars properly, only a trained human eye could do that. And thank God for it, too. Otherwise, she might be out of a job.

Double Claro, Natural, Claro, Maduro, Colorado, Colorado Maduro.

Since she started working in the packing department, she rarely noticed any numbness in her left hand. Now, it was her mind going numb. She could handle ten or twelve-hour days, but the stretch-out to fourteen for over a month was beyond the pale.

Natural, Oscuro, Colorado, Double Claro

She prayed to Saint Dymphna, patron saint against insanity.

Colorado Maduro, Claro, St. Dymphna, grant all those for whom we pray patience in their suffering and resignation to your divine will. Hint of red? No, just Claro.

She prayed to Saint Maurus, patron saint against the cold. But her most important prayer of all was her special intention Novena. She had completed nine of the nine days the night before. She had been praying to Saint Therese, the Little Flower of Jesus, for a special intention: that after Christmas, the stretch-out would stop and the workday would go back to ten hours and only five on Saturday.

"Girls, announcement. Girls," Miss Sweeny called out as she came into the packing department with Mr. Godfrey.

Maduro, Claro—

"No lunch break today," said Mr. Godfrey.

"Lord, have mercy," Cassie blurted out.

"It's Christmas Eve and we decided that you girls should skip the lunch break. That's right, no lunch break on account of the fact we gonna close the factory at 2 P.M."

Cassie and the others cheered in joyful surprise. They hugged one another, laughing at the ruse he had played on them.

"Merry Christmas, girls," he hollered out.

Thank you, Saint Dymphna, Saint Therese, Jesus, Mary, and Joseph, thought Cassie. Then she went back to work.

Claro, Maduro, Double Claro—

Not since the summer had Cassie left the factory while it was still daylight. She didn't wait for Brigid, jumping instead on the first trolley she saw coming. Cassie got off at Market Street, determined to find her oysters.

"E not yah not yet wid de oshtuhs," said the man.

Cassie pulled her coat tight and took off down Church Street, hoping to see or hear one of the street vendors with his cart. In the winter, their ice didn't melt as fast and they often made another pass before supper. She walked by Saint Phillip's, the Huguenot church, and by the Dockstreet Theater. Lots of people were out and about. The damp salt air cut through her thin coat, but the mood was festive. She prayed to Saint Anthony to help her find oysters.

Several blocks later, near Saint Michael's Gate, Cassie found not only the fishmonger with just enough oysters for her pie, but the vegetable lady, as well.

"T'engk Gawd," Cassie declared, and to the fishmonger she asked, "How much yuh tek fuh dem oshtuhs yuh got left?"

"Fifty-cent, yes maum."

The only problem was that she didn't have a container to carry them in since she hadn't gone home first. Observing Cassie's dilemma, the flower lady, surrounded by her children as she sat on a box sewing a sweetgrass basket, looked up. "Come yah," she said, "I gib oonuh sump'n." The flower lady motioned with her head to tell one of her children to bring Cassie the bowl from next to her flower cart.

"I'm mek'n an oshtuh pie fuh suppuh, an oshtuh pie, you understand, and I come down here straight from work without a bowl to put them in. Thank you so much. I bring it back to you, I swaytogawd, I bring it back next week."

"Yes, maum, next week be fine. I stay late T'ursd'y. That cigar factory they keep you from dayclean to fus' daa'k."

"Feel like dey keep'n us f'um dayclean tuh dayclean," Cassie replied.

"Shooo," the flower lady responded.

"I'm telling yuh now," said Cassie, enjoying not being rushed and taking time to banter. "Dayclean tuh dayclean. Shooo." And then both women shook their heads in the same way, at the same time.

Cassie paid for her oysters and an onion. The fishmonger, Francine, and the vegetable lady, all wished Cassie a Merry Christmas.

"Merry Christmas," said Cassie in return. As she turned to go, a young Negro woman wearing the blue uniform of the cigar factory walked up to buy something next. "Merry Christmas," said Cassie to her, as well.

"Merry Christmas to you maum," she replied.

Cassie blessed herself when passing Saint Mary's Church on her way to get the urchin. Maura O'Brian had been laid off when the factory went to the team system. She managed to marry one of the Santolini boys. Cassie couldn't imagine how.

Charleston harbor was full of shoals and strong currents. Until the jetties were built ships could enter Charleston harbor only during high tide. The harbor pilots were taken out to meet incoming ships, no matter the time of night or the weather. A harbor pilot, very often a Santolini or a Lockwood, took the helm of any ship coming or going from the wharves to the Clyde Line buoy. Everyone in Charleston respected the harbor pilots, and how Maura O'Brian, with the way she used to show out when she worked at the cigar factory—how she had managed to snag a virile Santolini boy was beyond Cassie. If only Brigid had married a Santolini.

"Maura, would you mind putting these in your icebox?" asked Cassie as soon as Maura opened the front door. "It's so nice to be outside during the daylight, I wanna take Patrick cross the way to look at de watuh." She didn't bother making small talk with Manus's cousin. To see her in that nice solid house with a chandelier in the hallway, well, it just put Cassie in an ill kind of mood.

Cassie held Patrick's hand and together they watched a pelican plunge into the water for a fish while seagulls cawed overhead.

"Don't look up with your mouth open," Cassie warned. She had never cared for small children. Too noisy, always oozing something from somewhere. But Patrick was clearly Brigid's son. Their facial expressions were so much alike.

The passenger ship S.S. *Seminole* was in the process of being docked. A tug was going out. "Your daddy on a ship and he coming back to see you for Christmas."

"That's not Daddy's ship," said the boy, pointing toward the harbor. "That's a tugboat."

"I found you," Brigid called out, running over and kneeling to hug Patrick. "I can't believe it, can you, Aunt Cassie? We've got the rest of the day off, and tomorrow we get paid for half-a-day without any work at all! My goodness, I am a lucky girl, that's the trute."

Cassie turned away and blessed herself, feeling certain Brigid's carrying on would bring bad luck.

"I bought ham and turnips from Tomboli's, and Maura told me you found your oysters. Oh, what a wonderful meal we're gonna fix."

Cassie watched how Brigid looked out beyond Fort Sumter, beyond Sullivan's Island. The eternal expression of a sailor's wife looking out to sea.

The tide was out. The wind was picking up, and soon, it would begin to turn. Cassie was not in a rush despite the cold. She sat on a bench to watch the harbor activity, breathing in the smell of the winter marsh at low tide. She coughed a few times and spat into her handkerchief.

The urchin ran about with Brigid chasing him, the green smock of her uniform flapping beneath her coat. She, too, stopped to cough, and Patrick waited patiently, well accustomed to the sight, and when she had cleared her lungs, she began to chase him again. Cassie pulled her beads from her coat pocket and said a rosary for her niece to always know such happiness.

"The sun's about to lean," Cassie called to Brigid.

"Should we go?" she called back, coming closer, holding Patrick's hand.

"Tide's turned. Wind's picking up. Will it be too cold for him?" Cassie asked.

"Oh Aunt Cassie," she said, "He's part McGonegal and part O'Brian. I doubt a stronger child has ever been born in Chaa'ston."

They stood at the edge of the old abandoned wharf, neither of them ready to go.

"I want to see Daddy's ship," said the boy.

"You and me both," said Brigid. She looked out to the mouth of the harbor again. "A pilot boat is coming back in."

Cassie looked, but there was no ship yet on the horizon. Neither of them budged, it was simply understood they would wait a while longer. Brigid buttoned Patrick's coat, and put his hat upon his head. The three of them huddled together for warmth on the bench. The sun leaned for down, and in the gray winter evening, the green and red of the kerosene lights marking the channel could be seen.

"A ship's coming in," said Cassie. Neither said another word. They waited silently as the ship got closer and closer, till finally they could make out a flag, a Union Jack. Cassie felt her niece sink against her shoulder with disappointment.

"I guess we should go home," said Brigid taking hold of Patrick's hand.

"I suppose," Cassie replied.

When they were at the edge of the field, Cassie turned back to look. Brigid stopped and turned to look at the harbor one more time, as well. They both saw the same thing, and without having to ask the other, they walked back to the bench and huddled together with little Patrick snug between them.

Again they waited. And waited. Ten or fifteen minutes later, as the ship came around Castle Pinckney, Cassie, Brigid, and the boy, walked to the railing at Bennett's Wharf.

"I think I see the Dutch flag," said Brigid.

"Daddy's ship! Daddy's ship!" Patrick began jumping up and down, which irritated Cassie. If it weren't Manus's ship after all, the boy would probably blow a gasket and start wailing.

Cassie could barely make out the flag over the stern, three horizontal bars: red, white, and blue. And as the ship passed, there was just enough daylight left to make out the name upon her bow, S.S. *Arabella Anke.*

Chapter 17

"Thank you, Jesus," said Meliah Amey looking up to admire the late afternoon winter sky as she and the other stemmers exited the building from the Bay Street door. No one could believe that Mr. Godfrey was letting them go early on account of it being Christmas Eve. Now she might have enough time to get to the Market. And with the factory being closed on Christmas day, she would have plenty of time to fix her family a good meal and keep the house warm all day. A trolley stopped up ahead and she and two other stemmers ran after it. As they made their way to the back, some of the white ladies pulled their scarves or coat collars over their nose.

After getting her ham bone and peas in the market, Meliah Amey went over to Saint Michael's Gate to buy parsnips from Maum Hannah and Francine. Kofi was six now and stayed alone when he wasn't with the Sisters at the Immaculate Conception School. Francine had proven to be a reliable caregiver for the boy, and never once did Meliah Amey regret that difficult choice she had made. Maum Hannah turned her back to Meliah Amey whenever she approached. The loss of the older woman's respect pained Meliah Amey.

Saint Michael's bells chimed. Meeting Street was busy with sedans and Studebakers vying for space among trolleys and the occasional horse-drawn dray. The automobiles were becoming common. Pea must be doing all right up there in Detroit.

As Meliah Amey approached the vendors on the corner, she saw the old buckruh woman from the cigar factory turning to leave after buying oysters. Meliah Amey had seen this woman walking to work in the mornings on Columbus Street, and it wasn't that she was really old, she wasn't yet a ma'magole, but she was older than most and this made her stand out. The not-yet-ma'magole never smiled at Meliah Amey, who wondered what she was thinking sometimes. Meliah Amey figured she was thinking about how much she didn't want to be walking alongside so many Negro women.

The not-yet-ma'magole wished Maum Hannah, Francine, and Mr. Gaillard a Merry Christmas, and when she turned and saw Meliah Amey in her uniform, she actually smiled. "Merry Christmas," she said to Meliah Amey as she passed.

"Merry Christmas to you, maum," said Meliah Amey, as friendly as if the two of them spoke every day.

"I can't believe they let you out early!" Francine nearly shouted. "How's my boy Paul doing?"

"He learning his numbers and letters. Say he wanna be an altar boy. I tell him he gonna have to study he head to learn the Latin for the Mass, that for true now."

"He a smart boy," said Francine.

"He helping he daddy keep track of the money in the big card game going on," said Mr. Gaillard.

"Say what?" Meliah Amey wanted to know.

"Shooo," Maum Hannah scoffed, shaking her head, her back still turned.

"Where he at? That dump on Tradd Street?" Meliah Amey demanded to know.

"Oh no, Joe Rabenel got a big card game at he own house."

Meliah Amey nearly fell on the uneven bricks of Bedon's Alley she was walking so fast. When she pushed open the door, through the smoke and carrying on, she saw Kofi rolling the dice across the table while his daddy whooped and hollered for his number to show. Meliah Amey's voice came out full throttle in the old-time talk.

"E time fuh gone!" she shouted. "E time fuh gone!" Meliah Amey took the bottle away from him, "Andunu! Andunu!" she yelled and shook the table causing the coins and some of the cards to fall.

"Watch yuh se'f!" Joe cursed back.

The front door opened and Binah came inside. Her face shocked by the sight she saw.

"Eee Eee!" Meliah Amey pleaded to Binah, "Tek Kofi, tek em now! Tek foot een han'," she cried, pointing to the door.

"Hol' on," said a man puffing on a cigar, still sorting his cards. "Me not ready not yet."

"Dis how yuh let she be wid yuh, Joe?" The voice came from a woman with Colorado Claro skin and tired happy dust eyes standing in their bedroom doorway. "No odduh man let dey woman speak dat way."

"Mek so? Oonuh a fine man once'd. E arms big an strong," said Meliah Amey looking at Joe, then to the rest of them. "E a Captain wid de Mosquito Fleet till e join up wid de Naby fuh e country. Dat buckruh Naby do um bad, hol'um cheap. Befo, Joe be Olowo like Denmark Vesey. Denmark Vesey be proud. E stay proud an stand up eben when dey hang him fuh try'n to set e own people free. Joe not like dat no mo. E don't tek de boat out. E no feed up e fam'ly. Buckruh Naby hol'um cheap, now e hol' me cheap. E spend de money fuh Kofi to go to de Abery. I pay dat nigger call e'sef de Mayor de last of de money to keep e sorry ass fum duh chain gang. But come teday, teday, Joe hol' Kofi cheap, an I won't stand fuh dat." Meliah Amey pushed the card table over. Bottles, coins and cards crashed to the floor. "Tek yuh clap-hat-bitch an get out. Andunu! Andunu!"

By the time Binah came back, Meliah Amey had cleaned up the mess, changed her clothes, and was sitting at the table, staring at the black-eyed peas, the parsnips, and the ham bone she had bought for Christmas dinner.

"Kofi playing with some chillun in front of Miss Huger's house," said Binah, taking a seat at the table. "You can't give up on Joe."

"Oh Binah, me haa't hebby. The buckruh Navy broke that man. He used to be like Denmark Vesey to me, but he ain no mo. He ain true-mouth no mo."

"Life's strange," said Binah. "Ray—he like to worry. You know, he scared of the water and what not. Yet he come out the Army with the world by the tail. People say the white folk in Paris can't get enough of Ray's music. I don't think I'll ever see him again."

Meliah Amey got up, put kindling in the stove, and struck a match. After she got the fire going, she put the ham bone in a pot with some water and started it cooking.

"Ray a hound dog," said Binah, taking the parsnips and cutting them up. "But Joe, Joe not the kind a man a woman should throw out."

"Mek so?" Meliah Amey asked. "I won't stand for Kofi being round the happy dust. Joe, he done start with it, too. He don't go to Mass anymore. Binah, without Gawd, nothing good gone come of that man."

"Study your head," said Binah, "Everybody got a time in they life they shamed to speak about." Binah peeled an onion. "When the Navy broke Joe Rabenel, the pieces had a long way to fall, and they got that same stretch to go back before he whole again."

Meliah Amey picked a pebble from the black-eyed peas and threw it hard across the room.

"You gonna be sorry for making that man go, and don't blame this here onion for making your eye leak. Another thing, don't be talking bout Denmark Vesey to Kofi. You want him to grow up to get his self killed? Meliah Amey, hab yuh head tek way? The high buckruh in Chaa'ston don't let the Ku Klux come in here so long we say good mawnin and don't cause trouble. The high buckruh gives us they hand-me-down clothes, and they hand-me-down places to live and the hand-me-down water to drink. Long as they keep the Ku Klux up the country and don't let'um come to Chaa'ston, all that is fine with me. You be careful talking bout Denmark Vesey. And on Christmas Eve, I swaytogawd yuh head tek way. You feeling alright? Did you eat crab today? Did you eat the dead man finguh?"

Meliah Amey put a streak-o-lean in the pot with the peas and set it on the stove.

The front door swung open and Kofi came inside, his clothes, face, and hands black with soot.

"You covered in coal dust, mek so?" Meliah Amey demanded to know.

"Isaac say a boo hag live in the Pinckney's underneath-the-house. I wanted to see for myself if I could find it."

"Shooo. You look like a Roo-Roo boy. Now get washed up. We going go Mass tonight."

"What's a Roo-Roo boy?" he asked while his mother took a wet rag to his face and hands.

"Boys not much bigger than you that clean white folks' chimneys. The smallest one goes up the chimney, cleaning it as he climbs up. When he pun-top, he call out, Roo Roo."

"Santa Claus gonna land puntop a Roo-Roo boy," said Kofi, laughing in a way that made Meliah Amey hug him close despite the soot. "Where's Tata? Sister Madelene said I can bring up the gifts at the middlenight Mass. I want Tata to go with us this time."

"Tata gone out," Meliah Amey said quickly. "Listen here, did I ever tell you the Denmark Vesey story?"

A metal stirring spoon slammed against the iron skillet. Binah cut her eyes to Meliah Amey.

"Go change and I'll come tell you a story," she said.

Meliah Amey sat down on his bed. "This is a story from slavery time. My Gkumma tell me this story. She say Denmark Vesey bought his own freedom with money he won in the lottery, but he couldn't be happy being free when the other Negroes were still slaves. Denmark Vesey planned what they call a rebellion. The field slaves an the house slaves in town here were all getting ready for the time when they going go and start killing the white peo—"

Kofi's eyes grew wide.

"Lord, have mercy!" Binah wailed from the kitchen. "Can't you tell him bout all through the house not a creature be stirring, not even a mouse?"

The rhyme made the boy laugh and Meliah Amey stopped. No, she could not tell her young son the truth about how the Charleston Negroes had planned to fight for their freedom by rising up together at once to kill all the white people. Kofi looked up at her, ready to hear what happened next. "I'll finish that story another time."

"Sister Madelene say Vincent de Paul was a slave but he ran away." The boy stood up, put his fists in the air as if he were fighting. "That's what I would do," he said, dancing around throwing punches. "I'd run away."

"That so? Well, you know my great-grandparents were alive when Denmark Vesey planned that rebellion. And my Gkumma, she heard them stories. She tell me, and now I'm telling you." Meliah Amey motioned for Kofi to sit down on the bed beside her.

"Gkumma say there's only three kinds of slaves. One kind be bad through an through and nothing gonna change'um. The other kind, freedom be the only thing that matter. Freedom for he self, and sometimes freedom for the other slaves, too. No matter what, you understand?" He nodded.

"The third type, well, to them, being loyal mean a whole lot more than being free. No matter what, he gone be loyal to he massuh, even if being loyal gone be why he not free. Gkumma, she say they always be least one slave the massuh gonna give the extra blanket. Gkumma say don't ever, I say don't ever, trust the slave that gets that extra blanket. See, Denmark Vesey—the buckruh didn't figure out bout the rebellion. Lord, No! Gkumma say it was one of the slaves that told on him. Listen to me, Kofi, listen to me now. See, the slave that gets the little extra sump'n, he no more free than all the rest. He scared the life he don't know gone be worser than the one he do. And just because slavery time over, don't ever trust your secrets or your freedom to the one that gets the extra blanket, you understand?"

"Did Denmark Vesey run away or did he go back to being a slave?"

"Freedom matter more to Denmark Vesey than anything else. No chile, he didn't ever go back to being a slave."

"Did your Gkumma that know'd that man, did she run away?" he asked, tracing the pattern on the quilt with his finger.

"No, your great-great grandparents were born into slavery and they died in slavery. And your great-grandparents they were born into slavery and President Lincoln gave them they freedom before they died. My maum and Tata, your grandparents, they the first of our people born into freedom. But listen here, Kofi. A person don't run away because he not smart or he not strong, you understand? It's more tangledy than that.

She didn't know how much of what she had told him made sense. But she wanted him to hear it. And then she thought of something she wanted him to see. Meliah Amey got down on the floor and pulled a box out from under the bed.

"Vincent de Paul," she said, "I'm gonna give you sump'n tonight that you can't ever give away sept to your own chillun some day." She pulled out a small box, opened it, and removed an old metal badge. She handed it to her son. He was fascinated by it, and she needed to make sure he understood that it wasn't a play thing.

"That belonged to your great-grandfather. That's what you call his slave badge. See on my mauma's side, her parents were sold to the Comings in town here. My grandfather, your great-grandfather, he a mighty fine carpenter. Everyone wanted him to do work for them. So Mr. Coming did what they called back then, hiring out. Most all the slave owners hired out they slaves with de mores skill at one thing or another. Might be a woman to make a wedding dress or a party dress or sump'n like that, or a man to make a wrought iron gate, or build some furniture, or lay the bricks, or even build a house. By hiring out my grandfather, Mr. Coming made extra money, and my grandfather, he got a little money for he own, too. They was so many Negroes going round at night on account of the hiring out, that the buckruh got nervous, you know, they get nervous that way. They wanted to be able to know if a slave was trying to run away or if he hired out. So the town come up with these badges, and Mr. Coming, he paid the city for this badge and my grandfather wore it when he gone from he quarters to the place he doing the extra work. I'm giving you this badge because I want you to understand about your people. Your great-grandfather, he one of the finest carpenters. He built some of the most beautiful homes in Chaa'ston."

"One-eight-five-six," the boy read the numbers aloud; 1856, the year the badge was issued.

Meliah Amey stood up. "Come yah," she said. "I wanna show you a house your great-grandfather help build. Get your coat."

By then it was first dark, and a steamer ship was coming into port just as Meliah Amey and Vincent de Paul stole up onto High Battery. A cold winter wind whipped from different directions.

Automobiles and a few carriages were arriving to one of the mansions on East Battery. White people dressed in furs and tuxedos with top hats rushed to get inside and out of the biting wind.

"See, the one with the half-circle porch on one side and the big square column porch on the other." The house was decorated with candles in the windows and it seemed they had electric lights in every room, and every one of them had been switched on for the party.

Vincent de Paul looked away to the arriving steamer.

"Listen to me," she insisted. "Your great-grandfather built that house, you hear me?"

"Then how come we don't stay there?" he asked.

Oh, he was going to be smart and he was going to be trouble. "Listen to me," she repeated, squatting down beside him. "Don't cut your eye away from them fancy houses when you walk by. Look at them. Kofi, look at the beautiful things in Chaa'ston. And when you look at them, remind yourself that it was your people, your people, you understand, that built them beautiful houses, the gardens, and the iron gates. Your people brought the know-how to grow the rice that made the buckruh rich. So don't cut your eye away like you're not even good enough to look at the work they did."

After supper, Meliah Amey let Vincent de Paul lie down until it was time to wake him to go to Mass.

"Where's Tata?" he asked, as Meliah Amey helped him into his jacket. "I want him to see me carry the gifts. Where is he?"

"He had to go see bout sump'n," she answered.

They made their way down Bedon's Alley. There was no wind to speak of, and she was glad. Vincent de Paul did not have a true winter coat.

They took the trolley north to Shepard Street. Meliah Amey stopped to pin her veil into place before walking up the wooden steps to the chapel.

"Sister Madelene say I got to be early to bring up the gifts tonight. Are we early?" he asked.

"Yeah, we early," she whispered, dipping her finger into the holy water font to bless herself. Vincent de Paul did the same.

The humble chapel with its tin roof looked lovely with all the candles lit and the smell of incense in the air. She saw Vincent de Paul's eyes linger on the manger scene beside the altar. He started to bolt in that direction and she pulled him back. "We'll go up after Mass to say a prayer."

Sister Madelene, wearing her grayish-blue habit, came out onto the altar, genuflected, and blessed herself before coming to speak with them. Meliah Amey hoped she would be able to understand her; sometimes she struggled with the nuns' accent.

"Merry Christmas, Sistuh."

"Joyeux Noel," Sister Madelene replied. "Vincent de Paul will bring up the gifts tonight for the special Mass," she said, smiling. "He will come with me a moment, s'il vous plaît."

Meliah Amey thought that Sister Madelene had the kindest face of just about any white woman she'd ever met.

Meliah Amey nodded. "Of course, Sistuh."

"Merci," said the nun, as she guided Vincent de Paul to the altar to show him what to do when the time came.

Meliah Amey was relieved for her time to pray before the crowd arrived. There were a few people scattered here and there, but one man caught her eye: off to the side, kneeling with his head bowed in prayer, as if he were trying to hide from everyone, himself included.

It was Joe.

Meliah Amey watched him. Her breath quickened and she felt the rattle of phlegm inside her chest. She didn't know what to do.

Then from the sacristy, Vincent de Paul walked out, he genuflected respectfully in front of the crucifix, and seeing his father, slid into the pew with him. Joe turned, tears streaming down his face, to hug the boy close.

More people arrived. The pianist began to play. Meliah Amey watched from the back of the church for some time, studying her head about staying or going. She found herself singing softly along, *Shepherds, why this Jubilee?* The processional began and as Father Joubert came down the aisle, Vincent de Paul had a look of panic upon his face, unable to comprehend why his mother would abandoned him at such an important moment in his life.

What if the boy were like Maum Hannah? What if he never forgave her for leaving after he had been selected to bring up the gifts for the most special Mass of the year?

"In nomine Patris, et filii, et spiritus sancti," began Father Joubert.

Meliah Amey genuflected and blessed herself before sliding in the pew to join her family.

"Ut apti simus," Father Joubert asked them to call to mind their sins.

Joe offered his hand to Meliah Amey as he responded, "mea culpa, mea culpa, mea culpa."

Through her veil she studied his opened palm, its deep lines, calluses, and fishhook scars. Joe's hands. They knew their way about her most intimate places. What did his hands offer her now? Whatever that might be, she was not ready, not yet, to accept. Throughout the Mass, Joe kept his hand opened to her. Meliah Amey closed her eyes in prayer, but it was the words of her Gkumma she heard: Forgiveness is not given; it must be earned.

Father Joubert, facing the altar of the little chapel on Shepard Street in the middlenight, intoned in the accent of his homeland, "Gloria in exelsis Deo, et in terra pax hominibus bonae voluntatis."

Yes indeed, thought Meliah Amey, Glory to God in the highest, and peace to his people on earth. It was Christmas middlenight. The hours would pass. In time, the sun would wash darkness away. Dayclean.

Chapter 18

JUNE 1924

By mid-June, memories of winter's damp were deep within cedar, keeping company with a gallant moth busy nibbling the family woolens.

Brigid sat on the beach blanket at the Isle of Palms wearing the new bathing suit, the *maillot de bain*, Manus had brought her from Marseilles. It covered her legs only to mid-thigh, and had no sleeves whatsoever. The material fit snug, revealing the lovely shape of her body, a fact Manus found quite appealing. Aunt Cassie, however, was so appalled she opted to stay home rather than be a party to indecency on the Lord's day.

Patrick joyfully shoveled sand into his bucket. Manus dozed in the shade of the umbrella and when he awoke, his bushy eyebrows and boyish yawn made Brigid laugh, and when she laughed, she coughed.

"Excuse me," she said.

"That place is the reason we can't get in the family way again. I mean it. They breaking the law keeping you girls so long every day."

"They ain breaking the law."

"I don't know bout that now. Either way, it's not right."

Brigid pushed sand into a mound beside the one Patrick had made. He laughed, happy for his mother's attention. She wanted Manus to change the subject. No sense in ruining her only day off in the final week before he went back to sea.

"I can't read Dutch, German, or French, but I talk to guys and they tell me what's going on. And I do read the papuhs in Newark and New York an let me tell yuh sump'n, Royal Cigar pays the girls in them factories up North a hell of a lot more than what they pay you."

"Can we please just enjoy today? Patrick, you wanna go in the surf?"

"Will you at least talk with the guy I know from the IWW?"

Brigid stood and put her hands down as if to pull Manus up, too. "They'll be no talk of unions round Aunt Cassie, you understand? Come on, get up. Let's go in the surf to cool off."

"I ain fooling," he said, putting his hands into hers. "Your Aunt Cassie's wrong. You won't have to do the colored jobs or work alongside them. The unions don't consider the stemmers skilled craftsman so they can't join. The company is trying to scare you girls with lies." Then he pulled her down beside him on the blanket.

"Manus!" she pushed at him, embarrassed to be in his arms in front of a beach full of people. "Come on, I wanna go in the surf and try out my new what-you-call-it, my *maillot de bain*." She wiggled out from his grasp and stood up. "Besides, you're not listening to me. It don't matter if we want to join or not. The union don't want us, either."

"You're wrong, the CMIU takes women now," he insisted.

"You're not listening to me! And I can't stand to talk with you when you won't listen. Come on, Patrick."

She wanted to have fun, and besides, she had her own way of seeing the matter.

Hiyak–Hiyah–Hiyak

"Don't look up at the seagulls with your mouth open," she warned Patrick. "Look here, a sand dollar." She reached down in the ankle-deep water to pick it up and show it to Patrick. He took it in his hands, admiring it thoroughly. "To you, that's a million dollars, isn't it?"

"What is it I'm not listening to you about?" Manus asked, as he ran up to join them.

"Luella Schultz met with a man from the Cigar Makers International Union and he say we can't join because we on the team system. They say making cigars this way don't require skill. It's not, what you call it, craftsmen work. To the CMIU, I'm no different than a stemmer and that's the Gawd's truth. They only want the cigar makers who are still making the entire cigar, start to finish, like we used to. Now let's hush talking bout this and try to enjoy the little time we got left before you leave."

"Oh alright," he said, his eyes revealing that he might smile. He picked up Patrick in his arms. "Only one more thing I wanna say, and then I'll be quiet. The Democrats are talking about adopting the KKK plank and if they do, you can't vote for Coolidge because the Ku Klux hate Catholics. I won't be here come Election Day but you got to promise me you gonna vote for the socialist, Lafolette."

"Eee! Eee!" she hollered, rushing into the surf to get away.

It was so much easier to swim in her new suit without the extra material weighing her down. She floated, letting the water cover her ears, the gentle swells raising and lowering her body, only sky above. Manus and Patrick were nearby. He was teaching the boy how to hold his breath and put his head under water. They went under, and when they both popped up, Patrick smiled, and Manus praised him for having done such a good job. Then all three of them lowered their heads under water. Laughing and smiling, they played together like a family of otters.

"Manus, I love my bathing suit," she said. Patrick was napping on the blanket and she and Manus were sitting close enough to touch.

"I wish I could buy you all sorts of stuff, Brigid. I wish you didn't have to work in that stinking place."

She didn't want him to brood. When Manus got quiet for too long, his thoughts inevitably went back to things he had done in the war. Once those thoughts took hold of him, he was even harder to manage than when he was talking about the union. Manus felt the war had been "a big con," as he put it. She never stopped admiring him for wanting everyone to get a fair shake, but Lord, some times were harder than others to love him for it.

"Manus, you know what I truly want to have?" she said, hoping he would look up at her. And when he did, she knew she had pulled him back from the edge. "I want an electric fan. Aunt Cassie and I saw one in the window of Rubin's Electric on King Street. It sits puntop the table and you plug it into the light socket. Oh my, can you imagine having your own portable breeze? That's what the sign says, 'Imagine Having Your Own Portable Breeze.'"

He didn't answer right away. She could see that he hadn't yet decided to make the turn.

"Yeah well," he answered and she could barely hear his voice at first. "We got a light socket in nearly every room now. What else Brigid, if you could have anything you wanted?"

She thanked the Virgin Mary. "I'd like a chiffon georgette dress from Kerrison's, and then next Saturday night, I'd want you to take me to that fancy new hotel, the Francis Marion. I could wear my dress an we'd dance like we did that time on the Isle of Palms when we missed the ferry back." Recalling that night, and how skilled he had been at the oars when it really started blowing, she leaned against him. "The orchestra's playing Rimsky-Korsakov's "Song of India." Doesn't that sound romantic?"

"I ship out T'ursd'y for Rotterdam," he answered, as if that were the only reason they wouldn't be going.

"I know," she said, "but wouldn't it be grand if we could go?"

Some Citadel cadets were horsing around in the sand, challenging one another to push-ups and handstands. The haircuts were unmistakable even though they were out of uniform. She and Manus watched to see what they would do next. Patrick woke up from his nap and came and sat on Manus's chest. Manus lifted the boy up in air with one hand, raising him up and down.

"Manus, please!"

"I got him, I got him," he said, annoyed that she thought otherwise. Patrick couldn't stop laughing.

"Hey Manus, we gonna lift Friday night at the YMCA. Can you come?"

It was Julian Jones. He and Manus belonged to the Charleston Barbell Club. Both had the muscles to show for it, too. "Wish I could, Julian, but I ship out Thursday."

"Look at them," said Julian, meaning the cadets. "Punks. I bet they sew lace on their panties."

Manus laughed. Brigid had to think about what Julian meant by that.

"Hey Brigid," said Manus, suddenly perky. "How much does Rubin want for that electric fan?"

"$14.95 plus tax," she said.

Manus stood up, "Julian, will you help me take some candy from the babies?"

"Nothing I'd rather do," he answered.

The two men walked down the beach to join the cadets.

"Come on Patrick," she said. "Your father's up to sump'n." She took the boy by the hand and went after Manus.

"You fellows look in shape. Bet the Citadel don't tolerate sissies."

At the mention of the word sissies, the young men began punching one another in the arm or in the stomach, trying to prove themselves anything but.

"Yeah, you think your tough, don't you?" he said.

"Look, shorty," said the cadet, "what you want f'um us?"

"I want to take you on, that's what. Show me what you got. I bet you two dollars you can't even lift Mr.—"

"—Rutledge," the other one answered.

"I bet you two dollars you can't lift Mr. Rutledge."

The cadet picked up the young Mr. Rutledge a few feet off the ground and set him down. Then he opened his hand, ready for the money. Brigid held her tongue, wanting to tear into her husband for wasting money that way.

"No, peckerhead, I didn't mean lift him like a girl," Manus scoffed. "I meant lift him ovuh yuh haid like a man."

The cadets were offended, and Brigid knew that was the intention.

The two cadets spoke to one another and then turned around. "Okay," said one, "I'll lift him over my head and you'll give me two dollars, right?"

"Right," said Manus. More people walking along the beach began to gather.

One cadet crouched down while the other positioned himself to be lifted.

"One-two-three," the crowd chanted.

But the cadet managed to lift the young Mr. Rutledge only to his waist level before his arms gave way. They changed positions, but it didn't help.

"How bout you, shorty," shouted one of the men who had gathered to watch. "Bet you can't do it either."

"Oh, I can do it," said Manus. "I can do it. Hey Julian, come over here. Let me show them how it's done."

Brigid couldn't believe it. She had never seen Manus like this before. Was he like this in the bars of Aruba and Marseilles?

"Brigid, give me your hat," he demanded. "Whatever money goes in the hat, I'll give it to the fine Mr. Rutledge if I can't pick Julian here up over my head. And you might notice, Julian is taller and weighs a lot more than Mr. Rutledge. If I can do it, I take all. Come on now," Manus urged the crowd. "Sweeten this pot." Some threw in change and one or two put in dollar bills.

"You're too short," someone yelled as he put in a quarter.

The cadets huddled together again. Manus cut his eyes to Brigid and Patrick. If he lost their trolley money back to the ferry she would never forgive him.

"De man crazy. Here's faw-ive dollars." Mr. Rutledge was irritated and his Geechee was coming out in the way he spoke.

"Make it interesting," Manus cajoled. "If one of you boys puts in another ten, I'll hold Julian here over my head with one hand. I say one hand."

The crowd stirred and hollered.

"Alright, I'll mek it interesting," said another cadet, throwing a ten spot into the kitty.

"Shooo, chile," Brigid stammered, aghast. "Manus O'Brian, you crazy. Have you lost your durn mind?"

Julian positioned himself. Manus got into a half-kneeling position, blessed himself, and bowed his head.

In one quick jerk, Manus lifted and stood, and briefly Julian Jones hovered at chest-height before Manus took one step back, bent slightly in the left knee, and pressed the man up overhead. Julian did his part by holding his body completely rigid, like a plank. The crowd gasped, waiting now for the next move.

Manus got his hands close together, his face stern but not contorted as he let his left arm down. He stood holding Julian Jones above his head with only his right arm.

The crowd went crazy. Manus turned side to side for everyone to see. His thick bushy eyebrows nearly crossed in concentrated effort. "On two," he yelled. "One—two," and then he let his arm bend, tucking fast and using his other arm to make sure Julian didn't fall as he came down.

The next morning, just after dawn, Brigid and Aunt Cassie joined the sea of young women walking to work on Bay Street.

"Mawnin," said a Negro woman.

"Good mawnin," answered Brigid.

"Mawnin," said Cassie.

Luella fell in beside them. "How'd you like them bringing in that piano player last week?"

"They brought her up to the packing department round six, and I thought she played grand," said Cassie. "Oh yeah, made the time go by real fast. It was wonderful."

"How'd you like it, Brigid?"

"I liked it fine," she said.

"I hear they got a woman coming next week going to tell us how to fix our hair an put on rouge and stuff like that. They playing us for suckers if you ask me."

"What you talking about?" Cassie wanted to know.

"Shooo! None of us going go to Saint Cecilia's ball! They trying to get us to stop complaining bout the stretch-out. That's all they trying to do."

"You can piss on me but don't try to tell me it's raining." Brigid said matter-of-factly.

"Brigid!" Her aunt implored. And even Luella took pause at hearing such words from Brigid.

"That's what Manus says when a man is taking advantage of him and wants him to act happy about it," said Brigid.

"I like it," said Luella. "Listen, I talked to Mr. Gresham, you know Mr. Gresham the new foremen. He say they need to shorten the day or pay us more money. That's right, that's what Mr. Gresham say."

"Mr. Gresham say that?" Brigid asked.

"Yeah! He going to talk with Mr. Rolands." Luella was stirred up. "And anudduh thing when I told Mr. Gresham bout that sorry wrapper leaf full of holes, he say to me, he say, 'Don't worry bout it.' He say he won't fine me the forty cent for not meeting the quota because it ain my fault."

"All the girls sure like Mr. Gresham," said Cassie sarcastically. "Mr. Gresham this and Mr. Gresham that. If you ask me, it's disgusting the way ya'll carrying on bout that man."

It began to rain and like always, this caused a tangle as white and colored tried to get to their respective doors before getting soaked.

Cassie went as far as the second floor to the packing department. Luella and Brigid continued up the steps.

"You know," said Luella, leaning close to Brigid's ear. "I saw Gretta getting into Mr. Gresham's car over on America Street."

"Oh yeah? He has a car, too?" answered Brigid, more surprised by this fact. She looked up to see Gretta on her way back down the stairs with the nurse beside her.

"You going the wrong way," said Luella.

Gretta didn't answer.

Brigid put her initials down and the stock boy handed her one bundle of binder leaf and another of filler.

"We're behind before we even get started," said Luella, taking her knife from her smock pocket to cut the string on her wrapper leaf. "Shooo! Not this sorry stock again."

"Looks like bugs got into it," said Brigid.

"The darkies spray it to kill the bugs," said Luella.

"Maybe the bugs ate it before they put the poison on it," said Brigid.

"Ours isn't any better," said a girl from the table behind them. From all across the room, cigar makers began holding up wrapper leaves to the morning sunlight. Most were full of holes.

"I ain putting up with this no more," said Luella, pushing her way out from the narrow space between the long tables across the factory floor. The normally busy hands of hundreds of cigar makers came to a stop. "I'm going go find Mr. Gresham."

Just as Luella was about to enter the stairwell, Mr. Godfrey came out of it along with a young girl Brigid did not recognize.

"This here Karina or sump'n like that," he said. "She going to work with you and Brigid while Gretta takes a few days off."

"What's wrong with—" Luella stopped herself. Brigid looked down at her filler leaves. Nervously, she began to form a bunch. She'd heard whispers from time to time for why a girl might be out a day or two after visiting the company doctor. But no one was ever sure. Such as that was not proper conversation. But a nice girl like Gretta?

"Wuh de mattuh?" Mr. Godfrey said to Luella. "How come you leaving the floor?"

"I'm wanna talk to Mr. Gresham," she said. "He understands how we got a bad shipment of stock and it's not our fault we can't meet quota."

"You must not be smoothing out the leaf good enough before you cut it," he said, irritated.

"Beg yuh pardon, sir," Luella interrupted. "I know how to smooth out the leaf. The problem is bugs have et this shipment of wrapper leaf. Mr. Gresham, he agrees with us."

"Mr. Gresham don't know what he's talking bout. That's why we let him go."

A collective gasp went across the expansive floor. Even Brigid's hands went still upon hearing the news.

"Why?" Luella demanded to know. "Why?"

"This ain no damn tea party. We running a business here, but I don't spect ignorant girls to know what that means." He stomped off, leaving Karina to take Gretta's place.

A few hours later, Luella wrote a note and passed it to Brigid, who passed it to the next girl.

Are we going to take this? They fired the one man who speaks up for us. Tomorrow at 10 a.m., put your hands in your lap. We will not go back to work until they bring back Mr. Gresham. We will not go back to work until they agree not to hold us to the quota long as we have sorry stock.

The sun leaned for down as Brigid and her aunt walked home.

"Awful hot for June," said Brigid. Cassie did not respond.

The breeze came and went like the gentle waves she had enjoyed so much the day before playing in the surf with her family. "Your mouth tied up or sump'n?" Brigid asked.

They were passing in front of the Negro funeral home on Calhoun Street when at last Cassie spoke. "You better not be planning to stop work in the mawnin. You hear me, girl?"

"Aunt Cassie, please, I don't want you mad with me, but we got to speak up this time."

"Luella write that note?" Cassie demanded to know.

"What difference it mek who wrote dat note?" Brigid replied, her temper showing for a change.

"You don't know what you getting into or where this might end up," said Cassie, more angry than Brigid had ever seen her. "Mr. Gresham's an agitator and a rascal, too. They oughta hang that man from the highest tree."

"Aunt Cassie," said Brigid, stopping on the sidewalk. "I'm going to stop work with the other girls."

"You making a big mistake. Think bout the rest of us? The ones that don't agree with you. The ones that don't wanna end up in the basement stemming longside some colored woman."

Brigid knew there was no point in the two of them talking any further. She stood still while her aunt kept walking.

Brigid felt scared. Some said that when the coloreds did something like this, Mr. Godfrey fired all of them. And Brigid knew she would never go down in that stinking basement and stem tobacco. She could read and write, and even if it didn't pay as well, she'd go work in an office on Broad Street rather than go down in that basement. A lot of girls couldn't read or write very well and finding another job would be tough. Her Aunt Cassie was one of them. Brigid turned the corner, heading to Saint Mary's Church.

Father O'Shaughnessy slid the screen back in the confessional. "Bless me, Father, for I have sinned," she began. When she had finished the standard preliminaries, she explained the situation to the priest, the problem with the twelve- to fourteen-hour days, the bug-eaten wrapper leaf, firing the one foreman everybody liked. She told him about the plan to stop work and how some said they would fire everybody and some said they would make the white girls go stem tobacco in the basement with the darkies, and she just didn't know what to do.

"What does your husband say?" asked the priest.

"He won't mind one bit," she said. "He's planning to vote for Lafolette."

"I see," Father O'Shaughnessy replied, his brogue not as strong as when he first arrived. "I see. In that case, let me explain a few things. If you girls go on strike, you'll be committing several sins: greed, pride, and avarice, too."

"Avarice! Really Father, avarice, too?"

"Oh yeah," he said. "Royal Cigar pays you to do a job. They don't pay you girls to sit with your hands in your lap. If you do you'll be stealing from the company."

"But it's piecework, Father."

"And—And, I don't mind telling you, you'll be stealing from the church."

"The church? How could that be?"

"The church is like any family. We need money to pay our bills. And we have to pay the bishop his due, of course. Let me tell you, the Shepard Street Chapel, and the other Negro parish on Wentworth, they don't raise their share of the expenses. But, the church is a family and like any wise family, we invest money to earn money. I happen to know for a fact that the church owns quite a bit of stock in the Royal Cigar Company. So if you girls do anything that hurts Royal Cigar, you'll be hurting the church as well, and that young lady, is a mortal sin."

It took Brigid nearly an hour to say all the Hail Marys she had been assigned for penance. The sun had set but it wasn't fully dark as she walked tiredly up the front steps to the house on Bay Street. Standing on the porch, she realized no one was talking or carrying on at all, not even little Patrick. Silence was a bad sign. She opened the door slowly. And there they were, the three of them, stripped down to the lightest of clothes, all of them sitting, chins up, and hair blowing back as they enjoyed the portable breeze of a new electric fan.

Chapter 19

The streets of Ansonborough were empty at that hour. Cassie removed her uniform cap, placing her veil over her head before she pushed the door open and went inside the church.

She knelt at the sacristy altar to light a candle for the intention of Mr. Rolands ending the stretch-out and going back to the ten-hour day and for Brigid to have enough sense not to participate in the strike. Cassie blessed herself and hurried on her way to the factory.

"Give me the name of every girl who says she's going to strike today," Mr. Rolands Jr. demanded.

The girls would be arriving soon and Cassie did not want to be seen leaving his office.

"Your daddy listened to me when I'd come to him and I pray Gawd you do the same. There's three problems making the girls wanna strike. Firing Mr. Gresham is only what's brought it to a boil. The other reason is the worm-eaten wrapper leaf. And the third is the stretch-out every day, every day, to twelve hours."

"No one is required to stay over fifty hours a week," he said, clearly irritated.

"What about Gresham and the sorry wrapper leaf?"

"That's not how this works," he said. "Just give me the names of the ones who want the union in here," he insisted, his hand ready with pen and paper.

Son of a bitch, thought Cassie, he's not going to budge.

"No talk going round bout joining any union," she insisted.

"I don't believe that for a minute," he said. "The colored longshoremen have got some of their people in town from the West Coast. They're behind this, I know it." He motioned with his pen again, ready to start writing.

Cassie looked at the clock; she needed to be going.

"Do you and your Catholic girls have any special days coming up?" Mr. Rolands's tone was more congenial now. "Miss Cassie, you know how this works. You been doing it long enough. You help me and then I put a little extra in your pay envelope. Lots of girls would appreciate a little extra. I deal with you because my father asked me to, but he's gone, isn't he, Miss Cassie? I don't have to—"

Father forgive me, she prayed.

"Luella Schultz," she blurted out, "she the one stirring them up. It's all her doing, I swaytogawd, Luella Schultz is the one." Cassie got up to leave.

Cassie slipped into the stairwell as the morning whistle blew.

Colorado, Claro, Double Claro, Maduro

There wasn't a clock in the packing department, but Cassie guessed it was nearing ten o'clock on account of the fact she felt an urge to make water and she always had to go about two hours before the lunch break.

Claro, Colorado Claro, Double Claro, Claro.

Cassie thought she saw one girl put her hands down by her side but she wasn't certain, and then across the way, another one, and then another one, and after that, another.

Cassie refused to stop working. The company paid her to do a job, and she wasn't going to be disrespectful to the honor of Mr. Rolands Sr. He was a good man who treated her decent. Mr. Rolands Sr. understood that it wasn't only about her getting a little extra in her pay envelope from time to time. He knew to listen to what Cassie told him. With him, it wasn't all push push and no give.

Then Mr. Godfrey came into the packing department and began writing down the names of the girls who had stopped working. Some of the girls saw this and started back to work before he could take down their names.

When he left the floor, the ones who had not gone back to work walked to the window and—of all things—opened it. The windows were not to be opened under any circumstance because the breeze might dry out the tobacco. The girls leaned outside, laughing and acting the fool.

Colorado Claro, Maduro, Claro, Double Claro.

"Come on, y'all," shouted a jubilant girl who ran onto the floor from the stairwell, "Nearly one hundred girls on the other floor stopped work. Come on, let your hands be still today," Another one hollered from the stairwell, "The po-leeze are coming."

Christ, have mercy, thought Cassie.

Later, on her way to the lunchroom, Cassie went up to the third floor to check on Brigid. She saw her seated in the wide-opened window, laughing and carrying on with the rest of them.

They all cheered and began waving. "It's the man from the newspaper," one of them shouted. "Everybody smile and wave for the camera!" and did they ever.

"How come you girls not working?" a reporter shouted from below.

They started yammering at once. Cassie shook her head, embarrassed that the girls were being silly and it would be in the evening paper for everyone to see. Then one of them yelled, "Because they fired a good man, a foreman named Mr. Gresham and we want him to get his job back."

"Don't forget the tobacco," another one prodded.

"And we got some wrapper leaf that's full of holes—" but the girl couldn't continue for her own giggling at having her picture made and being the center of attention.

"The stretch-out," one of them goaded her. "Tell'um bout the stretch-out."

"Oh yeah, we wanna work ten hour days, not twelve," she yelled down to the reporter.

"You girls sure are pretty," the reporter yelled back.

The girls, including Brigid, began to wave and cheer.

After lunch, Cassie returned to her station. The work day felt twice as long and four times as hard.

At five, Mr. Godfrey called quitting time.

Well, thought Cassie, least they weren't calling for a stretch-out.

"Quitting time," he shouted. "Everybody out. Go home now."

"We not gonna go," said one of the girls. "We staying till our demands are met."

Cassie was not prepared for the commotion when she got outside the building. There was a police paddy wagon on Drake Street but even the policemen were chatting with the cigar makers hanging out from just about every window in the place, every one of them laughing and showing out. The Negroes began to come out from the Bay Street door. Cassie shook her head, thinking how even the Negroes understood what it meant to work for a living. Apparently they understood it more than her own niece.

Cassie heard a familiar voice. She turned back to see Manus the Bolshevik holding the urchin by the hand. Manus hollered up to Brigid and the other girls. "*I hear America singing, the varied carols I hear, those of carpenters, boatmen, and cigar makers—Sing with open mouths your strong melodious songs.*"

This was all his fault, thought Cassie. He'd put peculiar ideas into Brigid's head.

"Mama," the boy yelled, waving.

"Mama loves you, Patrick," she yelled back.

Cassie shook her head, utterly appalled. The girls were wasting everyone's time. No one would take them seriously for showing out that way.

"Ridiculous," said Cassie quietly.

"Brigid," Manus shouted up again, "I got you a plate of food. I caught some porgy fish today. I know how you like porgy fish with red rice an a little mungwa salt. You can share with your comrades there."

Hiyak—Hiyah-Hiyak

Gulls gathered, anxious for a handout. An onshore breeze blew and the palmetto fronds scraped against one another.

Manus looked over his shoulder and saw Cassie watching him. At least he had the decency to stop laughing long enough to nod his head.

"Too bad you don't make enough money so your wife don't have to work so hard," she said.

Hiyak—Hiyah-Hiyak

Manus tilted his head, putting his hand beside his ear. Between the gulls and the other commotion, he had not heard what Cassie had just said.

"Shooo!" said Cassie, motioning him away with her hand before turning to walk home. Oh, how she wished she could afford her own apartment again.

The evening newspaper ran a picture of the cigar makers hanging out the window, all smiles, and laughing.

Cassie turned on the electric fan and sat down to read the article. Mr. Rolands said the strike was the result of a misunderstanding because the man in question left of his own accord and wasn't even fired. He made it sound like it wasn't even a strike at all, talking about how hard the girls had been working lately and that it probably was good for them to let off a little steam. He said they would keep an eye on the ones that wanted to spend the night in the building to make sure they stayed safe.

"Crummy papuh," said Cassie, "They don't mention the sorry wrapper leaf or the stretch-out or nothing."

The next day, there wasn't any more trouble; everything was back to normal and the only one fired on account of it was Brigid's friend, Luella Schultz.

Chapter 20

Father Joubert kept up with the tides as much as the fishermen, knowing to have the Mass that morning at five rather than five-thirty to allow the men to catch the last of the ebb.

Meliah Amey stood at the wharf in the darkness just before dayclean, watching Joe and the other men preparing their hand lines with twelve hooks each. In Joe's father's time, a few of the boats were still dugout cypress logs. Now they were cypress planks supported by live oak ribs. Meliah Amey said another prayer that Saint Peter would keep the men safe from Ki'tuta, the demon who rules the water. The air was ripe with the smell of the pluff mud at low tide. Across the Cooper River, the first light pushed into the sky above Mount Pleasant. Joe and his crew, along with the others, cast off, destined for the Blackfish Banks, matching the rhythm of their oars to song:

> *Rosy am a han'some gal!*
> *Haul away Rosy—Haul away gal*

Fancy slippers and fancy shawl!
Haul away Rosy, Haul—Away
Rosy gwine ter de fancy ball!
Haul away Rosy—haul away gal!

Meliah Amey watched the boats of the Mosquito Fleet until they reached Castle Pinckney, the name her father's people took when slavery time ended.

The wind calmed. She walked along the waterfront, enjoying the song of an e'ria 'ria bird, wishing for Joe to come home with a red snapper. "Oh yeah!" she said aloud. "Mek a perlo fuh suppuh. Marriage'um tuh sibi beans, tummetuh an rice, oh yeah! Red snappuh be good-eatin now."

A newspaper on the ground caught her eye. There was a picture of the cigar makers hanging out the window, laughing and waving like they were at a party. "Look like they having a grand time. They don't even know what they got to complain about." She shook her head in disgust as she read the article. If the stemmers had stopped working, they would have fired every one of them. "Shoo!" she said, letting the paper fall. "Don't ever trust silly white girls."

Slack tide made the swampy air of the basement even worse. She took her rag from her smock pocket, trying to wipe the taste of the insecticide from her mouth.

"Mawnin," she said to Sam Maybank.

"Mawnin," he replied. "Gonna be bad today. Monkey fixing to get hold of a lot of folks."

Sam was right, by lunch time, the heat monkey had taken down four stemmers.

Meliah Amey and Binah ate their lunch outside under a live oak tree.

"Too hot to eat," said Binah.

"Monkey get you, you don't eat," insisted Meliah Amey, offering Binah a bite of cornbread.

Binah wiped her face with a scarf that was too nice to be called a head-rag.

"Where you get that?" Meliah Amey reached for it, wanting to check the label. "Kerrison's! Since when you shop Kerrison's?"

Binah snatched it back. A breeze kicked up and the palmetto fronds scraped against one another. Binah kept looking back to the building trying to find someone.

Meliah Amey followed her gaze and was surprised to see Mr. Rolands standing on the steps by the Bay Street door. He was looking in their direction.

"E eye tie up on yuh," said Meliah Amey.

"Let them thoughts leave your head," said Binah, standing up to go. "He not like he used to be. Not with me he ain."

Mr. Rolands Jr. walked around to the Blake Street side of the building. Except for men bringing garbage to the incinerator, there wasn't much reason to go that way. Meliah Amey was disgusted but not completely surprised to see Binah following after him.

The wind increased and the direction changed. The sky, overcast and low for days, now had a distinct line of dark towering clouds offshore to the east. A squall line.

Meliah Amey had been assigned to sort tobacco leaves by grade after they had been stemmed, and she spent the afternoon praying for Joe as she sorted, barely noticing the woman who continued to bring her more tobacco to sort, or that the rag the woman took away from her mouth after she coughed was tinged with blood.

Late-afternoon storms were common in the summer and that was why the fleet made sure to be back inside the jetties by that time of day. At midday however, they would be nowhere near safe harbor.

Finally, Mr. Godfrey came through the basement, telling them to go home.

Meliah Amey got off the trolley at Broad Street and hurried to Adger's Wharf. A crowd had gathered, the fleet was late, and everyone had seen the squall line. Vincent de Paul stood with Julata, Mr. Arthur's wife.

"I tell him don't go out in that trus-me-Gawd boat no mo," Julata cried. "I tell him last night, I did."

"Julata, them not trus-me-Gawd boats," Meliah Amey tried to comfort her. "They very good boats, an the men—ain no better men on the sea than the Mosquito Fleet. No better men."

Father Joubert arrived to lead a rosary.

Vincent de Paul blessed himself and said in his awkward Latin, "Nomnay Paw-tray—an fill-in an spirit-toe." Meliah Amey couldn't help but smile, squeezing his shoulder to let him know she was proud of him for trying.

The crowd continued to grow as the news spread across the peninsula. Francine and her children were there, and so was Maum Hannah, and Miss Huger from down the alley, and Binah, too. Mayor Stoney was there, along with the former mayor, John Grace. Negroes and whites gathered together at Adger's Wharf, waiting and praying for the safe return of Charleston's Mosquito Fleet.

As the sun leaned for down the first of the patchwork sails appeared on the horizon. Everyone cheered but then grew silent, straining to see and to count, wanting to be sure that all twenty boats were coming home.

"A pilot boat and a lightship are coming in with them," said a white man with a telescope. "Harbor pilot's pulling three of the fleet boats and the lightship's got a line out to two boats. The rest of um's sailing on their own steam."

Meliah Amey watched and counted as they came closer. The small boats with their sails began to overtake the pilot boat and the lightship which were weighed down by their tows. "One, two, three, four . . . ," softly but urgently, she counted up to seventeen. Three boats were missing.

"Eee, Eee!" Julata wailed.

When Meliah Amey recognized Joe's haint blue sail, she fell to her knees in thanks. She pulled herself up to the railing, straining to see if Joe was on-board, and yes, thank Gawd, he was at the tiller. Father Joubert comforted Julata; Mr. Arthur's boat was one of the three lost in the storm.

As the crews tied up to the wharf, the wailing of loss and the wailing of joy grew louder, interspersed with details of the storm.

"It come up bout seb'n miles off the Isle a Palms," said one man as he climbed up the ladder from his boat. Meliah Amey pushed in close to hear, pulling Vincent de Paul by the hand.

"Ki'tuta mek the ocean swell up an slam us fum ebry side," he said. "De bo-it fill wid watuh. Us can't steer into de waves no mo. I wash out in dat angry sea, pray Gawd, let me see my fambly again. I come up an dare Captain Joe in e bo-it, but waves big an e can't get e bo-it tuh me. Captain Joe tie a line to een se'f an jump in de watuh. E start swimming." The man wiped his face on his arm, taking a deep grateful breath before continuing. "E go under sometimes, an I go under sometimes, but ebry time I come up, e still swim-ming tuh me. Then e head pop out of de watuh an e grab ahold of me. Men on e bo-it, dey start pulling de line. Captain Joe wulula me, I swaytogawd, he wulula me f'um Ki'tuta."

Two days later, Meliah Amey and Binah went to buy corn and tomatoes from Maum Hannah and Francine at Saint Michael's Gate. When they walked up, Meliah Amey knew she was seeing a haint, because standing beside them, just as he often did in the evenings, was Mr. Arthur, smoking his corncob pipe. It was just like Meliah Amey's Gkumma told her it would be. No words would come out of her mouth, no matter how hard she tried to yell.

Francine spoke up. "Ain you hear? The Clyde Line steamer coming from Jacksonville to Chaa'ston pick up Mr. Arthur and he crew. He done gone to Florida in dat leetle boat he got."

Twelve men had been thought dead in the storm. Now it was down to six. For years, the men of the Mosquito Fleet put aside fifty cents every month to go to the family of any man lost at sea. The money saved was divided among the six men's families.

And four days later, with the sails repaired, and the pine-tar set on the hulls, Captain Joe attended the early Mass before he and his crew, along with the remaining boats in the fleet, set out on the ebb tide, rowing together in song, bound for the Blackfish Banks.

Haul away Rosy—haul away gal

PART III

1929–1933

Chapter 21

MARCH 1929

"Damn it, girl! You gotta be faster than that!" Mr. Godfrey yelled over the deafening noise of the cigar-making machines. "Keep feeding um! One leaf aftuh de odduh. You too damn slow."

Despite the morning chill, Brigid felt the back of her uniform grow damp with sweat.

American Machinery and Foundry Company had finally built a reliable cigar-making machine that did all the rolling and bunching. Gone was the sense of accomplishment from making cigars by hand. The machines, when not awaiting repair, were loud, nearly too loud for Brigid to hear her own thoughts. Conversation became a thing of the past.

Four girls were assigned to each machine: One to feed it filler leaves, the other to apply a binder leaf on a preset die, and another to do the same with the wrapper leaf; the fourth girl inspected the cigars. In 1929, the long-revered "good five-cent-cigar" was born again when Royal Cigar introduced the Cadora, a machine-made cigar using Cuban wrapper leaf.

During the war, once Brigid became proficient at hand-rolling, she earned up to $12.00 a week for making a thousand cigars. When the company went to the team system, she and her two partners rolled close to eight hundred cigars per day for $9.00 pay per week. In 1929, each machine turned out three thousand cigars every day, and Brigid earned $10.00 for six full days of work. For Charleston's working women, it still paid better than most.

Brigid's Aunt Cassie was sent back to the cigar-making floor to work as an inspector.

"Shut it down," Brigid yelled to the girl nearest the lever to stop the machine when it jammed.

"Damn this machine," said Brigid, searching across the floor for Eric, the mechanic.

She waved her hand, hoping he would notice. He was working on Lydia's machine at the moment, and Brigid knew it would be hard to pull him away from her. Brigid offered up a prayer seeking forgiveness for what she was about to do. She waved her arm again until he looked in her direction, and when he did, she pulled up her dress a little to show him her leg above the knee.

Eric slapped Lydia on her round behind before pulling the lever to restart the machine.

"Your aunt baked me a pie," he said, his voice raised so she could hear. "Sure was good, too. Her machine ain't broke down since." Eric took out his screwdriver to remove the plate and clear the jam. "I love apple pie," he said with his hill country accent. "Course, there's some things a man likes even more than pie."

Since they were still on the piecework system, time spent waiting on Eric to fix the machine was money lost, and he took full advantage of his power. After Cassie baked him the pie, Sally brought him some cookies. Not long afterwards, a rumor went around that Lydia had given him a whole different kind of sugar, and since then no one could keep up. Brigid's Aunt Cassie declared she was too old for foolishness and vowed to learn how to fix the damn machine herself. She began looking over Eric's shoulder whenever he worked on her machine. Then she went home to the house on Bay Street to find the tools in Manus's toolbox, knowing he would never miss them.

Gone were lunchtime talk about boyfriends and dances at the Isle of Palms pavilion. Lunchtime became a time for girls to ask Brigid's Aunt Cassie questions.

"Miss McGonegal," a girl would ask, "how yuh fix a jam?"

"Take this here what they call a flathead screwdriver," and Aunt Cassie would take the tools from her smock and put them on the table to demonstrate. "Take the screws off the cover plate, you understand, then you reach in there with your hand an move that flywheel toward you—always toward you, never away—if the tobacco that's jammed don't fall out, then take your tweezers an reach in there. Make sure that flywheel turns good and smooth before you put the cover back on. I sometimes put a drop of this sewing machine oil on them gears, too."

At last the girls appreciated her aunt for being generous with her time and skills during the break. Even Brigid learned how to keep the gears oiled so they wouldn't overheat and crack, but sometimes a belt would break or a part would need replacing, and at some point, everyone had to play Eric's game on his terms.

One evening Brigid stepped outside onto Drake Street to find that spring had arrived. Throughout winter's cold damp, she had come to accept that she could not get pregnant again. The resulting grief weighed heavily upon her small frame. As she walked along, her strength improved with each passing blossom. Yellow jasmine bloomed upon a gray weather-worn fence, and in the yard next door, a white camellia. In another week, the azaleas—red, white, and purple—would take center stage from below Broad to clear up on the Neck.

As she neared the corner of Bay Street, she looked up to see the incomplete metal spans of the Cooper River Bridge rising above the marsh. John Grace's dream of a bridge to Mount Pleasant would soon be fulfilled. The bridge was being built simultaneously from the Charleston side as well as the Mount Pleasant side. A very large gap existed between the two spans. Large cranes sat on either end to lift the massive steel beams of the cantilevered center into place.

A four-masted sailing ship passed beneath the incomplete bridge. Now that it wasn't dark when she came out of work, one of the first things Brigid did was to look to see if the two sides had gotten any closer.

Crossing the Mall, she saw Manus striding toward her, racing Patrick across the field. She opened her arms to her precious boy. "I'm so happy to see you both. I can't believe it," she said, hugging Patrick close despite his nose wrinkling from the ammonia smell.

"A promise is a promise," said Manus, "and I promised we'd walk to the edge of the bridge and wait for the stars to come out. Let's all go. We might get to see Orion's dog, Canis Minor."

Together, they walked north on Bay Street toward the entrance of the bridge.

"Ebenin," Manus said to a passing Negro woman with a sweetgrass basket upon her head filled with fresh cut flowers.

"Ebenin," she answered nodding her head in return.

Brigid looked up at the bridge ahead of them. Some thought it magnificent and others, the ladies with the Preservation Society, called it an eyesore upon the horizon, a metal monster ruining the old charm of Charleston.

She had never walked up hill before, and the effort quickly took its toll. She rested. Behind her the sun hovered over downtown while the incinerator of the cigar factory belched smoke. Below her, the faded brown marsh grass gave way to a tender green. The seasons manifested themselves in the marsh grass and spring was certainly here. She continued climbing, determined to make it to the top.

But she kept falling behind. Brigid rested, coughed, and continued. Soon, she was higher than the cigar factory and the white capped waves of the harbor were beneath her.

Manus and Patrick came back to her. "Guess what?" he asked.

Brigid managed to smile despite her difficulty getting a good breath.

"I heard Ravenel's shipyard's hiring. I went by there today, an you won't believe it, but . . ."

"Oh Manus," she said, still somewhat out of breath, "did they?"

"They did!" he said, hugging her. "I start in de mawnin."

They stood together, looking out over the harbor and downtown as the sun began to set.

Manus nearly shouted, "Look, pawpus. I see two, no—three of them." Brigid looked over the railing, amazed by the perspective of seeing them from snout to tail as they leapt out of the water.

"You people gonna be arrested for trespassing," she heard a man call out from an approaching car.

It was John Grace. When he lost re-election, he returned to his law practice, determined to find private financing for the bridge. John Grace was no longer mayor, but he had become president of the Cooper River Bridge Company.

"Mr. President," said Manus. "I don't own no automobile an I hear you gonna charge a toll for us to use your bridge when it's finished. Thought I better take my family half-way cross while I can still afford it. How you been John?"

"Couldn't stand it any better, Manus. What do you think of her?"

"Shooo—you shown'um this time John Grace," Manus replied.

"Once I got the Preservation Society to acquiesce, meeting the demands of the U.S. Navy was nuttin, yuh understand? Nuttin."

"You're a brave man, John," said Manus. "I wouldn't wanna go two rounds with them Preservation Ladies."

Grace smiled and laughed heartily. Then he revved his engine for it sounded like his car might stall. "Pulling this hill ain easy," he said. "I better be going. Come down to the Hibernian Hall, Manus. I'll buy you a cold bay-uh." And with that, he turned the car around and took off down the hill.

"He ignores Prohibition, doesn't he?" said Brigid.

"Him and the rest of Chaa'ston," said Manus. "That's one thing the men below Broad and John Grace agree upon. Funny thing is, I've never seen John Grace take a drink."

She looked back over how far they had come, and then she looked ahead and how much further they had to go. Her legs felt weak. "Manus, you go on with Patrick. Go on but keep him close or I'll throw you off this bridge and don't think I can't find the strength to do it."

The two of them went on. She looked out across the harbor, wondering if she could see the jetties the fishermen talked about. She would love to see them from a boat someday. They were mysterious, a gate to another world, the world, Manus's world. She looked back over downtown. The sun leaned over the city. She watched Manus standing beside Patrick at the edge of the bridge. She wondered what he was saying to the boy. Was he talking about the porpoises that played in the bow spray of the *Arabella Anke* when he was at sea? Was he telling his son that he was proud of him for doing so well with his reading in school? What was he saying? Patrick would be their only child, and she wanted so much for him. With Manus at sea, his time with his son had been limited. Now that would change. She felt a rush of things she wanted Manus to teach Patrick. The boy loved to read, and she wanted Manus to teach him to recite poetry. She wanted their son to always have books to read, but she wanted him to have more than book learning. She would insist that Manus take Patrick fishing beyond the jetties when he was old enough. Manus had so many good traits to pass on. If only the beer didn't get the best of him. She wouldn't stand for that. No matter what, she wouldn't stand for that.

Evening did not linger. She watched her husband and son standing at the edge of a great precipice. Below, porpoises swam. Soon, maybe Orion's dog would appear overhead. Brigid buttoned her coat against the night air, and set off up the hill.

Together, they waited.

Chapter 22

With the days a little longer, Binah and Meliah Amey went after work to pull grass from behind Magnolia cemetery. Binah would dry it in the sun before using it in her coiled baskets that she sold to the buckruh in the office on East Bay Street downtown.

Meliah Amey straightened up, stretching her back. She studied the gigantic steel monster crawling across the sky high above the marsh. Maybe when the two sides were married it wouldn't seem so scary. She pictured a car driving off the unfinished bridge and out into the air. "I don't ever wanna ride in a automobile going cross that bridge," she said.

"Nobody we know own a car," said Binah. "Looks like you ain got to worry."

"How your people feel about the bridge?" Meliah Amey asked.

"They like it fine, but they not going to pay no toll to cross the water when they can take they boat for free," answered Binah.

Meliah Amey went back to pulling grass. An e luke'luke bird took flight when she got too close. She looked over to Binah, who looked different. She'd taken to wearing colorful scarves upon her head. And earbobs, too. But she was studying her head about something and not saying a word. It was nearly first dark and they were in a cemetery and Binah hadn't even noticed. Meliah Amey kept on pulling grass, filling her croaker sack, cutting her eyes now and then to Binah, trying to figure out what might be wrong. Binah had been transferred to the department making cigar boxes on the fifth floor a few months back, and Meliah Amey didn't talk with her at work much anymore.

"How you like making cigar boxes?" Meliah Amey asked.

"Everything hurry up, hurry up," she said. "You got to make sure the label don't go on crooked."

Ever since the cigar-making machines came into the factory, everything was hurry up, hurry up. And nobody got paid any more money for all the hurrying. Well, maybe the white girls making cigars were getting more money. Meliah Amey heard there wasn't anything hard about their jobs now that the machines did all the difficult parts like the cutting and the rolling. She heard the white girls just had to stand there and feed tobacco into the machine, and how hard could that be?

"Ee time fuh gone," said Meliah Amey. They secured their croaker sacks full of sweetgrass and started for home. Meliah Amey couldn't stand it any longer.

"Mek so yuh worry?" she asked as they walked through the cemetery.

Binah replied, "I got misery een my haa't."

"You get a letter from Ray?"

"Ray hol' me cheap," she said. Binah stopped beside a grave marker for one of the Ball family members, her eyes filled with tears, "Enu fole, enu fole."

"Who baby you carrying, Binah? Who the Tata?" Meliah Amey demanded to know, fearing the answer.

"I don't know. I don't know, Meliah Amey," she answered. "It may be Sam Maybank."

"Who de odduh man, Binah? Who yuh t'ink de Tata be fuh true?"

"Mr. Rolands Jr.," Binah finally answered.

Meliah Amey grabbed Binah by the shoulders. "Did he force you? Look at me Binah. Did he force you?"

Meliah Amey studied her friend's brown eyes for the answer.

Binah shook her head. "No, Meliah Amey, he don't force me."

"Shooo!" Meliah Amey exhaled, shaking her own head in disbelief and walking in circles around the headstone. "Fuh true? Binah, fuh true?"

"Fuh true," she answered softly.

Meliah Amey's hands dropped by her side. She reached up to touch Binah's print scarf. "No, I spect not. He give you he wife old clothes, and earbobs from the fibe an dime. Maybe he put an extra dollar in your pay envelope come Saturday."

"Shet yuh mouth, Meliah Amey."

"They say some of the white girls go to the company doctor. Mr. Rolands Jr. such a nice buckruh now, maybe he take care of that for you."

"Meliah Amey, listen to me. You an Joe got a son you both love mo'nuh anybody in the world. All them dimes you keep, you keep them dimes so he can go to the Avery Institute some day. I wanna baby, too. I want my baby to have a chance. This baby gonna be light. This baby have a chance."

"I won't have that buckruh's baby in we'own home, and that's the Gawd's truth."

They walked on in silence amid the live oaks, and blooming magnolias. They passed the headstones of the old names: Ball, Pinckney, Vanderhorst, Shaftesbury, Manigault, Ravenel, Coming, Rutledge, Maybank, Alston. Carrying their croaker sacks full of sweetgrass, Meliah Amey and Binah weaved their way to the cemetery gate, passing among the three thousand graves of rebel soldiers who had died "for the cause."

The wind picked up and the palmettos scraped against the houses on East Bay near High Battery.

They turned the corner at Elliot Street, where Meliah Amey looked down the road to see Vincent de Paul punch a white boy wearing a fancy scout uniform, knocking him down.

"Eee! Eee!" Meliah Amey screeched. "Come yah. Come yah!" she shouted. Vincent de Paul's eyes grew wide when he saw his mother and Binah rushing toward him. The Boy Scout had enough wits about him to take the opportunity to run away.

"Mek so? Mek so oonuh beat dat white boy?" Meliah Amey demanded to know as she twisted her son's ear. "Hab yuh head tek way?"

"That uniform," Vincent de Paul shouted. Her son was almost equal to her in height, and he cut his eyes away.

"Mek so?" she asked again.

"We were walking past one another, and I say, hey, where you get that uniform? He say he got it for being a Boy Scout. I say I like to have a uniform like that myself. Then he say, you crazy. Niggers can't be Boy Scouts."

Meliah Amey let go of her son's ear. "That boy ignorant. He getting a bad education at some fancy school." The boy looked down at his feet. "Listen to me, Kofi, you better not be showing out or they won't let you in the door to the Avery Institute, you understand?"

He nodded his head though still not meeting his mother's eye.

Binah added her two cents. "Them little dandy ones be the high buckruh chillun. He Tata might be a Broad Street lawyer. You beat up a white boy like that and they put you on the chain gang. Phosphate mine gonna be the only place you ever work."

Meliah Amey looked down the narrow road, worrying that the law could be on its way.

"Mek track fuh home," she insisted. They rushed down the alley, Meliah Amey continuing to admonish her son. "You need to learn bout penance. Come Saturday, you gone learn penance helping your Tata fix he nets and fishing lines."

She was stern with the boy, but in truth she was almost glad for the distraction the scuffle provided when they got home. Otherwise, she would have been trying to figure out how to tell Joe they were going to be needing more money come summer on account of the fact that Binah would be moving out.

Chapter 23

The factory closed at noon that Saturday so the cigar makers could attend the first annual company picnic at Hampton Park. A man named Mr. Hewitt was to address the crowd from a large stage set up near the bandstand.

Brigid greeted Mr. Rolands Jr. and his wife, as she, Manus, Patrick, and her Aunt Cassie passed the head table. It seemed to Brigid that Mr. Rolands Jr. had become oddly sullen over the years.

A brass band played amid the blooming oleander and azaleas. Brigid took the first empty seat she came upon.

"You need to see a doctor," Manus insisted for the third time that day. "You shouldn't get short-winded that bad. Miss Cassie, tell her to see a doctor, and not that goon at the factory, either.

"She in a bad way. I tell her, but she don't listen to me," said Cassie.

"Hush, the both of you. I just need a minute," she said, relieved to be sitting down. "Patrick, help your father carry the plates. And not much for me," she called out. In truth, she feared going to the doctor. One of the girls on her floor went to Roper Hospital with the same kind of cough and they kept her in the hospital for so long the company fired her. Some said all the Negro women in the basement had consumption.

"Don't be shy," Mr. Rolands Jr. announced from the stage. "Come on up here and fix a plate. We got plenty of fried flounder. Don't be shy, help yourself."

"This ain no damn flounduh," scoffed Manus after taking a bite of his fish. "This here whiting."

"That man don't know a flounduh from his own behind," said Cassie, tasting her first bite.

Of all times for her aunt and Manus to agree on something.

"Come on up," Mr. Rolands hollered again. "Plenty of fresh fried flounder."

"They'll fry up anything these days then tell you it's a better fish," said Cassie.

"This here whiting," Manus hollered out. "It ain no damn flounduh."

Fortunately, the band began to play the "Stars and Stripes Forever," drowning out Manus and Cassie's tirade over the misrepresented fish.

After lunch, Mr. Rolands introduced the guest of honor. Brigid watched with concern for the effort it took Mr. Hewitt to unseat himself from his place at the head table and to get himself to the podium. He appeared to be a man who never enjoyed any less than a generous portion of whatever he chose to partake.

"We're entering a new era in cigar making," he began. "Here in Charleston, we average three hundred fifty thousand cigars per day. We want to make that one million per day. Ladies and gentleman, I'm here to tell you we intend for the Cadora to be the world's number-one selling cigar.

"There's going to be some changes but when we're done, the Charleston cigar factory will be the single largest producer of cigars and cigar boxes in the world!" His voice boomed out across the park. "I insisted on having this picnic for you girls today to show you how much I appreciate the work you do." Everyone clapped and hollered.

"Starting next year, if you're sick and you go see the company doctor and he writes you a note that says you have to miss work, guess what? We're going to pay you seventy-five cents for the day of work you miss. And next Christmas, we're going to pay you for a full day on the holiday rather than a half-day."

Mr. Rolands Jr. and Mr. Godfrey clapped until everyone else did too.

"And here's the best part," he said. "We want you all to have fun and get some exercise, so starting this summer we're sponsoring a softball team. That's right, going to call you the Petite Royales, and I want every one of you to sign up to play. We want the city of Charleston to see our fine healthy workers enjoying themselves."

"He's full of crap," said Manus. "I don't see any darkies here. I bet some of them women would be good at softball. Hey, you gonna let the darkies play on the team?"

"Manus O'Brian," Brigid snapped. "Shut your mouth with that kind of talk."

"I'll be over at the track." Manus ripped his napkin from his shirt.

"Oh Manus, please don't lose any more money this week," Brigid pleaded. Keeping him inside the harbor jetties for this long a time had proved a mixed blessing. The extra money he made from the shipyard was too often lost to the horse track and the Blind Tiger behind Saint Phillip's Church.

"Quit your bellyaching," he said, his voice turning mean as he stood up to leave. "Least a good whore knows not to nag a man all the damn time."

Brigid tried to make his words different, as if she had misheard. Unfortunately, the look on her Aunt Cassie's face left no doubt. She often wondered if he did such things when he was away. She had found peace by convincing herself that she would know. She had thought that she would know. Aunt Cassie always said that only a damn fool would ever get married. Oh, she hated for her to be right. Brigid watched Patrick concentrating on the fish and trying to pick out the bones so he wouldn't choke. She kissed him on the head, forcing herself to smile, the way she would after a hard fall, too ashamed for anyone watching to see how much she hurt. Aunt Cassie put a forkful of whiting in her mouth, looking away to the speaker, trying to give Brigid a little privacy in which to bear her pain.

"Now we all know that a machine-made cigar with a Cuban wrapper leaf is as satisfying a smoke as any hand-rolled cigar. We know that, but men are creatures of habit, and sometimes they need facts and science to be convinced. It's time men learned what they are really putting between their lips."

"Shooo!" exclaimed Cassie, "de man crazy."

"I'm talking about spit!" Mr. Hewitt yelled out across Hampton Park. "Yes, I said the word spit! Spit is filthy, especially when it's on the tip of your cigar."

"Man crazy," Cassie harrumphed. "Shooo!"

Mr. Hewitt pulled a sheet from a large advertising-poster standing on an easel beside him: *Cadora, the no-spit cigar.*

"Hand-made cigars spread disease! Cigar makers who roll by hand are yellow-fingered people prone to all sorts of personal habits. Imagine those kinds of people licking the tip of every cigar they make." The crowd was aghast. "We have a government official willing to state on record that sealing a cigar tip with spit spreads disease. Royal Cigar is going to tell the truth. That's right. Before long, everyone will know that Cadora cigars are the only cigars certified clean and sanitary. Why? Because they're made by machines and never touched by the human hand. It's time the public learns why that makes for a safer more satisfying smoke. Okay girls, come Monday morning, let's get started making the Charleston cigar factory the biggest and best in the world."

When Monday arrived, Brigid had to stop halfway up the steps to the third floor to catch her breath. Her starched uniform chafed against her skin as sweat rolled down her entire body. When she reached her machine, Mr. Godfrey handed her a pink slip. She was being let go. Mr. Godfrey held a large stack of pink slips. She couldn't have been more shocked if he had slapped her.

"We're getting rid of the girls who learned to hand-roll," he said. "We need new girls who ain having to unlearn the old way. Makes em too slow."

Brigid felt strange walking down the steps to leave. Chief Papakeecha looking back over his shoulder at her from every neatly pressed green smock she passed.

She saw Gretta from her old team. When Gretta saw the pink slip in Brigid's hand, her mouth dropped. Gretta's no count husband had left her to support their daughter and Gretta's elderly mother on her own.

"Maybe you didn't get one," said Brigid.

Gretta rushed up the steps, anxious to know her fate.

Outside, the sun rose above the two approaching spans of the new bridge. She started across the field everyone called the Mall.

When she stopped to rest, her body felt on fire. She tore at the pins securing her cap, wanting it off her head. Her chest heaved and panic set in. She pulled the green smock over her head, throwing it to the ground, along with her cap. The oleander bush began to move, slowly at first, then faster, as if it were dancing a tarantella. She heard the clop clop of a horse.

"Miss, you alright? Miss, can I get somebody for you?" She didn't recognize the voice but it sounded as if a Negro man was speaking to her.

"Manus O'Brian," she said, "Ravenel Shipyard." Her own words sounded faint and far away. The edges were turning gray. She wondered how far she would fall and if there would be water where she landed.

The last thing she heard was the man's voice. "Oh Lord, she gone fall out."

Brigid heard talking far away. The words sounded like prayers. Yes, someone was praying, and she tried to keep up, *Hail Mary, full a-grace, de Lawd is wid dee.* It was her Aunt Cassie, but Brigid kept getting lost among the words, and then she saw a porpoise leap out of the water.

Sometime later, again she heard praying, and this time, she felt her eyes wanting to open. But why struggle when the wind was up, the tide high, and the sound of a loose halyard slapping against a mast made her turn around. A porpoise rose, curling in a perfect "C, as it dove under the dock. Brigid's mother and father wanted her to come aboard the schooner *Magnolia*.

Hiyak—Hiyah-Hiyak

Seagulls urged Brigid to open her eyes again. And when she did, it was daylight, and Manus was there in the room, looking out the window.

"Manus," she said, "where you been?" He came over and put his hand on top of hers. His face was unshaven and for the first time in all the years she had known him, he was out without a tie.

"You at the Baker Sanatorium," he said. "I been right here with you the whole time."

"How's Patrick?" she wanted to know.

"He fine. They won't let him come see you."

She closed her eyes. Sleep was so appealing.

"Everybody at Saint Mary's praying fuh yuh," he said. She felt his hand on top of hers again. "The doctor wants to do surgery, not a major kind at all so don't worry. You're not scared, are you?"

Hiyak—Hiyah-Hiyak

The seagull outside the window called, and again, Brigid opened her eyes. A breeze blew through the room.

"Should I be?" she asked, watching the curtains lift and fall.

"No, not at all. The doctor says the surgery will let your lung rest so it can get better. You got to stay here while your lung heals, but he say you gonna be fine. It will take time, but you gonna be alright."

"Oh Manus, how we gonna pay for a surgery with me not working?" she said, feeling more awake.

"Hush," he said. "Don't worry bout nuttin."

The next morning she awoke to find Manus by her bed, his head bowed in prayer. They would be coming soon to take her down to surgery. The doctor called the procedure a therapeutic pneumothorax. He said tuberculosis needed oxygen to grow in her lungs. By piercing the lung in surgery, it would get less oxygen but would slow the spread of TB. She would have to remain in the hospital to rest afterwards.

Manus blessed himself and kissed the crucifix when he finished.

"Next fall when the weather cools off an you got your strength, I'll take you on a trip. Just the two of us."

Here he was, her street angel, his wingtips forever soiled, holding her hand, staying by her side as she went ten rounds in the ring for want of a decent breath. Of all the things she may not know about him, of this she was certain: if it would help her get better, Manus would fight one hundred rounds against any weight class, for that was both the depth and the limit of his love for her.

"Just the two of us," she asked, making the effort to speak.

"Just the two of us. We'll take the Clyde Line steamer up to New York."

"Will I go through the jetties?" she asked, her voice getting a little stronger.

"Oh yeah!" he said. "Shoo! We got to go through the jetties to get anywhere."

"I've always wanted to see them jetties you men talk about. I never been no further west than Summerville and no more south than Savannah, and dat's de Gawd's truth an you know it."

"This thing the doctor doing this mawnin, it gone help your lung get better."

"Manus, listen to me, I got twenty dollars in a tin next to the Infant of Prague. I been saving it so Patrick can go to Bishop England. I want him to have a proper Catholic education. I want him to graduate from Bishop England, yuh understand?"

"Jesus woman, hush," he said harshly. "Typical Irish, talking dat way. All doom an gloom. Nuff tuh drive a man tuh drink."

"As if you needed persuading. Yuh bettuh not spend all my money on de bay-uh, yuh hear me, Manus? Do right by yuh son. Promise me that much, will yuh?"

"Ahh, for the love of Gawd, woman—shut your mouth wid dat kind of talk."

Two Negro women knocked on the door. "Mawnin," one of them called in a friendly voice.

"Good mawnin," said Manus, in a huff as he and his shame left the room.

One of the women helped Brigid over onto the gurney. "I hear yuh tell Mister don't spend de seed-corn money on the beer. Oonuh got lots a fight inside. Oonuh gone be fine, that's right."

Chapter 24

When Cassie asked Mr. Rolands Jr. if she could leave early the day of Brigid's surgery, he told her no. May Gawd save you from the fires of purgatory, she thought to herself. When she finally got to leave that evening, she had to get to the exact opposite point of the peninsula from the cigar factory and it took her three different trolleys before she stepped off the car on Rutledge Avenue at the corner of Colonial Lake and Baker Sanatorium. The tide was high. Couples relaxed in little rowboats on the lake, and boys fished from the walkway beside it. She reminded herself to tell Patrick never eat any fish caught in Colonial Lake. The Baker Sanatorium sewer pipe emptied into the small tidal pool known as Colonial Lake. The tide came in. The tide went out.

Brigid's bed was empty and someone had moved it again. "I told them nurses don't move this bed every time I get it right." Cassie believed that a sick person's bed must face north to south, and that they won't get better in a bed facing east to west. She put her purse down and went to work putting the bed back the way she had it. When that was done, she sat down and took out her beads to pray.

She was well into the Glorious Mysteries, eyes closed in prayer, when she heard Manus plop down hard into the chair.

"If I couldn't smell the beer, I'd ask where de hell yuh been." Cassie kept her eyes closed, continuing with her rosary. When she finished she blessed herself, lightly kissed the crucifix, and opened her eyes to face him. "Were any of the men in that tap-room the seventh son of a seventh son?"

"Aunt Cassie, I've asked men at the Hibernian Hall, the Knights of Columbus, and every Blind Tiger in between bout that an all I've found is a man who's the seventh son of the fourth son. Won't that do?"

"No, it won't do," she said. "I've asked everybody at work, and I asked Father O'Shaughnessy to make an announcement from the pulpit an you know what he had the nerve to say to me? He say, Woman, you should be ashamed for believing that West Ireland nonsense. Shoo! Wish my grandmother from Sligo was here to tell him what she's seen cured by the seventh son of a seventh son."

There was a soft knock at the door. Dr. Brooks entered. Cassie blessed herself. Manus stood up.

"Ether is such an improvement over chloroform. Even still, sometimes, well—seldom, but occasionally," Dr. Brooks labored to choose his words, "a patient will have a mild reaction to de ether. Rarely is it ever fatal. Unless of course there are other complications. Complications such as the presence of another lung condition, for example, in this case, asthma. Mr. O'Brian, your wife had an asthma attack while her lungs were full of ether. I'm very sorry to have to tell you, but we were unable to save her."

Manus shoved Dr. Brooks so hard only the wall prevented him from falling over backwards.

Everything went white.

Hiyak–Hiyah–Hiyak

The pale colors of the room slowly returned. The curtains whipped about in the breeze.

"Miss Cassie, who you want us to call to come for the body?" the nurse asked.

Cassie realized she was alone; Manus was gone. "McAlister's," she answered.

The rosary was held at McAlister's on Wentworth Street the night before, and in the morning, the funeral Mass took place at Saint Mary's.

Brigid McGonegal O'Brian was buried in Saint Lawrence cemetery next to a cedar tree. The new bridge crept onward across the sky above, seeking its mate approaching from the other shore.

Patrick, in his knickers and pressed shirt, stood between his great-aunt Cassie and his father for the graveside blessing. Father O'Shaughnessy anointed the casket with holy water as he led the Hail Mary: "Ave Maria, gratia plena; Dominus tecum: Benedicta tu in mulieribus et benedictus fructus ventris tui, Jesus. Sancta Maria, Mater Dei, ora pro nobis peccatoribus, nunc et in hora mortis nostrae. Amen."

An egret that had been keeping watch from the nearby marsh took flight.

Chapter 25

AUGUST 1929

The Shepard Street Chapel was crowded with fisherman gathered before day-clean.

"Ite, Missa est," said Father Joubert, the Mass is ended.

"Deo gratias," responded Vincent de Paul, thanks be to God.

Meliah Amey mouthed the words along with her son. This was his first Mass to serve and she was very proud of him. She made the sign of the cross, and gave thanks once again for the many blessings she and her family had enjoyed. She gave thanks for Vincent de Paul's gift of a strong memory. If it weren't for him being able to recite all that Latin, she didn't think the principal at the Avery Institute would have accepted her boy, but he did. Now her son would get a good education. And, with all the people in town for the opening of the bridge, Joe had never sold as many fish nor at the prices he was able to get that week.

"I'm proud of the boy," said Joe as he and Meliah Amey walked toward Bay Street. "He growing to be he own man."

"He not a man not yet, Joe."

"Tana, it's time to take him on the boat with me."

Meliah Amey stood still, rearing back her shoulders, and blessing herself no less than three times.

"Cut that out woman, right now," Joe insisted. "He needs to learn how to be both, for he self and for the other mens, too. No better way to learn them lessons than to go outside the jetties in a little boat. That's right, no better teachers than the men of the Mosquito Fleet."

Her heart boiled with fear. But when she studied her head she reminded herself that she wanted her son to be Olowo, a respected person.

"I come your side, Joe," she said. "I come your side. He can go with you but only in the summer when he ain got school."

They passed the carpenters hammering and sawing, trying to get the bleachers finished in time for the bridge celebration. Even the cigar factory was going to close the following day. When they got to the corner of Bay Street, Meliah Amey and Joe saw the people, mostly women, lining up to be inspected for hire by Mr. Godfrey.

Joe stepped in front of her, facing her, and put his hands on her shoulders.

"Tana, if I could sell the fish every week for what I charge this week, you wouldn't have to work for that sorry buckruh no mo. That would please me very much. Very much." And then he kissed her.

"Shoo! Now I got to pray Gawd because yuh mek me tuh worry wid yuh sweetmouth," she said, embarrassed but smiling. "Go on, catch them fish, man. Go on."

Meliah Amey turned, unable to watch the women as they reached up, bent over, or whatever else Mr. Godfrey asked.

Everyone had heard about the company picnic for the cigar makers. Some big shot came down from New York and the company fried up a bunch of flounder and told them how wonderful they all were. The company must have bought the fish up in Georgetown because Joe didn't sell them any flounder. She knew a woman from Bedon's Alley who was there serving the food, and she told Meliah Amey the man said they were going to be changing things at the factory, moving into a whole new era. That was the word he used, era.

Down in the basement that August morning, it sure didn't look, feel, or smell like a new kind of anything.

"If there be one man so little as to seek power by division, let him learn by the joy that marks this day, that man loves to be linked to his fellow man," shouted John Grace as he addressed the crowd of thirty-thousand gathered for the opening of the new bridge.

Meliah Amey handed her parasol to Binah, who was now quite big. Joe and Vincent de Paul stood nearby. Banners hung across the streets all over town, cars were in line as far as the eye could see, even though it was still hours away before the bridge officially opened.

"In the physical union which this bridge forms, there will be strength. From the double rainbow, which its lines suggest, there will grow hope. Long may its graceful silhouette be etched against the morning sky of Charleston."

"As President of the Cooper River Bridge Company, I welcome everyone to our historic three-day celebration. When I cut the ribbon at noon, there will be no toll from noon until 4 P.M." And with that, he raised his hands above his head, the champion. The band played, and a Navy gunboat fired its cannon to mark the beginning of a the parade of ships.

"They should have asked the Mosquito Fleet to be in the parade," said Joe with deep disappointment. "Kofi, come here, let's see what they selling good to eat."

A breeze picked up among the palmettos.

"Thank Gawd," said Meliah Amey.

"I remember what you say to me," said Binah. "Now the bridge open, sister say I stay with her in Scanlonville."

"How you gone get to work?" Meliah Amey asked.

"Uncle know a farmer with an old jalopy truck."

"That toll take all your money," said Meliah Amey.

Binah was quiet. Meliah Amey felt bad about insisting Binah move out, but she wasn't changing her mind, either.

"I want this child to have a chance. If he a boy, gonna name him Chance."

"What if you have a girl?" Meliah Amey asked.

"Hope," said Binah. "That's right, Hope."

Meliah Amey smiled. "I like them names," she said. "Mr. Rolands Jr. know he the father?"

Binah shook her head. "This my child. Mr. Rolands Jr., he got plenty of he own Chance an Hope."

"Us take you to your sister's in the boat."

"Uncle bringing the jalopy over in the mawnin. Sistuh say now the bridge open, we gonna build up a stand on the highway. Sell the baskets we se'f. No mo money for the buckruh on East Bay Street, you understand. That's right, we put up a stand on the new highway and keep the money in the family."

At noon, under the torment of the August sun, with a Marine gun salute, while standing beside Mayor Stoney, the former mayor John Grace, along with an old rebel soldier, cut the ribbon opening the Cooper River Bridge to automobiles.

Meliah Amey and the others rested under the shade of a live oak tree.

"Sure wish we had a car so we could go cross the bridge," lamented Vincent de Paul.

"We can take the boat over to Riverside Beach," said Joe, trying to cheer everyone up.

"We always go there," said Vincent de Paul. "Ain nothing special bout that."

They were all quiet then. Joe lit his pipe to keep the mosquitoes away while Meliah Amey and Binah fanned themselves.

"Least we ain in that cigar factory," said Binah.

"Shoooeee! Ain that the trute now!" Meliah Amey agreed.

Then a Negro woman pulled up in a Ford Model T beside where they were sitting on the grass.

"What the matter with you folks?" the woman yelled out the window. "Must be a bunch of sad-sack dummies who ain got no car to ride over the new bridge."

"Pea!" Meliah Amey, Binah, and Joe, all shouted at once.

Pea opened the door for them. "I seen the newsreel bout this bridge an I had to drive down here myself to see it. Get in, we going go have us a big time."

Pea shifted into gear and they joined the line of more than ten thousand cars waiting for the parade of floats to get across the bridge ahead of the general public.

People turned off their engines and stood outside the car to wait. Some had strapped ice-filled tubs of lemonade, tea, and home-brew onto the back of their cars. White and colored stood together, laughing and talking, carrying on about this and that.

"Yeah, my mauma work for your people, that's right," said Pea to a high buckruh lady from the car waiting in front of them.

"I was born a Rutledge but I married a Vanderhorst," the woman said. "I will nevuh—I say nevuh—forget yuh mother. Nevuh! Yuh mother was my favorite—my favorite—Dah," she said. "How she doing?"

"Oh, my mauma crossed over a long time ago," said Pea. "A long time ago."

"I am so sorry tuh hear that," said Mrs. Vanderhorst. "I truly am. Listen, help yuh se'f tuh a bottle ub Coca-Cola from our ice tub. Go on, all ub yuh now. I mean it."

And they did. There were no strangers, colored or white, waiting in line that afternoon to drive across the bridge for the first time.

By the time they started up the first span it was 3 P.M. smack in the middle of the heat of the day.

"Damn, Pea," said Joe. "You the one built this here car?"

"Shut your mouth, Joe," Pea snapped. "Never had to drive up a hill this steep with so many people in the car." The Model T coughed and sputtered. Meliah Amey, Vincent de Paul, Joe, and Binah moved their shoulders in a pumping action, urging the car onward and upward. At last they crested the first span and began the joyous coast down over Drum Island and then the bridge began to climb again, the second span being even steeper than the first.

But this time, they were not as lucky.

"The car done monkied," said Joe, as he and Vincent de Paul and Meliah Amey got out to push. They were far from alone in their predicament as many cars had also overheated, and lots of people were out pushing their automobiles to the top of the second span.

As they crested the top, Joe made sure Meliah Amey got in first. Then he and Vincent de Paul stood on the running board, enjoying the downhill breeze.

"Get in this car right now," demanded Meliah Amey, opening the door over Pea's objections.

When Joe and Vincent piled back into the backseat with Meliah Amey, they were all laughing like they never had before, higher than any of them had ever been above the marsh. Meliah Amey had a whole new way of looking at her home.

"Why we turning left?" Vincent de Paul hollered out. "Everybody going right. Follow them, Pea. That's where all the stuff going to be. The boxing match, the lifesaving demonstration. It's all that way. Come on Pea, you got to turn around."

No one said anything. Joe finally spoke up.

"The white folks going that way. Our beach obuh yah."

"I don't wanna go to the same old place we always go to," the boy whined. "It's not even a beach. Ain got no surf less a harr-y-kin's coming."

Pea continued on toward Riverside Beach.

Meliah Amey looked to Binah sitting up in the front seat. She wondered how light Binah's child would turn out to be. Light enough to become one of Charleston's Brown Elite? What if Binah's child turned out to be light enough to pass? What would it be like never having to tell your child, No, you can't go there; it's not for colored?

When they got out of the car, Vincent de Paul sulked off by himself. Binah's sister ran up to welcome her back home. Joe made a beeline for where the men had gathered under a clump of live oaks. A wooden stage had been built and musicians were warming up to play.

Scanlonville women walked with sweetgrass baskets full of vegetables and strawberries upon their heads. Men had pots boiling over fires, ready for steaming crab and shrimp. Meliah Amey said a prayer that her son would hold his head up and look around. Yes, they were at the place they had to go, and once it got rolling, there wasn't going to be any place with better food, or better music, than Riverside Beach.

Pea hadn't changed much except for the way she sounded sometimes when she talked.

Sam Maybank walked by ignoring Binah. "Binah," said Pea. "Ee eye tie up on you, but I can't tell if he wants to love you or kill you."

"We done with one another," she said. "And once I have this baby, not gonna let another man touch me. Too hot to be this big come summer."

By nightfall, sacred music and spirituals were over. Musicians took the stage with saxophones, trombones, clarinets, and trumpets. All of them making it up as they went along, playing the crazy new style they called syncopated rhythm.

One of the musicians invited Vincent de Paul up on stage during the break. When the man set him down at the piano and showed him how to play a simple scale, Meliah Amey was relieved to see her son smile. She said a prayer of thanks to the Virgin Mother for returning the light to her son's eyes.

They were on the leeward side of the point, and at slack tide, the mosquitoes came out in force. Tobacco smoke was supposed to keep them away. Pea had traded her old cigars made from scraps for cigarettes. Meliah Amey was tempted to try one, but then she thought of the chicken shit that she picked off the leaves and changed her mind.

Shortly before middlenight, a man onstage made an announcement. "News of the celebration for the opening of the Cooper River Bridge went out on the newsreels all over the world. We wanna welcome home our brothers and sistuhs who left us to make a better life someplace else. This next group, they came de mores miles. Everybody please welcome, from Paris, France, Ray Gaillard and the Fabulous Syncopated Orchestra."

It took both Pea and Meliah Amey to keep Binah from falling out.

"I don't want him to see me like this," Binah pleaded with her friends.

"You too big to run," said Pea.

"Too big to hide," said Meliah Amey.

It was too late. "Right over there, that's the woman I came back to see," Ray announced from the stage. Meliah Amey and Pea stood close, trying to block his view of Binah's stomach.

"Binah," he said, "I never stopped thinking bout you." Then he counted down, and the band started to play.

"Who knows how many chillun he got running round Paris," said Pea.

Binah had her eye tied up on Ray the whole time his band played. Meliah Amey looked around for Joe and saw him on the ground, leaning up against a live oak, sound asleep. "'E ass gone be et up," she said quietly. "Time for me to get my mens home, Pea."

Fortunately, Vincent de Paul was strong enough now to help his father into the backseat of the car. Meliah Amey and Pea watched from a distance as Ray approached the table to talk to Binah. When he leaned to kiss her, he saw the status of things. He wasn't prepared for this and Meliah Amey wanted to go over and curse him up one side and down the other. What did he think Binah was gonna do when she stopped hearing from him?

"It's all his fault," Pea snarled. "Think he can see the world till he tired of it, then come back yah to find her waiting for him to jump the broom."

It wasn't but a minute before Ray went back to his band, leaving Binah alone at the table.

They were loaded up and set to take off. Meliah Amey was exhausted, her son sound asleep in the front seat, and her husband beside her in the back, passed out cold. She knew she might be the only one capable of getting out to push the car up the steep hill of the new bridge. But that would have to wait. Meliah Amey clawed and climbed in the most undignified way, determined to get out of that car and go comfort her friend.

Chapter 26

Let this bridge be the emblem of unity.

Cassie had nearly busted a seam at the sight of John Grace talking about unity while standing next to his archenemy, Tom Stoney, and beside him, some dried up Confederate colonel. But there he was, smiling as if among close friends, talking about the strength of steel and promises of prosperity.

That was back in August.

Things had not turned out the way he had hoped, but she would always remember the grand speech he gave that day and how much the three of them needed to hear it. That was the only reason a sensible woman like Cassie McGonegal, wearing the black dress of mourning, stood in sweltering midday sun listening to John Grace pontificate.

Earlier, she had demanded that Manus get out of bed.

"I don't give a damn bout your headache," she had insisted. "Now get out of that bed an come with me an your son to the damn parade."

"Can we ride over the bridge today?" Patrick asked as the ships decorated with colorful flags and pennants went past in the harbor.

"How the hell you think we gonna do that?" Manus snapped.

Cassie hated to see the day become another disappointment for Patrick. She cut her eyes to Manus.

"Alright, alright," Manus scoffed and walked away.

Cassie didn't know where he was going but she didn't try to stop him.

She had never seen so many people before. The Negroes were certainly enjoying themselves, thought Cassie, feeling equally irritated and envious. To her they seemed not to have a care in the world.

She looked about for Manus, wondering if he had gone off to a Blind Tiger to drink. A Negro man needed to pass in the crowd and Cassie stepped back to allow him to get by. He tipped his head, taking note of her black dress, "sorry for your loss," he said as he passed.

"That's very kind of you," she replied, tipping her head in return.

Then she saw the top of Manus's straw hat pushing toward them. "I do hope you grow up taller than your father," she said to Patrick.

"I ran across Dan Cahill. De Cahills got a place on de island. We can ride ovuh wid him."

It was so hot. Going in the surf would feel good, but Cassie knew that it wouldn't be proper to put on a bathing suit while she was still in mourning.

"We gotta go if we're going," said Manus impatiently.

"The two of you go ahead," she said. "How you gonna get back to town if the Cahills are staying on the island?"

"I'll figure that out when the time comes," said Manus, "stay close to me," he instructed Patrick as he began pushing through the crowd.

It was after ten that night when Cassie heard a commotion on the front porch. She opened the door to see young Patrick trying to help his father up the steps.

"You should have left him on the beach," she said, lending a hand. "The crabs know what to do with the likes of him."

In the light, she saw that Manus had been beaten.

"Eee! Eee!" she shrieked, "Who beat him?"

Manus's straw hat fell off his head, and his trademark bow tie hung loose around his neck. "There," he said, taking a wad of money from his pocket, "fifty bucks, I won fifty bucks. I got money to pay dem bastards fuh killing my wife."

"I'll get you some water, Pop," said Patrick.

"I don't want no water," said Manus, stumbling away to his room and slamming the door behind him.

"Your daddy done ruined the day, didn't he?" she asked.

"Gosh no," he replied. "I got to see Pop box, and we rode in a car over the bridge. Aunt Cassie, today the best day ever."

That was August.

In only three months, everything had changed. Cassie had seen John Grace at Mass that morning, on his knees in feverish prayer. Since the market crashed in October, he wasn't the only one. Six weeks after it opened, the Cooper River Bridge was behind in taxes, John Grace couldn't afford to do any maintenance, and the state refused to buy it. John Grace and his bridge were on the edge of bankruptcy.

She couldn't get the sight of him that morning at church out of her mind. Never had she seen John Grace on his knees in utter despair. And that was why she was thinking of him, recalling the day the bridge had opened, as she packed her belongings to leave the house on Bay Street. They had to go. The bank was taking the house. Not long after the crash, the shipyard had a big layoff. The cigar factory was the only place in Charleston still hiring, but for the jobs they had available, they hired only women.

Cassie folded her black dresses into her suitcase. She was in the second six months of mourning and the custom required she wear white until it had been a year since Brigid passed.

Manus and Patrick were going to his Cousin Maura's house in the Borough. Cassie had found a two-bedroom apartment upstairs in a house on Poinsette Street with its own water closet and a nice porch. She had never lived that far north of town, almost on the Neck, in fact. Growing up, people said that a white person wouldn't survive spending a night on the Neck between June and September because of the poisonous vapors of the low-lying land.

The risk of yellow fever aside, Cassie looked forward to having her own place again, even if it was nearly on the Neck.

Cassie carried her things down the steps and set them on the porch. Maura O'Brian Santolini and her husband had arrived. They had borrowed a car to help with the move.

"Hey, Patrick," Manus yelled outside into the yard, "come inside. Cousin Maura's here."

"They done turned off the juice," said Cassie. "But I could heat you some coffee on the stove."

"No thank you, Miss Cassie," said Maura.

Cassie had always thought of Maura as a floozy. But Maura wasn't the one being put out on the street.

"Listen here," said Manus, as everyone came into the living room. "I've made up my mind and I need to talk with ya'll. I promised Brigid I'd make sure Patrick graduates from Bishop England." He paused to swallow. He had aged a lot since Brigid's death, and now he was losing his family's home. Even Cassie felt sorry for him. No man deserved to lose so much in one year. Not even Manus-the-Bolshevik.

"Patrick, I want you to have my poetry book." Manus handed Patrick the worn copy of Whitman's *Leaves of Grass*. "I don't see any way round it. I got to go back to sea," he said. "I won't make much money but I'll have a place to sleep plus rations. I'll send whatever I can back here. I already talked with a man and I leave in the mawnin for Jacksonville to pick up another Nederland steamer there."

Cassie couldn't be mad at him. He was only doing what he had to do.

"So, Patrick," he said, looking his son in the eye. "I need you to decide where you wanna stay. You wanna stay with Maura? I bet David would take you out on the pilot boat. Or, you wanna stay with your Aunt Cassie?"

The boy looked from Maura to Cassie. She said a prayer for him. Eight was a young age to be asked to make such a decision. Cassie knew that she was not the doting type. Maura was more that sort. Cassie was nothing like Brigid. Brigid had been gentle, kind to any stray animal on the street, freely giving her affection to the boy. But that wasn't Cassie's nature and it never would be.

Between her own mother and young Brigid, she couldn't bear the thought of having to take care of anybody else ever again.

She looked about the room. Yes, she would miss that house in the summer, with its upstairs porch overlooking the harbor, where the breezes were grand. But in the winter, the breezes were also grand and that was a problem. Then she noticed that Patrick was looking to her, as if he wanted her to say something. But it was his decision to make, not hers. She looked away, unwilling to meet his eye.

"I wanna go with Aunt Cassie," the boy answered softly.

Chapter 27

"You got to finish up more sooner tomorrow night," Vincent de Paul insisted to his mother.

Meliah Amey was in the middle of ironing sheets for one of the white families that lived around the corner on South Battery. She had begun taking in laundry to do in the evenings to help pay for Vincent de Paul's music lessons that weren't included in his tuition at the Avery.

"Mek so?"

"Mr. Logan told me to bring my mother and father to the concert at Morris Street Baptist Church. He said it will make you feel better about paying for the piano lessons."

"Baptist Church! We Catholics, not Baptists," she protested. She couldn't get her work done before midnight as it was.

"You don't have to be Baptist to go the concert," he insisted.

"Come yah. Help fold these sheets. Oonuh gonna wear me down to drybone."

Vincent de Paul took hold of a corner of the sheet. "Tomorrow, when we get back from the concert, I'll help you with the laundry," he said.

"Shoo!" she said, knowing she couldn't say no to that offer. "How come you so set on me coming to hear this music?"

"The singer named Marian Anderson. Mr. Logan say—said—Mr. Logan said Marian Anderson may have the best contralto voice in the whole world. Mauma, don't fret that laundry. Come tomorrow night. Please?"

"Kofi, do you see how hard I have to work—tie my mouth," she said. "Hand me that sheet."

Lots of people talked about how bad things were since the crash. Meliah Amey wanted to tell the buckruh how she and her family were using a privy down the alley before the crash on account of Mr. Shaftesbury being too cheap to put in a commode for them, and since the crash, the only thing different was that she knew not to even bother asking for one.

The only thing new at the cigar factory since the crash was that Mr. Rolands Jr. decreased the stemmers pay back to $6.00 a week.

"Go on if you think you can do better someplace else," Mr. Rolands Jr. had said to them. "One thing about the crash, I got hundreds of men, women, and children, waiting outside to come in here out of the cold and take your place."

The next evening after work, Vincent de Paul was waiting anxiously for her when she came around the corner to Bedon's Alley. "Maum, hurry," he yelled to her as soon as he saw her.

"Tek foot een han', Tana," Joe called out. He, too, was already dressed in his pressed white shirt and creased trousers.

Meliah Amey changed out of her smelly uniform and into a clean dress as quickly as possible. The three of them rushed out the door to catch the trolley to the Morris Street Baptist Church.

Out of habit, Joe and Meliah Amey blessed themselves and genuflected as they entered the pew. Joe kept clearing his throat, something he did when he felt uncomfortable. She dared to look around, realizing everyone was dressed so much nicer. The men in their vested suits with watch chains dangling. And women in dresses cut from fine wool. Most of all, Meliah Amey took note that she and her family were among the relatively few dark-skinned Negroes in attendance. For the first time ever, she was attending an event with Charleston's Brown Elite.

Joe leaned over looking for a kneeler to pull down. Seeing none, he sat in the pew, nervously opening and closing his hands. Any second she expected the jumping legs would take hold of him. She put her hand on top of his to calm him. She wondered if he was thinking the same thing as she: All his life, this is what we said we wanted for him. We've worked hard to give our son this opportunity to be a part of this other world. Why does it feel so wrong?

Meliah Amey looked over to Vincent de Paul. He looked happier than she had ever seen him. Then, as if sensing her fear, Joe squeezed her hand. "Trust in Gawd, Meliah Amey," he said softly. "Trust in Gawd."

"I'm glad you could join us," said the most distinguished Negro man Meliah Amey had ever met. "I'm Mr. Logan, Vincent's music teacher. Nice to meet you, Mr. Ravenel," he said, shaking Joe's hand. "I noticed you didn't pick up a program. Please, have this one."

Before Meliah Amey could finish reading, the pianist, dressed in a fine tuxedo, came out and took a bow. The only other Negro she'd known to wear a tuxedo was that scoundrel calling himself the mayor that used to drive the congressman's carriage.

And then Miss Marian Anderson came out on the stage in a snug-fitting satin dress, her shoulders nearly bare. This woman carried herself unlike any other woman, white or colored, that Meliah Amey had ever seen. Everyone clapped, and Meliah Amey and Joe both startled. They had never heard clapping inside a church before.

The sight of Marian Anderson, standing so sure of herself, somehow eased the ache Meliah Amey felt in her left knee from standing all day at the factory. And as the piano played the first few bars, a little of the ache in her back drifted away, and soon after Miss Anderson began to sing "He's Got the Whole World in His Hand" there was no ache left anywhere at all in Meliah Amey's body.

Meliah Amey, Joe, and Vincent de Paul joined in the burst of applause when she finished.

"Thank you," Miss Anderson said, bending at the waist in a poised bow of mutual respect for her audience. "Next, I am going to sing 'Let Us Break Bread Together' as arranged by my accompanist tonight, Mr. William Lawrence, a graduate of the fine Avery Institute here in Charleston."

Sometimes in the summer when she walked past a high buckruh's home, Meliah Amey had heard the sound of opera coming from a phonograph. But she had never heard a Negro singing a spiritual in that style before.

Again, when the song ended, the church broke into applause. They quieted and the pianist began to play the introduction to the next piece. Meliah Amey took note, this one sounded familiar but from long ago, really long ago when she was a child and still in school with the Sisters of Charity.

Vincent de Paul leaned forward, giving his mother a look that said, "See, I told you that you needed to come."

Meliah Amey glanced at the program, Schubert's "Ave Maria." As Marian Anderson sang, Meliah Amey's haa't ached. It ached from being full. It was 1929, the year the bridge opened and the stock market crashed, the year Meliah Amey heard the magnificent Marion Anderson sing at the Morris Street Baptist Church.

A few days later, as Meliah Amey walked across the Mall on her way to work in the morning, she saw Binah coming across the field from the direction of the waterfront. Since no one could afford the bridge toll, Binah's uncle had begun using his boat as a ferry service to cross the river. He only charged a dime each way.

Meliah Amey had not seen Binah since the baby was born.

"How's the baby?" Meliah Amey called out, happy to see Binah alive and well. So many women died in birth. She said a prayer of thanks.

"She good," answered Binah. "She healthy, t'engk Gawd."

"A girl! You can teach her to make the sweetgrass baskets."

"That's right," said Binah. "That's right."

Meliah Amey studied her friend's face, trying to determine if everything was alright with the baby.

"So," said Meliah Amey. "Is this baby like her daddy? Is she light?"

Binah stopped in her tracks. "Meliah Amey, I done had a black baby. I mean black. My girl adu."

"Adu?" said Meliah Amey, surprised. "Adu like Sam Maybank?"

"Yeah, chile," answered Binah. "She black like Sam Maybank black."

"What you name this black baby girl?"

"I study my head long time," Binah said. "Then I name her Carolina."

"Carolina?" said Meliah Amey, a little disappointed.

"That's right," said Binah. "Her true name Carolina."

Meliah Amey was speechless.

"Her true name Carolina," Binah repeated as the two of them started walking. "But her basket name, the name I give her soul you understand—that name be Hope."

Chapter 28

MAY 1933

It was Ascension Thursday and for the first time ever, Cassie had not been granted permission to come in late in order to attend eight o'clock Mass at Saint Mary's.

When she asked, Mr. Rolands Jr. explained it this way, "Mr. Roosevelt and his thirty-cent per hour and forty-four-hour work week has put the clamp on me. My hands are tied. It's not like it used to be."

Indeed. The next morning, stepping out onto sidewalk in front of the house on Poinsette Street before first light, she said to herself, "He treats me no better than them that work in the basement."

A Holy Day of Obligation was a promise to God, and Cassie was determined to observe before going to work. She looked up at the stars in the sky.

"I'm offering this up," she said, before setting off at a brisk pace to find the colored chapel on Shepard Street.

It was a modest little wooden church. Cassie genuflected and took a seat in the back pew beside a white man wearing waders and an old sun-eaten cotton shirt. She knelt to pray, glancing up now and then to watch the Negroes filing past to take seats up front. The women, like Cassie, wore veils, and she realized that without short sleeves, she might not have been able to tell some were colored at all. Like Cassie, nearly everyone wore some sort of uniform, be it fishing waders and rubber boots, or a railroad porter's coat, or a city garbage man's blue shirt. Many of the women wore a black dress with white trim. Cassie guessed they worked for a family below Broad, or maybe at one of the hotels. And she recognized the uniforms from the housekeepers at Baker Sanatorium, and the Medical Hospital. There was even a woman in the blue uniform of the cigar factory.

"In nomine Patris, et Filii, et Spiritus Sancti," the priest began. Cassie joined the rest of the congregation in blessing herself and bowing her head in prayer.

When it came time for Communion, Cassie hesitated on what she should do. She pushed back in the pew to allow the white fisherman to get by. She watched him approach the Communion rail, wait for an opening, and then kneel beside a Negro man.

Oh, what the hell, thought Cassie, and she got in line with the others. An opening came available at the altar rail between a Negro woman in a housekeeper's dress and a Negro man in his rubber boots and dungarees. Cassie McGonegal knelt between them. And like them, she bowed her head in prayer, waiting to receive the body and blood of Christ.

By the time Cassie walked beneath the Cooper River Bridge on Bay Street the sun was coming up, but it was cloudy and looked as if it might rain. She heard the metal grates rattle high above as a car climbed the first span of the bridge. A public health report had come out predicting a milder than usual polio season for the upcoming summer. Everyone was grateful for the news, especially John Grace, who had told Cassie the news after Sunday Mass.

"One good summer of toll-paying traffic is all I need to get me out of bankruptcy," he had said. "I'm going to see this through if it kills me."

"May Gawd rest your soul, John, when it does," Cassie replied. Of course, she and Patrick would continue to take the ferry over to the island for Sunday outings. Cassie admired John for not giving up, and honestly, what could he do now that the bridge was built? Tear it down and sell it for scrap?

The closer it got to 7 A.M., the less patient everyone became on Bay Street. With over three thousand people now employed at the cigar factory, and all but a hundred or so of them being women, the Eastside neighborhood was a laughing, shouting, car-honking throng of young women twice a day.

Several blocks before Blake, Cassie was in the street because the sidewalks could not hold them all.

"Pardon me, may I get by," said Cassie to a young woman leaning into a car window and talking to a boy.

"Who the hell you think you is?" said the woman, pushing away from the car to see who had spoken to her.

"Pardon me," said Cassie. The young woman scoffed, moving so close to the boy in the car that her breast nearly touched his nose. Definitely not from Charleston, thought Cassie.

Cassie shook her head and pushed on through the crowd. The Negro men in the lumber area worked a gang saw to split the tupelo wood into thin sheets for making the cigar boxes.

Cassie had risen to the coveted position of final examiner in the packing department. She made one dollar and seventy-five cents extra a week and got to sit down while she worked. By living nearly on the Neck, she was able to pay her rent to Mr. Shaftesbury at the bank and still have a little left over.

In some ways, during this time when so many people were being thrown out of their homes and going hungry, she and Patrick were doing all right. Cassie took fifty cents of what she made per week to pay a Negro woman to iron her work smocks and Patrick's uniform for Bishop England.

Cassie affixed her inspector's label, #37, to a box of Certified Cadora cigars and sent them on the line to be sealed and brought to shipping. Box after box, she opened each, applying her keen eye to the four S's: Shade, side, shape, and size. The top layer of cigars had to be a perfect match in shade, be it Claro, Colorado, Maduro, or the darkest of dark: Oscuro. Every cigar in each box had to be rolled to the same side, either a left or a right wrap depending on which side of the leaf had been used. And each cigar had to be a uniform perfecto shape, meaning tapered on both ends with a slight bulge in the middle. If one looked the slightest bit questionable, she would put that cigar through her ring gauge to be sure.

Cassie examined the box itself, making sure that nothing was crooked, not the lettering promising *"Certified" for Your Safety* or the label picturing the exotic young man of the tropics, holding brown tobacco leaves in each hand, a blue tie tucked into a bright red shirt, green pants tucked into tall black boots, and a big straw hat upon his dark head of hair. He stood on a fertile shore, a blue sea of boats and a yellow sky behind him. A box of cigars was a work of art, and Cassie's job was to make sure that each and every one met the exacting standards of the Royal Cigar Company.

All day long, the boxes came one after the other.

"Goddamn, lady, it's a box of cigars, not the *Mona Lisa*. Step it up, will you?" The supervisor yelled at Cassie like this at least once a day. She had the best job in the factory but some things never changed.

Cassie wished he would take his bad breath down to the shading department. She pulled a reddish Colorado Claro from a row of otherwise light tan Claros, held it up for the wise guy to see before putting her reject label on the box.

"Well, anyone can find a mistake if they stare at it long as you," he said, huffing and walking away.

"Lui é uno stronzo," said Salvatore Giordano. "Don't let him worry you, Miss Cassie."

Salvatore worked in the shipping department and he and the rest of the Giordano family went to Saint Mary's.

"Thanks, Sal," she said, keeping her eyes on the boxes as they came to her on the conveyor belt.

"Say Miss Cassie," he said, "I coach the softball team, and Saturday the Petite Royales are gonna play the Rinky-Dinks. Bring that boy of yours to the ball field to watch the game. I'll put him to use collecting bats or sump'n."

Cassie kept her eye on her work, but wondered what he was getting at. "That's kind of you to think of Patrick, Sal. Any special reason you got this idea Patrick should enjoy picking up your bats stedduh going fishing with me like we normally do come Saturday afternoon?"

"I know you got your hands full is all," he said.

"What you getting at, Sal?" she wanted to know.

"Let me finish this here and I'll come tell you."

Later, Sal came back over. "Last Sunday I was in my boat below de bridge, when I see a boy look like your Patrick. He and two other boys jumped in at the Columbus Street dock and swam over to Drum Island."

"My Patrick wouldn't do no such thing," Cassie insisted.

"That ain the worst of it," said Sal, getting more agitated. "Your boy needs supervision. He and them other two, they climbed the hand ladder on one of the pillars. Miss Cassie, I saw him climb all the way to the top of the bridge. I'm not kidding you."

"Say what?" She shut her line down she was so alarmed.

"I'm telling you, your little angel climbed up the Cooper River Bridge. Miss Cassie, I have sons. A lady can't keep up with a boy that age. I thought maybe putting him to work on the ball team might keep him out a trouble, that's all."

"What's the problem down there?" the supervisor shouted.

Sal left to return to his station. Cassie pulled the lever to restart her line. "I swaytogawd I may kill that boy myself for being such a damn fool." She vowed to go home and sew a Miraculous Medal on the inside of Patrick's bathing suit to keep him safe in the water.

Patrick was twelve. He needed someone to keep an eye on him but she worked late most nights and Manus came home only once or twice a year.

Wrappers all left. Shading natural tan. Shape uniform perfecto. Passed.

Maybe Sal was mistaken.

Shading Claro. Wrappers to the right, Shape uniform perfecto. Passed.

Manus had set up an account for the boy at Tulio's Tavern so he could get his supper there when Cassie worked late. She expected to get out on time that evening and wanted to go to Tombolies's Market to buy them each a pork chop after she went to the bookstore. Manus had sent an extra dollar that month to buy Patrick some book he was excited about. Cassie stole a glance to check her watch. Patrick was out of school. For the first time ever, her mind drifted to what sort of trouble he might be getting into. "I can't worry bout that," she said quietly. "It's up to Gawd to look out for that boy."

After work, while on the King Street trolley, she took the money from the envelope Manus had sent her to buy the book. She pulled out his letter one more time.

Miss Cassie,

I won at poker last night. Three of a kind in one hand, and a flush in the next. Please buy Patrick The Wild Swans at Coole *by the Irish writer William Butler Yeats. Make him read "An Irish Airman Foresees His Death." At his age fighting a war sounds grand. I want him to know the truth. This man Yeats has won a big prize. The Irish love good verse.*

Some guys onboard are fine but others want to cut you with a rusty knife. I wish I were there to teach my boy how to know the difference. I read in a paper about the Ku Klux up in Indiana. They beat a man leaving the Knights of Columbus and branded the letters KKK on his chest. Don't coddle the boy or hide this kind of news from him. He needs to know what the world is really like.

Manus

The bells on the bookstore door jingled. She read the newspaper best she could but had always felt that books were for people with more schooling. She walked along the narrow aisles, not knowing where to begin to try and find this book. All the letters ran together in a blur. She started for the door. Then she thought of Brigid and how important it was to her that Patrick keep up his reading.

"Pardon me," she said to the shopkeeper.

"Yes," he said, putting his finger beneath his nose to block the ammonia smell.

Cassie thrust Manus's letter out, pointing at it. "You got this here book?" She realized she sounded abrupt and she felt ashamed that he would think her even more ignorant than she felt at the moment.

"Let me see, poker, three of a kind—"

Her face burned with embarrassment.

"*The Wild Swans at Coole,*" he said finally. "Yes, it's in the poetry section. I suppose you need me to find it for you?" he asked.

Cassie felt sweat gathering beneath her arms. She hoped her smock would hide it from his view.

"Yeah," she said. "I need yuh tuh find it fuh me." She felt like telling him to keep it for himself and wipe his behind with it.

"That will be two dollars," he said. The drawer of the cash register opened with an abrupt, even critical, slam and rattle. "Sump'n wrong?" he asked impatiently.

"Shooo! Ain nuttin wrong wid me," she said, taking her coins from her purse and spreading them out on the counter to make up the difference. "Ain nuttin wrong wid me," she repeated, although she was worrying about what she could buy to fix for supper now that she had spent the money she intended for the pork chops.

She was in a foul mood as she walked down King Street to Tombolies's Market. Across the street in Marion Square, she happened to notice Bishop England boys playing ball, and Patrick was among them. She stood and watched. "Couldn't you have changed out of your nice clothes first?" she said to no one in particular.

He and his friends were playing against some Boy Scouts, and Cassie did not recognize the children as being from any of the families she knew. Patrick was a good athlete, anyone could see that. Then of course, with the Mighty Manus for a father, she shouldn't have been surprised. A boy like that needed meat to grow strong. She decided to buy one chop for Patrick and that she would make do with rice and beans. She set off for Tombolies, hoping to get there before he closed.

With the chop and the book in hand, Cassie started back home. Reaching Marion Square, she saw the boys were gone except for her Patrick and one of the ones she didn't recognize. She was about to pass on by, when she heard the sound of a scuffle.

She looked to see a Boy Scout give her Patrick a shove.

As she got closer, she heard Patrick yelling at the boy. "Give me back my book bag," he demanded.

"What book bag?" The boy taunted with Patrick's bag over his shoulder.

Again, the Boy Scout shoved Patrick.

Cassie hurried toward her shy and quiet boy. Before she reached him, however, her precious Patrick landed a right punch across the Boy Scout's chin, and followed it with a left jab to the belly. The Boy Scout doubled over momentarily before lunging. They toppled to the ground in a full-blown fight.

"What in the name of Gawd are you doing?" she yelled, grabbing Patrick by the ear. Both boys ceased at the sound of Cassie's voice. They stood, staring in shock at the sight of the gray-headed lady in her white uniform with the green smock bearing the Chief Papakeecha logo, holding a bag of groceries in one hand and Patrick in the other. The Boy Scout had a bloody nose and a cut lip. Patrick was dirty and his uniform shirt was ripped, but the only blood seemed to be from the knuckles on his right hand.

"What's de mattuh," the Boy Scout taunted. "You got to have your grand-mother come get your satchel back for you?"

Cassie snapped, "Shet yuh mouth." She let go of Patrick's ear and stepped closer to the offensive boy.

"PEW-weeee!" the Boy Scout exclaimed, making an ugly face, fanning the air with his hand, and stepping away from Cassie. "Mother was right. Cigar maker's smell like cat pee."

Patrick dove at the boy, knocking him fast and hard into the ground.

"Patrick," she said, not yelling or even with much anger in her voice at all, "Leave him be."

Patrick gave the boy a final kick in the rear, reclaimed his book-bag, and took the sack of groceries Cassie was carrying. The other boy scrambled to his feet and ran off.

"Boy Scouts are jerks," said Patrick in his usual soft-spoken voice. "Let's go home," he said, taking his great-aunt by the hand.

The sun was setting and they walked in the shadow of the Francis Marion hotel. As they made their way across Marion Square, high above them, in silhouette, the statue of John C. Calhoun stared out, presiding over all of it.

Chapter 29

Dere's no rain to wet you.
Oh yes, I want to go home,
Want to go home.

"Put some elbow to it, Kofi, you row like a gkumma." Joe commanded impatiently.

"Tata, don't call me a gkumma," Vincent de Paul shot back.

Meliah Amey cut her eyes to Joe, a look asking, Why that tone of voice?

Joe prepared the sails for when they were ready to come about. "Not much left on the flood an he bout to miss it. If the wind die when the tide go slack, Kofi gone be the one rowing us to Riverside Beach."

They were on their way to the Riverside Pavilion to hear Cat Anderson on trumpet and another musician people were talking about by the name of Duke Ellington.

Meliah Amey turned around in the boat so as not to face her men. She wanted peace. She took a breath, pulling the redemptive smell of the marsh deep into her body. The sun leaned. With each slice of the oars into the water, Adger's Wharf fell away. She imagined the pier pylon where the pelican sat as Mr. Godfrey's head. The bird stood, flapped her wings, shifted her weight, and then laid her droppings. Feeling better, the pelican took flight.

Dere's no sun to burn you.
Oh yes, I want to go home.

"Eee! Eee!" The women on the line had screamed, including Meliah Amey, when the third woman that day fell out from the heat and stench. Sam Maybank ran to fetch the nurse one more time, and when she came, the men took the woman away on the stretcher.

A moving belt had been installed in the basement and hundreds of Negro women had been hired to clean the debris off the tobacco and send it down the line to the stemmers, and then on to the sorters.

The shipment that morning had more than the usual amount of chicken-shit caked upon the leaves. Meliah Amey took her rag from her head and put it over her mouth, trying to keep from getting sick at the stomach.

Dere's no whips a-crackin'.

A woman started singing, and the others joined. "Mr. Godfrey say President Roosevelt be the one to make it so my chillun can't come here no more to work," said the woman on the line next to Meliah Amey. "Berry well den, now pay me more money if my chillun can't work. Mr. Godfrey say blame de president."

Dere's no stormy weather.
Oh yes, I want to go home.

A woman way back in the sorting department changed up the song:

Brudder George is a-gwine to glory
Take car' de sin-sick soul.

All the women knew to keep working but to look up, look around, be ready. That's how they used the song "The Sin-Sick Soul." It was a way to communicate that one of the girls needed looking after on her way to use the restroom that had been put in way back in the darkest corner of the basement.

Sam Maybank knew what the song meant, too, and Meliah Amey saw him looking around, trying to make sure all the buckruh supervisors stayed where they were and didn't go following after the girl.

Brudder George is a-gwine to glory
Take car' de sin-sick soul.

The women sang that song until the girl was safely back at her work station.

"Me not going go in that room, no sir, Mr. Godfrey," a man protested. "They put pizen in there."

"It ain poison! It's a government-approved compound!" Mr. Godfrey shouted back. "By the time you open de door, it's evaporated. It's gone."

The man shook his head. "Not gonna do it. No, sir."

The heat monkey making everybody crazy, thought Meliah Amey.

"Let me go back to the lumberyard, Mr. Godfrey. I work that gang saw in the hot sun all day long, but please don't make me go in that room with the pizen."

"I don't have time fuh yuh bellyaching." Mr. Godfrey walked away. "Sam," he yelled. "Get the tobacco out of the conditioning room. Come on, I ain got all day."

"A boat coming up starboard, you see it, don't you?" Joe barked.

Meliah Amey turned around, the look on her face asking her husband, *What's the matter with you?*

"Leab me be," Joe snapped.

Meliah Amey turned back around. "Can't wait to hear Cat Anderson hit the high notes, that's what I'm waiting on."

Cat Anderson and Ray were friends. They had known one another at the Jenkins Orphanage. Cat, like many of the boys there, went on to play with bands in the clubs in Harlem. That connection to Jenkins Orphanage brought the biggest names to Riverside Beach: Louis Armstrong, Count Basie. Meliah Amey, Joe, and Vincent de Paul heard them all.

The swells picked up when they reached the deeper water of the shipping channel.

"Hold portside oar!" Joe ordered angrily from the stern.

"Joe," she hollered. "Mek so wid de mean mouth?"

"I ain got no mean mouth, woman," he snapped. "Leab me be."

It became quiet then except for the sound of water slapping the starboard side of the hull. The boat began to turn, gently at first, until the wind caught the sail with a whoosh.

"He's mad at me," said Vincent de Paul, speaking loud so she could hear him over the wind. "I told him today that I don't want to work for the fleet this summer."

"Mek so?" she asked.

"Avery's got a summer scholarship to send one student to study at the Royal Academy of Music in London. Mr. Logan says I stand a good chance of winning the scholarship this year. The competition is next week."

Vincent de Paul talked different now that he had been at the Avery. Except when he was mad or excited and then he—like everybody from the lowcountry —no matter how much schooling they had—couldn't stop the Geechee from coming out their mouths.

"I swaytogawd I knew sump'n wrong with the two of you. I knew it." Meliah Amey decided to tie her mouth and study her head to figure out why

Joe didn't want Kofi to go to London. Mr. Gaillard was getting old and Joe wasn't getting any younger; he needed Kofi's help on the boat, but Meliah Amey didn't want Joe depending on Kofi to work for him.

She looked back at Joe, shifting among his boxes, not really looking for anything in particular, just not wanting to look her in the eye. Joe must have told the boy no. If she talked it up right then without speaking to Joe first, well, that would make him plenty mad at her, too.

"Kofi, going to London sounds grand, but Tata and me need to talk bout it first."

The look on both their faces told her she had managed to keep the peace for the time being.

The ferry *Sappho*, filled with cars and passengers, passed a safe distance in front of them. Gulls swarmed overhead while a tourist held up food for them on the upper deck. Meliah Amey turned back at Joe. He had relaxed. His hands were behind his head, his feet propped on a bailing bucket. Vincent de Paul's hands rested on the oars. They were in trim and the wind in the sail was doing all the work.

She spotted a porpoise swimming off the bow. "Pawpus." Meliah Amey smiled and pointed. The dorsal fin curled as it dove under the water, surfacing again a little further away.

Just before they reached Drum Island, they fell off the wind and the sail began to luff. They were alongside the island in the middle of the harbor when the wind died completely. A mosquito buzzed her right ear. She heard the sound of Joe striking a match and soon the smoke from his pipe settled around them.

"Slack tide," he announced, as if anyone needed it confirmed.

The bridge was still ahead of them and Meliah Amey watched as a car made its way over going toward the beaches. She heard Vincent de Paul adjusting the oars. They began to move again. Slowly at first, and each pull required much strain, but soon, the young man fell into rhythm and he began to sing, his voice deep.

> *King of Kings, and Lord of Lords*
> *And He shall reign forever and ever*
> *King of Kings—*

"Come on, Maum," said Vincent de Paul. "Principal Cox makes every class sing Handel's "Hallelujah Chorus" at graduation. I'm practicing so I'll be ready when the time comes. When I get to King of Kings, you sing, Forever and Ever, okay?"

Vincent de Paul rowed, and he began again, and this time when he got to King of Kings, Meliah Amey sang out, pronouncing it Fuh eber and Eber.

"Wait a minute," Vincent de Paul stopped her. "It's forever, E-V-E-R," he spelled out as he continued to row. "There is no B in it at all. You say it like an old Geechee woman: For eber and eber. And Maum, gwi and gwine are not words. You need to say go, going, or gone. And our last name, you say Rabenel. Our name is Ravenel, with a V." He formed the letter with his finger as he chided her. "You know, the letter that comes between U and W."

His words hurt her deeply and she was glad her back was to him.

"Mr. Dixon says if the black man wants to gain respect in the white man's world then we've got to pronounce our words same as the King of England. Maum, do you even know the letter V exists?"

"Wa'yiba!" Joe shouted, calling Vincent a bad person in the old-time talk. "Shet yuh mouth and get out my way. Let a man row dis boat because only a fool chile gone talk tuh e maum dat way."

Meliah Amey thought she did speak proper, unlike so many of the women down in the basement, especially the ones who had only recently moved into town from the islands. She could recite her prayers in Latin just as the nuns at the Immaculate Conception School had taught her. And she had passed every one of the six grades the school offered back then. They were going under the bridge, and she looked up at the bottom of the roadbed over one hundred feet above, thankful her son could not see how deeply his words had hurt her.

"Sit down Tata; let me row de boat," said Vincent.

"No!" insisted Joe.

Meliah Amey felt the boat rock. She turned around.

"I'm de captain. Change yuh seat boy."

"Oonuh not my captain!" Vincent shouted back, coming to his feet, facing his father eye to eye.

Meliah Amey blessed herself. Joe's chest swelled with anger. Vincent de Paul braced for a punch. Joe shoved his son with a quick thrust, as if he knew from experience the amount of force that would knock a man off-balance but not enough to knock him overboard. Vincent steadied himself before returning an identical shove to his father.

"Eee! Eee!" Meliah Amey shouted. "Sancto Maria, Mater Dei—"

Vincent de Paul pulled off his shirt, followed by his shoes.

"Kofi!" she yelled. He removed his trousers and then even his drawers. "Joe, stop de boy," she pleaded. "Kofi, no. Joe, stop him."

"Man, wuh yuh want fum me?" Vincent de Paul, his jaw tense, demanded of his father. Then he raised his arms up, shouting as if he wanted the cars passing on the bridge overhead to hear, as well. "What do you people want from me?"

Clearly, Vincent was no longer a boy, and Joe did not try to stop him as he dove into the water.

"Eee! Eee!" Meliah Amey cried as the boat rocked. She went down on her knees, overcome in prayer-filled emotion. But then almost as quickly, she raised her head, as if only then realizing that diving in was not the same as drowning. She looked across the smooth surface of the water. There he was, her son, swimming back to Charleston. She looked to Joe, standing in the back of the boat, his hand shielding the sun from his eyes as he watched Vincent's progress.

"Slack tide last ten maybe twelb minutes more," he said softly. "He be past Drum Island when the ebb starts. Ebb slow at first. He know that. He cross while the ebb slow an by the time he on de odduh side, the ebb pick up. When it do, he may eben lay on he back an float home. He know de watuh because I taught him good."

"Wuh us gwi do?" she pleaded.

Joe moved to the seat with the oars and got into position to row. "Don't tek yuh eye off Ajani. 'E no mo Kofi. E Ajani now. Watch him. Mek sure no ship coming tuh run him obuh. Us stay close. T'row him a line e need it, but us let him go, Meliah Amey. Us let him go."

PART IV

1934–1940

Chapter 30

Cassie stood at the Drake Street door looking out at the rain. Patrick had a ballgame later and she wanted it to clear so he could play. The next day the factory would be closed for the Fourth of July. Patrick loved anything to do with boats and the two of them were going to the Battery in the morning to watch the boats of the Mosquito Fleet race against one another.

Because of the wet, Cassie brought her sack lunch to the cafeteria. The only seat she could find was next to the rude girl who had been in her way on the sidewalk a while back.

"When I want him to come fix my machine, I do my lips like this," said the vulgar girl, demonstrating her flirtatious skills. "Did ya'll hear what Daphne done? Daphne, ain't no man in this place gonna ask you out after acting that way."

"Sue Ann, I don't want none of the men that work here asking me out," said Daphne, throwing a cracker at Sue Ann.

"No man south of Greenville gonna wanna go out with you when he hears," Sue Ann responded.

"Daphne, did you really show out like you belonged in the loony bin?"

"I sure did," she answered proudly. "When I was coming out the ladies I saw him standing behind the post with that look in his eye." Then she made her face go blank, and she started twitching and shaking. "Oh yeah, honey, shooo! I sure did. Let me tell you sump'n, he went on by. Without saying a word, or laying a finguh on me, he went on by."

"Every time I go to the ladies' room, when I come out, I swaytogawd, he's by that post" said another. "I try to hold it til the lunch break so I have company, but I can't an he knows it, too."

"He told me he'd put two hundred extra cigars on my sheet for the week if I'd go watch the Negro boat race with him in the mawnin," said another girl.

"How bout you, memaw? Have you always been the queen-bee examiner," asked Sue Ann. "Did you ever have to figure out how to get the mechanic to come fix your machine?"

"Sue Ann," snapped Daphne. "Show some respect. Miss Cassie's been yah longer than anybody. She knows all there is to know bout mek'n cigars. That's how come she's an examiner. Miss Cassie, tell Sue Ann what it used to be like making cigars by hand."

Cassie wished she could eat her lunch in peace. She watched the rain blowing against the window, thinking of Patrick's ballgame. When she looked about the table again, she saw the girls were waiting for an answer. Sue Ann, her makeup smeared from sweat, and the girl beside her with teeth that reminded Cassie of a shark's mouth, why should she explain to these girls what it meant to take pride in mastering a craft and learning to roll a Perfecto as well as a Panatela?

"I'm sorry ma'm. Maybe I forgot my manners down here in the city," said Sue Ann. "If you been here as long everyone says, I guess you done seen it all before, ain't you?"

"Shooo! Everything ya'll talking bout for trying to keep the men off of you when you go to the ladies' ain no different than it's ever been, an that's the Gawd's truth."

"You don't say," said Daphne.

"Oh yeah! A girl used to act like she had scrambled marbles to keep this one foreman from bothering her. Oh yeah! But see, back when we made the cigars by hand, we was free to get up an go to the ladies' when we needed to, and if we had a foreman who was trouble, well, we'd go two at a time. When the machines come, that changed. You got to get permission and wait till Miss Sweeny can take over. My advice is don't drink more than a half-a-cup coffee in the mawnin so you can hold your watuh till the lunch break."

"My mother told me that Miss Cassie learned how to fix the machine herself an that she taught the others on her floor," said Daphne. "Could you teach us how Miss Cassie?"

Before Cassie could answer, the shark-mouth girl spoke up.

"I don't wanna know how to fix the machine," she said. "That mechanic needs to do his job and leave me be to do mine."

"Tools are for men to use," Sue Ann insisted. "It wouldn't look right, a girl knowing what to do with a man's tools. I wouldn't want a man to get the wrong idea about me."

"Don't make no difference to me, chile," said Cassie, "Don't make no difference to me."

"If they keep increasing the quota an speeding up the machine," said another girl, "they gonna be taking me to the loony bin on Barre Street and it won't be no joke."

Everyone at the table agreed to that.

"What was the machine set at when you worked it, Miss Cassie?" Sue Ann asked.

"The girl doing the wrapper leaf, she had eight seconds, that's right, she had eight seconds to put that wrapper leaf on the die for the machine to cut it."

They all reacted to that.

"I put the wrapper leaf on," said the shark-mouth girl, "and when I started I had six seconds, now I got four."

"And the daily quota is four thousand," said Daphne.

"They fixing to raise it," said Sue Ann. "Just when you get the hang of one speed, Mr. Rolands Jr. comes up on the floor and tells the foreman to move it up again. And if you complain Mr. Godfrey says—"

"—There's women waiting outside right now to take your place," they chimed in together.

With the Depression on and times being so hard, Cassie knew of a few women who stayed below Broad who had come to work at the cigar factory.

"See, back when we made the cigars by hand, they had to work with us some because it took so long to train each girl," said Cassie.

"Mr. Godfrey says with the machines, they can train a cigar maker in ten days," said Sue Ann.

"Okay girls," yelled one of the foremen from across the cafeteria. "You got five minutes to be back at work. Five minutes."

"I ain't putting up with a quota over four thousand," said Sue Ann.

Cassie attempted to stand and a twinge of pain in her knee made her sit back down.

"There's a man I been talking to after work some days," Sue Ann continued.

"What you talking with this man about?" asked Cassie.

"He's with the CIO union. He wants me to arrange a time and a place for him to meet with the girls. My sister works in a cotton mill up in Greenville, and she joined a union. This man I talk to, he wants me to help him get a lot of the girls to come to a meeting. You wanna come?"

"Maybe," said Cassie. "Depends on when it is."

"Saturday July 25th," she answered. "I don't want to join the union but looks like they going to keep on speeding up the line till we all got the scrambled marbles."

Cassie smiled. Sue Ann was starting to grow on her. "I may be interested in that meeting," said Cassie. Sue Ann smiled and hurried off for her station.

Cassie knew that she had to tell Mr. Rolands Jr. about Sue Ann and the union man. Everyone else had left the cafeteria. The Negro women who cooked and served the food were coming out with their buckets of soapy water and rags to clean up. Their expressionless faces made Cassie wonder what they were thinking, and were their thoughts at that moment much different from her own?

Cassie bent and straightened her knee until it popped. She stood up and this time her leg held. She made her way to the stairwell. When she reached the landing, she paused to look out the window. It was raining again. A gray sky made her prone to strange thoughts. And Lord, her thoughts were tangled up in her head like some big ancient barnacle growing on a pier. Talking to Mr. Rolands Jr. wasn't anything like talking to his father. His father made her feel that the information she provided kept the factory open and that helped the girls she knew—and she knew most everybody back then. But things were different now. Used to be they hired a lot of Italians and Germans, and lots of them were Catholics, so they knew one another through church, but lately, they were hiring girls from Russia, Poland, and others from up in the hill country. They weren't her people. In fact, those women cleaning the cafeteria tables were probably more her people.

Cassie knew what Mr. Rolands Jr. would tell her if she went to his office. He'd say that if the union got in there, they would demand wages he couldn't afford to pay and the factory would have to close. He'd tell her that if the union got in there demanding he pay colored and white the same, he would shut the place down and then reopen it and hire only colored because everybody knew the colored could live on $7.00 a week.

No, she wasn't going to tell Mr. Rolands Jr. this time. She turned to go back to her station.

The stairwell darkened as a gust of wind blew, followed by rain beating hard against the window. Patrick's game would be cancelled for sure. She paused there on the steps, suddenly thinking of Brigid and how much it meant to her that Patrick graduate from Bishop England. Cassie would rather lie down and die than not see his mother's wish fulfilled.

What kind of a job could a woman her age get with times being so hard? What if the union got in there and she and Patrick were forced to live on $7.00 a week? Palmetto fronds slapped hard against the window.

"Shooo! You mess with barnacles, you going to get yuh s'ef cut." She turned around again, heading for Mr. Rolands's office.

Cassie slept poorly that night. In a foggy half-awake state, she thought she heard Brigid calling her, but then it sounded deeper, much deeper, and she realized that it was Patrick.

172

"Aunt Cassie, it's time to get up if you still wanna go with me to watch the sailing race."

Patrick had fixed her a cup of coffee. He was dressed and ready to head out the door. Cassie washed her face, pinned her hair, and got dressed as fast as possible. It was rare for her to have a day off in the middle of the week and for them to do something together. Soon, he would be too old to want to spend time with his great-aunt.

They took the trolley down to Broad Street. As they walked toward the waterfront, Cassie opened her parasol to shade her eyes from the blinding glare of the morning sun. They turned onto Church Street for the shade. Birds sang, and they heard the soft chime of Saint Michael's bells.

When they reached South Battery and Oyster Point, Patrick kept looking back, cutting his eyes to Cassie, as if in doing so, he could make her walk faster.

"Go ahead," she said. Much to their mutual relief, he ran on, dodging in and out of the Negro families arriving with pots of food, ice chests filled with drinks. The Fourth of July in Charleston was understood by those living below Broad to be a Yankee holiday. Thus, it was given to the Negroes as their day to have Oyster Point as well as High and Low Battery for their family reunions and picnics. Cassie knew that she and Patrick, and the other whites, would stay only long enough to watch the Mosquito Fleet sailboat race.

Charlestonians loved boat races, and this event had become as popular as the Azalea Festival tugboat races or any regatta put on by the Carolina Yacht Club.

Cassie climbed the steps to the Battery and joined Patrick at the iron railing looking out across the harbor.

"I read in the papuh that five boats are racing a twelve-mile course," said Patrick. "Mayor Stoney is gonna give twenty-five dollars to first place. They start at Adger's Wharf, come round this Oshtuh Point buoy, then out to Sullivan's Island Cove, round that buoy there, then they go way out to the Clyde Line buoy, then back here round this one again before heading to the finish line at Adger's Wharf."

She had never seen him so excited.

"Mawnin," said a Negro man to Cassie as he and his children positioned themselves beside her and Patrick at the railing.

"Good mawnin," she answered in return.

"Mawnin," said the man's wife.

Cassie smiled, nodding her head to acknowledge the wife, too.

They waited for a tugboat to pass.

"Miss Cassie, how you this mawnin?"

Cassie turned to see Sal Giordano from the shipping department at the cigar factory.

"Mawnin," Cassie said to him. "Patrick," she called. "Do you remember Mr. Giordano from that time we watched the Petite Royales play the Rinky-Dinks?"

Patrick reluctantly turned away from the water to say hello. Cassie gave him a slight kick in the ankle to improve his manners.

"Good mawnin, Mr. Giordano," he said.

"Sal," said Cassie. "You got a boat. Is it a trus-me-Gawd or is it a good seaworthy boat?"

"Oh Miss Cassie, ain nothing trus-me-Gawd bout my boat. I bought her from a man who builds for the shipyard. She's a fine boat."

"Well, Sal, I was wondering if you wouldn't mind taking my Patrick fishing with you sometime when you going to the jetties."

"Sure," he said. "He can come with me and my boy Tony next Sunday after the fisherman's Mass."

Patrick looked to his aunt as if he couldn't believe she was arranging such a wonderful thing for him. "Gosh, there's nothing I'd like better! Thanks, Mr. Giordano."

"Summer trout and drums are running good this time a year," he said. "We bring you back some good-eating fish, Miss Cassie."

Cassie made a note to herself to get up early Sunday to take Patrick to the fisherman's Mass.

The tug had at last cleared the harbor. Mayor Stoney, standing aboard a Charleston lightship, blasted the ship's horn to start the race.

From the Custom's House at the foot of Market Street, all the way to Low Battery, the crowd, some with telescopes and others binoculars, pressed closer to the water's edge, trying to get a better view of the multicolored patchwork sails racing toward the first buoy near Oyster Point, where the Cooper and Ashley River meet. Cassie and Patrick stood upon the gray slate of High Battery with the others, Negro and white, shoulder to shoulder in the bright sun of a summer morning.

The captains of these small brightly painted boats could be heard yelling commands to their crew. The crews moved rapidly into position, getting ready to change the setting of the sails as they rounded the buoy. A boat with a faded red-and-green sail took the lead. People clapped and yelled for each boat as it came about. Soon, all of them were making fast across the harbor, passing Fort Sumter to starboard, Sullivan's Island to port, while behind them, Charleston cheered.

Chapter 31

Joe's boat was in third place going into the turn at the Oyster Point buoy. He began to catch the second-place boat as he and his crew made their way out of the harbor. Mayor Stoney had taken an interest in the fleet and it was his idea to offer cash rather than trophies that year to the top three contestants. Joe had written to the mayor personally when he heard about the plan for the prize money:

> *To the Honorable Mayor of the City of Charleston,*
> *We as fishermans of the Mosquito Fleet of this City are Making ready to give you a race on the 4th Day of July, better than our former Race. We are in trim to do it.*
>
> *Joe Ravenel, Captain*

Meliah Amey stood at the railing on High Battery, cheering along with everyone else as the other boats came around the buoy and headed out. She couldn't help but notice how many white people there were in the park on what was supposed to be their day. Before long, the buckruh would probably take back the only day of the year when her people were allowed to enjoy a picnic at Oyster Point and be up on High Battery. The ancient live oaks filled with Spanish moss provided shade all day. A breeze could be found there when there wasn't one anywhere else. And that was why it was the most desirable place and only the highest of the high buckruh could afford the grand old homes beside the park. The homes built by the families of the people gathering now in the bittersweet shade.

The Ravenels and the Pinckneys set up near the bandstand, and Meliah Amey brought the gunjuh, a molasses cake, over to the table.

"Come yah, come yah, Meliah Amey," called one of Joe's cousin's to her. "How come Ajani not helping he Tata win de race?" The woman kept her head down as she spoke, keeping her eye on the coil she was bending for the sweetgrass basket she was making.

"He gone obuh to England to study music for the summer," answered Joe's Aunt Lizzy, also keeping her head down, as her fingers worked a filed nail to keep the intricate color pattern in her basket even.

"I'm telling oonuh," continued the aunt, keeping her eyes on the knot she was tying, "that boy gone graduate next year from the Avery Institute. That's right, the Avery Institute on Bull Street," she repeated. "I gwi see that boy when he sing the Hallelujah song. That's right Meliah Amey, you gots to save me a seat, because I swaytogawd I wanna hear that boy sing the Hallelujah song."

"Maum Lizzy," said Meliah Amey, filled with pride to hear the family acknowledge the sacrifice she and Joe had made. "You will sit next to me when that glorious day come."

Meliah Amey left her gunjuh cake on the table and hurried over to the High Battery seawall, anxious to see if the boats were on their way back yet. As she was passing the flank of old cannons that had defended Charleston, first against the British, and later against the United States in rebel time, she couldn't help but notice the white man sitting on one of the cannons talking to Sam Maybank. She looked back over her shoulder one more time as she crossed East Battery Street. The two of them were still talking. All the white people that had come that morning were up at the railing watching the race. But that man talking to Sam was facing the wrong direction.

When she got to the railing and looked out, she did not see any boats in the fleet. She glanced over her shoulder, and the white man remained on the cannon, intent on whatever he was discussing with Sam. Sam appeared to be mostly listening, but every now and then, Meliah Amey could see that he was explaining something to the white man. And the man did not look like a Geechee. It was funny, the white people kind of all looked alike, at least the low buckruh looked like the other low buckruh and the high buckruh looked like the other high buckruh but still, Meliah Amey could tell that this man was from away because he didn't look like either. Then Sam and the white man began talking with their hands moving in the air, but they weren't fighting because a moment later, they shook hands and the white man got up off the cannon and walked away.

Meliah Amey turned back to the harbor, shielding the sun from her eyes with her hand, trying to see if any boats were on the horizon.

"I see one," shouted a white man down the railing, with a telescope to his eye.

"Yes," another man with binoculars cried out, "The one in the lead got a blue sail."

Meliah Amey clinched her fists, suppressing the urge to shout out "Lord, have mercy." A blue sail—that was Joe's boat. She had insisted on a haint blue cloth for the sail to keep away Ki'tuta. She blessed herself and said a Hail Mary.

Joe's boat neared Fort Sumter, but the one in third place was moving up. Meliah Amey wished that there weren't so many white people there to watch the race. She wanted to jump up and down and yell, "Eee! Eee! Come on, Joe!" but she would never let herself holler like that in front of whites. She knew they would look down their skinny noses at her if she did. Besides, Mr. Chisholm's wife was doing a fine job of whooping it up now that his boat was about to pass the one in second place.

The sails of the second-place boat began to flap when the boat passed on its starboard side.

"Second place has had its wind blocked," shouted the man with the telescope. "He's going to catch the one in first."

"He sees him," shouted the other man with the binoculars. "I saw the captain with the blue sail look over his shoulder. He sees the boat gaining on him."

Do something Joe, Meliah Amey wanted to scream.

"He's gonna jibe! The one with the blue sail is gonna jibe. He's a better skipper than I would have thought," said the telescope man.

Meliah Amey wanted to kick him.

"He's going to starboard," shouted a young boy to his Gkumma. Meliah Amey was surprised to see it was the ma'magole from the cigar factory. "He knows he can't let that boat pass him on the upwind side," her boy hollered out.

Meliah Amey understood that the race was not a direct line back to Adger's Wharf, instead, it was now a schemy contest to see who could pass on the upwind side of another boat to steal the wind momentarily and get ahead. Both boats were tacking and jibing, trying to get into position to be the one to make a move close enough to the finish line that the other boat would not have time to recover.

The zigging and zagging of the first- and second-place boats allowed time for the third-place crew to gain enough ground to become a serious threat again. As the three boats approached the Oyster Point buoy everyone went wild. Negro and white, it didn't matter, they hollered out, shaking and shimmying, jumping up and down with excitement as the crews engaged in a furious dance of shifting their weight about the boat, changing the set of the sails, anything to catch a little more lift, a little more push through the water, trying to get into position to make that final move. The boats darted in and out so close to one another, Meliah Amey feared they would collide.

"Eee! Eee! Come on, Joe! Tek foot een han'," she shouted, not caring who heard her yell to her husband. "Tek foot een han', Joe! Now!" And then, Joe made his move, barely eclipsing the second-place boat, but it was enough to snatch the wind away.

Chapter 32

Mr. Rolands Jr. fired Sue Ann and hastily arranged for a company picnic to be held at Hampton Park on the same Saturday the union man planned his meeting. At Cassie's urging, Mr. Rolands Jr. agreed to pay the trolley fare for every employee and family member planning to attend.

Cassie had no desire to attend the picnic, preferring instead to stay home and put on a pot of red rice and sivy beans. She switched on the radio bought at a rummage sale, and positioned the electric fan to blow directly on her as she chopped the onions and tomatoes.

She'd heard it all before. Mr. Rolands Jr. or somebody from the office up North would come down and tell the girls what a good job they were doing. Citadel cadets would be driving by in their cars, hollering out, "Hey Cadora College girl, you wanna take a ride out to the island with us?" Oh yeah, and lots of the girls would jump in the car with them boys, not giving a thought to how it looked, or what the cadets were really after. Cassie had seen and heard it all before. Maybe this time the company would fry up a bunch of mullet and call it red snapper. Then Mr. Rolands Jr. would get up to talk about the union menace and how it could lead to the white girls having to go down in the basement to stem tobacco alongside the darkies.

Cassie did not doubt Mr. Rolands Jr.. Nor did she have the slightest intention of supporting the union. She was simply weary. Weary from fighting the devil. Maybe it was the age her body carried now. Lately, she felt like she was constantly trying to sort out and remember exactly who was the devil in this situation. She turned up the radio.

Ladies and gentleman! Royal Cigar, the makers of the Certified Cadora cigar are pleased to bring you the smooth sounds of Tom James, the Cadora Singer. While you're enjoying the music, light up a Cadora and experience the pleasure of a smooth clean smoke. And remember, you can't tell by looking if your cigar is clean or made in unsanitary conditions. Fifty-eight health officials approve Cadora's campaign for cleanliness, and now, here's Tom James . . .

She heard the slam of the door and the sound of Patrick bounding up the stairs to the apartment.

"I need a knife," he called out, rushing past her and pulling open the kitchen drawer.

"What you need with a knife?" she asked, rising from her chair.

Patrick had her longest, sharpest cooking knife in hand. Cassie blocked the doorway to the kitchen. "I swaytogawd you better tell me what you fixing to do with that knife?"

"I got in a fight with a colored boy an we not done yet. He's waiting for me on Rutledge Avenue right now. Aunt Cassie, I got to go."

"Patrick O'Brian, you ain leaving out this house with my knife."

They were staring eye to eye, and for the first time Cassie realized that Patrick was taller than she.

He set the knife down on the counter.

Cassie blessed herself. "Who started it, you or the colored boy?"

Patrick stared at the floor, shifting his weight around, not wanting to talk.

"Listen to me," she insisted. "Now I don't ask much of you, do I?"

Still looking at his feet, he nodded in agreement.

"The only thing I ask you to do is to keep up with your schoolwork because that's what your mother wanted. You ain got to fix you own food or do your own wash. If you wanna be a damn fool and get into trouble, you gonna be out on your own. I won't have it in my house, you understand? Now who started it?"

"Tony Giordano, Shrimpy, and I were walking home—"

"Tony Giordano? Sal's boy?"

Patrick nodded his head. "It's going along fine until these three colored boys come out from a side street. We didn't want to let them pass and they didn't want to let us pass. Then Tony yelled that Pompey was coming so we all acted like nothing was wrong."

"What you talking bout? Who Pompey?" Cassie asked.

"Pompey Rides the Rooster," said Patrick. "He's the po-leeze-man that rides the red bicycle. He won't let you skate unless he's closed off the street from the cars. If he catches you, he takes your skates down to the po-leeze station and says only parents can pick them up. I can't believe you never heard of Pompey, Aunt Cassie. If he catches you ringing doorbells or turning over garbage cans, he makes you pick up trash from around Colonial Lake. He got a bike rather than a motorcycle just so us kids can't hear him coming."

Cassie knew so little about how Patrick spent his time.

"Why you say he rides the rooster?" she asked.

"When he got the bright red bicycle, Sally Blake said the bike looked like a red rooster, and then she sang something like "Pompey rides the rooster but he ain like he used to." I don't know Aunt Cassie, it's just what we sing whenever we see him coming. Pompey yells at us to be quiet. He hates it. Tony once hid Pompey's bike behind the bushes at Colonial Lake and gosh, that really made Pompey mad."

It occurred to her that Pompey knew more about her Patrick and his friends than she did. But at least the boy had calmed down. He took a seat in the chair at the kitchen table.

"Why you wanna get in trouble with the colored boys?"

"One says, 'You wanna fight' and Tony said, 'Yeah, we fight you.' Then Tony said to one of the coloreds, 'What you wanna fight with?' Then, the colored boy, he said 'Knives.' Well, none of us had a knife. Then Shrimpy, he spoke up and said, 'Let's all go home to get a knife and meet back there behind that service station on Rutledge Avenue.'"

"Leave the colored alone," she said. "I mean it. When I was growing up, used to be some boys your age like'd to hang out in the cemeteries to scare the old darkies walking home at night. Patrick, don't ever do that, you hear me?" She waited for Patrick to nod his head and agree. "And for Gawd's sake, don't ever pick a knife fight with a colored. Let them be, you hear? If we let them be, they'll let us be, and we won't have no trouble. That's how it's always been in Chaa'ston and that's how it's got to stay."

Tom James sang on the radio. She looked at the boy sitting there, and if Cassie ever worried that she might forget Brigid's face, all she had to do was look at Patrick.

"Patrick," she said, "how you spend the day during the summer when you not in school?"

"What do you mean?"

"Just what I say, that's what I mean."

"Well," he began, "Tulio says that I've got an $8.00 a month tab. Most days I get breakfast from him. Then, if it's raining, I go to the library. If the weather's good, I go down to the water. If I'm real lucky, one of the tugboat captains will take me along with him a few hours. Rita Hagerty's got one of them big inner tubes and if the tide is running right, sometimes she and I ride that tube from the Columbus Street dock over to Sullivan's Island. Then we walk around on the beach until the flood tide comes to take us back to town.

"The colored man named Seasar that works the train switch down the street gave me and Tony one of his old cast nets. He's teaching us how to throw it, and how to catch mullet by calling de pawpus."

"Shooo! How you call a pawpus?"

Patrick began to tap out a rhythm on the table. "No, it's more like this," he said, changing it up. "Seasar showed us, and it works, too. You do this on the side of your boat or take a board into the water if you're on the shore. Seasar says you won't catch any bait fish without the porpoise nearby to drive them to shallow water."

Patrick let his hands rest. "We've been using a hand line to catch crabs. See, there's a train for Charlotte comes in round one in the afternoon. We sell the crabs to them cooks and soon as we learn the cast net, we gonna be able to sell them shrimp, too. The Mosquito Fleet sells to the evening trains, but Tony and I figured out there weren't nobody selling to this one o'clock train for Charlotte. Now, if I got ball practice, I spend the afternoon at Hampton Park."

She listened, amazed at all the things she had no idea he did. She felt sorry for him not having either of his parents to see him grow up. And she knew the time wasn't too far off when he would leave her. She regretted not having more patience with him in the evenings when she came home late from work, worn-out to the bone, with her own supper to fix and both their washing still to do.

"Patrick," she said. "I've been putting a little seed-corn money aside since I been a final examiner. I ain getting any younger, and a roundtrip ticket on the Clyde Line steamer from Chaa'ston to Jacksonville is twelve dollars. If your Pop wins some decent money at poker this month and sends it to us, how about you and I take the boat after work some Saturday and come back Sunday evening. What would you think about that?"

His hair was a mess and his face and shirt were dirty, but when he smiled, she saw Brigid smiling, too. And that was the only answer she needed.

"I fixed red rice to go with the sivy beans," she said. "Let's bring our plates out on the porch to eat. Tide must be coming in. I see a little breeze picking up."

Patrick put the knife back in the drawer, opened the cabinet and took down two plates.

Chapter 33

Dear Cassie,

I am sorry I won't be home for Christmas. The ship is being dry-docked here in Rotterdam for a major repair to her ballast pumps. We set out but had to turn back while we still could. I am sending money I got from that short-haul I did over Thanksgiving for you to buy Patrick a shotgun for Christmas. I got Patrick's postcard. He wrote, "I am on the high seas aboard the S.S. Seminole bound for Jacksonville. Cassie, I know that set you back.

Things are squirrelly because of the new German Chancellor. Maybe jobs will improve in Charleston soon. Some guys on the ship were in San Francisco when the longshoremen there went on strike. I hear there are as many picket lines this year in America as there are breadlines.

Merry Christmas to you and my boy.

Your Bolshevik,
Manus

Cassie folded the money and put it in the tin can she kept inside her top drawer. Patrick would be crushed to hear that his father wasn't coming home. But it couldn't be helped and he would just have to accept it.

"Patrick," she called softly at his bedroom door. "I'm leaving for work. You need to get ready for school. Here's fifteen cents on the table for you to buy us some kerosene. Feels like a cold wave is coming."

She waited for his sleepy acknowledgement.

"Get your supper from Tulio tonight. I'm putting a letter from your father on the kitchen table next to the money for the kerosene."

She propped the letter against the Infant of Prague, who was, once again, waiting for glue to dry before being returned to the sill. His head had come off so many times, the best Cassie could manage was an odd tilt as if he were now trying to figure out why he had to hold the entire world in his hand.

She walked to work in the dark, wearing her heavy coat, regretting how it would smell of ammonia the next time she wore it to Mass.

Unlike summer when the girls chitchatted, everyone stepped briskly, anxious to get inside. As they came down Columbus and Bay Street, the white and Negro workers were intertwined. Cassie found that getting out of each other's way to enter through the proper door was even more tedious when done against a cold and salty wind.

"Scuse me, maum," said a Negro man who had to stop short in front of Cassie in order to let a white woman cut in front of him to get to the Drake Street door.

"Pardon me," said Cassie in return.

Normally, the whites were inclined to stay to the left side of the sidewalk and the Negroes to the right, since their door came after, but when it was cold or raining, everyone got all tangled up together.

Cassie hung her coat in her locker and put on the sweater she left there to wear at work. Some supervisors didn't allow the girls to wear a sweater on the cigar-making floor. To see a girl on the line wearing a sweater on a cold day usually meant she had done a little extra something for a supervisor to give her that privilege. Being a final examiner, Cassie no longer had to put up with that sort of thing.

Cassie got situated on her stool and opened the first box of the day.

"Come on now," said the supervisor as he walked past. "We want these ready fuh Santa not de damn Easter bunny."

At lunchtime, despite the cold, Cassie went outside to eat her boiled egg rather than go to the cafeteria and sit with the cigar makers. The cold air made her cough, and it took a while to get her lungs to clear. In the distance, a bell rang three times. "I knew it," she said, shaking her head. "A durn cold wave is coming."

When the temperature was going to go below freezing, the fire departments in Charleston rang their bells three times every twenty minutes to warn people to buy more coal or kerosene, and to cut off the water so the pipes didn't burst. She hoped the man living downstairs at the house would shut off the water. Last thing she'd want to do when she got home after dark would be to crawl under the house trying to find that knob.

When she went back inside, she ran into Daphne coming up the stairwell.

"Did you hear what happened to the new Polish girl?" she asked. "The mechanic forgot to put the guard plate back on her machine. She's like most of them; don't speak hardly any English, but when she shoved a bunch of filler leaves in there she lost two fingertips."

"Oh Lord!" said Cassie, coming to a standstill.

"They say it was a bloody mess, too. So much for certified clean."

The two of them started up the stairs together as more girls came into the stairwell from the cafeteria. Daphne leaned in close and kept her voice down, "Some say this mechanic had been sweetmouthing her for days but she wouldn't have nothing to do with him."

"That's awful," said Cassie.

"Oh yeah, I'm telling you, it's bad up there on the cigar-making floor, Miss Cassie. It's bout the worst I ever seen it. They got it set for me to have three seconds to put on a wrapper leaf. Three seconds."

Cassie shook her head. "Shoo! The man crazy to set the machine that fast."

The stairwell was jammed now and Cassie weaved her way over to the door when they got to her floor and Daphne continued up the stairs.

Gretta, the cigar maker who had worked on the team with Brigid, had recently been made a final examiner. She and Cassie fell in beside one another as they went back to their stations. "Did you hear bout the Polish girl?" she asked.

"Terrible," said Cassie, "Just terrible."

"Well, let me tell you what I heard," said Gretta, looking around to make sure the supervisor wasn't nearby. "The mechanics aren't happy because they've got twenty machines to each one of them, and they heard that in the factories that's got the union, the men only have ten machines a piece. Plus, they compared pay envelopes and even some of them's not paid the same for doing the same work. For us it's been that way long as I can remember, but the men, the men won't stand for that."

"What they gonna do?" asked Cassie before Gretta got too far away.

Gretta looked around again, making sure the coast was clear. "The men talking to the AFL union."

"Shoo!" said Cassie. "I don't know bout that now."

"No, listen to me," said Gretta. "The AFL ain like what we been told. One of the mechanics I talked to up on four, he said the AFL won't allow the Negroes in their union. He says it's only for skilled craftsman like the mechanics and cigar makers."

Mr. Godfrey walked onto the floor and Gretta drifted away soft as a fairy to her stool and opened a box of cigars.

The air that day might as well have been filled with gunpowder as tobacco dust.

Later that afternoon, Cassie told her supervisor she needed to be excused to go to the ladies. "And don't hang round outside the door, neither," she said to him when he gave her permission to leave her station.

In the midst of a rather indelicate moment for Cassie, the supervisor yelled from outside the door, "Hey come on, ain you done yet? What's tek'n so long?"

"What in Gawd's name has come over the men in this place?" she said, pushing past the supervisor, heading directly to Mr. Rolands's office.

"Miss Cassie McGonegal! Don't think I haven't noticed you haven't been to see me this week," said Mr. Rolands with a smile on his face. "Union talk around here is so loud even I can hear it. I keep waiting for you to bring me some names. Okay, I'm ready, give them to me."

"I didn't come to give you names," she said, still furious.

"Well, that's all I'm interested in hearing," he said, leaning back in his chair, no longer smiling. "I honor the deal you made with my father because he asked me to before he died. But you got to keep up your side of the bargain, Miss Cassie." He came forward again in his chair, and picked up the pen. "I need the names."

"And I need you to listen to me," she insisted. "What has got into the men in this place? Long as I been here there's always one or two foremen that will try to mess with the girls, but my Lord! All of a sudden—all of a sudden— seems like none of them show any respect for us being ladies."

"Give me the names of the girls talking about the union?" he insisted again.

"You need to look into what happened to that Polish girl that got her fingers cut. You need to look into that on account I heard the mechanic that left the plate off her machine was upset she wouldn't go out with him. And anudduh thing—"

"Hold on, Miss Cassie. Hold on—have a seat, please" he said, standing a little as if his manners were finally coming to him. "You want some coffee?"

"No thank you, Mr. Rolands," she said, taking a seat.

"Christmas will be here in no time," he said, taking his seat. "I bet you could use a little extra in your pay envelope this time of year, couldn't you? A little extra to buy something special for that—what is he, your nephew or something, right?"

This caught her off guard, and when she looked at him, and the picture of his father on the wall behind, Cassie had a moment of pause. She took a deep breath. It had been unlike her to go storming into a man's office like that.

"Well, thank you kind, Mr. Rolands, but that's alright. We're doing okay this year."

"No, no, I insist," he said. "You've helped keep this factory open many times. And we go way back, don't we?"

"Yes," she answered, even smiling as a memory came to mind of how she used to look forward to seeing Mr. Rolands Sr. come onto the cigar-making floor. Often, he would pull up a chair beside her table and they would talk about any old thing. Mr. Rolands Sr. had always behaved like a gentleman to her. Always.

"Some of the Negroes are talking with the CIO," he said. "Charleston won't stand for the likes of the CIO. What are the cigar makers saying?"

Cassie hadn't come to talk about the union. She wanted Mr. Rolands to do something about the way the foremen were treating the girls. But there was that picture of his daddy, staring right at her with that smile.

"There is a mechanic talking with the AFL," she said.

"AFL? Well, I'll be damn. I could just wait and let the AFL and the CIO shoot each other in the foot. They always do, you know." He rocked back and forth in his chair, contemplating this development. "Okay, let's start with the mechanic," he said, putting pen to paper. "What floor does he work on?"

"Fourth floor," she said, and as the words left her mouth, a sour feeling came over her.

"Excellent!" he said. "And the girls he's been talking to?"

Cassie did not want to tell him about Gretta or her daughter, Daphne. She knew their families well from growing up in the Borough. And with Christmas a few days away, she hadn't come to talk about agitators and she saw no reason to tell him that Gretta and Daphne were both likely to want to join the union if they could.

"Mr. Rolands, sir, I don't know of any of the girls that are interested in joining the union right now."

He leaned back in his chair, looking at her in a most peculiar way.

"Why, Miss Cassie, I do believe this is the first time I've had to wonder if you were telling me the truth. And that's not good. That's not good at all. Are you telling me the truth?"

"Oh yeah!" she said nervously, "I'm telling you the truth." She had never lied to anyone ever before, and the feeling that came with it now was as horrible as she had ever imagined. To lie was to set a trap for oneself, and she had just bitten the cheese.

"Tell you what," he said, his voice more relaxed. "I want you to go back to work, and when you go home tonight and you're fixing supper or whatever for your family, I want you to think about all of this we talked about today. I'm gonna give you until the day after tomorrow, but that's all, you understand. Day after tomorrow, I'm expecting you to come in here and give me a list with the names of the girls willing to cause trouble and bring hardship down on all the rest. And Miss Cassie, don't ever lie to me again."

That night when she got home, Patrick had the radio turned up and he was covered in blankets listening to the Citadel Drama Club performance of *A Christmas Carol*. Not only had he bought the extra kerosene but the stove was going as high as it could without flames shooting out the top.

What reason have you to be merry? You're poor enough?

"That's Mr. Scrooge talking," said Patrick.

What reason have you to be morose? You're rich enough?

"That's Mr. Scrooge's nephew," he added.

From outside, in the distance, the fire department bells rang slowly three times. Cassie went to fill a kettle but only a little water came out.

"Mr. Klein downstairs showed me the knob under the house to turn off the water." Patrick called out from the other room. And then he sneezed.

"Bless you," she said, and she went to her room to change out of her uniform and smock. She saw the letter she had left for him from his father on the table. The boy was being good-natured, and this made her feel even worse.

What's Christmas time . . . but a time for paying bills without money.

She joined Patrick in the living room and together, wrapped in blankets against the cold draft, they listened to the story of Mr. Scrooge.

When they were going off to bed, Patrick asked, "Aunt Cassie, what's a Bolshevik?"

This made her smile. "Ask your father next time you see him." She looked at Patrick then, thinking he looked pale. "You feeling alright?"

"I'm alright," he said.

"Take this blanket here," she said, handing him one of hers.

"I'm fine, I got plenty," he said.

"Take this one," she insisted. And she was glad when he did.

The smell of coal burning all over town drifted in between the boards with the cold night air, and Cassie slept poorly.

The next day, when Mr. Rolands didn't call for overtime, Cassie was relieved because she wanted to get down to her old church in the Borough and talk to Father O'Shaughnessy about her troubles. She arrived at Saint Mary's just as Father O'Shaughnessy was leaving.

"Miss McGonegal," he said. "I hope you're not wanting me to hear your confession. I have an engagement this evening and I'm about to be late."

"Oh Father, my mind is all tied up. I need your advice. I promise Father, I won't keep you."

"Well, all right then," he said rather gruffly, buttoning his coat and pulling his hat down tight upon his head.

"It's bout my job, you see."

"Yes, that's the problem indeed. Women should be at home and not taking a good job away from a man trying to look after his family." The priest had a way of shrugging his shoulders and smiling as he did so, even when he was expressing displeasure. "All right, go on, I'm about to be late to me supper engagement."

"Thank you for taking the time to listen to me, Father."

He shrugged his shoulders again.

"See, I've worked at the cigar factory since I was twelve. But—they doing an awful lot that ain right, you understand? I don't wanna lose my job. I don't want any girl to lose her job, specially here at Christmas time. Oh Father, it's all tangled up. It's hard for me to explain but the men in that place . . . and the machines, see they set the machines too fast and one of the men didn't put the cover back on and this girl, she got two fingertips cut off and Father, I sway-togawd, I feel I got to do sump'n."

"Do something?" he said. "Are you a surgeon now Miss McGonegal? Can you sew the poor girl's fingers back on for her?"

"No, I'm an examiner. I got the best job in the whole place. I don't wanna lose it but—"

The priest pulled his watch from his coat pocket to check it. "If you've got the best job in the place, then why are you sticking your nose where it don't belong?"

"Father," she pleaded, "They ain treating the girls fair. And I ain never said what I'm bout to say to no one, but it's been on my mind and I got to let it out: if they treating the cigar makers this bad, how are they treating the colored down in the basement?"

"Dear Lord! You're making me late to supper because you've only now come to realize the world is not fair? Woman, get a hold of yourself. I know Mr. Rolands. His wife is a Catholic. She comes from a prominent family up North. They had me over for supper last week. Quite the spread, too. Lace curtain all the way," he laughed, shrugging his shoulders again. "He's a smart man; a good businessman, Mr. Rolands. Royal Cigar is a very profitable company. Do you claim to know more than the man put in charge to run the place?"

"Of course not, Father. I pray Gawd to clear my mind of these thoughts, I do. I suppose you're right and Mr. Rolands knows what's best—"

"You suppose? Listen to me, the man in charge knows what's best for the company. As for the other, you might do well to remember that in 1820 when Bishop England came to Charleston, he nearly got himself lynched for starting up schools for the Negro children. Bishop England had to make a choice between teaching the colored or saving his church. And if he had lost the church, think of how many souls would have suffered the fires of hell. So you know what he did, he closed all his schools, even the ones for the innocent white children. You be careful Miss McGonegal. If you let your mind get away from you, they'll be plenty of innocent ones hurt all over again."

Daylight was dying. In the distance, Saint Michael's bells chimed.

"The Lord has a plan," he said to her. "These things work themselves out over time. Doesn't Bishop England have a fine school named after him today? And the colored children have got the Sisters teaching them at Immaculate Conception. See, it will all work out in time. Listen to me woman, do as Mr.

Rolands tells you to do. I mean it. He knows what's best and *that's* what's best for all concerned."

The next day, she waited until late in the afternoon to excuse herself to go to the ladies', and this time, the supervisor left her completely alone. She went down the stairs to Mr. Rolands's office. When she was about to open his office door, a Negro woman flung open the door from inside. Cassie stepped back into the hallway as the woman rushed past her, pulling at her blue uniform, her hair a mess, tears streaming down her face. She ran to the stairwell.

Cassie stood in the quiet empty hallway.

Mr. Rolands's secretary came out of the payroll office down at the other end.

"Miss Cassie," she said when she got closer. "Do you need to see Mr. Rolands?"

Cassie didn't know what to say.

"You alright, Miss Cassie? Do I need to get the nurse for you?"

"No," she answered. "I'm alright."

"Okay, if you're sure. I think he was expecting you to come by. You wanna see him now?"

"No," said Cassie. "Not today."

Chapter 34

Meliah Amey sat at the kitchen table shucking oysters for a pot of oyster-mush. In the distance she heard the bells from the fire station on Meeting Street, warning that a cold wave was coming.

Since the little house on Bedon's Alley did not have indoor plumbing, Meliah Amey and Joe did not have to worry about any pipes bursting. When Joe heard the bells, he brought in extra jugs of water from the cistern down the alley in case the pump-handle froze.

Meliah Amey would take the oysters and marriage'um with the onion and cornmeal boiling on the stove. She couldn't decide if she was going to attend the meeting that Sam Maybank had arranged that night at the Longshoremen's Hall near the Vendue Range wharves. The slow tolling of the fire bells did not help.

"Too cold to be out," she said, thinking out loud.

"Too cold to be in here," said Vincent de Paul, pulling his coat tighter around him as he sat doing his homework at the simple desk Joe had built for him from scrap washed ashore.

"Nobody going to listen to what a bunch of colored women has got to say. Just be a waste of time to go to that meeting."

"Tana," said Joe, taking his pipe from his mouth, about to say more, but then he considered Vincent de Paul within earshot and put his pipe back in his mouth.

Meliah Amey watched the oysters in the pot, waiting for them to curl.

Charrrrrr-Coal.

The lonely call of the charcoal boy came from over on Tradd Street. "Ajani," said Joe, "Take fifteen cent, fetch us another sack a coal for tonight."

"Tana," said Joe as soon as Vincent de Paul was outside. "They hol'um cheap. President Roosevelt passed the law for the least pay and the most hours. But the cigar factory still don't pay you what the law say you ought to make for the time you put in."

"Vincent de Paul rushed back inside. "Maum, can I bring a bowl of mush to the charcoal boy?"

"Yes, Ajani. Fix him a bowl," she answered.

When Vincent ran out the door again, Joe continued. "You never tell me bout the men in that place. But I know, Tana, I know."

She could not look her husband in the eye, and he, seeing this and knowing why, knocked over a tin cup of water so hard, it hit the wall. Steam droplets hissed as they landed on the stove.

"And I can't do nuttin bout the way they treat you. I hold all that nuttin inside my haa't. One day—one day, Tana, that plenty of nuttin gone kill me dead."

In the distance, the fire bells rang slowly three times.

Vincent de Paul burst through the front door with the sack of coal and the empty bowl and spoon. "Only thing good about being out is that it makes you feel warm when you come back in." He saw his mother taking off her apron. "You going to the union meeting tonight?"

"Don't let the stove go out," she said, reaching for her coat and hat. "Now move out the way before I change my mind."

The damp wind coming off the harbor went right through her cotton coat. Up ahead, under the dim glow of street light, she saw the small boy selling charcoal from his little cart pulled by a little donkey.

Charrrrrr—Coal.

The boy held both notes for a four-count beat, ending on the lower of the two when he sang *Coal.* Meliah Amey never heard a more mournful sound.

And watching the little boy and his donkey-cart moving slowly down East Bay and into the dark shadow of the night brought her to a standstill. Again, the fire department bell rang.

Walking into the brightly lit meeting hall was like walking from winter to summer. There were close to one hundred Negro workers from the cigar factory, and unlike at work, they sat talking freely amongst themselves. Binah was laughing and cutting up with Sam Maybank, and Meliah Amey went over to say hello.

"How you doing, girl?" Binah asked. Binah looked happier than Meliah Amey had seen her in years.

"Sam, come up yah so we can get started," announced an extremely good-looking man at the podium.

"Should we wait an see if more people come?" Sam asked.

"The cold wave got folks scared to come out," the man at the podium replied. "Don't worry, Sam. This is a good turnout for your first meeting. After Christmas you have another meeting and that's when folks will start signing the union cards. We get a big crowd here that night. Now come on up here and tell us what's happening at the cigar factory."

Meliah Amey didn't realize that she had made a little noise.

"Meliah Amey! I ain hear you make that sound in a very long time." Binah nudged her, and Meliah Amey laughed. She missed laughing and acting the fool sometimes the way she and Binah used to do.

"He don't work at the cigar factory," said Meliah Amey.

"Oh no, chile," said Binah. "He the head of the Longshoreman's Union here in Chaa'ston. They say he make seven thousand dollars a year. A year! That union is good to them men now."

Meliah Amey turned to Binah. "Binah, what you doing at a union meeting? Never thought I'd see that. Sump'n different about you. Who got he eye tie up on you now? Whoever the man is, I swaytogawd you must be in love for true this time."

"Sam and me got married last month," she said smiling. "That man, he a very good father, I mean it. I love that man for it, too. That's right, I do."

Meliah Amey hugged Binah. "We stay on America Street now. He maum take care of Hope when I go to work."

"That's grand," said Meliah Amey. "Since you up on the box-making floor, I don't hear bout none of this you telling me."

"Sam's a very good man. He not Ray, but in some ways, he more better, and I got to look out for my chillun," said Binah.

"Chillun?"

"Yes, maum," said Binah. "It early, very early. I ain even tell Sam yet—but I know. I know."

Meliah Amey leaned in close to Binah. "How bout the buckruh debble?"

"Oh no," said Binah. "He eye tie up on the new girl Rachel that work with you in the basement."

"All the mens eye tie up on that one. I worry bout that girl, Binah. I worry bout that girl and that's the Gawd's truth."

When the whistle blew at seven-thirty the next morning, all hands sprang to work in the cold damp of the basement. The men began to pry open the large wooden crates containing the raw tobacco. "You can't be wearing that sweater over your smock," Mr. Godfrey shouted at Meliah Amey. "Put it back in your locker."

When she returned from her locker, she saw that Binah was working in stemming.

"Mek so oonuh down yah?" Meliah Amey asked.

"Don't know," she said. "Mr. Godfrey come up on the box floor to tell me go work in the basement."

Mr. Godfrey stood up on a crate to keep a better eye on the stemmers. "Damn it," he yelled, "You got to be faster than that, now hurry up."

In the cold, Meliah Amey's fingers did not want to work fast, and she knew she wasn't the only one.

"That ain right," said Mr. Godfrey jumping down from the crate and standing behind Rachel. "You leaving too much of the leaf on the stem." And as he stood behind her, Meliah Amey saw Mr. Godfrey running his hand over Rachel's backside.

Before he stepped away, he said to Rachel, "Why don't you go to your locker and get a sweater."

No more peck o' corn for me—Meliah Amey called out in song. It was the first time she had ever taken the lead.

No more, no more—responded the other women.

No more pint o'salt for me—sang Meliah Amey.

No more, no more—the other women responded.

"That's better," Mr. Godfrey called out over their singing. "When you sing, I know you're happy. That's good. I like it when you people sing."

When the whistle blew at five-thirty, Meliah Amey and Binah walked together up Columbus Street.

"They know," said Meliah Amey.

"It don't matter if they do," said Binah. "Sam say it's the law now. Once we get enough people to sign them cards the company can't stop us from joining the union."

The sun leaned. "I'm going to Henderson's department store with Ajani," said Meliah Amey. "We wanna see if we can find something we can afford to buy Joe for Christmas."

"I promised to take Hope to see the lights on King Street one evening," said Binah.

"Come with us," said Meliah Amey. "I want you to see Ajani now."

Henderson's Department Store on King Street had a Santa Claus right up front when they entered the store. One white boy sat in his lap and two other white children waited in line to be next.

Meliah Amey, Binah, and Vincent de Paul tried to walk fast and ignore the Santa, but Hope stopped, fascinated by the man in the red suit, with the shiny black boots and white beard.

Binah gently took Hope by the hand, not wanting to make a scene. But the girl pulled away. "I wanna sit in Santa's lap," she said.

"Carolina," said Binah, her voice soft but very stern. "Come yah, right now."

When white children came in the store, Santa called out, "Merry Christmas" and waved. No matter what Carolina did to try and get his attention, Santa turned his head, going out of his way to ignore her even when there were no white children waiting to sit in his lap.

"Carolina," said Vincent de Paul, holding out his hand to her. "Will you help me pick out a shirt for my Tata for Christmas?"

"How will Santa know what I want?" she asked.

"I'll help you write him a letter," said Vincent de Paul. "We'll mail it to the North Pole."

Vincent de Paul kept his promise to Hope. Then he and his friends wrote their own letter to the newspaper. A few days later, he brought a copy of the morning paper home so that his parents could read the letter he had helped write. It appeared with a headline.

SANTA AND NEGROES

All children, regardless of color or creed have a right to believe in Santa Claus. It's been brought to our attention that the Santa Claus in our local stores where Negroes trade do not converse or pay the slightest attention to the Negro children who wish to talk to them. This tends to destroy their faith in the spirit of Christmas.

For surely the Christ Child was sent to save all men and thus Christmas belongs to all. We cannot afford in a Democracy to say that Santa Claus must discriminate between black and white.

A Group of Students of Avery Institute

With the Christmas rush on, the workdays stretched out to fourteen hours. Mr. Rolands and Mr. Godfrey had taken to hanging out in the basement, keeping an eye on things. Meliah Amey couldn't tell who they were watching most, Sam, to see if he was trying to recruit for the union, or young Rachel.

The next morning before dayclean, Meliah Amey knelt in prayer at the chapel, praying to Saint Martin de Pores, Saint Jude, and all the angels and saints to please hear her prayers and keep Rachel safe from the wickedness and snares of the devil.

Late in the afternoon, when Sam had finished up in the sterilization room and was back on the stemming floor trying to make sure the women didn't run out of tobacco to stem, Mr. Rolands Jr. came up to Binah just as Sam was turning around from setting down a box next to her.

"Binah," said Mr. Rolands Jr., "I need to see you in my office. I want to talk to you about something."

"What's the matter with you, Sam," said Mr. Rolands Jr., "I pay you to do what I tell you to do. And I told you to unload tobacco from these boxes."

Must have been a full hour before Binah came back down to take her place beside Meliah Amey. Binah's eyes were leaking and she kept gasping a little like she was trying to hold on to keep from breaking down."

Meliah Amey didn't think she could ever hate that man any more than she already did, that is until she saw Binah at that moment. Mr. Rolands must have found out about their plans to join the CIO, as well as who was leading the effort, too.

The next morning, as Meliah Amey came around the corner at the factory, people were walking in all directions, and no one was going in the door.

"The factory is closed," someone yelled. "Sign on the door says closed until further notice. Pay envelops can be picked up after eight o'clock."

Sam came up. "The whites over on Drake Street say they don't know any more than we do. A woman that stays in that house there, she say she saw trucks and people coming and going all last night."

Around eight in the morning, Mr. Godfrey came accompanied by two policemen. "The cigar factory is closed," he said. "If you don't move on after you get your pay envelope, we will arrest you for trespassing."

"When you gone open back up?" someone yelled out.

"We got no plans to reopen this factory," he answered.

Just like that, the week before Christmas, and one month before tuition was due for Vincent de Paul's final term at Avery.

Meliah Amey went back to the Shepard Street Chapel. She lit a candle, and fell to her knees in prayer.

"Madame Ravenel, ce qui est mal? What is wrong?"

She turned to see Sister Madelene, her grayish-blue habit stained with dirt from working in the yard. "Oh Sistuh," she said. "I need you to pray for us. The cigar factory locked the doors and shut down because we was fixing to sign the union cards right after Christmas."

Sister Madelene knelt down to pray, placing her hand on top of Meliah Amey's. "Blessed are the merciful, for they shall obtain mercy."

Chapter 35

By March, winter began to yield to spring, but the factory remained closed. Among the things Cassie chose to do without, one of them was voting. She couldn't spare the $1.50 for the poll tax, and because the amount accumulated each year, if she wanted to vote next time, she would have to pay $3.00. In the past, Mr. Rolands Jr. would offer to pay the tax for her provided she agreed not to vote for a New Deal candidate.

Cassie managed to pick up some work arranging flowers for McAlister's Funeral Home. Manus took on an extra transport to Rotterdam from Aruba just so they would be able to cover Patrick's spring term at Bishop England, as well as the rent for March. She despised being beholden to Manus for the roof over her head.

For a woman accustomed to working ten to fourteen hours a day, she hardly knew what to do with herself. Regardless of her knee pain, she walked every day all the way down to her old neighborhood to attend Mass and light a candle for the cigar factory to reopen and hire her back as an examiner. Patrick had mastered using the cast net for bait fish, but with the water still cold, pickings were slim. Cassie had some luck with speckled trout using a hand-held line she made herself. If they could hang on till the water warmed, maybe she could catch some good eating fish like flounder.

In the meantime, with his two-time-one gun, as the Negroes called a double barreled shotgun, Patrick hunted in the marsh behind Saint Lawrence and Magnolia cemetery. He brought home rabbits and marsh hens for her to cook. The marsh hen was not particularly good eating, no matter how long she soaked it in vinegar and water. As the saying went, the only thing she had plenty of was time.

And that was why she was home the morning Patrick came in early from school because he didn't feel well. She put him to bed with a hot-water bottle to ease the stiffness in his back and neck. In a few hours, however, he was worse. She went downstairs to Mr. Klein's apartment to use his phone and send for the medical doctor.

"It appears to be the beginning of the infantile paralysis," the doctor said. "Though it could be spinal meningitis. Bishop England has had cases of both recently. It's early in the year but looks like we're gonna be in for a bad spell this time." He spoke to Cassie on the landing outside the apartment so the boy wouldn't hear.

"Eee!" she exclaimed, cupping her hand over her mouth to silence herself. "Gawd in heaven, doctor, what can be done for him?"

"There's horse serum for meningitis, but more than half get the serum sickness."

"Eee!"

"His muscles are tender all ovuh, an he's very weak. Looks to me like poliomyelitis coming on."

"Doctor, can't you do sump'n for him at the hospital? We can't pay much but I swaytogawd, we get you the money in time. I swaytogawd we will."

"We only got one iron lung machine and the Alston girl is in it now. Let's watch your boy over the next few days and see how things go."

Cassie went downstairs to Mr. Klein's again.

"Mr. Klein," she pleaded, banging on his door. "You got to help me, please. I need you to find Father O'Shaughnessy from Saint Mary's parish down in the Borough. Please, tell him come quick. Tell him Cassie McGonegal's boy is very sick."

Two hours later, Mr. Klein returned. Patrick was sleeping.

"Father O'Shaughnessy said to tell you he has an engagement this afternoon and he doesn't have time to come this far north beforehand. He suggested you try the chapel over on Shepard Street since its closer to where you live now. You want me to run over there and see if I can find somebody?"

"Oh Mr. Klein, would you please. Thank you so much. And before you go, would you come in here an help me move Patrick's bed so it's lined up north to south?

Mr. Klein returned with Father Joubert. The priest anointed the boy with oil and a blessing to heal the sick. Then he joined Cassie in saying a rosary aloud.

Patrick started mumbling about his friend Seasar, the man who operated the train switch, the one who had taught him to throw the cast net. When he stopped mumbling the steps to casting, he started talking jibberish about seeing elephants and tigers on King Street.

"I will have one of the Sisters arrange to come over every day to help you nurse the boy," said Father Joubert as he was leaving. "I am here whenever you need me. The Sisters and I will keep him in our prayers."

"Thank you, Father," she said, closing the door behind him. She sat beside Patrick's bed all night, praying and keeping vigil.

The next day Patrick's fever continued to rage. Cassie went downstairs and knocked on Mr. Klein's door.

"How is he?"

"No better," she said. "Mr. Klein, I know I've burdened you already, but I need to ask you if you could please go find out where we are with the tide just now?"

"Excuse me?" he said.

"The tide," she said. "Is it ebbing or flooding? I can't see the water from here and I need to know."

"Well, I suppose I could go find that out," he answered with some reluctance.

"And Mr. Klein," she added, "we need a car."

"A car! Good God, woman, anything else?"

"Yes, I know your back is bad from the war, stay with him while I go find somebody that can carry him. I'll be back as fast as I can."

Cassie rushed down to the end of the street and started down the railroad tracks to the little box where the switch-man stayed.

"Your name Seasar?" she asked the Negro man sitting inside.

"Seasar not yah not yet," he said. "He come dayclean."

"Where he stay?" Cassie asked. "He an my boy Patrick are friends. I need his help." Cassie knew if she didn't explain, the man would never tell her the truth of where Seasar lived.

"Patrick your boy?" he said. "He an Tony be here all the time jabbing with Seasar."

"Patrick's very sick," she said.

"Seasar stay on Congress Street. Twenty-four Congress Street."

Some three hours later, they were loaded in the borrowed car with Mr. Klein at the wheel and Seasar beside him, Patrick wrapped in blankets in the backseat beside Cassie.

"Head for the bridge," she said, "We going to Sullivan's Island."

At the toll booth, Mr. Klein rolled down his window, and looked back to Cassie for the money.

"Shoooo! I don't have money for no damn toll" she snapped, leaning forward from the backseat. "Tell John Grace that Cassie McGonegal is gonna put the money for the toll in the collection basket at Saint Mary's Church on Sunday. Tell him that, now. Come on Mr. Klein, kick it in the fanny, we've got to get there while the tide is coming in."

Mr. Klein looked to the man sitting beside him for support. "Don't ask me," said Seasar. "I take the chance with the law over making she mad."

Mr. Klein stepped on the gas and they lurched away from the toll booth with the attendant waving his arms behind them.

The car labored up the steep span of the bridge.

When they reached Station 22 on Sullivan's Island, Seasar carried Patrick down the sandy path and through the dunes to the beach. Waves folded, broke, and raced up into the sand with white foamy margins leading the way. Cassie had wrapped Patrick in every blanket she owned.

"Kamba'boli bird singing," said Seasar, "tide not done risen not yet."

"Thank goodness," said Cassie, making her way through the thick sand. Seasar laid the boy down just above the high tide line, and Cassie pulled the cap down over his ears. Patrick's eyes opened a little and then he drifted back to sleep.

Gulls gathered overhead, but didn't linger. Neither did Mr. Klein.

"Too bad the big hotel burned," he said. "I'm gonna see if I can find a tavern open this time of year." He walked off down the beach.

Seasar sat in the sand beside Patrick. After awhile, Cassie did the same.

"My grandfather from Sligo once'd cured a man's fever this way. He said that when the tide turns, the waves carry the fever out to sea."

"Miss Cassie, it gonna be sun-lean before the ebb starts," he said. "And it won't be running good till f'us daa'k. But if it help this boy, that's alright," said Seasar, "that's alright."

The ebb peaked after dark. At fourteen, Patrick wasn't easy to carry, but Seasar managed. Cassie hoped to find Mr. Klein back at the car.

"You know," said Seasar as they made their way back through the dunes. "One of me'own brothers got stiff in the legs. Maum, she make a salve with lard from a buzzard. That's right, she make that salve and she tell me rub he legs with that buzzard salve. Miss Cassie, come dayclean, he moving he legs and that's the Gawd's truth."

Crazy darkie voodoo, she thought to herself.

"Seasar, how many brothers you got?"

"Eight," he said. "Maum had one girl and eight boys."

Cassie stopped suddenly. "Seasar, of your brothers, when were you born? You know, first son, second son?"

"I'm number seb'n," he said, shifting the boy in his arms to get him better situated.

"Really?" she said with interest.

"Yeah! And me'own Tata, he number seb'n of he brothers same as me."

"Shooo, chile!" said Cassie smiling. "Seasar, you're the seventh son of the seventh son. That means you got the healing gift. That's what cured your brother, not that ole buzzard salve. Put him down, put the boy down." Cassie pulled the blankets from Patrick's legs.

"Seasar, put your hand on his forehead and then rub his legs." Seasar did as she asked.

"Thank you, Seasar. Thank you now." Cassie knelt right there on the path to pray, never minding the sand spurs tearing her stockings.

Chapter 36

Meliah Amey stood outside the gate of the Avery Institute on Bull Street, looking up at the grand three-story brick building with its cupola on top. There was still a bite to the wind. This was the last day to pay for the spring term and she was far behind on the money to Mr. Logan for Vincent's music lessons. She had come to withdraw her son from the school.

Meliah Amey pushed open the gate, crossed the yard, and went up the front steps. Inside, it was quiet and full of promise. First, she heard the piano. A violin joined. She recognized Vincent's playing and went up the stairs to the auditorium where she had heard him play before.

The auditorium was a beautiful room with large windows and high ceilings that allowed the instruments a rich, abundant sound. She hung back from the doorway. Vincent de Paul on the piano, and Mr. Logan himself on violin. She did not know the names of the students on the other three instruments.

The piece had a pained beauty to it, as if it came from someone who knew what it meant to be on your knees in a storm and then, come dayclean, to stand up tall again.

And by the time he played the last note, Mr. Logan's violin bow was shedding long strands of hair. He wiped his brow with a crisp handkerchief and returned it, still neatly folded to the breast pocket of his suit. "Vincent, would you please accompany Miss Simmons for the spiritual. Let's start with 'Honor, Honor.'"

The young woman student did not sing a spiritual in the style of the women in the stemming department, but like Marian Anderson did when she came to the Morris Street Baptist Church.

"Mrs. Ravenel?" Mr. Logan spoke softly as he came out into the hallway. "Do you need to speak with Vincent?"

"I'm sorry," she said. "I didn't mean to disturb."

"Is anything wrong?" he asked.

She didn't want to say it. "What was that music you played just now?"

"Samuel Coleridge-Taylor's 'Piano Quintet.'"

"Sir, it was beautiful. I thank you very much for teaching my son all these years. Mr. Logan, I hardly can speak what I come to say. See, we can't pay you the money we owe for the lessons. Can't pay for the term neither. Today gone be Vincent's last day here at Avery."

"Mrs. Ravenel," he said sternly. "I've been working on a concert program to which we have invited Mayor Maybank, and Mr. Shaftesbury from the bank, among others. They need to learn that Charleston has a tradition of Negro musicians and composers trained in the classical style of playing. We're calling it *An Evening with Colored Composers*. Our people have used Negro melodies in the same way Brahms did with his Hungarian folk music. All of us here at Avery feel this is an extremely important concert. Mrs. Ravenel, no one can learn your son's part this close to the concert."

"I'm real sorry bout that, I am, but—" she swallowed hard—"see he didn't win the scholarship this term. Sir, we ain got the money."

"Let me speak to Mr. Cox. If I could get him to extend your deadline to May, could you pay then?"

In April, the fleet would return to the Blackfish Banks, and Joe would bring home more money. Maybe she could find work by then that paid more than washing and ironing. By May, maybe times wouldn't be so hard.

"Oh Mr. Logan, that'd be wonderful—wonderful—if you could talk with Mr. Cox." No matter what, she figured they couldn't make her son give back what he had learned come May.

She was crossing Meeting at Broad Street when she saw Binah seated in a chair sewing one of her baskets. She had set out other baskets on a blanket on the ground for the tourists to see. Francine was next to her selling flowers.

"Cigar factory gonna open back up again," said Binah.

"Shooo! True-mouth?" Meliah Amey asked.

"Oh yeah chile," she said. "Sam down there now. They already hired him to clean the place. He say they putting in machines down in the basement to do the stemming."

"Yeah? Before they say only thems that work the machines get paid for skill. Oh Binah, you think we gonna make what the white girls make?"

"Listen here, this the best part, Sam say the debble done gone to Cuba. They put him in charge of buying the tobacco down there. They got a new buckruh at the cigar factory now. Sam say he big an red in the face like he ain used to the Chaa'ston air."

"The Lord answered my prayers two ways: he opened the cigar factory and he got rid of the Gafa. Shooo! Today a good day, Binah. A very good day."

"I loss the baby on account of what that man done to me," said Binah. "And then we liked to starve with that place close up. I tell Sam, if the cigar factory hire me back, he gots to promise me—promise me—we ain messing with no more unions."

"Fuh true," answered Meliah Amey, smiling and blessing herself twice. "I swaytogawd that's fuh true."

Unlike Mr. Rolands, the new manager was friendly and never cussed at them. But the rate for piecework didn't change, and to earn Mr. Roosevelt's minimum wage he set the quota so high, Meliah Amey ended up soaked in sweat from collar to garters trying to meet it.

At first, Mr. Godfrey based the women's pay on the weight of the leaves after the machines discarded the stems, but when he realized their sweat was adding to the weight of the leaves, he went back to having their tobacco weighed before the stems came out.

Meliah Amey kept her mouth shut, considering herself lucky to have a job that paid three to four times as much as washing and ironing.

Come June, every indignity she had ever endured at that place paid off when she, Maum Lizzy, and Joe took their seats in the auditorium of the Avery Institute on Bull Street to hear the graduating class of 1935 sing Handel's "Hallelujah Chorus."

Chapter 37

Patrick called out in the wee hours of the night, and Cassie rushed to his room, where she found him sitting up. "Aunt Cassie," he said. "There's sand in my bed," he said. Slowly, he pushed off the covers and cautiously stood to brush away the sand.

When two weeks passed without the boy experiencing paralysis, the doctor insisted that Patrick must have had the nonparalyzing form of the disease. Manus took leave of his ship when it docked in New York and caught the train for Charleston. For days, he hardly left the boy's bedside.

Soon after, word went out all over town that the cigar factory was going to reopen.

Columbus Street was packed with men and women. A barker directed the Negroes to Bay Street and the white workers to Drake.

The new manager, Mr. Wilkerson, said everyone had to fill out a piece of paper and write down his or her name, and if they had worked there before, what sort of job they used to do.

Cassie worried about her spelling but did the best she could as she wrote down *e-x-a-m-n-e-r* on the paper, blessed herself, and then walked back to Poinsette Street. The camellia blossoms had never looked prettier, and soon, the azaleas would bloom again.

"I liked that one," said Patrick. "Read 'Oh Captain, My Captain' again."

"Manus, really," said Cassie. "You wearing the boy out."

Manus stopped mid-sentence, offended.

"No, Aunt Cassie," Patrick insisted. "I love it when Pop reads that way. Honest."

Manus needed no further encouragement and continued. *"The ship has weathered every rack, the prize we sought is won—"*

Green Peas! Sugar Peas!

The vegetable lady sang out down in the street. She didn't always come that far north. Cassie grabbed a bowl from the cupboard and hurried out to catch the woman with the basket of fresh vegetables upon her head.

Manus was still carrying on as Cassie rinsed the peas and put them in a pot upon the stove.

Manus got a beer from the icebox. "I think I'll go down to that Poetry Society with them blue bloods, see if they'll let an old Geechee like me join."

"Oh Manus," she said, "don't be ridiculous."

"I'm serious," he said, taking a long sip. "You ain got to have money to know poetry. Shooo! There was this colored sailor on the ship with me once. Langston was his name, Langston Hughes. He was all the time writing stuff down. So one evening, I saw him, and I said to him, 'What you writing?' and he said, 'Poetry.' I'll be damn, I thought to myself, a Negro poet. When we made call here, me and him were behind one another on the gangway. I asked him if he knew anybody here—you know, I didn't want him getting in trouble going someplace he shouldn't. He says to me, 'I'm going to see Teddy Harleston, the artist.' I said, 'You mean the colored undertaker Teddy Harleston?' He said, 'I don't know if he's an undertaker, but I know he's a fine artist.' Miss Cassie, did you know that Teddy Harleston is a painter and that people outside of here have heard of him?"

"Since I never had need for a colored undertaker, why would I know sump'n like that bout the Harlestons?"

"How many times do you think I've walked past their funeral home on Calhoun Street going to the K.C. Hall with no idea one of them was an artist."

Cassie didn't feel the need to respond. She kept her attention on mixing egg and milk for macaroni pie, hoping he would make his point soon and be done for a while.

"I'd like to read what that colored sailor has to say. I would. If I ever see a book on the shelf with his name on it, Langston Hughes, I'm gonna buy it, and that's the Gawd's truth."

"You go to the library all the damn time. Don't they have enough books to read for free without spending money on the jabberings of some colored man?" Cassie added a spoon of mustard to her mixing bowl.

By the time the macaroni pie was done, Manus had fallen asleep on the sofa. Cassie woke him with a nudge. "Run this plate down to Seasar before it gets cold."

The new manager, Mr. Wilkerson, hired both Gretta and Cassie back as final examiners. Mr. Wilkerson, unlike the Rolands men, always made a point of saying how much he appreciated Cassie's hard work.

"I've got a responsibility to three folks," he liked to say. "My stockholders, my customers who smoke the cigars, and my employees. You girls do what's good for the company and the company will do what's good for you."

But other than him smiling and patting them on the back, things weren't much different than before. Cassie found herself recalling Brigid when she had shocked Cassie by casually repeating the words of her sailor husband: *You can piss on me but don't try to tell me it's raining.*

Cassie would come home to find Manus and Patrick practicing to see who could render a more dramatic recitation of poetry. Cassie was more than ready for Manus to head back to sea, but it was obvious that the best medicine for Patrick had been the time spent with his father. However, as Patrick got stronger, Manus slipped further into old habits.

One evening in May, Cassie turned onto Poinsette Street and heard Manus carrying on while she was still a block away. He was on the porch downstairs with Mr. Klein.

"People see things different ovuh dare," Manus babbled loudly.

Manus and Mr. Klein were passing a bottle between them.

"I got a girl in Rotterdam," said Manus proudly, slapping Mr. Klein on the back, who winced in pain from the force.

Cassie's jaw dropped. She stopped in her tracks.

"Listen to me, Klein," Manus continued. "I know you fought in the war, same as me. Everything we fought for is going down the hole and nobody gives a damn. Germany has retaken Saarland. You remember Saarland; lots of manufacturing plants there. When I think about it, I go nuts. We can't fight that same war over again. If a guy like me can see that Germany is rebuilding its army, how come France and the U.S. don't do something?"

"Don't think about it," said Mr. Klein. "It will only make you crazy."

"No, no, listen to me. They've passed a law forcing the Jews into jobs for guys like me, you know, picking up garbage and stuff, even though the men are educated. Hell, I heard some of the Jew garbage men were college professors and such, but they won't let them work at the universities, either. And there's talk of passing a law that says if you got any Jew blood in you at all—at all—they gonna take away your rights to be a German citizen. So Klein, what do you make of it?"

Mr. Klein stood up indignantly. "I'm an American. I have no opinion of how Germany treats its citizens. Why are you telling me all this?"

Cassie walked toward the porch. If Manus didn't go back to sea soon, none of the neighbors would be speaking to her.

"I tell you because I think you need to know. If you have any family over there, well—"

"I'm just like the next guy, an American with my own troubles. Leave me be."

As Cassie came up the steps, Mr. Klein went inside his apartment, slamming the door behind him.

Manus was standing now, holding to the railing for support, his eyes red and watering.

"I didn't mean to make him mad, Miss Cassie, but he needs to know. If any of his people ask him for help, he needs to understand how bad it is over there."

"Did you look for a job today?" she asked.

"Shipyard ain hiring," he said, sitting down hard in Mr. Klein's chair and taking another sip from the bottle.

"You must not be looking hard enough," she said. "I hear the asbestos plant is hiring. Shooo! They pay good money at the asbestos plant."

Three days later, Manus went back to sea with his old shipping company, the Nederland Line. In April the Azalea Festival marked spring's arrival. Cassie lit a dollar's worth of candles at Saint Mary's giving thanks that Patrick was strong enough to go with her to the Battery to watch the annual Tugboat Fleet race between the Cooper and Ashley River Bridges.

It would be 1939 with Holland barely clinging to neutrality and most of Europe at war before Manus came home for a full-time job as the Charleston Navy Shipyard shifted to a wartime footing. Because Manus was home, he and Cassie were both in attendance as the choir sang *Panis Angelicus* while Patrick and the rest of the Bishop England class of 1939 marched into the auditorium for graduation.

PART V

1941–1946

Chapter 38

It was so warm that first week of December that an azalea bush near Brigid's grave bloomed. Cassie and Patrick had taken the bus to Saint Lawrence cemetery to pay their respects, just as they did every Sunday after Mass.

"Gawd rest her soul," said Patrick blessing himself after kneeling in prayer.

"Gawd rest her soul and all the souls of the faithful departed," said Cassie, also kneeling on the marble step that marked the O'Brian family plot.

Patrick and Cassie pulled weeds that had begun to grow in the unseasonably warm weather.

"Paper say it going to go to seventy-two degrees today," said Cassie, reaching for Patrick. With one hand, he easily helped her up. Carrying stacks of empty bins for the cigar makers had put muscle on his bones. Patrick had not grown much taller than his father, but he was every bit as strong.

When he graduated from high school, Patrick tried and tried to get on with one of the tugboats or to work with the harbor pilots, but those men had their own sons to hire. The shipyard wanted skilled electricians and machinists. After several disappointing weeks of looking for a job on the waterfront, Patrick went to Cadora College, where he was hired on as a stock boy.

"It's warm enough for me to go swimming and poor Pop's out there somewhere in the cold North Atlantic."

"Your daddy a damn fool for leaving a good job here in town," said Cassie, brushing dirt from her dress. When Germany bombed Rotterdam and the call went out for merchant seaman to help transport vital supplies to Europe, Manus dropped everything—and everyone—and went to sea. Cassie realized she shouldn't speak to Patrick of what she saw as Manus's supreme lack of judgment. Why go to sea when every day brought news of Germany sinking another merchant ship bringing aid to Britain?

"I'd rather take my chances at sea than spend ten hours a day at stinking Cadora College."

"Quit if you hate it that much. Shooo! Don't mek no difference to me where you work, long as you got a job."

He walked ahead of her then, his head down as if he were trying to figure something out. Cassie could see that he was wanting to break free of her.

They stopped at John Grace's grave. His Cooper River Bridge towered above the marsh where he lay in eternal rest, no doubt counting the cars.

"I still owe you one toll," she said, smiling. "Listen here, Patrick," she said as they continued on their way. "I got tummetuh sauce and bacon to make us some red rice. That sound good to you?"

"Aunt Cassie, I won't be home for dinner. I'm going to the movies with Tony and some other people."

"What's showing?"

"It's got Errol Flynn and Olivia de Havilland."

"I love Olivia de Havilland," she said, regretting it right away.

"You wanna come?" he said, straining to sound as if he meant it.

"Me? Why would I wanna go? I got to iron my smocks. Shooo! I don't wanna go to no picture show."

They were on Meeting Street and it was time for her to cross over since she was heading back home and Patrick was on his way downtown. As she started across the street, she got a shooting pain in her right knee and it buckled. She caught herself and managed not to fall. A car horn blew.

"Go to hell," Patrick cursed the driver as he charged in front of it to get to Cassie's side.

"Aunt Cassie, you alright?" He took her arm to help across the busy street.

"Let go of me," she snapped, pulling her arm away from him. "I ain no invalid. Patrick go on and leave me be."

Cassie was in the kitchen washing up the dishes and listening to the radio broadcast of the football game. The New York Giants were playing the Brooklyn Dodgers.

> *We interrupt this program to bring you a special news bulletin. The Japanese have attacked Pearl Harbor Hawaii by air. President Roosevelt has just announced that he will be asking Congress for a declaration of war . . .*

Still in her apron, Cassie went downstairs, hoping to see Mr. Klein out on his porch. But he was not there. The news was too terrible to bear alone. She went out on the sidewalk and walked up to King Street. Cars were stopped and people were getting out to talk about what had happened. When she went back home, she smelled cigarette smoke beneath Mr. Klein's door. Despite the mild weather, he had his windows closed and his curtains drawn.

Not long after, she heard Patrick pounding across the front porch and running up the steps. "Aunt Cassie, did you hear what's happened? We're at war with Japan!" he yelled, bursting into the living room with a special edition of the paper. Cassie sat in her chair, head bowed, rosary beads in hand, the room nearly dark.

He would not be able to tell her that night; in fact, he would not be able to tell her at all. He would leave her a letter upon the kitchen table, beneath the Infant of Prague. In it, he would say how much he loved her and how hard it was for him to leave her all alone. Of course, she knew all this long before the night she would come home from work to find the letter on the table. She knew it beyond any doubt from the way he bounded up the stairs that Sunday afternoon. And that was why she continued to pray even as he waited for her to look up and say something about what had happened. And only after she had blessed herself and kissed the crucifix did she summon the strength to raise her head and meet his eye.

"My Patrick," was all she said.

Chapter 39

Miss Huger was the only one on Bedon's Alley who had both electricity and a radio. Every night since the attack, Meliah Amey and her family went to Miss Huger's house to listen to the latest news. That night, Mayor Lockwood addressed the city, informing them of President Roosevelt's order banning the sale of tires for three weeks so that military vehicles could be supplied first. The mayor reminded them that the Navy base and the shipyard made Charleston an enemy target, and to that end, he called upon citizens to forget personalities and inconveniences and to assist in the country's war effort. National guards had been requested for the Cooper River Bridge, and he called upon residents of Folly Beach and the other islands to register for Civil Defense Work. To help pay for war-related projects, Mayor Lockwood let them know that he was canceling the Azalea Festival for the following year.

They walked home with a wind blowing in come-and-go bursts. People living on the alley sat on their porches, discussing the attack and if Charleston might be next.

"I'm joining the Navy," said Vincent de Paul. "I talked to a recruiter today on King Street."

"Mother of Gawd," Meliah Amey shrieked.

"You smart, Ajani," said Joe. "But this I know better. Recruiter say it gone be one way, but when you get there, they say nigger clean them dirty dishes. Say nigger can't be puntop deck."

"Mr. Roosevelt signed an order for the Navy to integrate," Vincent de Paul replied. "The recruiter said a colored man can pick between the Attendant Branch and the Seaman-Fireman Branch. The president himself gave the order. We got a chance to prove ourselves."

"I thought you were saving your money for the college in Orangeburg," his mother said. "Ajani, please, listen to your Tata. He true-mouth."

"I won't sign for you," said Joe, walking away.

"I don't need your signature," he called to his father. "Maum, please, come my side."

"Eee! Eee!" Meliah Amey cried out, "Ajani, don't join the Navy. Please."

Vincent de Paul put his arms around his mother. "This war gonna change everything for us. Please, Maum, come my side."

The cigar factory was considered a wartime industry as it supplied the military with an endless stream of Petite Royales and Cadora cigars. Fewer women showed up in the mornings on Bay Street, but Mr. Godfrey continued his inspections as he had always done, requesting this one to bend, that one to reach, all of them to stoop—he kept an eye for the ones that most pleased him, but with so many cooking and cleaning jobs at the Navy base, most weeks he had to take whoever showed up.

There were so many white people coming to Charleston for shipyard jobs, the government built them apartments north of the Neck near the Navy base. New houses went up west of the Ashley River and even east of the Cooper. Meliah Amey had never seen so many white people. The buses could be so crowded sometimes one wouldn't even stop for her. Because of the extra time it now took to get to work in the mornings, she had to skip the fisherman's Mass with Joe.

Despite all the new housing built for the influx of white workers, the residents of Bedon's Alley still had to use an outdoor privy. And when the city ran electricity to Meliah Amey's house, she didn't mind paying the power company for the juice to operate the lights. What galled her was the fact that the Shaftesbury family decided to raise the rent $10.00 a month. Like many things, electricity arrived as a Drunken Dick.

Drunken Dick was an area of water off Sullivan's Island near the north jetties. For years she had heard Joe and the men of the fleet speak of it and the danger it presented to the unsuspecting sailors. Never having been near the jetties herself, Meliah Amey imagined that the name referred to a place where the current held people or objects, swirling them left and then right, just as she had observed Joe's boozed-up member to behave under similar circumstances.

When Joe eventually clarified to her that Drunken Dick was not a current at all but a shoal named for sailor named Dick who got drunk, ran aground there and drowned, Meliah Amey was disappointed. She refused to give up her own definition for the term, using it to describe any situation that on the surface appeared to be smooth sailing and a step forward, but instead turned out to be merely a lurch to the side. It didn't matter if she stemmed tobacco by hand or fed it to a machine, the company had a way of lengthening the workday, or raising the quota so they never got the wage the law guaranteed. When they met the minimum, Mr. Godfrey would say the law didn't apply to them because they were agricultural workers, same as a field hand, and the minimum wage law didn't apply to farmers and field hands. Meliah Amey never got ahead, nor did she sink to the bottom. Her pay envelope bobbed around all those years, stuck in a Drunken Dick kind of current.

"I swear, you bout the slowest darkie I ever seen," Mr. Godfrey shouted over the noise of the stemming machine. Meliah Amey looked up to see that he was again yelling at Francine. With the demand for workers up, she had set aside her flower basket and come back to the factory.

During the break, Meliah Amey and others rushed to the ladies' room. There were no doors surrounding the commodes. While waiting her turn, Meliah Amey spoke with Francine.

"How your chillun?" Meliah Amey asked.

"They good," said Francine. "I got one boy in the Army; he work in the mess hall for the camp in San Francisco. Another, he in the Navy working to load and unload they ship. An another boy, he work at the asbestos plant, same as my girl."

When it came Francine's turn, Meliah Amey stood in front, with her back to Francine. This was a system the women had learned to give one another a little privacy, and to provide a shield against the foreman's intrusions.

"How bout your boy?" Francine inquired.

"He up in the snow at Camp Robert Smalls where the Navy trains the colored sailors."

"Camp Robert Smalls," said another woman. "Shoo! Smalls be a Chaa'ston name."

"My name Smalls," said the woman next to her, adjusting her uniform back in place.

"Can't you women take a piss any faster?" Without knocking or anything, Mr. Godfrey came right on in the ladies' room. "I'm docking every one of you by two pounds. Now hurry up." He had inherited Mr. Rolands's riding crop and he slapped it against the sink to emphasize his point. He stood there, waiting for them to leave.

"'E de mores Gafa," Meliah Amey said quietly to herself as she walked past him, looking down at the dust-covered shoes of the most evil spirit.

Meliah Amey got off the bus and walked down Saint Michael's Place in a cold drizzle. The blackout curtains and the absence of street lights made it even darker. She hurried by the cemetery. Inside, Joe had a fire going in the wood-stove. He sat in his chair with the evening paper in one hand and a magnifying glass in the other.

"I need practice reading," he said. "Ajani not here no more to make out the words for me. You read good, Tana. You could have been a teacher like the ones they got at the Avery. With more schooling, you could have been a teacher."

"You sweetmouth me," she said.

"Naw, Tana. I tell the trute," he said.

She went in the bedroom to change out of her uniform.

"Got speckled trout for supper," he called out. "We gone up the Wando today to get out the wind."

"Joe, is that camp where Ajani be, could it be named for one of the Chaa'ston Smalls?"

"Oh yeah!" he said. "That camp named for the slave that dressed up in the rebel captain's clothes when the captain came in town one night to go to West Street."

"Shooo! You don't know that," she said, sticking her head in the living room.

"The white officers went ashore, now where you think they going go?" Joe put the magnifying glass down and lit his pipe. "Robert Smalls in the fleet. He say the back-back Robert Smalls took the ship named the *Plantar*—them rebels must have thought a colored man didn't know how to sail a big ship like that."

Meliah Amey went to stand by the woodstove to get warm, and listen to the story.

"He plan it all out. That night he pick up he family at the wharf. Then he sail that rebel gunboat past Fort Sumter. He hoist the white flag when he getting near to the union blockade. Robert Smalls give the union the map to show where the rebels put the mines. Then he teach them the currents, shows them where they might run aground at low water. He teach them everything he know bout this haa'buh. President Lincoln say he going to make Smalls a Navy officer, but even back then, the union Navy say no to having a colored captain. Very well then, said the president, I make Robert Smalls an Army officer but he still gone be the Captain of the *Plantar* gunboat an he still gone fight for the Union."

It was different, just the two of them in the house. So quiet. Almost lonely. Meliah Amey looked over at Joe beside their one reading lamp, the paper falling out of his lap and onto the floor. She smiled, walked over and kissed him on top of his shiny bald head. Then she went back to the cupboard, pulled the iron skillet down from the shelf, put it on the stove to heat, while she married up the flour and egg for the fish.

Chapter 40

Cassie placed her label, # 37, in the cigar box, closed the lid, and sent it down the line to Salvatore in shipping.

"Good job," said Mr. Wilkerson, all smiles, as he made his daily rounds through the packing department. "Miss Cassie, how's that nephew of yours? He's in the Navy, right?"

"He in the Aleutian Islands," she said. "I pray Gawd every day—every day—to keep him safe."

"Amen," said Mr. Wilkerson, placing his hand on her shoulder. Her neck was bothering her from looking down and the pressure of his hand only made it worse. "Keep up the pace, Miss Cassie. We've all got to do our part for the soldiers."

"Mr. Wilkerson," she called to him as he was walking away. "How bout that five-cent raise I asked you bout last month?"

"Oh that's right," he said. "To tell you the truth, I haven't had time to put pay raise requests into the War Labor Board. Government's got to approve any change in pay these days. Ridiculous if you ask me, but I haven't forgotten."

She liked Mr. Wilkerson fine. However, it was beginning to dawn on her that all his pats on the back never amounted to more money in her pay envelope come Saturday.

"Buon giorno, Salvatore," she heard Mr. Wilkerson say. "My neighbors back in Philly were Italians. Listen, thanks for staying late yesterday to help move equipment. Tell me, how's your boy? He's in the Army, right?"

"Marines," Salvatore corrected him indignantly. "Lance Corporal Anthony Giordano with the U.S. Marines."

Cassie kept her head down. Patrick had written to her how he and Tony went to the Navy recruiter's office on King Street together. Only, the Navy didn't take Tony so he went next door to the Marines, and they accepted him.

At lunchtime, Cassie and Gretta walked to the cafeteria together.

"I don't know any of these girls," said Cassie. "Seems they hire new ones every day."

"I saw Sue Ann at the A&P, you know the one from up in the hills. She's got a job at the shipyard now. She said building a destroyer is easier than making cigars. They pay fifteen cent more an hour. Lots of girls wanna work at the shipyard, but the Labor Board won't approve for them to leave the cigar factory."

"The Labor Board know that if they let everyone leave for the shipyard, won't be no girls left making cigars for the soldiers."

"Ain you heard?" said Gretta. "Salvatore and all the men had to work late last night. Say they brought in new cigar making machines for the third floor."

"Shooo! Who they gonna get to run them?"

"That's what everybody's talking bout," she said, keeping her voice low. "One of the mechanics told me that Mr. Wilkerson gonna put colored women on the third floor to make cigars."

"Say what?" said Cassie, not believing her ears.

"Yes, ma'm. Colored women gonna be making cigars."

They sat down at the table with their sack lunches.

"We never gonna see another raise out of this place, and that's the Gawd's truth."

It was dark when she left work. A cold silvery mist hung in the air. The cigar factory had become a night-and-day operation, and Cassie weaved her way through the crowd of women arriving for their shift.

"Hey, Cadora College girl," a sailor yelled out his window to the young woman walking in front of Cassie. "Come on, sugar, let me buy you a drink."

The young woman stopped suddenly, considering his offer, and when Cassie bumped into her, the abrupt stop sent a sharp pain through her right knee. "He won't be so interested when he gets a whiff of yuh uniform," she said into the girl's ear. Cassie normally kept such comments to herself but she was cold, tired, and in pain.

"Durn bus," she said when she reached Meeting Street. "They never run on time like the trolleys did." She bought an evening paper to read the article about the ongoing battle for the Solomon Islands. She hadn't heard from Patrick in weeks.

Traffic was at a standstill. Charleston simply wasn't big enough to hold all the sailors stationed at the Navy base plus all the civilians coming for jobs at the Navy Shipyard. And the people, thought Cassie, with their funny accents and bad manners. A man and a woman stood next to her waiting on the bus without as much as a nod of the head.

A Negro man walked past, "Ebenin" he said to her, tipping his hat.

"Good ebenin," she returned enthusiastically, looking at the couple as if to say, See? We greet one another in Charleston, no matter who you are.

Finally, a crowded bus arrived. Cassie thanked the man who gave up his seat for her near the front. Before the bus pulled away, three Negro sailors boarded, paid their fare, and took hold of a pole next to Cassie.

Must be from somewhere else, thought Cassie. She didn't care if they stood there or not, she just wanted to get home.

"You boys got to move to the back," said the driver.

The sailors appeared not to be listening.

"Hey, fellows," said the driver, "Don't know where you're from, but I know where you at, and you got to move back."

"No, sir," said one of them.

"Say what?" the driver snapped.

"No, sir," said another. "We're American citizens. We're not moving to the back."

"Like hell you ain," said the driver, opening the door, with a gun in his hand.

"Eee! Eee!" screamed Cassie and the other women.

Cassie blessed herself.

"Crazy cracker," said one of the sailors.

"Get off my bus," the driver insisted.

The three of them got off the bus without another word.

Lord, have mercy, she thought. What if that driver had fired his gun on this crowded bus?

When she finally got home, she was cheered to find a letter from Patrick in the box. She poured herself a shot of Jameson to calm her nerves and ease the pain in her knee.

Dear Aunt Cassie,

I have been on this transport ship for three days now. Scheduled to arrive Frisco tomorrow then leave for South Pacific. I skippered an LST. Felt bad

217

for them soldiers in Kiska. I would get the LST close as I could to shore and then lower the ramp in the bow and those poor soldiers with all their gear would charge out into the cold waves trying to make their way to the beach in the dark. Some of them don't make it.

When we were leaving Temnac Bay we came upon a ship, the S.S. Hascall, that was on the rocks. We searched for survivors in the water but saw no traces. Figured another ship must have picked them up. I secured a line to her and managed to jump on deck despite heavy seas. No one was onboard but the chow was still on the men's plates. Don't tell anyone but I raided the liquor supplies and brought it back to my guys.

On Sunday morning they announced that we were having a church service on this tub. I asked the Petty Officer if it was a priest having the service. He said no, a Baptist Preacher. I said, no thank you, I'm a Catholic. So it was me, a Jew, an atheist, and some guy, I don't know what he was— Hindu or something, and the four of us played cards because it wasn't our religion at the prayer service. They're good guys. I had three of a kind one hand and a full house the next. I won $20.

I miss you and I pray for you every day.

Love,
Patrick

The apartment was too quiet without Patrick. And Manus? She hadn't heard from him in months, which was unusual. She wondered how she would know if something had happened to him.

She read in the paper about the battle in the Solomon Islands, and then she read about a court case the Negro teachers of Charleston had brought against the school board. They were asking to be paid same as the white teachers. She poured herself another sip of Jameson. That was interesting to her. The Negro teachers were suing for more money? She'd never heard of such a thing. She thought of the plan to have Negro women cigar makers. Maybe Mr. Wilkerson didn't understand the darkies the way Mr. Rolands did. All the businessmen in Charleston said if you wanted a Negro to show up six days a week, you had to pay him for the four days that you'd pay a white. Otherwise, the Negro would go fishing the other two days.

She read the article. A Negro lawyer named Thurgood Marshall had come down from up North to represent the colored teachers. And Judge Waring, a man from a good South of Broad family, had decided the case in favor of the colored teachers. "I swaytogawd," said Cassie out loud. She took a sip of whiskey. "Sump'n bout this war has gotten into the coloreds and Judge Waring, too."

Chapter 41

At 3 A.M. on June 6, 1944, the bells of Saint Michael's began to ring. Meliah Amey and Joe went out into the alley, joining others walking to Miss Huger's house, where the light was still on. With the radio broadcast playing in her living room, she came out on the porch to tell them the news. "He say the liberation of Europe has begun. They calling it D-Day."

Meliah Amey and Joe blessed themselves as they bowed their heads, joining the others in prayer.

Vincent de Paul was stationed along with 150 other Negro men on the destroyer U.S.S. *Mason*, or as he said in his letter: "The rest of the Navy call our ship *Eleanor's Folly* on account of it being no secret Mrs. Roosevelt was the one that wanted full integration in the military."

Meliah Amey prayed for all the soldiers who were, at that very moment, making their way onto Normandy Beach, though she didn't know if her son's ship was involved.

Saint Michael's bells rang throughout the night, muted only by the sound of the wind before dayclean. Then other churches began to ring their bells as well. Meliah Amey walked to work; it was faster than riding the bus. Everywhere, she observed men and women, colored and white, their faces concerned, their eyes puffy from lack of sleep. She and Joe were out of rice—unthinkable for anybody from Charleston—because they had used up their ration coupons for it already. As the bells rang throughout the peninsula that morning, even the lack of rice was not a burden. The sound of the bells peeling, chiming, and clanging bound them all together in purpose and resolve. She passed a poster at the corner of Calhoun and Bay Street, showing a soldier with muscles rippling, and the words: *Support Our Men Overseas: Pay Willingly Your Share of Taxes and Obey Rationing Rules.*

She heard the bells even from inside the Bay Street stairwell as she climbed the steps. She heard them as she and Binah and the other Negro women collected their tobacco bundles from the stock boy. She heard the bells right up until the roar of the cigar-making machines consumed every other sound.

Every four seconds, Meliah Amey applied a wrapper leaf to the preset die for cutting. Binah worked a few machines over, feeding a filler leaf, one after the other, after the other. Meliah Amey couldn't even look away for a few seconds without risking getting out of sync, tearing the wrapper leaf, or any number of ways it seemed that caused the machine to jam.

"I thought colored women were supposed to be fast," Mr. Godfrey shouted. "If you can't do better, I got plenty more down the basement to take your place."

The church bells celebrating the cause of democracy in Europe were still ringing as Meliah Amey, Binah, and Sam Maybank sat in the shade of a live oak tree eating their sack lunches.

"Yeah, I like the extra three dollars a week fine," said Binah. "But we still wear these ugly-ass blue uniforms, and we can't eat in the cafeteria with the white girls."

"I don't wanna eat with them so much as I wanna get paid same as them for doing the same job," said Meliah Amey, slicing up a tomato, and taking a bite. "Oh Lord! This tummetuh good." She offered some to her friends.

"Thank you," said Binah, taking a slice. "They paying us better to make cigars but the foreman still coming in the ladies' room, and they still trying to fumble our behinds."

"I'm telling you, it's hot all over the country," said Sam.

"Ummm, you said that right, this yah tummetuh good," said Binah.

"Royal Cigar know they beat," said Sam. "The War Labor Board done ruled that every one of us gets a ballot to vote for one of three choices: AFL, CIO, or no union. It's got to be the CIO. They not afraid to say equal pay for equal work. Now the company, they gonna be trying to get the white girls and the mechanics to join the AFL. See, the AFL say they for fair wages for the Negro, but they don't want the stemmers or any of us down the basement in they union. I'm talking with a man in the shipping department named Salvatore an he supports the CIO. Salvatore true-mouth."

"All I know," said Binah, "is the last time we bout got the union, they shut this place down and we liked to starve."

"Shooo! Ain gonna happen this time," said Sam. "The War Labor Board going to be in charge of the election and counting the votes. With the shipyard hiring white girls, Royal Cigar got to give sump'n up for a change."

Chapter 42

"Alright, them bells have got everybody rattled," said the foreman. "Best thing for our boys overseas is make them a good cigar. Now let's get busy."

Cassie took a seat on her stool, turned on her light, and opened her first box of the day. Color, shape, and direction of the roll were consistent, and the bands were aligned perfectly. She flipped the box upside down, opening the lid slightly to view the edge of the top row. The filler tobacco appeared uniformly brown, and spaced evenly—neither too tight, nor too loose. She put her # 37 on the box and sent it on to be sealed for shipping.

Cassie went to the lunchroom and actually bought a plate lunch. She had not slept for listening to the radio and saying the rosary after the church bells had begun to ring.

As Cassie was taking her seat, one of the Flaherty girls at the table said, "I'm voting for the AFL because we don't need outsiders telling us how to get along with our colored."

"Listen here," said another, "they're paying us twenty-three dollars a week to make cigars and they're paying them thirteen. If the niggers don't get paid the same as us, who you think gonna be out of work before long?"

"Sal told me that the CIO plans to set the pay rates for each job," said Gretta. "If you ask me, that's what we need. I been here a long time. It don't ever change. Supervisor gonna pay some girl more than another. And too many times, what he put in her pay envelope got more to do with what she done for him than how many cigars she made."

"That part sounds fine," said the Flaherty girl, "but I don't want to work alongside the coloreds."

"The head of the CIO told Sal that the white and the colored gonna be kept separate," said Gretta. "We won't have meetings with them or have to work next to them, but they going to get paid same as us. I don't see how anybody—anybody—can object to that. You can't vote for the AFL," she implored the Flaherty girl. "The AFL won't recognize the packers as being skilled and them girls only bringing home eighteen dollars a week. A week!"

"The war is making Chaa'ston crazy," said another girl. "My boyfriend's a bailiff an he told me that Judge Waring made a rule that Negroes in his courtroom must be called Mr. or Mrs. Whatever. My boyfriend say if you got any case coming before Judge Waring these days that's got to do with a darkie, Waring's gonna rule for the darkie."

"Shooo!" the entire table scoffed.

"Say what?" said Cassie.

"I heard the families below Broad won't even speak to Judge Waring. Not since he divorced and married that Yankee they call the Witch of Meeting Street. I swaytogawd, I heard the Warings have the colored sitting with them at the suppuh table."

"Oh Lord! Shoo!"

"My mother told me that Judge Waring's morals are questionable," said the Flaherty girl. "She told me he used to spend a lot of time on West Street."

"What man in this town ain?" asked Gretta.

"Miss Cassie, who you gonna vote for, the CIO or the AFL?" the Flaherty girl asked.

Cassie wasn't about to share her voting intentions with anyone. "I haven't decided," she said, standing up to take her tray back to where the Negro women washed them. "I did have some questions for Sal. Anyone seen him today?"

"Out sick is what I heard," said Gretta.

"Sick!" Cassie couldn't believe it. Sal was like her, and the two of them never stayed out sick, no matter how bad they felt.

With the five-thirty change of shift, Cassie made her way up Columbus toward Meeting Street to catch the bus. The bells were silent. A breeze was up and the palmetto branches made their stiff scraping sound as they whipped back and forth. Girls waved for their rides, car horns honked. The somber tone of the morning had lifted.

Cassie felt lucky to find a seat on the crowded bus, even if it was in the colored section. "Ebenin," she said to the woman wearing a black dress with a white apron.

"Ebenin," the woman replied.

It was the same driver who had pulled the gun on the Negro sailors. Cassie found herself imagining what she would say if the driver stood up, pointed his gun at her, and told her she couldn't sit next to the Negro woman. The driver shut the door when the last passenger boarded and they were off without delay.

Cassie closed her eyes, giving in to the relief of not having to look at another cigar that night. When she heard the woman next to her sniffle, she knew it was the smell of ammonia from her uniform that irritated the woman's nose.

The bus slowly made its way north toward the Neck. When Cassie opened her eyes she noticed, under her shoe, a dirty morning newspaper. She would always wonder what compelled her to pick up that nasty paper. But something did, and that is where she read that Lance Corporal Anthony Giordano with the U.S. Marines had been killed in the Solomon Islands. Patrick's best friend. "Gawd rest his soul," she said softly.

Cassie took the steps to her apartment one at a time. She heard the sound of her radio and briefly paused before turning the key. She opened the door slowly. The electric fan was on, too. She stepped inside. There on the sofa was Manus, sound asleep. His sea bag beside him on the floor. His nose twitched, detecting something unpleasant, and then he woke up.

"Ah, the sweet smell of the cigar factory," he said. "Aunt Cassie, how you been? You glad to see me?"

"For the moment, I guess I am," she answered. "Where in the hell have you been?"

"Ever heard of Murmansk?" he said. "I been stuck in the Russian Arctic waiting for enough ships to make it over to form a convoy back home. That's where I been. How's Patrick? He alright?"

"Far as I know, he alright," she said. "I pray Gawd for him every day."

Manus blessed himself, and said a prayer of thanks. Cassie had no idea of these places Manus described. But she did know that arctic meant snow and ice.

From outside came the song of a street vendor.

Old Joe Cole—Good old Soul
Porgy in the summer-time
An e whiting in the Spring
Don't be late I'm wait'n at de gate
Don't be mad—Here's your shad
Old Joe Cole—Good old Soul.

"You don't know how beautiful that Negro singing sounds to me," said Manus. "I mean it. Nearly lost my mind in the Russian Arctic where everything's white and gray."

"Don't hear the hucksters like you used to," she said. "People say the fleet may be out of business before long. Say they being outdone by the fishermen with the big boats that have the frigerator on board."

Porgy in the summer-time.

"You younger than me," she said to Manus, "run catch that man an buy us some porgy. I ran out of coupons for rice, but I can slice up a tummetuh and some okra. Once you eat, you know where you at."

That night after supper, they sat on the upstairs porch. Manus prepared to light a cigar.

"Do you mind?" he asked.

"Shooo! Don't make no difference to me, chile."

"It'll keep the mosquitoes away," he said, striking a match.

"Look like a La Preferencia," she said. "Perfecto Superior. We used to make them here in Chaa'ston. May I see it?" Manus handed her the cigar.

Cassie turned it over, ran her fingers along the sides. "I used to make these here by hand. No machine gonna make these here," her voice proud and regretful, too. She had once made something of value. She admired the tip on the end, that most difficult part to get just right. She sniffed it. "Smells like

Cuban filler." Cassie gently pressed the cigar between her thumb and fingers from one end to the other. "How much they take for this?"

"Buck-fifty," he answered defensively.

"Shoooeee!" she said, rearing back in her chair. "You been had. That cigar got a hard spot in the middle. Filler packed too tight in the middle. It won't draw easy."

"Give me that," Manus insisted, reaching to take the cigar back. "You're being too finicky." He tried to light it.

"Shouldn't have to work that hard to get it to light," she said, laughing a little. "You gonna fall out, you keep that up."

Finally, when he seemed to have it going, he sat back in his chair, putting his feet up on the railing.

"In the Arctic there were months at a time without any darkness," he said. "It was horrible. One of my uncles told me bout such a thing, but I didn't believe him. That was the uncle who left Chaa'ston to go to Alaska for the Gold Rush." Manus tried to puff on his cigar but he had to inhale deeply again to keep it lit.

"I didn't know your uncle went to Alaska," she said. "Did he find gold?"

"Not one nugget," answered Manus. "Not one. But he came back to Chaa'ston and opened an icehouse on Calhoun Street. He did alright."

The evening was pleasant with a breeze that came and went with the rhythm of a calm sea.

"Ebenin, Miss Cassie," called Seasar as he passed on his way home from working the railroad switch. "You heard from Patrick lately?"

"Not since last month," she called down to him.

"Tell him Seasar say hey next time you see him," he said.

"Seasar," she called out again. "I got bad news. Very bad news. You remember Tony, Patrick's friend?"

"Oh yeah, I taught both them boys how to throw the cast net. Naw! Don't tell me, Miss Cassie."

"I read in the mawnin papuh that Tony was killed in the Solomon Islands."

"Oh no! I sure am sorry," said Seasar. "I always enjoyed talking with them boys. And I been looking forward to hearing bout what they did and what they seen in the war. I sure am sorry to hear that news, I sure am." Then he tipped his head. "Ebenin to you both."

"Ebenin," Cassie and Manus responded together.

Manus gave up trying to keep his cigar lit. "I talked with some guys when I got off the ship today. They say the Maritime Union gonna help get a local set up here for the Food, Tobacco, and Agriculture Union. I swaytogawd, between the Wagner Act an the War Labor Board—Shooo—even them fat cats at Royal Cigar can't weasel out of paying a fair wage much longer. Yeah, I heard all about the cigar factory today." Manus smiled.

"Don't look so happy," she scoffed.

"You got to vote for the CIO. You know that, don't you?"

"Hush your mouth," she said. "I'm a final examiner. I got the best job in the place. I don't want no union."

"How can you say that? Look at how they treated Brigid? The more hours she work'd the less money she made. An I won't ever forget the way she used to cough. In the night, in the mawnin. That dust made her lungs weak before she even got consumption."

"And what makes you think the union gonna look out for us women any better than the company? I don't want them taking the dues money out of my paycheck."

"For crying out loud, you got to have the check off," said Manus. "Once guys get their pay envelopes they go downtown and spend it fast as you please. Money you don't see, you don't miss."

"Like hell," she said. "I miss every cent I never seen."

"If we didn't have the check off, the whole system wouldn't work. We couldn't have the strike fund, or put money to the politicians supporting labor. Naw, Miss Cassie, you got to have the check off."

"I ain voting for either one of them unions come next week," she said in a huff. "Where you think they gonna put an old lady like me? They'll be giving their buddies the good jobs. Shooo!"

"I got one more convoy next week for England," he said. "When I come back I'm gonna work with the Maritime Union to organize the cigar factory. I wanna do it for Brigid."

"You going to hurt more people than you help," she answered.

His voice became angry. "Call me a sucker but I believed the man when he said it was the war to end all wars. I cut a man's throat with my own bayonet. A blue-eyed man with a crucifix hanging round his neck. And for what? You should see what's been done to them people over there. People I cared about. God damn it, Rotterdam's been bombed to hell. And for what? Miss Cassie, for what?"

She turned away from him. The street was dark and still. Moths circled in the light. Cassie waited for a breeze to come along and cleanse the air between them.

When she spoke, she kept her tone grave, letting only her eyes smile a little. "From the first day I met you, I knew you was a Bolshevik."

Manus looked like he was about to hit her. Then he shook his head and smiled. "Only you, Miss Cassie, only you."

"You should have stayed in Russia," she said, keeping her tone as if she meant it. "Why'd you even bother to come back here?"

"Oh now, look out," he said, beginning to laugh. "You know why?"

"Shooo!"

"Couldn't stand the thought of never seeing you again."

She pushed at the air, unable to keep from smiling. "I got to go to bed." As Cassie went to stand, her knee gave.

"Miss Cassie, let me help you," he said, jumping up.

"Leave me be," she snapped, no longer kidding with him. "I don't want yuh help." She limped toward the door. "Leave me be."

The next week, everyone on the payroll at the cigar factory was handed a ballot, and the representatives from the War Labor Board were there to count them and monitor the election.

Cassie and eleven other workers voted for no union. Nineteen votes were voided for not being clear. Six hundred and ninety-one voted for the AFL, and seven hundred and seventy-two voted for the CIO.

Chapter 43

The sign on the wall said:

A MEETING OF THE WHITE MEMBERS OF THE FTA LOCAL 18 WILL BE HELD MONDAY NIGHT AT 8 P.M. IN THE NATIONAL MARITIME UNION HALL, 102 CHURCH STREET. NEGRO MEMBERS WILL MEET AT THE SAME TIME AND LOCATION ON TUESDAY NIGHT. ALL MEMBERS ARE REQUESTED TO ATTEND AND ALL EMPLOYEES ARE INVITED.

When Tuesday night came, Meliah Amey rushed home from work to get supper on before she had to leave for the meeting. The wind was up as she made her way down East Bay near the Battery. A large wave broke against the seawall, sending water pouring across the slate slabs and into the street.

"We fixing to have a big storm," she said to Joe. Vincent de Paul had sent them a radio when he learned they finally had electricity in the little house. Joe sat by the radio, listening.

"Man say we might get a harr-y-kin, but they don't know. I know," he said, "tide been over three feet higher than normal this week, and the currents be crazy mixed up—crazy mixed up, you understand. This harr-y-kin gone be a bad one."

Meliah Amey took a bowl of leftover succotash from the icebox, and started water on the stove to cook some rice. "Joe," she said, "if you don't go out in the boat in the mawnin, could you bring that pail of grease to Mr. Tomboli? President say take your cooking grease to the butcher once a week. They using it to make gunpowder or sump'n."

"I done that already," he said. "We stay in the harbor today. I come home early. Tana, you have foot een han' since you come in the door. You didn't even see the letter from Ajani."

She stopped everything and sat down at the table to read the letter.

Dear Maum and Tata,

We have just returned from our fourth mission escorting merchant convoy ships carrying supplies across the North Atlantic. I am lucky to be alive and to be writing you this letter. Eleanor's Folly may never be called that name again. Before we reached England we ran into a bad storm. The convoy was forced to separate and the Mason escorted a smaller group of ships. We had just sighted land when a tremendous wave split the forward deck and our ship nearly broke apart. Two men were able to get out there, hang on in heavy seas, and get a temporary weld in place. I was on the bridge helping to keep the Mason from getting broadside to the waves. It took all hands to save our ship. And still, our gunners kept every one of the merchant ships in our group safe. Captain Blackford and the convoy commander are recommending the crew of the Mason for commendations for heroic action.

When we got liberty in Plymouth, we headed for the USO because we heard they were serving free cokes and hot dogs. But when us guys from the Mason arrived, they refused to serve us. They said it was only for white soldiers. Some thanks, right?

I have been recommended for officers' training in a new program for Negroes at Camp Robert Smalls. I am considering it.

Tata, thank you for the rosary beads you made me out of the little shells.

Love,
Vincent Ajani

Meliah Amey blessed herself, and said a prayer to Saint Michael the archangel to keep him safe. Ajani had lived up to his name: *he who wins after a struggle*. She looked over at Joe, sitting with the filed nail and spoon he used for mending his nets.

"I am very glad you helped me with my words," he said, looking up and reaching across the table to take her hand. "I don't know what I'd do if I could not read all the words our son writes in his letters."

She placed his calloused palm against her cheek and closed her eyes. Together they had done it. Their son had a chance at opportunity. She held onto Joe's hand. He gently stroked her cheek. Yes, chile, she thought to herself. I love this man Joe Ravenel. I love him for true.

Meliah Amey woke up lying next to Joe. Now she really did have to take foot in hand. She dressed and hurried out the door without her supper.

Meliah Amey slipped into a seat as Sam Maybank was at the podium speaking. "The man on the radio say we might be in for a big storm. I say, those of us here tonight as members of the FTA Local 18, I say, we *are* the storm."

Meliah Amey smiled and joined in the clapping. She had never heard Sam sound so sure of himself.

"We wanna welcome Mr. Stanford with the CIO, and Mr. Lucio with the National Maritime Union, and some of these fine soldiers stationed at the Navy base hospital."

Everyone clapped except Meliah Amey. My Gawd, Sam, she thought, how come you got a bunch of buckruh men in here to talk? She looked at each of their faces, trying to see what they were thinking as they looked out over all the young Negro women. In her experience, with few exceptions, when the buckruh of any means looked upon a healthy young Negro woman, his mind went to one of two things, and both of them involved the woman on her knees.

When Mr. Stanford came to the podium to speak, he informed them that the War Labor Board agreed that Royal Cigar maintained substandard wages, and that each employee of the Charleston cigar factory would soon be getting a check in the amount of $70.00 for back wages.

Meliah Amey put aside her suspicion and cheered along with the others.

"And we're close to completing negotiations for a pension system, too," he said. "Some women have worked at the cigar factory for thirty years. We're trying to reach an agreement that those women will only have to put in another three years from the date we sign the contract to become eligible for a modest pension. It won't be much, but we hope it will be enough to keep them out of the state poorhouse and ease the burden on their children taking care of them."

Again, everyone clapped. Meliah Amey wiped her eye. Sometimes in the middle of the night, she watched Joe sleeping, worn out from rowing to the

Blackfish Banks and hauling in the heavy fishing lines. She wondered what would become of them if they lived to be too old to work.

"The CIO wants the newspapers, along with the mayor and every shop on King Street to understand—when the cigar factory workers have more money in their pay envelopes, that's more money to be spent here in Charleston. More money for your children's schools and playgrounds. The CIO is committed to the principle that every worker in that cigar factory deserves equal pay for equal work, and to be treated with respect, regardless of skin color."

Everyone stood up and cheered. The lights flickered twice as the winds outside picked up.

"And I want you to know, I said the exact same thing last night when we met with the white workers. I'm here to tell you tonight that all across the South, Negro and white are beginning to see the Jim Crow system is no different than when Hitler took away the rights of the Jews to be German citizens.

"Slavery made the plantation owners wealthy in the past, and while the South may have lost the war, don't worry, most of the plantation owners still owned enough land to sell off chunks over the years in order to send their kids to good schools and to start buying stock in Northern factories that make millions off the South's resources. I am convinced that the Jim Crow is not really about a true belief in the inferiority of the Negro, but instead, it is entirely about maintaining an endless supply of cheap labor. With the war industry booming, I dare say the bourbon is flowing freely again on the piazzas south of Broad.

"That's right," said a woman up front.

"So the factory owner up North pays the white worker a few dollars more a week than he pays the Negro and convinces himself not only that he isn't doing anything wrong but he deserves an award for hiring the Negro at all. The factory owner has his managers and supervisors down South constantly remind the white cigar maker that she better not ask for more money. She better not try to insist that the foreman keep his hands to himself."

Meliah Amey couldn't believe her ears. Did he say that the foremen mess with the white girls, too?

"No, she can't demand to be paid more or treated better because she knows that right on her heel is the Negro worker. The manager constantly reminds the white cigar maker that the Negro woman down in the basement is desperate to take her job and willing to do it for only a few dollars more a week than she's making now stemming tobacco." He slammed his fist to the podium. "The only way to break free of this age-old shackle is to unite the working poor of both races."

A few people timidly clapped. Meliah Amey and the others sat with a stunned look on their faces. She had never heard a white man talk this way before.

"We must do away with the poll tax that limits the poor of both races from voting. We must teach our members to read and write well enough to communicate effectively with management, the union, and the newspapers. And despite the setback issued by the governor of South Carolina this afternoon, we will press on to end the white-only Democratic primary here in South Carolina once and for all."

There was a loud boom of thunder. Everyone flinched and then laughed.

"What you mean setback?" a man yelled. "Judge Waring ruled in our favor."

"If you haven't seen the paper this evening, I have bad news," said Mr. Stanford. "When Judge Waring issued his ruling that the white-only primary violated the Fifteenth Amendment, the honorable governor of South Carolina, Governor Johnston, called a special gathering of the legislature and asked them to remove all references to state statutes to the Democratic primary. They voted to approve the changes and this afternoon made the announcement that the Democratic party of South Carolina is merely a private club, and thus well within its rights to deny ballots to Negroes." Mr. Stanford raised his hand to quiet everyone. "We won't let such an affront to justice stand. To that end, the soldier here and his wife, who, by the way, is from right here in Charleston—they're going to be holding classes at night for any cigar factory worker that wants to improve his or her reading and writing. They're gonna be having lectures to talk about government and what can be done to improve your schools and neighborhoods. The CIO is committed to extending the rights of citizenship to all Americans."

Meliah Amey was so inspired she signed up to help with the classes.

"I ain never," said Binah.

"Me, neither," answered Meliah Amey. "You really think the foremen fumble the white girls' behind?"

"Chile, them men fumble anything they want."

"Binah, do you think they do worse than that to the white girls?"

"Why don't you ask them?" said Binah. "When we walking down Columbus Street in the mawnin, say, 'Hey white girl, do the foremen fumble your behind? Yeah, okay. Is that all he do?'"

"Shut your mouth" said Meliah Amey, laughing at the idea of talking that way to the white girls.

Meliah Amey decided to wait with Binah while Sam was busy talking to Mr. Stanford.

"How's Hope?" she asked.

"All sass and no sugar," answered Binah. "She's going to the Immaculate Conception. I ain gonna become no pope-worshiping Catholic," she said, moving her hands around as if trying to bless herself, "but I can't say enough good about that Sister Madelene."

"Binah, who that man in the nice suit waiting to talk with Sam?"

"Don't you know who that is?" she said. "That's Mr. Lofton; he rich. Very rich. Sells fire insurance to the Negroes that can afford to buy it."

"If he were a tobacco leaf and I was sorting," said Meliah Amey, "he so light, I put him with the Claro."

"Wonder why he here," said Binah suspiciously. She motioned for Meliah Amey to follow her to get close enough to hear.

"Sam," said Mr. Lofton. "Quite the turnout. More than I expected."

"We're very pleased," said Sam. "Say they had just as many white members last night. We got to have them or we won't get far."

Mr. Lofton put his arm around Sam, guiding him away from the others. "You got someplace we can talk?"

Binah and Meliah Amey looked at one another. "In here," said Binah, grabbing Meliah Amey's hand and pulling her into a room. "He'll take him in the hallway door." They squatted down behind a desk.

"Sam," Mr. Lofton said, his voice sounding old and wise. "I've been talking with other men and those of us in the leadership are strongly opposed to going this route with the union, particularly the CIO."

Meliah Amey could see the men only from the knees down. Sam's pant legs and boots were covered in brown tobacco dust. Mr. Lofton's pant legs were pressed with a crisp crease, and his shoes sparkled from a recent shine.

"Some of the more prominent ministers agree, and I've asked them to speak out against any union involvement from the pulpit next Sunday. We need to stay together, Sam. We can't afford to let our cause get splintered in too many directions. More importantly, the CIO is stacked with Reds and everybody knows it." Meliah Amey watched how his feet moved when he was about to make a point. "We can't afford to be put into a position where we're forced to defend our allegiance to this country. There's a war going on, you know? Instigating labor unrest could be seen as unpatriotic and against the war effort." His feet shifted again. Meliah Amey never realized that a person speaks with his feet as much as his hands.

"Chaa'ston's not like it used to be. We got a bunch of crackers moving in here to work at the shipyard. They might even bring the Ku Klux with them. We've got to stay together and work through the federal court system. Thurgood Marshall with the NAACP is an excellent litigator, and Judge Waring is sympathetic to our cause. We won the case for equal pay for the teachers, didn't we? And we won the case over the Democratic primary. And Sam, we're making plans to bring a case against the separate schools. Listen to me, the union route is the wrong way to go. We won't get anywhere by joining up with a bunch of Reds and ignorant crackers."

Meliah Amey watched the shiny shoes turn quickly and walk away.

She and Binah struggled to stand up after squatting so long. Sam looked nearly gray.

"E scheme-y," said Binah.

Meliah Amey felt sorry for Sam. She could see him studying his head, trying to figure out what he should do, and of the two men he admired, Mr. Stanford and Mr. Lofton, who should he follow? Which one was true-mouth?

The rain blew sideways and Meliah Amey struggled to make her way back to Bedon's Alley. She kept looking over her shoulder, scared by Mr. Lofton's mention of the Ku Klux. She thought she might have heard someone running up behind her. Up ahead, water poured across the sidewalk from a gutter drain and she hurried to jump over it. Her Gkumma used to say that if you think a bad spirit is chasing you, cross some water because a bad spirit won't cross water. When she reached Broad Street, a trash can blew past. The hurricane flag had been raised at the courthouse.

There were no lights on in the houses and she knew the power had gone out. When she came to her front steps, she could see that Joe had taken heavy lines and lashed them across the little roof, securing them to trees and metal stakes he had set in the ground. He had done all he could to try to hold the roof intact. If Joe suspected that bad of a storm, she knew it was going to be bad. The kerosene lamp was going, and she helped him gather water in as many tubs and jars as they could find. They put blankets and towels in front of the doors to keep out the water if it should rise. And then they settled down to pray.

Chapter 44

Cassie's kerosene lamp flickered as the wind found the usual cracks and the rain found new ones. She exchanged the soaking wet towels beneath her porch door for dry ones. Then she settled down next to the lamp to read Patrick's letter.

> Dear Aunt Cassie,
>
> I am in Saipan. It's been rough. Bodies floating everywhere. Their eyes look at you. I'll never forget the smell.
>
> Any news yet from Pop? I have his book, Leaves of Grass with me. Sometimes I practice "Oh Captain, My Captain" like he and I used to do. Here's one for you. I went to the commissary yesterday and bought a box of Certified Cadora cigars, and guess what? It had your inspection number on it, # 37. Pretty amazing, isn't it?
>
> I can't wait to go fishing with Tony when the war is over. We always had a lot of luck over the oyster beds near Fort Sumter. Someday I want to buy a good sound boat so we can go out to the jetties whenever we want. Tell Pop hello if you run into him. I wish he would write. I know you're not much for writing, but even a word or two would be mean a lot to me.
>
> Love,
Patrick

She held the map from the newspaper closer to the kerosene lamp. They had printed a U.S. flag over Saipan. The next offensive would be the Bonin Islands, nine hundred miles from Saipan and only six hundred miles from Tokyo. The newspaper said they expected the Bonin invasion to have more casualties than Saipan. Cassie pulled out her rosary beads. Palmetto branches beat against the window. The wind howled outside as the house creaked, straining to hold together. Cassie prayed, not for herself but for Patrick.

For hours, the wind and rain beat against the house. Then it became eerily quiet. Cassie, lying fitfully in her bed, knew the eye was passing directly over Charleston. When the wind returned, it did not whistle, it moaned—a deep purgatorial moan, as if all the souls she had ever prayed for were crying out, demanding to be heard.

Cassie's mother had been able to see spirits. They say it was the people born at night that could see the fairies and such. Cassie had been born just before dawn, and she had been relieved not to have the burden that comes with the gift. But that night, Cassie felt the weight upon her chest, and in the blue flashes of light, she saw the first one sitting on her cedar trunk at the foot of her bed.

It was a Japanese soldier. "Please don't hurt my boy," she said. In another flash of lightening, he became bloated and lifeless. The room went dark. A tree cracked outside, and the moan rushed inside again with a pop of lightening. Cassie closed her eyes but all she could see was the sweet face of young Tony Giordano, proudly holding out a bucket of blue crabs he had caught. Behind her closet door stood the old Negro man she had seen beaten by two white men years ago. It happened early one morning when the streets were empty and she was on her way to work. Then she saw the young white girl on West Street, the one with the dirty mattress upon her back. And then, Brigid was there, smiling and waving as she had done when leaning out the window of the factory, and later, Luella Schultz. And while the others went as quickly as they had appeared, Luella arrived with her books and her newspapers, and the box upon which she would stand when she read to them.

"Oh Lord," Cassie said. "I heard you fell on hard times, Luella, after I gave Mr. Rolands your name and he fired you. I'm sorry to hear bout that, I am. I wish Mr. Rolands Sr. could explain it to you, like he did to me. I didn't want the factory to close. Not just for me, but for all them girls feeding they family with the money from making cigars. I'm sorry you fell on hard times, and I'm sorry I never let you know how much I enjoyed you reading that book *Jane Eyre* to us. Father O'Shaughnessy once told me that Saint Thomas Aquinas said there's three things necessary for going to heaven: to know what to believe; to know what to desire; and to know what to do. Luella, I believed I was doing what I ought to do. I believed I was doing right."

Luella picked up her box and walked out.

Cassie had never felt so alone. "The eye done passed, the end got to be coming soon," she said. The roaring train-like moan increased. Mr. Rolands Sr. checked his pocket watch. "May I sit with you awhile?" he asked, his voice calm, the same as it had been so many years ago. He pulled a chair beside her bed, took a seat and placed his hand on top of hers. "I'm going to look out for you, and let me guess, you never had anybody say that to you, have you?"

Dayclean arrived with bright sun and blue skies. Downed trees and sheets of tin and copper blocked the streets. The air smelled of the insides of things: old houses missing roofs, oak trees split apart. The power was out. Cassie tried to make it to Meeting Street to catch the bus, but it was futile. She saw a Negro woman in the blue uniform of the cigar factory. The woman, seeing Cassie in her uniform, spoke up first, "Cigar factory not open not yet. The roof done blow away. Say it gone be weeks before they get the roof puntop."

Cassie stood on the corner, watching the people coming out. Everyone smiled and greeted one another, thankful to have survived. She wasn't ready to be alone but it was hard to get about because of the debris.

"Extra, Extra," the newspaper boy yelled, "Mosquito Fleet destroyed by powerful storm. All boats moored in harbor sunk or severely damaged. Extra, Extra. Mosquito Fleet destroyed."

Chapter 45

SEPTEMBER 1945

"Ite, Missa est," said Father Joubert. The Mass is ended.

"Deo gratias," Meliah Amey responded quietly. Thanks be to God.

The early morning Mass at the Shepard Street Chapel did not have near the crowds it did before the war. And Joe's attendance had also fallen off in the year following the terrible hurricane that destroyed the boats of the Mosquito Fleet. But Meliah Amey and Joe wanted to attend that morning to give thanks for the news of Japan's surrender and to pray for the people of Hiroshima and Nagasaki. When the news broke, church bells all over the peninsula peeled, and fireworks lit the night sky.

"Bonjour Madame et Monsieur Ravenel," said Sister Madelene. Joy of the war's ending spared no one.

"Never thought I'd be walking with you to the cigar factory," said Meliah Amey as they headed toward the waterfront.

After the storm, Joe went to the bank to talk to Mr. Shaftesbury about a loan for one of the new style fishing boats with the diesel engine and a refrigerator. Even though Joe and Meliah Amey had never missed a rent payment in all their years of renting from Mr. Shaftesbury, he wouldn't give Joe a loan. And neither would any other bank in Charleston. Joe went to work at the shipyard, but soon as the war began winding down, he was laid off.

Now, Joe worked in the lumberyard preparing the tupelo wood to be made into cigar boxes.

"When oshtuh season come, I take the bateau up the maa'sh and make a leetle extra," said Joe.

"If we ever have more money," said Meliah Amey, "I wanna stay some-place that's got the toilet inside."

The roar of the machines came to life when the forewoman blew the whistle. The only good Meliah Amey could see in having a woman foreman was that at least she kept her hands to herself.

Brown tobacco dust floated in the air. The sun rose over the Cooper River Bridge, and the heat of a September morning began to build.

Meliah Amey and her partner worked at a feverish pace trying to meet the new quota of five thousand cigars per day.

When Meliah Amey saw she was about to run out of wrapper leaf, she glanced about the floor, trying to spot one of the stockers. Normally, the young white boy kept their bin full.

"I get it myself," she said over the noise of the machines.

Meliah Amey flung her empty box onto the stockroom counter. "I need wrapper leaf," she said. "How come you not keeping up? Cost me money to wait on you."

"I'm waiting for it to come up from the basement," said the stock clerk.

The freight elevator opened with Sam pushing a cart piled high with wrapper leaf.

The stocker removed an armful to weigh and record before issuing to Meliah Amey.

"Meliah Amey," said Sam, putting his arm around her, and grinning. "My my—you looking fine this victory mawnin."

"Shut your mouth, Sam," she said, unable to keep from smiling. She let her arm go around his waist. "Dust in my hair and stinking to high heaven."

The stock clerk handed her the bin, and as she turned around, the forewoman was right there, the look on her face worse than a haint hag.

"I'll not have foolishness on my floor," she yelled over the noise of the machines. "What's yuh name?" she asked Sam.

"Say what?" Meliah Amey interrupted.

"My name Sam Maybank," he said.

"Yuh fired," she said.

"Fuh what?" Sam demanded to know.

"For having familiarities with a woman while yuh supposed to be working."

"I did no such thing," said Sam, getting nervous. "No such thing."

They were shouting over the machine noise. The Negro women cigar makers began to notice the conflict. One by one, they shut off their machines. Soon, the floor was completely quiet.

"I saw you with my own eyes," the woman foreman insisted.

"I did nuttin wrong," Sam pleaded. "Tell'um Meliah Amey."

"What'd he do?" asked Mr. Godfrey from the other side of the room.

"Sam," said Binah. "What's going on?"

"Mr. Godfrey, I caught him having familiarities with this woman. She invited his advances rather than trying to stop him."

"Eee! Eee!" Meliah Amey screeched. "I did no such thing."

"I seen the two of you with my own eyes."

"Meliah Amey!" Binah cried. "Mek so?"

"I did no such thing," Meliah Amey begged her friend not to believe the buckruh woman over her.

"Go on, Sam. You're fired," said Mr. Godfrey. "Look what you done did. Every one of um's stopped work to gawk. Go on, you're done causing trouble here."

"It's not like you say," Meliah Amey pleaded. "Please, tell the trute. I got a husband."

"Woman, be quiet," demanded Mr. Godfrey, "or I'll fire de both ub yuh."

"We have the right to meet with a union representative before you fire eben one of us," said Sam.

"Like hell," said Mr. Godfrey. "Nuttin in dat union contract say we can't fire a man we ketch having his way with a woman. Now go on."

Sam left.

"Get back to work. All of yuh," yelled Mr. Godfrey.

"He just fired the union steward," someone said on the floor.

"Binah," Meliah Amey reached for her friend. "Believe me. Sam put he arm round me like a friend. Like a friend, that's all. I swaytogawd that's all."

"Get back to work," the forewoman yelled.

"I come your side," said Binah. "I know you true-mouth."

They walked back to their respective machines, but neither of them pulled the lever to start them back up. Others, seeing them, also stood by their machines without starting them.

The floor was silent.

"I request that Mr. Rufus Stanford with the union be called right this minute," said Binah to the forewoman. "We not going back to work till I speak with Mr. Stanford."

In the back, a woman began to sing.

No more mistress' call for me
No more, no more.

After an hour, none of the women had started their machines.

Meliah Amey turned off the radio when she heard the newsman say something about the Negro Women at the cigar factory sitting idle all afternoon while the white cigar makers kept working.

She sat down, put her head in her hands and cried.

Joe had told her he didn't believe the buckruh, but every time she looked at him on the way home, he cut his eyes away. And when they reached Bedon's Alley, he said he'd be home later and kept on walking.

There was a knock at the door. Sam and Binah were there with some soup and cornbread.

"We got word out," said Sam. "Mr. Wilkerson's refusing to meet with Mr. Stanford. Rufus say for me not to worry because nobody believes that white lady."

Joe didn't come home until the middle of the night, and when he crawled into bed beside her, he stunk of liquor. In the morning, when she got up to get ready, he didn't budge. The last thing she wanted was to arrive at work without him by her side.

The Spanish moss swayed in the live oaks as she crossed the Mall on Bay Street. She heard something like a person yelling but did not turn around. Then she heard it again. She turned around to see Joe, running to catch up.

Mr. Stanford had gone in the building to try and talk to Mr. Wilkerson. Hundreds of Negro workers had gathered at the corner, refusing to enter the factory until Sam was reinstated.

Mr. Stanford came out shaking his head. "I have left word with his secretary that Royal Cigar is about to be in violation of their contract and that I will be forced to contact the Labor Board. At this time, the union is not authorizing a strike. If you do not report to work today, I can't guarantee that your job will be protected."

Without so much as a mumble, the workers who gathered on the corner that morning, including Meliah Amey, Joe, Binah, and Sam, all of them turned around and started walking home.

They crossed the Mall. Meliah Amey looked back. Hundreds of Negro workers were walking away from the building. She smiled and Joe took her hand. A breeze rushed through the palmettos like a strong wave charging up the beach.

It was late in the afternoon of the next day before Mr. Wilkerson met with Mr. Stanford. He agreed not to fire Sam, and to pay him for the days he had missed. He refused to discuss any other concerns about the conditions under which the Negroes worked. For Meliah Amey, and the others, it marked the first time they stood up together and no one lost a job.

Chapter 46

Cassie was ironing her uniform and listening to the final game of the World Series when a loud knock came at her door. "Western Union," the delivery boy shouted over the noise of the radio.

"Oh for Pete's sake," she said after reading Patrick's telegram. He was still at the base on Guam and it might be six months before he was approved for discharge. Cassie took the Infant of Prague down from the sill and placed him on top of the telegram on the kitchen table so Manus would see it. Since he'd been home, Manus had thrown himself into something being called "The New South Lectures." With the war over, everybody wanted something new: a new range, a new electric icebox, a new house. Apparently some even wanted a new South.

Manus went about his day with an intensity of purpose that Cassie felt would have been better directed had he joined the monastery. Perhaps he could be useful training Saint Bernards in the Swiss Alps.

She put the iron to her uniform, releasing a waft of ammonia into the air.

Borowy takes the mound for the Cubs.

"Shooo, he arm worn out," she scoffed. "Don't put him in." She heard the crack of the bat followed by the crowd's cheer.

Nobody listened to her, especially Manus. Right then he was at the union hall helping to teach tobacco workers how to improve their reading and writing.

"That's all well and good," she had told him, "but it don't have a damn thing to do with making cigars." What got on Cassie's last nerve was him talking about how the white girls couldn't read or write much better than some of the colored. If Manus ever dared come right out and suggest that she attend one of those classes, well, that would be the end of it; she'd throw him out. Yes, ma'am. He wasn't blood relation and with each passing day she felt less obligated to provide a roof over his head.

It was bad manners to call attention to another's shortcomings. Of course she wished she had had more schooling. God knows she would have liked to have written nice letters to Patrick rather than merely short notes wishing him a happy birthday and such. Cassie felt pretty good about her reading, and she could figure out many of the big words in the evening paper on account of her knowing the Latin from Mass. But Manus shouldn't talk that way about the cigar factory. A lot of the girls that worked there were smart. Brigid certainly.

And Luella Schultz had some smarts to be able to read like she did. Oh Lord, thought Cassie, don't let my mind get tied up on what happened to that girl.

Durn Manus O'Brian, she thought, nearly burning a hole with the iron in her smock. The unwelcome memory of Luella Schultz stepped into her mind and stood up on that old crate she used when she read to them. "Okay," Cassie said aloud. "We going go through this one more time. You right, things don't square with how Mr. Rolands Sr. explained it to me. Mr. Wilkerson let the Negro women make cigars before we even had the union. No union forced him; he did it because he saw a way to make more money. There, I come out and said it. Yuh happy? Will yuh leave me be?"

Swing and a miss . . . Strike one!

The downstairs door opened and slammed shut, followed by the sound of Manus bounding up the stairs.

"It was the best meeting so far," he announced as he went to get a beer.

And Newhouser throws the pitch and . . . swing and a miss. Strike two!

"We're reaching more than tobacco workers now. The new principal from over at the Avery Institute, he was there, a colored preacher from Morris Street Baptist Church. But see, it's whites, too. There's a group called the Southern Regional Council, and some soldiers stationed at Stark Hospital on the Navy base. Shooo, I even saw Father Joubert from the chapel on Shepard Street."

Cassie wanted him to be quiet so she could hear the game.

"Who's ahead?" he asked.

"Tigers," she said, annoyed.

"You want the Cubs to win don't you?"

"I bet Salvatore fifty cents they would," she answered.

Manus took a long sip of beer, wiped his mouth. She could see he was torn between listening to the game and what was on his mind.

"We've got to get more people voting. First thing Hitler did was take away the Jews right to vote and go to schools."

"So now you're for the Jews as well as the darkies?"

Strike three! And the Tigers go to bat.

"Miss Cassie," he said, offended. "I been a lot of places; fought one war, an ran supplies on a merchant ship in another. All I've seen comes down to one thing. Guys like me, we're more or less garbage men, an everywhere there's trouble it's on account of a garbage man like me being made to go fight against a garbage man from someplace else."

Cassie set the iron on the counter to cool. "Telegram from Patrick's on the table. His unit's still on Guam. The Navy going to keep them there till at least March maybe even April."

"Son of a bitch," said Manus.

"When he come home, what you gonna do?" Cassie asked. "You gonna take him to your union meetings?"

"Patrick gonna be a man when he comes home, Miss Cassie. He going go his own way. You better think bout that now."

"I never coddled that boy," she insisted.

Swing and he—fly ball to right field, and he's—out! That does it. The Detroit Tigers beat the Chicago Cubs nine to three to win the World Series.

"Cubs lost in the first inning," she said, taking a seat at the table next to Manus. "Borowy's arm worn out. They should have put in Passeau or even Erickson."

Manus finished his beer and got another. "Too many of the best players still in the service. Baseball gonna be a lot better next year when they're all finally home." He took a sip. "Sump'n I wanna ask you," he said when he sat down again. "The girls say—I'm talking bout white and colored alike—they say the foremen get fresh with them, maybe even take advantage of a girl. I wanna ask you, did Brigid ever have any trouble like that?"

Cassie switched off the radio.

"Not long after she started to work there, a foreman by the name of Schmidt got a hold of her—"

Manus slammed his fist down on the table.

"—in the stairwell. I had a feeling when I seen her run off the floor by herself and all upset, so I went to check on her. When I saw him with her that way, I took my knife and said, 'I cut yuh throat. I swaytogawd, I cut yuh throat.' I meant it, too. He let her go and I went straight to Mr. Rolands—I'm talking bout the daddy Mr. Rolands—I went straight to him. Soon as I told him what had happened, he fired Schmidt right then and there. He fired him. He sure did, right then and there."

Manus reached across the table, put his hand on top of Cassie's. "Thank you," he said. "I mean it. I know you loved her, too."

Cassie pulled her hand away from his, having never forgotten how much she had wanted to cut *his* throat for hurting Brigid so deeply with his shameful talk of whores at the picnic.

"Shooo!" she said at last, waving her hand, trying to push those thoughts away. What good would it do either of them to fight about it now? "When the day comes to meet the Lord, we each gone have to worry about our own sins. Ain that right, Manus?"

She met his eye, expecting a worthy response. But it seemed that on that subject at least, Manus had nothing to say. She glanced at the Infant of Prague, with his questioning tilt of the head.

"Yes, Miss Cassie, you're right. And I hope you will pray for my soul when it is so long in purgatory."

A gull squawked outside the window.

"Me and Rufus talked with some of the Negro workers bout what it's like down in the basement."

"You're gonna do it. I knew it. You're gonna stir up trouble between us and the coloreds, aren't you?"

Manus kept his head down, not saying anything.

"Listen, since Mr. Wilkerson come to be the manager, I swaytogawd, things not that bad," Cassie insisted. "You stir up trouble this way and you don't know what's going to come of it, you hear me?"

"Rufus say he hears the same stories from women that work in the stemming houses for the cigarette factories in Winston-Salem. Miss Cassie, the union won't let them isolate one factory from the other. If they treat women bad in Chaa'ston, they treat women bad in Trenton an Philadelphia. It's gonna be like a flood tide. Everybody's gonna hear about it.

"The FTA local up in Philly went out on strike last week and the local here plans to join them. The National Maritime Union supports this strike so I'll be walking the picket line tomorrow at the cigar factory."

"Shooo," said Cassie, looking at her uniforms hanging on the bedroom door, pressed and ready to go. "I ain going against the company that keeps this roof over our heads," she insisted.

"The walk-out is set for tomorrow at ten o'clock," he said.

"Listen to me," Cassie pleaded, "I only got one or two years left in me to work. Manus, I'm old, I can't go back to mek'n cigars. I can't keep that pace and I don't qualify for the government's old-age pension because I never been married. I swaytogawd I'll jump off the Cooper River Bridge before I become a burden to Patrick when he trying to start a family of his own. And I know for damn sure that you don't wanna have to take care of me. I've got to make three more years to get that new pension. Can you promise me that all this you're stirring up ain gonna cost me my job as an examiner and that they won't just shut the place down like they did before? Can you promise me that?"

"No," he said quietly. "Miss Cassie, I can't promise nuttin bout how any of this is gonna turn out."

A little after ten the next morning, Salvatore and two other men from the packing department walked by Cassie's station.

"Where you men think you're going?" the foreman called out.

"Union called for a strike to start at ten o'clock. So that's what we're doing, we going on strike," said Salvatore.

"Gretta?" Cassie said, surprised to see her friend and fellow examiner walking out.

"Yeah, Miss Cassie, me too," she said. "My daughter, she a cigar maker on the fourth floor. You and me, we got a real good job being examiners, but I got to do this for my daughter."

Other women followed Gretta until only about ten workers remained in the packing department. Cassie got up and walked to the window overlooking Drake Street. She opened the window.

White women in their white uniforms and green smocks stood alongside Negro women in their blue uniforms and blue smocks. Union men passed out signs for them to carry and they began walking single file down the sidewalk. Cassie leaned out the window to get a better look. She saw cigar factory workers stretching as far as she could see down the palmetto-lined streets of Drake and Columbus. Cassie crossed the factory floor to the large windows facing Bay Street and she opened that one, too. The breeze off the harbor smelled of the marsh, and she breathed in deep.

The scene below was identical to the other: white and Negro picketers mixed in together, carrying the same signs. Signs that read BOYCOTT ROYAL CIGAR TOBACCO, DON'T BUY CADORA CIGARS, EQUAL PAY FOR EQUAL WORK. Another one read, DEMOCRACY ABROAD, DEMOCRACY AT HOME. Cassie reached over and shut off the conveyor belt. Without the motor running, she heard Negroes singing a spiritual song. And there was Manus, as short as ever but standing tall with his homemade sign that read: I HEAR AMERICA SINGING: A LIVING WAGE FOR ALL WORKERS.

In the distance, sirens wailed, coming closer.

"All right, all right," Mr. Godfrey hollered as he walked into the packing department.

Cassie turned to see Mr. Wilkerson and Mr. Godfrey. "Easy there," said Mr. Wilkerson, touching Mr. Godfrey on the arm to calm him down.

"We got some outside agitators stirring up trouble here in Charleston. Remember how the Negro cigar makers sat idle at their machines one day last month for no reason? They don't know what they want. The union takes advantage of their ignorance. It's a shame if you ask me. But fools are always willing to believe there's a pot of gold waiting for everybody in this life."

Hiyak-hiyah-hiyak

"Shut them windows," Mr. Godfrey snapped. "Damn gull bout flew inside. Okay, ladies, back to work."

Chapter 47

It was time. Meliah Amey cut her eyes to the other women on her machine, and their eyes answered back, *we ready*. She stole a glance to Binah, and Binah nodded. Meliah Amey shoved the lever of her machine into the off-position. The noise level on the floor did not change. She wondered if she and Binah would be the only two teams to summon the courage.

"What's going on here?" the forewoman called out angrily as she walked toward them. Another machine went silent, and then all down the row, others followed. Meliah Amey looked into the forewoman's eyes. "Answer me," she insisted.

Meliah Amey had no answer for this woman. Instead she turned and walked away. The expansive floor had never seemed as far to cross. "Gawd be with us," she said softly, knowing the other cigar makers were following. Their shoes left footprints in the dust-covered wooden planks of the floor.

Mr. Godfrey and Mr. Wilkerson both stood by the door looking plenty mad, but neither of them said a word. The Negro workers streamed into the Bay Street stairwell. The cigar makers from the third floor joined the box makers coming down from the fifth as the workers from the basement came up. Meliah Amey wondered if any of the white workers would keep their word to honor the strike.

A mild breeze, a beautiful blue of an autumn sky, and countless monarch butterflies welcomed the workers once outside. Meliah Amey nearly dropped to the ground with emotion when she saw several hundred white women in their white uniforms and green smocks pouring out onto the sidewalk from the Drake Street entrance. The short stocky man from the Maritime Union was there, too.

Sam passed out leaflets listing their demands:

THE WORKERS OF THE ROYAL CIGAR TOBACCO COMPANY
ARE ON STRIKE FOR:

EQUAL PAY FOR EQUAL WORK
NO DISCRIMINATION AGAINST NEGRO WORKERS
65 CENT PER HOUR MINIMUM WAGE
SIX DAYS SICK LEAVE WITH PAY

Salvatore, the union steward for the whites, handed out signs. Meliah Amey picked one that read: DEMOCRACY ABROAD, DEMOCRACY AT HOME. The young white girl beside her picked up EQUAL PAY FOR EQUAL WORK. The two women stared at one another. Meliah Amey felt the old resentment bubbling inside her: If this woman thinks she's got it bad, she doesn't have any idea what that basement is like on a hot summer day or cold winter morning. Bet they don't set her machine at more than four thousand every day. This lily-white girl would run back home to her daddy if a foreman came in while she was doing her business in the ladies' room.

The white girl stared back at Meliah Amey, perhaps thinking her own version of the same thoughts.

A monarch butterfly landed on Meliah Amey's hand holding her sign. It fluttered its orange and black wings and then lifted off, only to land upon the young white girl's shoulder.

"Mawnin," said Meliah Amey to the white girl.

"Good mawnin," she answered.

And they turned to join the line of a thousand other workers on the Columbus Street sidewalk to make their first trip around the block surrounding the factory.

Police cars arrived amid blazing sirens. Mr. Stanford took the bullhorn to speak. "Victory in this strike will be a blow to substandard wage industries across America. Victory here in Charleston will cut across the North-South wage differentials. Together we are laying the cornerstone for fair employment practices in this country."

Meliah Amey prayed for them to find the courage not to abandon one another if things got tough, if that Columbus Street sidewalk came to feel as if it were paved in pluff mud, if it came to feel like they were carrying their signs of protest across the marsh at low tide.

That first day, the strike had a picnic-like atmosphere. Many churches and civic groups supported the strike and brought food for the workers. Meliah Amey, Binah, Sam, and Joe sat under a live oak eating fried chicken and deviled crab. "Never ate this good for dinner," said Sam.

"Never ate this good in my life," said Meliah Amey.

All afternoon, reporters took pictures and asked workers to comment on why they were striking. That evening Mr. Stanford brought copies of the newspaper to hand out. "They didn't publish anything Sam told them," he said in disbelief, "only some ridiculous statement they claim a Negro woman made about not having any idea why she wasn't working today and how she was only doing what the union man told her to do. I bet she didn't say anything like that at all."

Meliah Amey didn't completely doubt a woman might say something like that, but she was being smart in the old way, she knew: When you're planning a rebellion the last person you tell the truth to is a white man with a pen and a piece of paper in his hand.

"Can you believe it," said Meliah Amey, handing her copy to Binah. "Sounds like Mr. Wilkerson thinks he has enough people still on the job to keep making just about as many cigars as we normally do."

"Dat man, e head tek way," said Binah.

"I ain believing this here article talking about the New South Lectures," said the stumpy little man named Manus. His mouth moved as he formed the words, and when he finished the editorial he crumbled the paper and threw it down. "He say what's wrong with the entire country right now is too much democracy and that South Carolina needs to have enough sense to go back to the way things were eighty-six years ago."

"Eighty-six years ago," said Sam, stunned. "Then he talking bout back in slavery time!"

The sun leaned and the workers returned their signs to the station wagon Mr. Stanford drove to carry them back to the office for the night.

"Let's sing one more song," said Lucille Simmons. Meliah Amey was tired of singing and tired of walking. "Come on, this gonna be our end-of-day song." Lucille began to sing: "*If in my heart I do not yield—*" She motioned with her hands for them to join in. It was an old field song and the women in the stemming department sang it now and then. "This is a song about a promise we going to keep. Now come on, sing with me. "*If in my heart I do not yield, We will see the Lord someday.*

"That's a silly song to pick for the end of the day," whispered Binah. "It's too fast."

"I just wanna go home," Meliah Amey answered. But young Lucille was determined they would all sing a final song together. Reluctantly, Meliah Amey and Binah joined:

If in my heart I do not yield
I'll be alright someday.

A military patrol shore wagon pulled up along with a police car. The officers got out and rushed toward a white sailor in uniform.

If in my heart I do not yield.

The military police grabbed the sailor, handcuffed him, and as they began dragging him toward the patrol wagon, the man named Manus moved to intervene. Binah cut her eyes to Meliah Amey before changing the words on the refrain and singing louder than anyone else: *"We will win our rights someday."*

"No more singing," yelled the city policeman. "Yuh disturbing de peace."

"No call for treating the sailor that way," Manus insisted. "Let him be."

"Mind you own business," said one of the officers, approaching as if he might arrest Manus, too.

"Ease off, Manus," Mr. Stanford shouted. "They want trouble. You got to learn not to fight back." They shoved the sailor into the wagon. "Same goes for everybody," Mr. Stanford shouted. "This has to be a peaceful demonstration. If it turns violent, the newspaper will be printing up a big story with lots of pictures."

The police drove away. First dark arrived. Palmetto leaves scraped against one another in the cool wind of a turning tide.

Softly, Miss Simmons, Binah, and Meliah Amey continued to sing.

If in my heart I do not yield
I'll overcome someday.

Two weeks passed and the company continued to refuse to negotiate. On the Feast of All Souls, Joe and Meliah Amey attended the early Mass before dayclean at the chapel on Shepard Street. Up ahead in the streetlight she saw the elderly white woman—ma'magole—with a bad limp making her way to the chapel.

"Look like she got a bad wheel," said Joe.

Meliah Amey saw the white uniform hanging out beneath the ma'magole's coat. She recognized her from the cigar factory. She had been there forever and used to buy crabs from Ray when he pushed the cart around Elizabeth Street.

"She not join the union; she not support the strike," said Meliah Amey to Joe. "Ma'magole always got a mean look on her face."

"Maybe she got that look because of the pain in her leg," said Joe.

The ma'magole stopped to put her veil over her head before going up the steps. Meliah Amey heard footsteps running down the sidewalk and turned to see Manus from the Maritime Union. "Cassie," he called out. "Why didn't you wake me up? I told you I'd walk with you."

"I don't need your help," she answered. "Sides, I heard you stumbling up the steps in the middle of the night. I heard the rest of it, too. I'm glad the drink makes you sick."

"Joe, Meliah Amey," said Manus. "Good mawnin."

"Mawnin," said Joe.

Meliah Amey nodded, studying the buckruh sailor. Was he really true-mouth if he was related to Ma'magole?

"Bonjour," said Sister Madelene. "I made soup for the workers. I'll have Father Joubert bring it over." She smiled and went up the steps.

Manus tried to help his aunt up the steps, but she pulled her arm away. "Let me be," she scoffed.

By dayclean Meliah Amey and Joe reached the factory, where several hundred workers were already walking the line. The morning had a first bite of winter and everyone had worn some sort of wrap.

"Joe, Meliah Amey," Sam called to them. "We out of leaflets and Mr. Stanford's not here not yet. Could you go over to the union office and fetch us two more boxes?"

Meliah Amey enjoyed the break from walking the line. She and Joe headed toward Meeting Street, walking past Ma'magole, who was doing her best to get to work on time but continuing to refuse to take Manus's arm for support.

When Meliah Amey and Joe were about to enter the union office, four husky men burst out the front door, jumped into a waiting taxi and sped off. When Meliah Amey and Joe ran into the office, they found Mr. Stanford on the floor, covered in blood. He had been stabbed and slashed across the face with a knife.

"Eee! Eee!" Meliah Amey screamed. She took off her sweater and pressed it against Mr. Stanford's belly to hold back the blood, and with her other hand, she held her veil to the gash across his face.

"Joe," she yelled, "dial the O for operator. Tell she we need an ambulance."

"Listen yah, a man been cut at the union office at the corner of Meeting Street and Mary Street. He hurt bad and—hello?" He looked at the receiver, and then put it back to his ear. "Hello?" Joe hung up the phone and ran out the door to find help.

"Jesus, Mary, and Joseph—hear my prayers. Please Gawd, help dis man. Please Gawd, don't turn yuh back on us now."

Chapter 48

"They say he's a member of the Communist Party," said Cassie, striking the match to light the oil heater for the first time that season.

"You saying he deserved to get stabbed?" Manus wanted to know.

"Don't be ridiculous," she said, putting the match to the wick.

"The police picked up the men that done it and they let them go! Let them go!" Manus declared.

Flames shot out the top of the heater. Cassie cut the dial back until the flames settled. "Mr. Godfrey told me that your Rufus Stanford served five years in prison in California for having a car full of dynamite at some strike he was leading out there. Did you know that?"

"For allegedly having car full of dynamite," Manus emphasized. He went into Patrick's room where he had been staying and came out with his sea bag. "I don't know if he's a Communist or not. So what if he is? He's working to help people get the right to vote."

A flame shot out the top of the heater and Cassie adjusted the dial one more time. "You got your bag in your hand. You going someplace?"

"I'm broke. I need to go back to work for a few months. I'm deadheading down to Jacksonville tonight. I'll pick up a ship there to take a load of new Pontiacs to Havana. I'll have to see what I can find after that."

"Oh," she said. "You won't be here for Christmas then, and neither will Patrick."

"I'll try to get back for at least a few days so you ain alone."

"Shooo!" she said, waving her hand. "Don't worry bout me. Chile, that's the last thing should be on your mind."

"I won a few bucks the other night, why don't you take it?" Manus removed the bills from his wallet. He put them on the table, setting the Infant of Prague on top for emphasis.

"I don't want your money, Manus O'Brian."

"Woman, keep the money," he insisted. "I won't ever be able to thank you enough for raising my son and taking care of him."

"Shooo," she huffed, waving her hand again.

"No, I mean it. We did it, Miss Cassie. Brigid wanted her son to have a proper Catholic education. She wanted him to have lots of books to read. And we did it, Miss Cassie. Me and you—the unlikely pair we are, we did it."

Cassie waved her hand again, not comfortable with sentimental talk.

"Take the money. It doesn't look like that place is ever going to come to the table and pay you people what's fair." Manus set his bag down. "Sump'n I wanna tell you."

Cassie wished he would sit down if he was going to start preaching about the union.

"I appreciate you letting me stay with you. But when I come back I'm gonna get a place of my own."

"Up to you," she said. "Until McAlister's takes me out feet first, my door swings both ways."

"Yeah, well—thanks, but when I come back, well, I've asked Eva Conrad to marry me. She works at the phone company. She the union steward for the switchboard operators. We think we can afford a little house over near the ball field."

Cassie couldn't have been more shocked. It never occurred to her that he was seeing a woman when he went out at night.

"Eva Conrad? Is she even a Catholic?"

"Of course she is," he insisted. "She goes to Saint Patrick's. Her husband died last year."

"How come he died?" Cassie wanted to know.

"He quit breathing! I don't know, a haa't attack or sump'n. She's in the Ladies Auxiliary down the K.C. Hall."

"Where her people stay?"

"She stay on Sumter Street. She was a Mueller before she got married. You know them, they stayed on Wall Street down in the Borough."

"A German Catholic?" she said, with apprehension. "All the discipline but none of the humor." She looked at Manus. His hair was beginning to gray but he was still as strong as a small ox. "Maybe that's what you need, Manus, a strict German woman to keep you in line. Well, she got her work cut out for her, and that's the Gawd's truth."

"It's time for me to shove off. I love you, Miss Cassie." He picked up his duffle.

"Shooo," she said, turning away.

"Scabs," the picketers yelled. The workers entering the factory, colored and white, entered now through the Drake Street door, where policemen, with their billy clubs drawn, kept a path clear. A policeman shoved a Negro man carrying a sign DEMOCRACY ABROAD, DEMOCRACY AT HOME. Cassie shook her head, and made her way up the steps, one at a time.

She found Mr. Godfrey sitting on her examiner's stool. "Miss Cassie, you need to go up to the fourth floor. We need you to make cigars for awhile."

Go to hell, was what she wanted to say to him, but then she remembered Father O'Shaughnessy admonishing her that men like Mr. Godfrey knew what's best for the company and that she should listen and do as told.

"I'll meet you up there," he said, going to the elevator and leaving her to take the steps.

"Don't worry, Miss Cassie," he said when she arrived to the fourth floor. "We gonna slow it down till you get back in the swing of it. Let me introduce you to the women you gonna be working with. This here Martha Sue. She normally works in clerical. And this here Sally; she work in payroll. This gone be temporary. More of our boys coming home every day. They gonna need jobs, too. Our boys gonna come home and run these Reds that's stirring up trouble with our darkies out of Chaa'ston. You girls done the right thing and the company appreciates your loyalty. Okay, let me show you how to work this here machine."

Cassie applied the wrapper leaf, but even with the machine set at a lower speed, she could barely keep up. She had grown unaccustomed to the strong fumes released when the filler leaf was cut and within an hour she had a splitting headache, and Martha Sue had thrown up twice.

"Feed the tobacco in this way," Cassie said to Sally, trying to show her how to be more efficient.

The morning wore on and the three women did the best they could to keep up. Then the sound of the machine began to vary, causing the belt carrying the filler leaf to change speeds, and when it stopped altogether, Cassie gave thanks to the angels and saints.

"What do we do now?" asked Martha Sue.

Cassie knew exactly what to do and her tools were still in her smock pocket. She could have the machine running again in less than fifteen minutes. And in the old days that was just what she would have done.

"We call the mechanic over and wait for him to fix this damn machine," she said, leaning up against the thing, trying to get some weight off of her leg. Even her left arm was starting to feel that old numbness in it from having her head cocked at that uncomfortable angle for so long.

The mechanic was new and it took him forty-five minutes to get their machine unclogged and operating again. Cassie had kept her mouth shut, not offering any advice.

The foreman didn't call the lunch break until nearly 2 P.M. Going down the steps was even worse than coming up.

She brought her tray to the table with Martha Sue and Sally.

"If them pickets get their way, I guess we'll have the colored in here eating with us," said Martha Sue.

At that moment, feeling as bad as she did, Cassie didn't give a damn who sat next to her at lunch, all she wanted was to go back to her old job and pray God she could make three more years to collect her pension.

"My daddy says if these Reds try to make me sit slap-up beside a nigger then I better get my behind back to Bamburg," said Sally.

Cassie pushed back from the table, tired of meaningless talk.

She started up the steps, each one more painful than the last. She stopped to rest, looking around that stairwell she'd been climbing since she was twelve years old. "Oh Lord!" When she reached the landing between the second and third floor, she realized she needed to use the restroom. Pulling on the railing so hard to take the strain off of her leg was making it hard to hold her water. She turned the corner and kept on.

By the time she reached the third floor, she knew she couldn't wait. "What the hell," she said, accepting that she would rather use the colored bathroom on the third floor than wet herself.

Out of the corner of her eye, Cassie saw the ten or so Negro women at their cigar-making machines cut their eyes in her direction, wondering why she was on their floor.

"Jesus, Mary, and Joseph," Cassie sighed with relief as she sat on the toilet, her knee not capable of holding a squat. There were no doors around the toilets as there were in the white bathrooms, but she could not care less at that moment. It felt good to have made it in time. She didn't give a damn whose fanny had been on that seat before her own, either. She blessed herself, bowed her head to say a prayer of thanks.

"I said lunch is over. Get your sorry ass off that toilet and—"

Cassie looked up from her compromised position to see Mr. Godfrey standing not ten feet away, staring eye to eye with her.

She tried in vain to cover herself with her smock. Mr. Godfrey stood frozen in shock from finding Cassie McGonegal where he least expected to. He turned and walked into the sink. She stood, not taking time to finish wanting only to pull her dress down and cover herself. Mr. Godfrey put his hands over his eyes as Cassie pushed by him, her Irish blood raging, overriding her knee pain. She hurried to the nearest stairwell, taking each step as fast as she could without falling.

In her rush, Cassie had not noticed which stairwell she had entered, she knew only that she was going to get out of that building. When she pushed the

Bay Street door open, nothing looked familiar. She lurched toward a palmetto tree to steady herself.

She did not see a familiar face. That is except one.

"Ma'magole, what's wrong?"

It was the Negro woman Manus knew. The one Cassie had seen at the chapel on Shepard Street on the Feast of All Souls.

"I'll be alright," she answered, praying for the Lord to give her strength so she wouldn't fall out right there on the sidewalk. She held tight to the palmetto tree and when she looked up, the woman was still there.

"I get yuh some watuh."

The wind picked up and Cassie tasted the salt in the air.

"Thank you so much," she said, still quite shaken, to the woman. "I'm sorry; I don't know your name?"

"Meliah Amey," she said.

"I'm Cassie," she replied before drinking the water. "Meliah Amey, what floor you work on?"

"Third floor," she answered.

"Pardon me for asking," said Cassie, still short-winded. "But does Mr. Godfrey ever come in the restroom when you're doing your business?"

"Oh yeah, chile," she answered. "Who you think gonna stop that man from doing what he wanna do?"

Chapter 49

"Sure didn't think we'd still be walking this picket line come the new year," said Sam, pulling his cap down over his ears, and placing his hands over the trash-barrel fire.

"Say most of the white folks going go back to work this week," said Binah, picking up her sign and leaving the warmth of the fire.

"Don't be talking that way," Sam called to her. "Company spreading that word. They trying to break our spirit. We been out here too long to give in now."

Father Joubert no longer walked the picket line. Joe had seen Bishop O'Shaughnessy driving by one day when Father Joubert was protesting. A few days later Sister Madelene came to tell them Father Joubert had been transferred to a parish up in the hill country. The Sisters stopped coming, too. Soon after, the civic groups and other churches didn't bring food as often. The union had to spend a large portion of the strike fund to get Binah out of jail. She was arrested for disturbing the peace but she was really just singing.

Meliah Amey didn't know how much longer they could hold out. If Vincent de Paul hadn't sent twenty dollars the week before, she and Joe would have been thrown out of the house on Bedon's Alley for not paying rent. The winter winds had been too strong for Joe to take the bateau in the marsh for oysters. For the first time since she was a little girl, she had gone to bed hungry and unsure of the next meal.

Meliah Amey looked over at Ma'magole sitting in a chair Salvatore had brought for her, holding her sign, ALL WORKERS DESERVE DIGNITY. Just when so many other white workers were giving up and starting to cross the line, here was Ma'magole, holding strong. Meliah Amey couldn't help but feel a little sorry for the old woman. She kept to herself, only occasionally talking to Gretta or Salvatore. Didn't seem like she had any family to speak of now that Manus the sailor had gone back to sea.

A bone-chilling wind blew in from the harbor. No one could remember a colder winter in Charleston. "Joe, bring Ma'magole's chair ovuh yah by the fire. She gonna freeze to death sitting out there like that. And don't let her tell you no."

Joe got the old woman settled closer to the fire, and then he returned to the line carrying his sign saying: *Boycott Royal Tobacco Products.*

"Meliah Amey, are you a cigar maker?"

"Yes, Miss Cassie, I am," she answered.

"You like that machine?"

"I don't like it one bit when it gets jammed up because you don't make any money waiting on the man to fix it," Meliah Amey answered.

"Oh yeah, Lord, that's the truth, now," she said, looking up and kind of smiling like she wanted to talk with her. "You need to fix that machine yourself. That's right, then you won't lose money waiting on the mechanic. In my day, the mechanic would make the girls show they behind or sump'n before he come over."

Meliah Amey couldn't help but laugh. "Miss Cassie, I know of what you speak. But they don't teach us how to fix them machines."

"Shooo!" said Miss Cassie, "I teach you. Yeah. I teach you right now."

Meliah Amey pulled up a crate and took a seat. "Here's the tools you need," and she took a pouch with two screwdrivers, a pair of pliers, some tweezers, and a small bottle of sewing machine oil. "I brought these for you," she said. "I want you to have'um. Not much you can't fix with them right there."

"Miss Cassie, you mean it? Won't you need'um?"

"Only one job left in there I can do, and that's being an examiner. I can't stand long and I can't keep up the pace of the cigar machine."

Meliah Amey received the offered gift. "Thank you, Miss Cassie. Can you tell me how to fix that machine when it sounds like it's going different speeds?"

Ma'magole explained everything she knew about fixing a jammed up machine, or a loose belt.

When she had finished, she sat back and smiled. "Someday, let me show how to make a cigar by hand. It was grand compared to them durn machines. Shoo! I could roll a Corona, a Pantella, a Victoria, a Perfecto. An with a left or a right wrap," she said, sitting back and nodding her head with pride. "We didn't make the five-cent cigar, no chile—we made La Coronas, La Preferencias, one called the Antonio Cleopatras—all of them fine cigars. And it was quiet. Except for the girls talking to one another. Sometimes one of the girls would get ahead on her quota and she would get up and read us a story, and that was real nice. Real nice." The ma'magole got a sad look on her face all of sudden.

Binah came back down the sidewalk, anxious to hand Meliah Amey her sign and warm up by the fire.

Meliah Amey started down Columbus Street. It wasn't long before her fingers ached from the cold. Her eyes watered from the wind as she looked up at the cars crossing the Cooper River Bridge. People said come summer there wouldn't be any toll charged to go across.

A car of white boys sped past, honking the horn and squealing tires. "Go home, Commie Reds," one of them yelled. She turned away so as not to have to look at their ugly faces. She didn't see them throw the bottle. When it landed on the sidewalk and broke, a small sliver nicked her leg.

As the sun leaned into the gray clouds, Meliah Amey felt little pecks, almost a sting, on her cheeks, on her forehead, on her cold ashy hands. It was sleeting in Charleston. By the time she had turned the corner, the sleet turned to snow.

Back at the trash-barrel fire, she joined Sam, Binah, Francine, Joe, Ma'magole Cassie, the white woman named Gretta, and Salvatore. Flakes of snow fell on their heads and quickly melted.

"Let's sing our end-of-day song an go home," said Lucille.

"Slow it down this time," Binah called out. "That song too fast. It would sound bettuh if we slow it down."

Miss Cassie stood up to leave as she always did when they began to sing the end-of-day song.

If in my heart I do not yield
I'll overcome and
We will win this fight someday.

From the look on Ma'magole's face, Meliah Amey and the others could see that she was worried about walking to the bus stop—and yet—she didn't seem ready to leave, either. The buckruh never sang, but that evening, they looked different, like their mouths almost wanted to form the words, their bodies wanting to sway but holding back. Francine saw it, too. And so did Binah, Lucille, Sam, Joe. The white folks—Gretta, Salvatore, Ma'magole, and the rest—not singing a word but looking on the edge, on the verge, until all of them were looking at one another, as if only now, after all this time, they were seeing one another for true. And when the promise of the refrain came around again, Lucille changed it up one more time:

If in my heart, I do not yield
We will overcome someday.

The snow began to stick. Meliah Amey watched Ma'magole trying to get home before the sidewalks got any worse. They were covered in a light dusting, a sight every bit as uncommon in Charleston as if the Virgin Mary herself had joined the workers there trying to get warm beside the trash barrel.

Joe saw that Meliah Amey was worried. "I mek she a walking stick tonight," he said. Meliah Amey put her hands in her pocket, her fingers wrapping around the tools Miss Cassie had given her.

"I meet you back home," she said to Joe.

"Mek so?" he said.

"First dark coming. I walk with Ma'magole so she don't fall."

Chapter 50

There was no point to looking in her cupboard that morning. Cassie knew the half-head of cabbage in the icebox was the last of her food. And the night before, she had added the last of her oil to the heater. If Patrick hadn't sent her fifteen dollars in his last letter, she wouldn't have made the rent. There was no money left beneath the Infant and she returned him to his perch in the windowsill above the sink.

She stood in her cold kitchen wearing only her slip, staring at the union card she had signed, declaring herself a member of the CIO. Cassie was trying to decide if she should put on her uniform and smock and cross what remained of the picket line. Her belly growled. She took the uniform off the hanger and slipped it over her head. First light fell upon the walking stick Joe Ravenel had made for her. This gave her pause. Then she took her smock from its hanger and slipped it over her head. She picked up her green cap and was about to pin it on when the light found Brigid's picture on the table.

I cut yuh right now. I swaytogawd, I cut yuh right now.

Cassie saw Mr. Schmidt in the stairwell with his hand on Brigid, and then Mr. Godfrey with that filthy look upon his face when he came into the ladies' room. She changed into her long drawers and a slightly moth-eaten wool dress.

The sidewalk on Columbus Street had patches of ice, rare for late March. Her knee ached even more, and she could not walk another step carrying her sign. Cassie stood beside the trash-barrel fire along with the Negro woman named Francine, who also had a bad leg.

"What a sight we must be," said Cassie. The both of them with their signs propped against them. Cassie's read: EQUAL PAY FOR CIGAR MAKERS ON BOTH SIDE OF THE MASON-DIXON LINE. Francine had the most popular sign that everyone liked to get: DEMOCRACY ABROAD, DEMOCRACY AT HOME.

"Did you sell flowers by Saint Michael's?" Cassie asked.

"Yes, maum," Francine answered.

Cassie smiled. "You let me borrow a bowl one time at Christmas when I got some oshtuhs."

"That's right," said Francine, smiling. "That's right. You bring me that bowl back like you said you would. I remember."

Cassie pulled her coat tight around her chest. She smiled, glad for someone to talk with by the warmth of the fire.

Gretta and her daughter walked up in their uniforms and green smocks. Sam and Salvatore hurried over.

Gretta put her hand up. "No," she said. "I thought about it all night long. We don't wanna go back but she got chillun to feed. I hear Mr. Stanford's back to work and even he can't get them to budge."

"Excess profits tax," said Salvatore.

"The company made so much money last year, any profit they made come October would have gone to the war tax," said Sam. "They didn't wanna pay their share of that war tax."

"You mean we never had any leverage, this whole time we been out here in the freezing cold?"

"Royal Tobacco don't play fair," said Salvatore.

"We been had! We been had!" Gretta exclaimed.

"The war's over and they done away with that special tax," Sam called out.

"The company's ready to start making money," Salvatore followed. "We got a little leverage now. Please, hold on a few more days."

Despite Sam and Salvatore's plea, Gretta and her daughter crossed the line and went inside.

By the end of the morning, only thirty or forty workers remained on the line. Cassie was one of them.

Cassie looked up at the old red brick building. She could see Brigid leaning out the window, laughing and giggling that day she and the other girls stopped working. Manus down below holding Patrick in one hand and a plate of porgy fish in the other while he recited poetry.

"Mek so yuh worry?" asked Francine.

"I worry bout getting old, being alone and not being able to look after myself."

"Thank Gawd we in Chaa'ston," she said, patting Cassie's hand. "Our people buried here. We not by we se'f."

Cassie pulled her hat down, trying to keep her ears warm. "Let's take a seat on this crate and take the weight off?"

The two women sat down beside one another.

"I got a thermos of soup from the pastor's wife at Mother Emmanuel Church," said Francine. "You want some?"

Francine unscrewed the top of the thermos. Steam drifted out, bringing the smell of beef, carrots, and celery to Cassie's nose.

"I don't wanna take your soup," she said.

"Not my soup," said Francine. "She made it for us out here on this picket line."

"Alright then," said Cassie as she watched the chunks of vegetables pour into the thermos cup. "I appreciate—" She hesitated as Francine shook the thermos trying to get more to come out, but none did. There was only one cup left.

"Go ahead," Cassie insisted.

"No, no," said Francine.

They cut their eyes to one another, not saying a word. Francine took a sip and without looking at Cassie, passed the cup. Cassie took the cup with its wonderful smell rising up. The soup was warm and delicious. Cassie couldn't remember when she had last tasted beef. She and Francine passed the cup back and forth and in no time it was empty.

"I done told you people, you can't block the sidewalk," the policeman shouted. "If yuh not able to walk, yuh ain got no business on a picket line. Now get up."

Cassie did as she was told, pushing herself to stand with the help of the walking stick. She had seen how rough the police were with that woman just for singing and she didn't want to be handled that way herself. Cassie didn't think her heart would hold up to a night in the Seabreeze Hotel, as everyone called the city jail.

In the commotion with the police officer, Cassie had not properly thanked Francine for the soup, but when she turned around, Francine was too far away.

A car pulled up and Mr. Stanford, with his unmistakable scar, got out in a hurry. Even if he was a Communist, thought Cassie, he was a straight shooter.

"Trenton and Philly are talking," he announced. "Wilkerson called me this morning and he's ready to meet. I want two women with me at the negotiating table. Binah, would you come?"

"Meliah Amey, you read and write better than me," said Binah. "You go with him."

"Who else?" he called out, looking around. No one had to look very far.

Men in suits filed into the conference room, but none of them took a seat. They stood, clearly not pleased to find Meliah Amey and Cassie seated at the fine table. Cassie cut her eyes to Meliah Amey. She looked just as nervous.

"This is a beautiful table," said Mr. Stanford real cordial, trying to break the strain. Cassie and Meliah Amey agreed as they touched the grain admiringly.

"Quite a bit of history behind it, too," said Mr. Wilkerson, also being friendly. "Mr. Rolands bought it from an old Charleston family and the story is that the man who had it made was a state senator. You see, a long time ago there was this slave named Denmark Vesey that tried to stage an uprising. Anyway, long story short—this table is made from the tree where they hung Denmark Vesey."

Cassie saw Meliah Amey's hands go quickly to her lap.

"Let's get down to business," said Mr. Wilkerson. "Ladies, if you will excuse us, but this is a matter for gentleman, and I would prefer the both of you leave so we can get started."

"Mr. Wilkerson," said Mr. Stanford, his voice serious. "These two women are well qualified to participate in these negotiations. Most of your workers are women."

Several of the men snickered. Mr. Wilkerson raised his hand to quiet them. "Let's keep moving. Cindy, pass out the papers." His secretary began passing out papers, stopping at Meliah Amey and Cassie, she looked to Mr. Wilkerson for approval. He nodded.

Cassie felt her heart leap with fear at the sight of all those words. One at a time, she told herself, take them one at a time.

"As you can see our offer stands at ten-cent-an-hour raise across the board," said Mr. Wilkerson.

"But that's no different than what you said before we even went on strike," said Mr. Stanford.

"The war is over, Mr. Stanford. The regulatory boards are disbanding and every day more GIs come home looking for a job. The market has changed considerably since we last talked."

Cassie studied the paper. One column listed the union's demands and beside all of them was the word NO. No to the sixty-five-cent minimum hourly wage. No to the company paying fifty-percent of a family's medical insurance. No to the seniority system for wages and promotions. The only one with a question mark was the demand to end discrimination against Negro workers.

"Let's talk about having a system to determine wages and promotions," said Mr. Stanford.

"Nothing to talk about," said Mr. Wilkerson. "We don't need it."

"Excuse me," said Meliah Amey. "May I say something?"

"Listen here—"

"Please address her as Mrs. Ravenel," Mr. Stanford interrupted.

The men harrumphed like a gaggle of geese.

"Mrs. Ravenel," said Mr. Wilkerson, somewhat pained, "tell us what you think we need to know to run our business."

"For years, the foreman pays the girls for lots of reasons that don't have nothing to do with how much tobacco they stem, or how many cigars her team makes. Everybody knows what goes in another's pay envelope. When it's not fair, people get mad. Makes them wanna work someplace else. If you had a system that everybody could see in writing, people will work harder to get the better pay."

Cassie raised her hand.

"Yes, Miss McGonegal. What do you have to say?"

"Mrs. Ravenel is right. We need a pay system in writing. An for those of us that's been here for ovuh twenty years, we need to be sure our pay can't go less than a certain amount. See, lots of us women never been married an we ain eligible for the old-age pension from the state. Out there on the line with the colored, I hear that lots of them ain eligible for the old-age pension or the minimum wage on account of y'all calling them in the basement same as a field hand on a farm, an that ain right."

"You know, John," said one of the men in suits. "If we graded the jobs by class, it might give them an incentive to stay longer. Might save us some on training new labor."

Mr. Stanford jumped in. "We want an end to the company classifying the tobacco processors as farm workers, and we want it in the contract that pay is based on job description regardless of age or race."

Mr. Wilkerson nearly fell out of his chair.

"I started work here when I was twelve years old," said Cassie, "an it's been the same all that time. A supervisor or a manager can put a little extra in a girl's envelope because she done a favor for him—and it's time for all that to stop."

"That's right," said Meliah Amey.

Cassie met Meliah Amey's eye. Both of them knew what had to be said next. Cassie studied Meliah Amey's brown eyes as hard as Meliah Amey was studying Cassie's blue ones. Who was going to say it?

It was Cassie who spoke. "We not going go back to work till you put in that there contract that the men that work here—I don't care if they on the line or in the manager's office—the men can't put they hands on a woman or make advances that way, and he can't set foot in the ladies' room."

The men shifted nervously, cutting their eyes away from Cassie. Meliah Amey took it from there.

"We want stalls with doors built around the toilets, and we wanna wear the same uniforms as white or no uniforms at all," said Meliah Amey. "We want to use the cafeteria, and the stairwells and doors, same as the white girls."

"Hold on, hold on," Mr. Wilkerson interrupted. "Maybe I share your vision, and maybe I don't, but I am bound to follow the law, and the law of this state is that colored and white must be kept separate."

"Mr. Wilkerson," Cassie was quick to reply. "Let me tell you sump'n. They's lots of ways Chaa'ston's not like the rest of this state. This town has always gone its own way in that department so don't sit there like you spect us to believe you men gonna let the law of the federal government, or the law of this state, stop you from doing what you want to do."

"My God—You two don't understand what you're talking about. Tell me, what it is you really want from us?"

"To be paid fair and treated decent," said the two women at the same time.

That evening as Cassie left to catch her bus, she heard them getting ready to sing the song they always sang at the end of the day. Binah was carrying on, laughing and being lighthearted, the way she could be sometimes.

First dark had set in, and Cassie could hear them singing as she crossed the next block. Seemed every time they sang it, they changed the words. She wondered if it would be the last time she would hear the Negroes singing that particular song.

If in my heart I do not yield
We will overcome some day.

Chapter 51

In April, a few days after the strike ended, the newspaper ran an article claiming that Communists were luring Negro workers at the cigar factory to join the union. And because so many workers crossed their own picket line as the strike wore on, the AFL filed papers with the Labor Board, requesting a new vote be taken to determine which union, if any, would represent the workers.

After the long bitter winter, a mild Sunday afternoon prompted Joe and Meliah Amey to take a walk along the waterfront.

"The man at the bank still won't give me no loan to buy a fishing boat like they all got now," he said. A flock of gulls squawked as their flight slowed against a stiff headwind. "Mr. Chisholm sell lots of his property in Scanlonville for them to build more houses. His son stay on Shem Creek an he bought a shrimp boat. No trus-me-Gawd, no no. He buy a big boat with a diesel engine and a big frigerator. Say come this season, I work for him."

"You used to being the captain," she said. "How you gonna take orders from this young man?"

"Long as he not Mr. Godfrey, I take orders fine," he said.

"How you plan to get over to Shem Creek before dayclean?" she wanted to know.

"The bus goes over the bridge now," he was quick to answer. "I gone take the bus over there."

"Alright, I come your side," said Meliah Amey.

The tide was out and yet small waves hit against the Low Battery seawall with a solid thunk. They walked along, without talking.

A dah lifted a boy dressed in a fine playsuit down from one of the Oyster Point cannons. The mainsail of a boat in the Ashley River began to luff, and the boat stalled. Meliah Amey and Joe watched the crew from the Carolina

Yacht Club as they scrambled about the deck, ducking to miss the boom when it swung unexpectedly across the stern.

Joe couldn't help but smile. "Too bad they can't sail as fine as they dress." The men barked orders at one another, trying to get the boat in trim.

"Do you think any good come from the strike?" Meliah Amey asked Joe.

"The most good is yet to be," he answered.

"What you mean?" asked Meliah Amey.

"Just what I say, that's what I mean," he answered.

Meliah Amey shook her head. "We nearly froze to death for ten cent more an hour. They put a few of us on other floors and we don't have to wear them sorry uniforms no more, but it's still all colored down in the basement. People calling it a victory. Don't seem like much of a victory to me."

"We can eat in the cafeteria," he added.

"Shooo," said Meliah Amey, waving her hand. "I hear Mr. Godfrey say this won't last. Say once more men come back from the war, they gone run these Reds out of the South and the cigar factory going to go back to being like it was before."

"Meliah Amey," he said, shaking his head. "Think about the folks you helped learn to read and write in the classes the union and them put on. Woman, you talk bout what Mr. Godfrey say. I say Mr. Godfrey can go to hell. Listen yah, all them people you helped teach got registered to vote. Shooo! We ain gone stop none of this we done started. Tana, think about all the good gone come someday!"

"Someday? Why not today? Shooo!" she said, ready to chew into him until she saw the look in his eye. To doubt his faith at that moment would be to love him less. She shook her head, "gone shut my mouth."

They continued walking along Low Battery, not talking, studying their own thoughts. When they were near to where the Ashley and Cooper Rivers joined, she cut her eyes at Joe. He was reading the water, interpreting the intentions and mysteries of that world he knew so well, and she, so very little. Sometimes at night if she couldn't sleep and he was turned on his side, she liked to prop up on her elbow just to look at his proud cheekbone, the angle of his jaw, his skin—his rich wonderful adu skin.

When he turned and caught her staring at him, this made him smile in a schemy kind of way.

"Tana," he said, "Yuh eye tie up on me."

She laughed, but didn't say a word.

"Gonna storm," said Joe, looking out over the harbor. The wind kicked up and within seconds, there was a crack of thunder and a squall was upon them.

Joe took Meliah Amey's hand and they ran for cover under the bandstand. He put his jacket over them against the blowing rain.

When the storm passed, they continued walking along the oyster shell path. As they neared High Battery, they heard a deep thud from the harbor. Joe ran up the steps, ahead of her.

"Mother of Gawd!" he shouted, pointing. Then she saw it, too. A large ship was sideways against the north side of the bridge. "Anchor line must have popped in that squall," Joe said, pointing for Meliah Amey to see. "The bow looks stuck in the pluff mud."

The yacht club sailboat was safely motoring back toward the dock, its mainsail down and loosely piled. The men onboard saw the ship's predicament, as well.

A strong gust came up and the ship pivoted fast and hard into one of the metal supports of the bridge. There came then a most horrible sound of metal on metal, a slow giving way to an unbearable force. Sparks flew into the gray sky above the ship as the power lines crossing the river on top of the bridge came down. And then, the unimaginable, the support pier gave way to the ship as it cut a large gash in the Cooper River Bridge. Meliah Amey and Joe could only watch as a car drove into midair before plummeting into the water below.

Chapter 52

Cassie made her way down Columbus Street with the help of her walking stick. They no longer wore a uniform, but all the girls, Negro and white, carried a green smock to wear over their street clothes while working. The camellias were blooming and soon the azaleas would be, too. Cassie was happier than she could remember.

Cassie's fellow examiner, Gretta, along with Francine and Binah, entered the Drake Street door at the same time. Binah now worked as an examiner on the box floor, and it turned out that Francine had a keen eye for sorting the cigars by shade.

"You gots pep in your step this mawnin, Miss Cassie," said Francine.

"Your boy must be coming home," said Binah.

"Oh yeah, Lord!" Cassie replied. "Got the telegram Thursday. His ship due in any time now."

"Will I get to see Patrick at the Azalea Festival this weekend?" Gretta asked as she moved ahead of Cassie on the steps.

"Shooo! Patrick wouldn't miss that tugboat race for the world! Not for the world!" Cassie replied.

"Mawnin, Maum Cassie," said Meliah Amey, appearing beside Cassie on the steps.

"Mawnin, Meliah Amey," she answered. "Did you get good news?"

"I sure did! He on the Navy ship due in this mawnin," she said.

Meliah Amey slowed so the two of them could walk together up the stairs.

"Miss Cassie, the machine be squealing and the mechanic, he put oil on the upper belt, but the squealing come back an now it tearing up the binder leaf."

"The mechanic put oil on the belt! What a chowder-head. Don't ever put oil on a belt," she said, shaking her head. They had reached the landing and they stopped as it was Cassie's floor. "You got to wipe that oil off the belt best you can. You might try taking a wire brush to rough up them pulleys so they can grab the belt again, but I don't know. You gonna be in the cafeteria at lunchtime?"

Meliah Amey nodded, "Yeah, I'll be there."

"I'll find you in the lunchroom; maybe I can think of sump'n by then."

They were on the landing with the window looking out over the harbor. Neither of them could resist it.

The sun rose above the glaring gaping hole in the Cooper River Bridge. The Corps of Engineers was already at work trying to repair it. The *Nansemond*, the old ferryboat, had been put back into service. Cassie and Meliah Amey watched the water churn behind it as it backed away from the pier.

Down on Bay Street, Mr. Godfrey had the Negro women lined up to inspect for hire.

"Gawd, have mercy on that man's soul," said Meliah Amey.

"Gawd, have mercy on all of us," replied Cassie.

Meliah Amey saw the ship first. Unable to speak, she nudged Ma'magole to get her to look.

The sailors were on deck in their white uniforms as the ship passed at the foot of Columbus Street, heading up the river toward the Navy base.

"Our boys are home," said Cassie.

"That's right, our boys are home," Meliah Amey responded.

Both of them blessed themselves and closed their eyes, giving prayers of thanks for the safe return of Vincent de Paul and Patrick.

"Time for you two to get to work," the foreman yelled.

Neither Cassie nor Meliah Amey budged from the window.

"Never thought I'd live to see a bridge cross the Cooper River. Never thought I'd live to see that," said Cassie.

"I know of what you speak," said Meliah Amey.

"Tide's too strong in that river," said Cassie. "No bridge gonna stand up for long. Soon as they build it back, some fool going to go run into it again."

"Shooo! An when he do, we going to go fix it, ain we Miss Cassie? Ain we now?"

The whistle blew.

Taking foot in hand, Meliah Amey turned and continued up the stairs.

ACKNOWLEDGMENTS

References to real people, events, establishments, organizations, or locales are intended only to provide a sense of authenticity and are used fictitiously. Telling "a story" requires liberties be taken and, I hope, indulged. Among these, certain dates were changed. For example, cigars were not produced in the building on Bay Street until 1903, but in the novel the building is already in use as a cigar factory in 1893. The *Nicaragua Victory* ship hit the Cooper River Bridge in February 1946; in the novel the incident occurs in April 1946.

So many people have given freely of their time and energy to help me complete this book. It has truly taken a legion of librarians, archivists, colleagues, and friends over the years. My deepest gratitude goes to two archivists in Special Collections at the College of Charleston library: Sharon Bennett and Harlan Greene. Sharon responded to my very first general email query seeking information about the cigar factory. In the years since, Sharon has become a very dear friend to my entire family. Harlan has answered or provided direction for the lion's share of my questions and always with a thorough and thoughtful patience.

I am grateful to Mayor Riley for his encouragement and support and to Shannon Ravenel for taking time to read an excerpt and provide advice.

A very special and heartfelt thank you goes to Ally Sheedy.

Thank you also goes to Brian Fahey, archivist with the Catholic Diocese of Charleston; the staff of the South Carolina Historical Association; Jennifer Scheetz with the Charleston Museum; Dr. Kerry Taylor at the Citadel; Leila Potts Campbell and the Avery Research Center; and also Libby Wallace Wilder, Becky Baulch, and Edward Buckley with the *Post and Courier.*

I cannot say enough about the intellectual and digital prowess of the modern librarian. My sincere thanks and praise to them all: Nic Butler and staff of Charleston Public Library; the research staff at the Library of Congress; and, at Piedmont College, Bob Glass, David Gibbs, and especially John Gehner, as well as Louisville librarians and friends Sarah Reed and Nikki Gaines. Like all classic heroes, they arrived on the horizon just in time to save the day and my sanity.

To the members of Piedmont College's English Department, I thank you for your encouragement, patience, and understanding.

The thought of editing this manuscript, with its heavy reliance on the Gullah-Geechee language, caused many to turn and run. But not all. For those who stayed, out of diligence and/or love for the beauty of the West African influenced speech patterns, I *knee bone* in Sea Island sand before you: Dr. Katherine Wyly Mille, Kristina McGrath, Benee Knauer, and especially Jonathan Haupt, Pat Conroy, and everyone at USC Press.

For my cousins, Margaret Moore Sibbald and Mary Moore McKay, thank you for telling me your memories of working at the cigar factory. Mary taught me about sorting cigars by shade. Margaret, I hope I did justice to the relentless headache you described. Tony Hyman answered my emails about cigar-making machines, cigar-making tools, boxes, and all things cigar.

Thank you to my amazing publicist, Katharine Walton.

Thanks also go to Joe Watson for all he does for the community.

Thank you to Peter Irvine, Paul Rossmann, and Mackenzie Brady.

The Kentucky Foundation for Women supported earlier writing projects, and I remain forever grateful.

For help with the setting and details of growing up in Charleston during the 1920s and 30s, the following family members and friends graciously agreed to be interviewed: Jack Moore, Trudy Moore, Ann Moore, Margaret Moore Sibbald, Mary Moore Mckay, Walter Duane, and Buddy Bennett. I will forever cherish Ann Moore's observation: "The seasons in Charleston are manifested in the marsh."

Rusty and Betty Harley, without your gracious generosity and hours spent on your porch, I would not have learned the movement of light over the harbor and the beauty of the setting sun over downtown. For Mallory School-field, I thank you for taking me beyond the jetties; going through them under sail with container ships coming and going is not for the neophyte. You are a master of your craft. Meg Randolph, there are so many reasons to thank you, none more important than your endorsement of me for my first physical therapy job. To my most respected mentors and friends from the Medical University Hospital of MUSC, this book would not have been written without my time at MUH and Charleston County Hospital: Jerri Anne Miller, Debbie Angelo, Erica Rouvalis, Martha Somers, and Charlyne Butler Raih.

Other friends proofread the manuscript at various stages, providing corrections, insights, and/or moral support. Deepest thanks to Rosemary Barnes, Trish Dare, Pam Weatherly, Susan Millar Williams, Valerie Salley, Amy

McGary, and Donna Denton. And to Riley Weatherly for alphabetizing the glossary.

For my siblings, Marian and Marty, I thank you for picking up my slack and understanding when I've been unavailable while working on this project.

For my agent, Charlotte Sheedy, I have nothing but love, praise, and gratitude for all that you have done on my behalf.

Trisha, more than anyone, you have given and sacrificed so that I could take the time to see this through. Together, we have stood against winds too often from the north, beneath a sky too full of winter constellations. A tight weave will endure. Summer returns. Always.

SOURCES

Many people in Charleston, my own family included, will probably agree with the sentiment "You don't say anything bad about the cigar factory." Details from cigar makers and tobacco processors in the time leading up to the 1945 strike are sparse at best. (Avery Research Center's transcript of an interview with Lillie Mae Marsh Doster refers generally to the "bad conditions" created by segregation at the factory in *Voices of Civil Rights Movement: Oral History of Charleston Civil Rights Movement*, and Peter F. Lau's book *Democracy Rising: South Carolina and the Fight for Black Equality since 1865* mentions the arbitrary nature of decisions regarding pay equity, time off, dismissals, and disciplinary measures.) To create the conditions inside my fictional cigar factory, I turned to accounts of women tobacco workers elsewhere. Three books stand out: Patricia A. Cooper's *Once a Cigar Maker: Men, Women, and Work Culture in American Cigar Factories, 1900–1919;* Dolores E. Janiewski's *Sisterhood Denied: Race, Gender, and Class in a New South Community;* and Robert Rodgers Korstad's *Civil Rights Unionism: Tobacco Workers and the Struggle for Democracy in the Mid-Twentieth-Century South.* Also helpful were Winfred B. Moore Jr. and Orville Vernon Burton's *Toward the Meeting of the Waters: Currents in the Civil Rights Movement of South Carolina during the Twentieth Century.* Especially important was Beverly W. Jones's article "Race, Sex, and Class: Black Female Tobacco Workers in Durham, North Carolina, 1920–1940, and the Development of Female Consciousness." Other important contributions included Robert Korstad and Nelson Lichtenstein's "Opportunities Found and Lost: Labor, Radicals, and the Early Civil Rights Movement," Patricia A. Cooper's "What This Country Needs Is a Good Five-Cent Cigar," and Joseph Clarke Robert's chapter titled "The Negro Slave in the Factory" from his 1938 book, *The Tobacco Kingdom 1800–1861.* Information on cigar inspection came from the online Cuba Travel source and Castros Cuban Cigar Store, 2001.

Charleston is as much a part of this story as cigar making, and the most influential book was by far Jason Annan and Pamela Gabriel's *The Great Cooper River Bridge.* Essential articles on Charleston included Stephen O'Neil's 1994 dissertation, "From the Shadow of Slavery: The Civil Rights Years in Charleston"; Trevor Weston's "Notes from a Musical Dawn: African American

Musicians in Charleston, 1900–1910; and, of course, James Bishop, Glenn Ulrich, and Henrietta S. Wilson's "'We Are in Trim to Due it': A Review of Charleston's Mosquito Fleet"; Suzanne Krebsbach's "Catholic, Black and Proud: An Essay on Black Catholics in the Diocese of Charleston"; Theodore Hemmingway's "Prelude to Change: Black Carolinians in the War Years, 1914–1920"; and Eli A. Poliakoff's "Charleston's Longshoremen: Organized Labor in the Anti-Union Palmetto State."

Other vital books included Edward Ball's *The Sweet Hell Inside* and *Slaves in the Family*; Mamie Garvin Fields with Karen Fields's *Lemon Swamp and Other Places: A Carolina Memoir*; Nancy Rhynes's *Before and After Freedom: Lowcountry Folklore and Narratives*; Mark R. Jones's *Wicked Charleston: The Dark Side of the Holy City*; Harriette Kershaw Leiding's 1910 collection, *Street Cries of an Old Southern City*; Walter J. Fraser's *Charleston! Charleston!*; *Renaissance in Charleston: Art and Life in the Carolina Low Country, 1900–1940*, edited by James M. Hutchisson and Harlan Greene; Harlan Greene, Harry S. Hutchins, Jr., and Brian Hutchins's *Slave Badges and the Slave-Hire System in Charleston, South Carolina, 1783–1865*; Joyce V. Coakley's *Sweetgrass Baskets and the Gullah Traditions*; Gadsden Cultural Center's *Sullivan's Island*; Jack McCray's *Charleston Jazz*; John Meffert, Sherman Pyatt, and the Avery Research Center's Black America series book *Charleston, South Carolina*; Tinsley E. Yarbrough's *A Passion for Justice: J. Waties Waring and Civil Rights*; *A Dubose Heyward Reader*, edited by James M. Hutchisson; Dubose Heyward's *Mamba's Daughter*; Alice Childress's play, *Wedding Band*; John Leland's *Porcher's Creek*; and Elizabeth Leland's *The Vanishing Coast*. Also helpful with the history of the Mosquito Fleet was the March 12, 2009, Regulated Wild Lecture "Fish" featuring the late Edwin Gardner and sponsored by the Avery Research Center at the College of Charleston.

For assistance with the Gullah-Geechee language, I consulted Virginia Mixson Geraty's *Gullah Fuh Oonuh* and *Bittle en' T'ing': Gullah Cooking with Maum Chrish'*; Lorenzo Dow Turner's *Africanisms in the Gullah Dialect*; Emory S. Campbell's *Gullah Cultural Legacies*; Ambrose Elliot Gonzales's *Gullah Stories of the Carolina Coast*; Patricia Jones-Jackson's *When Roots Die: Endangered Traditions on the Sea Islands*; Roger Pinckney's *Blue Roots: African-American Folk Magic of the Gullah People*; and Allen Mitchell's *Wadmalaw Island: Leaving Traditional Roots Behind*. Online assistance with the language came from Cengage Gale Learning, "The Dolch Basic Sight Vocabulary"; Michael W. Twitty's Afroculinaria blog, and Buddy Bennett's kindly prepared handwritten glossary.

Ken Burns's film *Jazz: The Story of America's Music* introduced me to the WWI Harlem Hellfighters and James Reese's 369th Regiment. Donald M.

Williams's book *Shamrocks and Pluff Mud: A Glimpse of the Irish in the Southern City of Charleston* helped with the role of the Irish Volunteers in WWI, my grandfather John, his brothers Alex, Arthur, and Charlie among them. Also helpful was Adolph W. Newton's *Better Than Good: A Black Sailor's War 1943– 1945*. A book vital to understanding the change WWII brought to Charleston was Fritz P. Hamer's *Charleston Reborn: A Southern City, Its Navy Yard, and WWII*. The most illuminating book on African American sailors during WWII was Mary Pat Kelly's *Proudly We Served: The Men of the USS* Mason. Their bravery and skill appear fictionally in the novel.

The *Charleston News & Courier* covered events at the cigar factory over the years. Two articles were particularly helpful, one from June 27, 1931, describing the job duties for each floor, and one for its description of the mass of women on Columbus Street on January 28, 1943. Two pictures worth a thousand words came from October 6, 1936, showing women leaving in their crisp uniforms and heels, and from October 3, 1940, with striking women (double entendre intended), laughing and smiling from a window.

Paul Rossmann adapted the 1861 Library of Congress map used for endsheets.

Jack Moore and Buddy Bennett provided details and advice for fishing in Charleston Harbor and near the jetties. Buddy said not to tell anyone this, but here goes: One day Buddy loaned me a very fancy crab trap—I suppose too fancy, because I managed to put it out upside-down, and we didn't catch even one crab. In memory of Buddy, someday, my generation of the family will expunge our record with a big enough catch to make crab cakes for all hands.

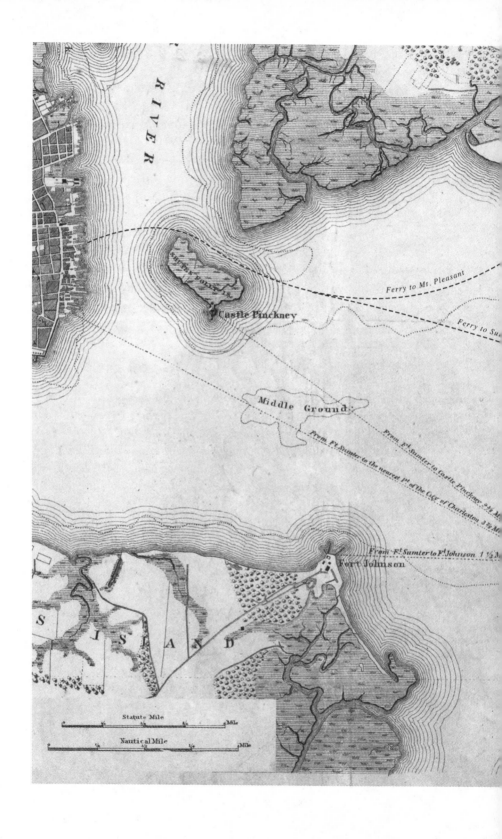

R I V E R

Ferry to Mt. Pleasant

Ferry to Sue

Castle Pinckney

Middle Ground

From F.t Sumter to Castle Pinckney 2⅜ M

From F.t Sumter to the nearest p.t of the City of Charleston 3⅜ M

From F.t Sumter to F.t Johnson 1¼ M

Fort Johnson

S I S L A N D

Statute Mile

Mile

Nautical Mile

Mile

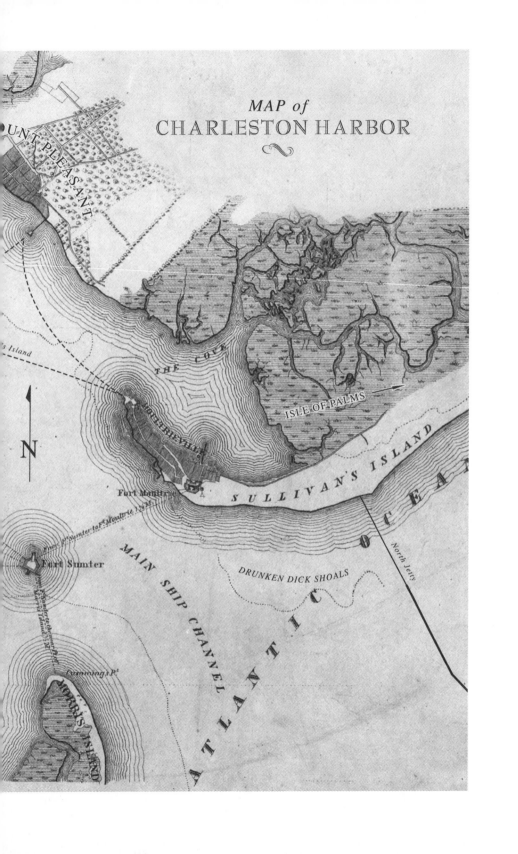

MAP of
CHARLESTON HARBOR

MOUNT PLEASANT

THE COVE

's Island

MOULTRIEVILLE

Fort Moultrie

ISLE OF PALMS

SULLIVAN'S ISLAND

N

From Fort Sumter to Fort Moultrie 1¾ M.

Fort Sumter

MAIN SHIP CHANNEL

DRUNKEN DICK SHOALS

ATLANTIC OCEAN

North Jetty

Cummings P

MORRIS ISLAND